Dear Reader,

I always love revisiting the McKettricks, especially at Christmas! If you missed it in hardcover, here's your chance to spend the holidays with these folks of Blue River, Texas. You'll find a bonus story included, *Daring Moves*—one of my favorites. I also hope you'll be watching for the final installment of my newest trilogy set in Parable, Montana, when *Big Sky River* hits stores in January.

In *A Lawman's Christmas*, who should appear in Blue River as the new marshal but Clay McKettrick, Jeb and Chloe's son from *Secondhand Bride*. His arrival puts Dara Rose Nolan in a tailspin.... What if the young widow with two daughters—and no way to earn a living—is forced out of her home by the new lawman? But 'tis the season for miracles, if only Dara Rose can allow herself to wish for the gift she needs most— Christmas in Clay's arms.

I would also like to write today to tell you about the scholarship program I personally finance— Linda Lael Miller Scholarships for Women, awarded to those seeking to improve their lot in life through education. You can find more information about this program on my website, www.lindalaelmiller.com.

With love,

Linda Lael Miller

LINDA LAEL MILLER

A Lawman's Christmas:
A McKettricks of Texas Novel

HARLEQUIN®

entertain, enrich, inspire™

ISBN-13: 978-0-373-77787-7

A LAWMAN'S CHRISTMAS:
A McKETTRICKS OF TEXAS NOVEL
Copyright © 2012 by Harlequin Books S.A.

The publisher acknowledges the copyright holder of the individual works as follows:

A LAWMAN'S CHRISTMAS:
A McKETTRICKS OF TEXAS NOVEL
Copyright © 2011 by Linda Lael Miller

DARING MOVES
Copyright © 1990 by Linda Lael Miller

Recycling programs for this product may not exist in your area.

This edition published by arrangement with Harlequin Books S.A.

For questions and comments about the quality of this book, please contact us at CustomerService@Harlequin.com.

® and TM are trademarks of Harlequin Enterprises Limited or its corporate affiliates. Trademarks indicated with ® are registered in the United States Patent and Trademark Office, the Canadian Trade Marks Office and in other countries.

www.Harlequin.com

Printed in U.S.A.

CONTENTS

A LAWMAN'S CHRISTMAS: A McKETTRICKS OF TEXAS NOVEL

In memory of Kathy Bannon.
We sure do miss you, Teach.

Chapter 1

Early December, 1914

IF THE SPARK-THROWING SCREECH of iron-on-iron hadn't wrenched Clay McKettrick out of his uneasy sleep, the train's lurching stop—which nearly pitched him onto the facing seat—would surely have done the trick.

Grumbling, Clay sat up straight and glowered out the window, shoving splayed fingers through his dark hair.

Blue River, Texas. His new home. And more, for as the new marshal, he'd be responsible for protecting the town and its residents.

Not that he could see much of it just then, with all that steam from the smokestack billowing between the train and the depot.

The view didn't particularly matter to him, anyhow, since he'd paid a brief visit to the town a few months back and seen what there was to see—which hadn't been much, even in the sun-spangled, blue-sky days of summer. Now that winter was coming on—Clay's granddad, Angus, claimed it snowed dust and chiggers in that part of Texas—

the rutted roads and weathered facades of the ramshackle buildings would no doubt be of bleak appearance.

With an inward sigh, Clay stood to retrieve his black, round-brimmed hat and worn duster from the wooden rack overhead. In the process, he allowed himself to ponder, yet again, all he'd left behind to come to this place at the hind end of beyond and carve out a life of his own making.

He'd left plenty.

A woman, to start with. And then there was his family, the sprawling McKettrick clan, including his ma and pa, Chloe and Jeb, his two older sisters and the thriving Triple M Ranch, with its plentitude of space and water and good grass.

A fragment of a Bible verse strayed across his brain. *The cattle on a thousand hills...*

There were considerably fewer than a thousand hills on the Triple M, big as it was, but the cattle were legion.

To his granddad's way of thinking, those hills and the land they anchored might have been on loan from the Almighty, but everything else—cows, cousins, mineral deposits and timber included—belonged to Angus McKettrick, his four sons and his daughter, Katie.

Clay shrugged into the long coat and put on his hat. His holster and pistol were stowed in his trunk in the baggage compartment, and his paint gelding, Outlaw, rode all alone in the car reserved for livestock.

The only other passenger on board, an angular woman with severe features and no noticeable inclination toward small talk, remained seated, with the biggest Bible Clay had ever seen resting open on her lap. She seemed poised to leap right into the pages at the first hint of sin and disappear into all those apocalyptic threats and grand promises. According to the conductor, a fitful little fellow bearing the pitted scars of a long-ago case of smallpox, the lady had come all the way from Cincinnati with the express purpose of saving the heathen.

Clay—bone-tired, homesick for the ranch and for his kinfolks, and wryly amused, all of a piece—nodded a respectful farewell to the woman as he passed her seat, resisting the temptation to stop and inquire about the apparent shortage of heathens in Cincinnati.

Most likely, he decided, reaching the door, she'd already converted the bunch of them, and now she was out to wrestle the devil for the whole state of Texas. He wouldn't have given two cents for old Scratch's chances.

A chill wind, laced with tiny flakes of snow, buffeted Clay as he stepped down onto the small platform, where all three members of the town council, each one stuffed into his Sunday best and half-strangled by a celluloid collar, waited to greet the new marshal.

Mayor Wilson Ponder spoke for the group. "Welcome to Blue River, Mr. McKettrick," the fat man boomed, a blustery old cuss with white muttonchop whiskers and piano-key teeth that seemed to operate independently of his gums.

Clay, still in his late twenties and among the youngest of the McKettrick cousins, wasn't accustomed to being addressed as "mister"—around home, he answered to "hey, you"—and he sort of liked the novelty of it. "Call me Clay," he said.

There were handshakes all around.

The conductor lugged Clay's trunk out of the baggage car and plunked it down on the platform, then busily consulted his pocket watch.

"Better unload that horse of yours," he told Clay, in the officious tone so often adopted by short men who didn't weigh a hundred pounds sopping wet, "if you don't want him going right on to Fort Worth. This train pulls out in five minutes."

Clay nodded, figuring Outlaw would be ready by now for fresh air and a chance to stretch his legs, since he'd been cooped up in a rolling box ever since Flagstaff.

Taking his leave from the welcoming committee with a touch to the brim of his hat and a promise to meet them later at the marshal's office, he crossed the small platform, descended the rough-hewn steps and walked through cinders and lingering wisps of steam to the open door of the livestock car. He lowered the heavy ramp himself and climbed into the dim, horse-scented enclosure.

Outlaw nickered a greeting, and Clay smiled and patted the horse's long neck before picking up his saddle and other gear and tossing the lot of it to the ground beside the tracks.

That done, he loosed the knot in Outlaw's halter rope and led the animal toward the ramp.

Some horses balked at the unfamiliar, but not Outlaw. He and Clay had been sidekicks for more than a decade, and they trusted each other in all circumstances.

Outside, in the brisk, snow-dappled wind, having traversed the slanted iron plate with no difficulty, Outlaw blinked, adjusting his unusual blue eyes to the light of midafternoon. Clay meant to let the gelding stand untethered while he put the ramp back in place, but before he could turn around, a little girl hurried around the corner of the brick depot and took a competent hold on the lead rope.

She couldn't have been older than seven, and she was small even for that tender age. She wore a threadbare calico dress, a brown bonnet and a coat that, although clean, had seen many a better day. A blond sausage curl tumbled from inside the bonnet to gleam against her forehead, and she smiled with the confidence of a seasoned wrangler.

"My name is Miss Edrina Nolan," she announced importantly. "Are you the new marshal?"

Amused, Clay tugged at his hat brim to acknowledge her properly and replied, "I am. Name's Clay McKettrick."

Edrina put out her free hand. "How do you do, Mr. McKettrick?" she asked.

"I do just fine," he said, with a little smile. Growing up on the Triple M, he and all his cousins had been around horses all their lives, so the child's remarkable ease with a critter many times her size did not surprise him.

It was impressive, though.

"I'll hold your horse," she said. "You'd better help the railroad man with that ramp. He's liable to hurt himself if you don't."

Clay looked back over one shoulder and, sure enough, there was the banty rooster of a conductor, struggling to hoist that heavy slab of rust-speckled iron off the ground so the train could get under way again. He lent his assistance, figuring he'd just spared the man a hernia, if not a heart attack, and got a glare for his trouble, rather than thanks.

Since the fellow's opinion made no real never-mind to Clay either way, he simply turned back to the little girl, ready to reclaim his horse.

She was up on the horse's back, her faded skirts billowing around her, and with the snow-strained sunlight framing her, she looked like one of those cherub-children gracing the pages of calendars, Valentines and boxes of ready-made cookies.

"Whoa, now," he said, automatically taking hold of the lead rope. Given that he hadn't saddled Outlaw yet, he was somewhat mystified as to how she'd managed to mount up the way she had. Maybe she really was a cherub, with little stubby wings hidden under that thin black coat.

Up ahead, the engineer blew the whistle to signal imminent departure, and Outlaw started at the sound, though he didn't buck, thank the good Lord.

"Whoa," Clay repeated, very calmly but with a note of sternness. It was then that he spotted the stump on the other side of the horse and realized that Edrina must have scrambled up on that to reach Outlaw's back.

They all waited—man, horse and cherub—until the train pulled out and the racket subsided somewhat.

Edrina smiled serenely down at him. "Mama says we'll all have to go to the poorhouse, now that you're here," she announced.

"Is that so?" Clay asked mildly, as he reached up, took the child by the waist and lifted her off the horse, setting her gently on her feet. Then he commenced to collecting Outlaw's blanket, saddle and bridle from where they'd landed when he tossed them out of the railroad car, and tacking up. Out of the corner of his eye, he saw the town-council contingent straggling off the platform.

Edrina nodded in reply to his rhetorical question, still smiling, and the curl resting on her forehead bobbed with the motion of her head. "My papa was the marshal a while back," she informed Clay matter-of-factly, "but then he died in the arms of a misguided woman in a room above the Bitter Gulch Saloon and left us high and dry."

Clay blinked, wondering if he'd mistaken Edrina Nolan for a child when she was actually a lot older. Say, forty.

"I see," he said, after clearing his throat. "That's unfortunate. That your papa passed on, I mean." Clay had known the details of his predecessor's death, having been regaled with the story the first time he set foot in Blue River, but it took him aback that Edrina knew it, too.

She folded her arms and watched critically as he threw on Outlaw's beat-up saddle and put the cinch through the buckle. "Can you shoot a gun and everything?" she wanted to know.

Clay spared her a sidelong glance and a nod. Why wasn't this child in school? Did her mother know she was running loose like a wild Indian and leaping onto the backs of other people's horses when they weren't looking?

And where the heck had a kid her age learned to ride like that?

"Good," Edrina said, with a relieved sigh, her little arms still folded. "Because Papa couldn't be trusted with a firearm. Once, when he was cleaning a pistol, meaning to go out and hunt rabbits for stew, it went off by accident and made a big hole in the floor. Mama put a chair over it—she said it was so my sister, Harriet, and I wouldn't fall in and wind up under the house, with all the cobwebs and the mice, but I know it was really because she was embarrassed for anybody to see what Papa had done. Even Harriet has more sense than to fall in a hole, for heaven's sake, and she's only five."

Clay suppressed a smile, tugged at the saddle to make sure it would hold his weight, put a foot into the stirrup and swung up. Adjusted his hat in a gesture of farewell. "I'll be seeing you, chatterbox," he said kindly.

"What about your trunk?" Edrina wanted to know. "Are you just going to leave it behind, on the platform?"

"I mean to come back for it later in the day," Clay explained, wondering why he felt compelled to clarify the matter at all. "This horse and I, we've been on that train for a goodly while, and right now, we need to stretch our muscles a bit."

"I could show you where our house is," Edrina persisted, scampering along beside Outlaw when Clay urged the horse into a walk. "Well, I guess it's *your* house now."

"Maybe you ought to run along home," Clay said. "Your mama's probably worried about you."

"No," Edrina said. "Mama has no call to worry. She thinks I'm in school."

Clay bit back another grin.

They'd climbed the grassy embankment leading to the street curving past the depot and on into Blue River by then. The members of the town's governing body waddled just ahead, single file, along a plank sidewalk like a trio of black ducks wearing top hats.

"And why *aren't* you in school?" Clay inquired affably, adjusting his hat again, and squaring his shoulders against the nippy breeze and the swirling specks of snow, each one sharp-edged as a razor.

She shivered slightly, but that was the only sign that she'd paid any notice at all to the state of the weather. While Miss Edrina Nolan pondered her reply, Clay maneuvered the horse to her other side, hoping to block the bitter wind at least a little.

"I already know everything they have to teach at that school," Edrina said at last, in a tone of unshakable conviction. "And then some."

Clay chuckled under his breath, though he refrained from comment. It wasn't as if anybody were asking his opinion.

The first ragtag shreds of Blue River were no more impressive than he recalled them to be—a livery on one side of the road, and an abandoned saloon on the other. Waist-high grass, most of it dead, surrounded the latter; craggy shards of filthy glass edged its one narrow window, and the sign above the door dangled by a lone, rusty nail.

Last Hope: Saloon and Games of Chance, it read in painted letters nearly worn away by time and weather.

"You shouldn't be out in this weather," Clay told Edrina, who was still hiking along beside him and Outlaw, eschewing the broken plank sidewalk for the road. "Too cold."

"I like it," she said. "The cold is very bracing, don't you think? Makes a body feel wide-awake."

The town's buildings, though unpainted, began to look a little better as they progressed. Smoke curled from twisted chimneys and doors were closed up tight.

There were few people on the streets, Clay noticed, though he glimpsed curious faces at various windows as they went by.

He raised his collar against the rising wind, figuring he'd had all the "bracing" he needed, thank you very much, and he was sure enough "wide-awake" now that he was off the train and back in the saddle.

He was hungry, too, and he wanted a bath and barbering.

And ten to twelve hours of sleep, lying prone instead of sitting upright in a hard seat.

"I reckon maybe you ought to show me where you live, after all," he said, at some length. At least that way, he could steer the child homeward, where she belonged, make sure she got there, and rest easy thereafter, where her welfare was concerned.

Edrina pointed past a general store, a telegraph and telephone office, the humble jailhouse where he would soon be officiating and a tiny white church surrounded by a rickety picket fence, much in need of whitewash. "It's one street over," she said, already veering off a little, as though she meant to duck between buildings and take off. "Our place, that is. It's the one with an apple tree in the yard and a chicken house out back."

Clay drew up his horse with a nearly imperceptible tug of the reins. "Hold it right there," he said, with quiet authority, when Edrina started to turn away.

She froze. Turned slowly to look at him with huge china-blue eyes. "You're going to tell Mama I haven't been at school, aren't you?" she asked, sounding sadly resigned to whatever fate awaited her.

"I reckon it's *your* place to tell her that, not mine."

Edrina blinked, and a series of emotions flashed across her face—confusion, hope and, finally, despair. "She'll be sorely vexed when she finds out," the girl said. "Mama places great store in learning."

"Most sensible people do," Clay observed, biting the inside of his lower lip so he wouldn't laugh out loud. Edrina might have been little more than a baby, but she sat a horse like a Comanche brave—he'd seen that for himself back at the depot—and carried herself with a dignity out of all proportion to her size, situation and hand-me-down clothes. "Maybe from now on, you ought to pay better heed to what your mama says. She has your best interests at heart, you know."

Edrina gave a great, theatrical sigh, one that seemed to involve her entire small personage. "I suppose Miss Krenshaw will tell Mama I've been absent since recess, anyway," she said. "Even if *you* don't."

Miss Krenshaw, Clay figured, was probably the schoolmarm.

Outlaw's well-shod hooves made a lonely, *clompety-clip* kind of sound on the hard dirt of the road. The horse turned a little, to go around a trough with a lacy green scum floating atop the water.

"Word's sure to get out," Clay agreed reasonably, thinking of all those faces, at all those windows, "one way or another."

"Thunderation and spit!" Edrina exclaimed, with the vigor of total sincerity. "I don't know why folks can't just tend to their own affairs and leave me to do as I please."

Clay made a choking sound, disguised it as a cough, as best he could, anyway. "How old are you?" he asked, genuinely interested in the answer.

"Six," Edrina replied.

He'd have bet she was a short ten, maybe even eleven. "So you're in the first grade at school?"

"I'm in the second," Edrina said, trudging along beside his horse. "I already knew how to read when I started in September, and I can cipher, too, so Miss Krenshaw let me skip a grade. Actually, she suggested I enter *third* grade, but Mama said no, that wouldn't do at all, because I needed time to be a child. As if I could *help* being a child."

She sounded wholly exasperated.

Clay hid yet another grin by tilting his head, in hopes that his hat brim would cast a shadow over his face. "You'll be all grown up sooner than you think," he allowed. "I reckon if asked, I'd be inclined to take your mama's part in the matter."

"You weren't asked, though," Edrina pointed out thoughtfully, and with an utter lack of guile or rancor.

"True enough," Clay agreed moderately.

They were quiet, passing by the little white church, then the adjoining graveyard, where, Clay speculated, the last marshal, Parnell Nolan, must be buried. Edrina hurried

ahead when they reached the corner, and Clay and Outlaw followed at an easy pace.

Clay hadn't bothered to visit the house that came with
the marshal's job on his previous stopover in Blue River. At
the time, he'd just signed the deed for two thousand acres
of raw ranch land, and his thoughts had been on the house
and barn he meant to build there, the cattle and horses he
would buy, the wells he would dig and the fences he would
put up. He could have waited, of course, bided on the Triple
M until spring, living the life he'd always lived, but he'd
been too impatient and too proud to do that.

Besides, it was his nature to be restless, and so, in order
to keep himself occupied until spring, he'd accepted the
town's offer of a laughable salary and a star-shaped badge
to pin on his coat until they could rustle up some damn
fool to take up the occupation for good.

"There it is," Edrina said, with a note of sadness in her
voice that caught and pulled at Clay's heart like a fishhook
snagging on something underwater.

Clay barely had time to take in the ramshackle place—
the council referred to it as a "cottage," though he would
have called it a shack—before one of the prettiest women
he'd ever laid eyes on shot out through the front door like
a bullet and stormed down the path toward them.

Chickens scattered, clucking and squawking, as she
passed.

Her hair was the color of pale cider, pinned up in back
and fluffing out around her flushed face, as was the fashion among his sisters and female cousins back home in
Arizona. Her eyes might have been blue, but they might
have been green, too, and right now, they were shooting
fire hot enough to brand the toughest hide.

Reaching the rusty-hinged gate in the falling-down

fence, she stopped suddenly, fixed those changeable eyes on him and glared.

Clay felt a jolt inside, as though Zeus had flung a lightning bolt his way and he'd caught it with both hands instead of sidestepping it, like a wiser man would have done.

The woman's gaze sliced to the little girl.

"Edrina Louise Nolan," she said, through a fine set of straight white teeth, "what am I going to do with you?" Her skin was good, too, Clay observed, with that part of his brain that usually stood back and assessed things. Smooth, with a peachy glow underneath.

"Let me go to third grade?" Edrina ventured bravely.

Clay gave an appreciative chuckle, quickly quelled by a glare from the lady. He didn't wither easily, though he knew that was the result she'd intended, and he did take some pleasure in thwarting her.

At that, the woman gave a huffy little sigh and turned her attention back to her daughter. She threw out one arm—like Edrina, she wore calico—and pointed toward the gaping door of the shack. "That will be quite enough of your nonsense, young lady," she said, with a reassuring combination of affection and anger, thrusting open the creaky gate. "Get yourself into the house *now* and prepare to contemplate the error of your ways!"

Before obeying her mother's command, Edrina paused just long enough to look up at Clay, who was still in the saddle, as though hoping he'd intercede.

That was a thing he had no right to do, of course, but he felt a pang on the little girl's behalf just the same. And against his own better judgment he dismounted, took off his hat, holding it in one hand and shoving the other through his hair, fingers splayed.

"You go on and do what your mama tells you," he said

to Edrina, though his words had the tone of a suggestion, rather than a command.

Edrina's very fetching mother looked him over again, this time with something that might have been chagrin. Then she bristled again, like a little bird ruffling up faded feathers. "You're *him,* aren't you?" she accused. "The new marshal?"

"Yes, ma'am," Clay said, confounded by the strange mixture of terror and jubilation rising up within him. "I am the new marshal. And you are…?"

"Dara Rose Nolan. You may address me as *Mrs.* Nolan, if you have any further *reason* to address me, which I do not anticipate."

With that, she turned on one shabby-heeled shoe and pointed herself toward the "cottage," with its sagging roof, leaking rain barrel and sparkling-clean windows.

Edrina and another little girl—the aforementioned Harriet, no doubt—darted out of the doorway as their mother approached, vanishing into the interior of the house.

Clay watched appreciatively as the widow Nolan retreated hurriedly up the walk, with nary a backward glance.

Chickens, pecking peacefully at the ground, squawked and flapped their wings as they fled.

The door slammed behind her.

Clay smiled, resettled his hat and got back on his horse.

Before, he'd dreaded the long and probably idle months ahead, expecting the season to be a lonesome one, and boring, to boot, since he knew nothing much ever happened in Blue River, when it came to crime. That was the main reason the town fathers hadn't been in any big rush to replace Parnell Nolan.

Now, reining Outlaw away toward the edge of town,

and the open country beyond, meaning to ride up onto a ridge he knew of, where the view extended for miles in every direction, Clay figured the coming winter might not be so dull, after all.

INSIDE THE HOUSE, Dara Rose drew a deep breath and sighed it out hard.

Heaven knew, she hadn't been looking forward to the new marshal's arrival, given the problems that were sure to result, but she hadn't planned on losing her composure and behaving rudely, either. Poor as she was, Dara Rose still had high standards, and she believed in setting a good example for her children, prided herself on her good manners and even temperament.

Imagining how she must have looked to Clay McKettrick, rushing out of the house, scaring the chickens half to death in the process, she closed her eyes for a moment, then sighed again.

Edrina and Harriet watched her from the big rocking chair over by the wood-burning stove, Edrina wisely holding her tongue, Harriet perched close beside her, her rag doll, Molly, resting in the curve of one small arm.

The regulator clock ticked ponderously on the wall, lending a solemn rhythm to the silence, and snow swirled past the windows, as if trying to find a way in.

Dara Rose shivered.

"What are we going to do, Mama?" Edrina asked reasonably, and at some length. She was a good child, normally, helpful and even tempered, but her restlessness and curiosity often led her straight into mischief.

Dara Rose looked up at the oval-framed image of her late husband, Parnell Nolan, and her throat thickened as fresh despair swept over her. Despite the scandalous way he died, she missed him, missed the steadiness of his presence, missed his quiet ways and his wit.

"I don't rightly know," Dara Rose admitted, after swallowing hard and blinking back the scalding tears that were always so close to the surface these days. "But never you mind—I'll think of something."

Edrina slipped a reassuring arm around Harriet, who was sucking her thumb.

Dara Rose didn't comment on the thumb-sucking, though it was worrisome to her. Harriet had left that habit behind when she was three, but after Parnell's death, nearly a year ago now, she'd taken it up again. It wasn't hard to figure out why—the poor little thing was frightened and confused.

So was Dara Rose, for that matter, though of course she didn't let on. With heavy-handed generosity, Mayor Ponder and the town council had allowed her and the children to remain in the cottage on the stipulation that they'd have to vacate when a marshal was hired to take Parnell's place.

"Don't worry," Edrina told her sister, tightening her little arm around the child, just briefly. "Mama *always* thinks of something."

It was true that Dara Rose had managed to put food on the table by raising vegetables in her garden patch, taking in sewing and the occasional bundle of laundry and sometimes sweeping floors in the shops and businesses along Main Street. As industrious as she was, however, the pickings were already slim; without the house, the situation would go from worrisome to destitute.

Oh, she had choices—there were always choices, weren't there?—but they were wretched ones.

She could become a lady of the evening over at the Bitter Gulch Saloon and maybe—*maybe*—earn enough to board her children somewhere nearby, where she could see them now and then. How long would it be before they realized how she was earning their living and came to despise her? A year, two years? Three?

Her second option was only slightly more palatable; Ezra Maddox had offered her a job as his cook and housekeeper, on his remote ranch, but he'd plainly stipulated that she couldn't bring her little girls along. In fact, he'd come right out and said she ought to just put Edrina and Harriet in an orphans' home or farm them out to work for their keep. It would be good for their character, he'd claimed.

In fact, the last time he'd come to call, the previous Sunday after church, he'd stood in this very room, beaming at his own generosity, and announced that if Dara Rose measured up, he might even marry her.

The mere thought made her shudder.

And the *audacity* of the man. He expected her to turn her daughters over to strangers and spend the rest of her days darning his socks and cooking his food, and in return, he offered room, board and a pittance in wages. If she "measured up," as he put it, she'd be required to share his bed and give up the salary he'd been paying her, too.

Dara Rose's final prospect was to take her paltry savings—she kept them in a fruit jar, hidden behind the cookstove in the tiny kitchen—purchase train tickets for herself and her children and travel to San Antonio or Dallas or Houston, where she might find honest work and decent lodgings.

But suppose she *didn't* find work? Times were hard. The little bit of money she had would soon be eaten up by living expenses, and *then* what?

Dara Rose knew she'd be paralyzed by these various scenarios if she didn't put them out of her head and get busy doing something constructive, so she headed for the kitchen, meaning to start supper.

Last fall, someone had given her the hindquarter of a deer, and she'd cut the meat into strips and carefully preserved it in jars. There were green beans and corn and stubby orange carrots from the garden, too, along with apples and pears from the fruit trees growing behind the church, and berries she and the girls had gathered during the summer and brought home in lard tins and baskets. Thanks to the chickens, there were plenty of eggs, some of which she sold, and some she traded over at the mercantile for small amounts of sugar and flour and other staples. Once in a great while, she bought tea, but that was a luxury.

She straightened her spine when she realized Edrina had followed her into the little lean-to of a kitchen.

"I like Mr. McKettrick," the child said conversationally. "Don't you?"

Keeping her back to the child, Dara Rose donned her apron and tied it in back with brisk motions of her hands. "My opinion of the new marshal is neither here nor there," she replied. "And don't think for one moment, Edrina Louise Nolan, that I've forgotten that you ran away from school again. You are in serious trouble."

Edrina gave a philosophical little sigh. "How serious?" she wanted to know.

"*Very* serious," Dara Rose answered, adding wood to the fire in the cookstove and jabbing at it with a poker.

"I think we're *all* in serious trouble," Edrina observed sagely.

Out of the mouths of babes, Dara Rose thought.

"Do we have to be orphans now, Mama?" Harriet asked. As usual, she'd followed Edrina.

Dara Rose put the poker back in its stand beside the stove and turned to look at her daughters. Harriet clung to her big sister's hand, looking up at her mother with enormous, worried eyes.

"We are a family," she said, kneeling and wrapping an arm around each of them, pulling them close, drawing in the sweet scent of their hair and skin, "and we are going to stay together. I promise."

Now to find a way to *keep* that promise.

Chapter 2

—⟨∞⟩—

THE SNOW WAS COMING down harder and faster when Clay returned to Blue River from the high ridge, where he'd breathed in the sight of his land, the wide expanse of it and the sheer potential, Outlaw strong and steady beneath him.

Dusk was fast approaching now, and lamps glowed in some of the windows on Main Street, along with the occasional stark dazzle of a lightbulb. Clay had yet to decide whether or not he'd have his place wired for electricity when the time came; like the telephone, it was still a new-fangled invention as far as he was concerned, and he wasn't entirely sure it would last.

At the livery stable, Clay made arrangements for Outlaw and then headed in the direction of the Bitter Gulch Saloon, where he figured the mayor and the town council were most likely to be waiting for him.

Most of the businesses were sealed up tight against the weather, but the saloon's swinging doors were all that stood between the crowded interior and the sidewalk. A piano tinkled a merry if discordant tune somewhere in all that roiling blue cigar smoke, and bottles rattled against the rims of glasses.

The floor was covered in sawdust; the bar was long and ornately carved with various bare-breasted women pouring water into urns decorated with all sorts of flowers and mythical animals and assorted other decorations.

Clay removed his hat, thumped the underside of the brim with one forefinger to knock off the light coating of snow and caught a glimpse of his own reflection in the chipped and murky glass of the mirror in back of the bar.

He didn't commonly frequent saloons, not being much of a drinker, but he knew he'd be dropping in at the Bitter Gulch on a regular basis, once he'd been sworn in as marshal and taken up his duties. Douse the seeds of trouble with enough whiskey and they were bound to take root, break ground and sprout foliage faster than the green beans his ma liked to plant in her garden every spring.

One glance told him he'd been right to look for Mayor Ponder and his cronies here—they'd gathered around a table over in the corner, near the potbellied stove, each with his own glass and his own bottle.

Inwardly, Clay sighed, but he managed a smile as he approached the table, snow melting on the shoulders of his duster.

"Good to see you, Clay," Mayor Ponder said cordially, as one of the others in the party dragged a chair over from a nearby table. "Sent a boy to fetch your trunk from the depot," the older man went on, as Clay joined them, taking the offered seat without removing his coat. He didn't plan on staying long. "You didn't say where you wanted your gear sent, so I told Billy to haul it over to the jailhouse for the time being."

"Thanks," Clay said mildly, setting his hat on the table.

At home, the McKettrick women enforced their own private ordinance against such liberties, on the grounds that it was not only unmannerly, but bad luck and a mite on the slovenly side, too.

"Have a drink with us?" Ponder asked, studying Clay thoughtfully through the shifting haze of smoke. The smell of unwashed bodies and poor dental hygiene was so thick it was nearly visible, and he felt a strong and sudden yearning to be outside again, in the fresh air.

Clay shook his head. "Not now," he said. "It's been a long day, and I'm ready for a meal, a hot bath and a bed."

Ponder cleared his throat. "Speaking of, well, beds, I'm afraid the house we offered you is still occupied. We've been telling Dara Rose that she'd have to move when we found a replacement for Parnell, but so far, she's stayed put."

Dara Rose. Clay smiled slightly at the reminder of the fiery little woman who'd burst through the door of that shack a couple of hours before when he showed up with Edrina, stormed through a flock of cacophonous chickens and let him know, in no uncertain terms, that she wasn't at all glad to see him.

There had been no shortage of women in Clay McKettrick's life—he'd even fallen in love with one, to his eventual sorrow—but none of them had affected him quite the way the widow Nolan did.

"No hurry," Clay said easily, resting his hands on his thighs. "I can get a room at the hotel, or bunk in at the jailhouse."

"The town of Blue River cannot stand good for the cost of lodgings," Ponder said, looking worried. "Having that power line strung all the way out here from Austin depleted our treasury."

One of the other men huffed at that, and poured himself another shot of whiskey. "Hell," he said, with a hiccup, "we're flat busted and up to our hind ends in debt."

Ponder flushed, and his big whiskers quivered along with those heavy jowls of his. "We *can* pay the agreed-upon salary," he stated, after glaring over at his colleague for a long moment. "Seventy-five dollars a month and living quarters, as agreed." He paused, flushed. "I'll speak to Mrs. Nolan in the morning," he clarified. "Tell her she needs to make other arrangements immediately."

"Don't do that," Clay said, quietly but quickly, too. He took a breath, slowed himself down on the inside. "I don't mind paying for a hotel room or sleeping at the jail, for the time being."

The little group exchanged looks.

Snow spun at the few high windows the Bitter Gulch Saloon boasted, like millions of tiny ghosts in search of someplace to haunt.

"A deal," Ponder finally blustered, "is a deal. We offered you a place to live as part of your salary, and we intend to keep our word."

Clay rubbed his chin thoughtfully. His beard was coming in again, even though he'd shaved that morning, on board the train. Nearly cut his own throat in the process, as it happened, because of the way the car jostled along the tracks. "Where are Mrs. Nolan and her little girls likely to wind up?" he asked, hoping he didn't sound too concerned. "Once they've moved out of that house, I mean."

"Ezra Maddox offered for her," said another member of the council. "He's a hard man, old Ezra, but he's got a farm and a herd of dairy cows and money in the bank, and she could do a lot worse when it comes to husbands."

Clay felt a strange stab at the news, deep inside, but he

was careful not to let his reaction show. He felt *something* for Dara Rose Nolan, but what that something was exactly was a matter that would require some sorting out.

"Ezra ain't willing to take the girls along with their mama, though," imparted the first man, pouring himself yet another dose of whiskey and throwing it back without so much as a shudder or a wince. The stuff might have been creek water, for all the effect it seemed to have going down the fellow's gullet. "And he didn't actually offer to marry up with Dara Rose right there at the beginning, either. He means to try her out as a housekeeper before he makes her his wife. Ezra likes to know what he's getting."

Someplace in the middle of Clay's chest, one emotion broke away from the tangle and filled all the space he occupied.

It was pure anger, cold and urgent and prickly around the edges.

What kind of man expects a woman to part with her own children? he wondered, silently furious. His neck turned hot, and he had to release his jaw muscles by force of will.

"Dara Rose is a bit shy on choices at the moment, if you ask me," Ponder put in, taking a defensive tone suggesting he was a friend of Ezra Maddox's and meant to take the man's part if a controversy arose. With a wave of one hand, he indicated their surroundings, including the half dozen saloon girls, waiting tables in their moth-eaten finery. "If she turns Ezra down, she'll wind up right here." He paused to indulge in a slight smile, and Clay underwent another internal struggle just to keep from backhanding the mayor of Blue Creek hard enough to send him sprawling in the dirty sawdust. "Can't say as I'd mind that, really."

Clay seethed, but his expression was schooled to quiet amusement. He'd grown up playing poker with his granddad, his pa and uncles, his many rambunctious cousins, male and female. He knew how to keep his emotions to himself.

Mostly.

"And you a married man," scolded one of the other council members, but his tone was indulgent. "For shame."

Clay pushed his chair back, slowly, and stood. Stretched before retrieving his hat from its place on the table. "I will leave you gentlemen to your discussion," he said, with a slight but ironic emphasis on the word *gentlemen*.

"But we meant to swear you in," Ponder protested. "Make it official."

"Morning will be here soon enough," Clay said, putting his hat on. "I'll meet you at the jailhouse at eight o'clock. Bring a badge and a Bible."

Ponder did not look pleased; he was used to piping the tune, it was obvious, and most folks probably danced to it.

Most folks weren't McKettricks, though.

Clay smiled an idle smile, tugged at the brim of his hat in a gesture of farewell and turned to leave the saloon. Just beyond the swinging doors, he paused on the sidewalk to draw in some fresh air and look up at the sky.

It was snow-shrouded and dark, that sky, and Clay wished for a glimpse, however brief, of the stars.

He'd come to Blue River to start a ranch of his own, marry some good woman and raise a bunch of kids with her, build a legacy comparable to the one his granddad had established on the Triple M. Figuring he'd never love anybody but Annabel Carson, who had made up her mind to wed his cousin Sawyer, come hell or high water, he hadn't been especially stringent with his requirements for a bride.

He wanted a wife and a partner, somebody loyal who'd stand shoulder to shoulder with him in good times and bad.

She had to be smart and have a sense of humor—ranching was too hard a life for folks lacking in those characteristics, in his opinion—but she didn't necessarily have to be pretty.

Annabel was mighty easy on the eyes, after all, and look where *that* got him. Up shit creek without a paddle, that was where. She'd claimed to love Clay with her whole heart, but at the first disagreement, she'd thrown his promise ring in his face and gone chasing after Sawyer.

Even now, all these months later, the recollection carried a powerful sting, racing through Clay's veins like snake venom.

Crossing the street to the town's only hotel, its electric lights glowing a dull gold at the downstairs windows, Clay rode out the sensation, the way he'd trained himself to do, but a remarkable thing happened at the point when Annabel's face usually loomed up in his mind's eye.

He saw Dara Rose Nolan there instead.

BY THE TIME DARA ROSE got up the next morning, washed and dressed and built up the fires, then headed out to feed and water the chickens and gather the eggs, the snow had stopped, the ground was bare and the sky was a soft blue.

She hadn't slept well, but the crisp bite of approaching winter cleared some of the cobwebs from her beleaguered brain, and she smiled as she worked. Her situation was as dire as ever, of course, but daylight invariably raised her hopes and quieted her fears.

When the sun was up, she could believe things would work out in the long run if she did her best and maintained her faith.

She *would* find a way to earn an honest living and keep

her family together. She had to believe that to keep putting one foot in front of the other.

This very day, as soon as the children had had their breakfast and Edrina had gone off to school, Dara Rose decided, flinging out ground corn for the chickens, now clucking and flapping around her skirts and pecking at the ground, she and her youngest daughter would set out to knock on every respectable door in town if they had to.

Someone in Blue River surely needed a cook, a housekeeper, a nurse or some combination thereof. She'd work for room and board, for herself and the girls, and they wouldn't take up much space, the three of them. What little cash they needed, she could earn by taking in sewing.

The idea wasn't new, and it wasn't likely to come to fruition, either, given that most people in town were only a little better off than she was and therefore not in the market for household help, but it heartened Dara Rose a little, just the same, as she finished feeding the chickens, dusted her hands together and went to retrieve the egg basket, hanging by its handle from a nail near the back door.

Holding her skirts up with one hand, Dara Rose ducked into the tumbledown chicken coop and began gathering eggs from the straw where the hens roosted.

That morning, there were more than a dozen—fifteen, by her count—which meant she and Edrina and Harriet could each have one for breakfast. The remainder could be traded at the mercantile for salt—she was running a little low on that—and perhaps some lard and a small scoop of white sugar.

Thinking these thoughts, Dara Rose was humming under her breath as she left the chicken coop, carrying the egg basket.

She nearly dropped the whole bunch of them right to

the ground when she caught sight of the new marshal, riding his fancy spotted horse, reining in just the other side of the fence, a shiny nickel star gleaming on his worn coat.

It made him look like a gunslinger, that long coat, and the round-brimmed hat only added to the rakish impression.

Already bristling, Dara Rose drew a deep breath and rustled up a smile. It wasn't as if the man existed merely to irritate and inconvenience *her,* after all.

The marshal, swinging down out of the saddle and approaching the rickety side gate to stroll, bold as anything, into her yard, did not smile back.

Dara Rose's high hopes shriveled instantly as the obvious finally struck her: Clay McKettrick had come to send her and the children packing. He'd want to move himself—and possibly a family—in, and soon. The fact that he had a fair claim to the house did nothing whatsoever to make her feel better.

"Mornin'," he said, standing directly in front of her now, and pulling politely at the brim of his hat before taking it off.

"Good morning," Dara Rose replied cautiously, still mindful of her rudeness the day before and the regret it had caused her. Her gaze moved to the polished star pinned to his coat, and she felt an achy twinge of loss, remembering Parnell.

Poor, well-meaning, chivalrous Parnell.

Greetings exchanged, both of them just stood there looking at each other, for what seemed like a long time.

Finally, Marshal McKettrick cleared his throat, holding his hat in both hands now, and the wintry sun caught in his dark hair. He looked as clean as could be, standing there, his clothes fresh, except for the coat, and his boots brushed to a shine.

Dara Rose felt a small, peculiar shift in a place behind her heart.

"I just wanted to say," the man began awkwardly, inclining his head toward the house, "that there's no need for you and the kids to clear out right away. I spent last night at the hotel, but there's a cot and a stove at the jailhouse, and that will suit me fine for now."

Dara Rose's throat tightened, and the backs of her eyes burned. She didn't quite dare to believe her own ears. "But you're entitled to live here," she reminded him, and then could have nipped off her tongue. "And surely your wife wouldn't want to set up housekeeping in a—"

In that instant, the awkwardness was gone. The marshal's mouth slanted in a grin, and mischief sparkled in his eyes. They were the color of new denim, those eyes.

"I don't have a wife," he said simply. "Not yet, anyhow."

That grin. It did something unnerving to Dara Rose's insides.

Her heartbeat quickened inexplicably, nearly racing, then fairly lurched to a stop. Did Clay McKettrick expect something in return for his kindness? If he was looking for favors, he was going to be disappointed, because she wasn't that kind of woman.

Not anymore.

"It's almost Christmas," Clay said, assessing the sky briefly before meeting her gaze again.

Confused, Dara Rose squinted up at him. Christmas was important to Edrina and Harriet, as it was to most children, but it was the least of her own concerns.

"Do you need spectacles?" Clay asked.

Taken aback by the question, Dara Rose opened her

mouth to speak, found herself at a complete loss for words and pressed her lips together. Then she shook her head.

Clay McKettrick chuckled and reached for the egg basket.

It wasn't heavy, and the contents were precious, but Dara Rose offered no resistance. She let him take it.

"Where did Edrina learn to ride a horse?" he asked.

They were moving now, heading slowly toward the house, as though it were the least bit proper for the two of them to be behind closed doors together.

Dara Rose blinked, feeling as muddled as if he'd spoken to her in a foreign language instead of plain English. "I beg your pardon?"

They stepped into the small kitchen, with its slanted wall and iron cookstove, Dara Rose in the lead, and the marshal set the basket of eggs on the table, which was comprised of two barrels with a board nailed across their tops.

"Edrina was there to meet Outlaw and me when we got off the train yesterday," Clay explained quietly, keeping his distance and folding his arms loosely across his chest. "The child has a way with horses."

Dara Rose heard the girls stirring in the tiny room the three of them shared, just off the kitchen, and such a rush of love for her babies came over her that she almost teared up. "Yes," she said. "Parnell—my husband—kept a strawberry roan named Gawain. Edrina's been quite at home in the saddle since she was a tiny thing."

"What happened to him?" Clay asked.

"Parnell?" Dara Rose asked stupidly, feeling her cheeks go crimson.

"I know what happened to your husband, ma'am," Clay said quietly. "I was asking about the horse."

Dara Rose felt dazed, but she straightened her spine

and looked Clay McKettrick in the eye. "We had to sell Gawain after my husband died," she said. It was the simple truth, and almost as much of a sore spot as Parnell's death. They'd all loved the gelding, but Ezra Maddox had offered a good price for him, and Dara Rose had needed the money for food and firewood and kerosene for the lamps.

Edrina, already mourning the man she'd believed to be her father, had cried for days.

"I see," Clay said gravely, a bright smile breaking over his handsome face like a sunrise as Edrina and Harriet hopped into the room and hurried to stand by the stove, wearing their calico dresses but no shoes or stockings.

"Do we have to go live in the poorhouse now?" Harriet asked, groping for Edrina's hand, finding it and evidently forgetting that the floor was cold enough to sting her bare feet. In the dead of winter, the planks sometimes frosted over.

To Dara Rose's surprise, Clay crouched, putting himself nearly at eye level with both children. He kept his balance easily, still holding his hat, and when his coat opened a ways, she caught an ominous glimpse of the gun belt buckled around his lean hips.

"You don't have to go anywhere," he said, very solemnly.

Edrina's eyes widened. Her unbrushed curls rioted around her face, like gold in motion, and her bow-shaped lips formed a smile. "Really and truly?" she asked. "We can stay here?"

Clay nodded.

"But where will *you* live?" Harriet wanted to know. Like her sister, she was astute and well-spoken. Dara Rose had never used baby talk with her girls, and she'd been reading aloud to them since before they were born.

"I'll be fine over at the jailhouse, at least until spring," Clay replied, rising once again to his full height. He was tall, this man from Arizona, broad through the shoulders and thick in the chest, but the impression he gave was of leanness and agility. He was probably fast with that pistol he carried, Dara Rose thought, and was disturbed by the knowledge.

It was the twentieth century, after all, and the West was no longer wild. Hardly anyone, save sheriffs and marshals, carried a firearm.

"I'm going to school today," Edrina announced happily, "and I plan on staying until Miss Krenshaw rings the bell at three o'clock, too."

Clay crooked a smile, but his gaze, Dara Rose discovered, had found its way back to her. "That's good," he said.

"Why don't you stay for breakfast?" Edrina asked the man wearing her father's badge pinned to his coat.

"Edrina," Dara Rose almost whispered, embarrassed.

"I've already eaten," Clay replied. "Had the ham and egg special in the hotel dining room before Mayor Ponder swore me in."

"Oh," Edrina said, clearly disappointed.

"That's a fine horse, mister," Harriet chimed in, her head tipped way back so she could look up into Clay's recently shaven face.

Dara Rose was still trying to bring the newest blush in her cheeks under control, and she could only manage that by avoiding Clay McKettrick's eyes.

"Yes, indeed," Clay answered the child. "His name's Outlaw, but you can't go by that. He's a good old cayuse."

"I got to ride him yesterday, down by the railroad tracks," Edrina boasted. Then her face fell a little. "Sort of."

"If it's all right with your mother," Clay offered, "and you go to school like you ought to, you can ride Outlaw again."

"Me, too?" Harriet asked, breathless with excitement at the prospect.

Clay caught Dara Rose's gaze again. "That's your mother's decision to make, not mine," he said, so at home in his own skin that she wondered what kind of life he'd led, before his arrival in Blue River. An easy one, most likely.

But something in his eyes refuted that.

"We'll see," Dara Rose said.

Both girls groaned, wanting a "yes" instead of a "maybe."

"I'd best be getting on with my day," Clay said, with another slow, crooked grin.

And then he was at the door, ducking his head so he wouldn't bump it, putting on his hat and walking away.

Dara Rose watched through the little window over the sink until he'd gone through the side gate and mounted his horse.

"We don't have to go to the orphanage!" Harriet crowed, clapping her plump little hands in celebration.

"There will be no more talk of orphanages," Dara Rose decreed briskly, pumping water at the rusty sink to wash her hands.

"Does Mr. McKettrick have a wife?" Edrina piped up. "Because if he doesn't, you could marry him. I don't think he'd send Harriet and me away, like Mr. Maddox wants to do."

Dara Rose kept her back to her daughters as she began breakfast preparations, using all her considerable willpower to keep her voice calm and even. "That's none of your business," she said firmly. "Nor mine, either. And don't you *dare* pry into Mr. McKettrick's private affairs by asking, either one of you."

Both girls sighed at this.

"Go get your shoes and stockings on," Dara Rose ordered, setting the cast-iron skillet on the stove, plopping in the last smidgeon of bacon grease to keep the eggs from sticking.

"I need to go to the outhouse," Harriet said.

"Put your shoes on first," Dara Rose countered. "It's a nice day out, but the ground is cold."

The children obeyed readily, which threw her a little. She was raising her daughters to have minds of their own, but that meant they were often obstinate and sometimes even defiant.

Parnell had accused her of spoiling them, though he'd indulged the girls plenty himself, buying them hair ribbons and peppermint sticks and letting them ride his horse. Edrina, rough and tumble as any boy but at the same time all girl, was virtually fearless as well as outspoken, and trying as the child sometimes was, Dara Rose wouldn't have changed anything about her. Except, of course, for her tendency to play hooky from school.

Harriet, just a year younger than her sister, was more tentative, less likely to take risks than Edrina was. Too small to really understand death, Harriet very probably expected her papa to come home one day, riding Gawain, his saddlebags bulging with presents.

Dara Rose's eyes smarted again and, inwardly, she brought herself up short.

She and the girls had been given a reprieve, that was all. They could go on living in the marshal's house for a while, but other arrangements would have to be made eventually, just the same.

Which was why, when she and the girls had eaten, and the dishes had been washed and the fires banked, Dara Rose followed through with her original plan.

She and Harriet walked Edrina to the one-room school-house at the edge of town, and then took the eggs to the mercantile, to be traded for staples.

It was warm inside the general store, and Harriet became so captivated by the lovely doll on display in the tinsel-draped front window that Dara Rose feared the child would refuse to leave the place at all.

"Look, Mama," she breathed, without taking her eyes from the beautiful toy when Dara Rose approached and took her hand. "Isn't she pretty? She's almost as tall as *I am*."

"She's pretty," Dara Rose conceded, trying to keep the sadness out of her voice. "But not nearly as pretty as you are."

Harriet looked up at her, enchanted. "Edrina says there's no such person as St. Nicholas," she said. "She says it was you and Papa who filled our stockings last Christmas Eve."

Dara Rose's throat ached. She had to swallow before she replied, "Edrina is right, sweetheart," she said hoarsely. Other people could afford to pretend that magical things happened, at least while their children were young, but she did not have that luxury.

"I guess the doll probably costs a lot," Harriet said, her voice small and wistful.

Dara Rose checked the price tag dangling from the doll's delicate wrist, though she already knew it would be far out of her reach.

Two dollars and fifty cents.

What was the world coming to?

"She comes with a trunk full of clothes," the storekeeper

put in helpfully. Philo Bickham meant well, to be sure, but he wasn't the most thoughtful man on earth. "That's real human hair on her head, too, and she came all the way from Germany."

Harriet's eyes widened with something that might have been alarm. "But didn't the hair *belong* to someone?" she asked, no doubt picturing a bald child wandering sadly through the Black Forest.

"People sometimes sell their hair," Dara Rose explained, giving Mr. Bickham a less than friendly glance as she drew her daughter toward the door. "And then it grows back."

Harriet immediately brightened. "Could we sell *my* hair? For two dollars and fifty cents?"

"No," Dara Rose said, and instantly regretted speaking so abruptly. She dropped to her haunches, tucked stray golden curls into Harriet's tattered bonnet. "Your hair is much too beautiful to sell, sweetheart."

"But I could grow more," Harriet reasoned. "You said so yourself, Mama."

Dara Rose smiled, mainly to keep from crying, and stood very straight, juggling the egg basket, now containing a small tin of lard, roughly three-quarters of a cup of sugar scooped into a paper sack and a box of table salt, from one wrist to the other.

"We'll be on our way now, Harriet," she said. "We have things to do."

Chapter 3

AS HE RODE SLOWLY ALONG every street in Blue River that morning, touching his hat brim to all he encountered so the town folks would know they had a marshal again, one who meant to live up to the accompanying responsibilities, Clay found himself thinking about Parnell Nolan. Blessed with a beautiful wife and two fine daughters, and well-liked from what little Clay had learned about him, Nolan had still managed to be in a whorehouse when he drew his last breath.

Yes, plenty of men indulged themselves in brothels—bachelors and husbands, sons and fathers alike—but they usually exercised some degree of discretion, in Clay's experience.

Always inclined to give somebody the benefit of the doubt, at least until they'd proven themselves unworthy of the courtesy, Clay figured Parnell might have done his sinning in secret, with the notion that he was therefore protecting his wife and children from scandal. But Blue River was a small place, like Clay's hometown of Indian

Rock, and stories that were too good not to tell had a way of getting around. Fast.

Of course, Nolan surely hadn't planned on dying that particular night, in the midst of awkward circumstances.

Reaching the end of the last street in town, near the schoolhouse, Clay stopped to watch, leaning on the pommel of his saddle and letting Outlaw nibble at the patchy grass, as children spilled out the door of the little red building, shouting to one another, eager to make the most of recess.

He spotted Edrina right away—her bonnet hung down her back by its laces, revealing that unmistakable head of spun-gold hair, and her cheeks glowed with exuberance and good health and the nippy coolness of the weather.

As Clay watched, she found a stick, etched the squares for a game of hopscotch in the bare dirt and jumped right in. Within moments, the other little girls were clamoring to join her, while the boys played kick-the-can at an artfully disdainful distance, making as much racket as they could muster up.

The schoolmarm—a plain woman, spare and tall, and probably younger than she looked—surveyed the melee from the steps of the building, but she was quick to notice the horse and rider looking on from the road.

Clay tugged at his hat brim and nodded a silent greeting. His ma, Chloe, had been a schoolteacher when she was younger, and he had an ingrained respect for the profession. It was invariably a hard row to hoe.

The teacher nodded back, descended the schoolhouse steps with care, lest she trip over the hem of her brown woolen dress. Instead of a coat or a cloak, she wore a dark blue shawl to keep warm.

Clay waited as she approached, then dismounted to meet

her at the gate, though he kept to his own side and she kept to hers, as was proper.

The lady introduced herself. "Miss Alvira Krenshaw," she said, putting out a bony hand. She hadn't missed the star pinned to his coat, of course; her eyes had gone right to it. "You must be our new town marshal."

Clay shook her hand and acknowledged her supposition with another nod and, "Clay McKettrick."

"How do you do?" she said, not expecting an answer.

Clay gave her one, anyway. "So far, so good," he replied, with a slight grin. Miss Alvira Krenshaw looked like a sturdy, no-nonsense soul, and although she wasn't pretty, she wasn't homely, either. She'd probably make some man a good wife, given half a chance, and though thin, she looked capable of carrying healthy babies to full-term, delivering them without a lot of fuss and raising them to competent adulthood.

Wanting a wife to carry over the threshold of his new house, come spring, and impregnate as soon as possible, Clay might have set right to courting Miss Alvira, provided she was receptive to such attentions, if not for one problem. He'd gone and met Dara Rose Nolan.

Stepping off the train the day before, he'd been sure of almost everything that concerned him. What he wanted, what sort of man he was, all of it. Now, after just two brief encounters with his predecessor's widow, he wasn't sure of much of *anything*.

Considerable figuring out would be called for before he undertook to win himself a bride, and that was for certain.

Over Alvira's shoulder, he saw a boy run over to where the girls were playing hopscotch, grab at Edrina's dangling bonnet and yank on it hard enough to knock her down.

The bonnet laces held, though, and the boy ran, laugh-

ing, his friends shouting a mingling of mockery and en-
couragement, while a disgruntled, flaming-faced Edrina
got back to her feet, dusting off her coat as she glared at
the transgressor.

"Looks like trouble," Clay observed dryly, causing Miss
Alvira to flare out her long, narrow nostrils and then spin
around to see for herself.

Edrina, still flushed with fury, marched right into the
middle of that cluster of small but earnest rascals, stood
face-to-face with the primary mischief-maker and landed
a solid punch to his middle. Knocked the wind right out
of him.

Miss Alvira was on the run by then, blowing shrill toots
through the whistle every schoolmarm seemed to come
equipped with, but the damage, such as it was, was done.

The thwarted bonnet thief was on his knees now, clutching his belly and gasping for breath, and though his dignity had certainly suffered, he didn't look seriously hurt.

Clay suppressed a smile and lingered there by the gate,
watching.

Edrina looked a mite calmer by then, but she was still
pink in the face and her fists remained clenched. She stood
her ground, spotted Clay when she turned her head toward
Miss Alvira and that earsplitting whistle of hers.

"What is going on here?" Alvira demanded, her voice
carrying, almost as shrill as the whistle. She reached down,
caught the gasping boy from behind, where his suspenders
crossed, and wrenched him unceremoniously to his feet.

Clay felt a flash of sympathy for the little fellow. Like
as not, he'd taken a shine to Edrina and, boys being what
boys have always been, hoped to gain her notice by snatching her bonnet and running off with it—the equivalent of
tugging at a girl's pigtail or surprising her with a close-up

look at a bullfrog or a squirmy garter snake, and glory be and hallelujah if she squealed.

Miss Alvira, still gripping the boy's suspenders, turned to frown at Edrina.

"Edrina Nolan," she said, "young ladies do not strike others with their fists."

Edrina, who had been looking in Clay's direction until that moment, faced her accuser, folded her arms and staunchly replied, "He had it coming."

"Go inside this instant," Alvira ordered both children, indicating the open door of the schoolhouse with a pointing of her index finger. "Thomas, you will stand in the corner behind my desk, by the bookcase. Edrina, you will occupy the one next to the cloakroom."

"For how long?" Edrina wanted to know.

Clay had to admire the child's spirit.

"Until I tell you that you may take your seats," Miss Alvira answered firmly, shooing the rest of her brood toward the hallowed halls of learning with a waving motion of her free arm. "Inside," she called. "All of you. Recess is over."

The command elicited groans of protest, but the children obeyed.

Thomas, clearly humiliated because he'd been publicly bested by a girl, slunk, head down, toward the schoolhouse, and Edrina followed in her own time, literally dragging her feet by scuffing the toe of first one shoe and then the other in the dirt as she walked. Finally, she looked back over one shoulder, caught Clay's eye and gave an eloquent little shrug of resignation.

He hoped the distance and the shadow cast by the brim of his hat would hide his smile.

That kid should have been born a McKettrick.

DARA ROSE MADE THE ROUNDS that morning just as she'd planned, swallowing her pride and knocking on each door to ask for work, with little Harriet trudging along, uncomplaining, at her side.

There were only half a dozen real *houses* in Blue River; the rest were mostly hovels and shanties, shacks like the one she lived in. The folks there were no better off than she was and, in many cases, things were worse for them. Thin smoke wafted from crooked chimneys and scrawny chickens pecked at the small expanses of bare dirt that passed for yards.

Mrs. O'Reilly, whose husband had run off with a dance hall girl six months ago and left her with three children to look after, all of them under five years old, was outside. The woman was probably in her early twenties, but she looked a generation older; there were already streaks of gray at her temples and she'd lost one of her eye teeth.

She had a bonfire going, with a big tin washtub teetering atop the works, full of other people's laundry. Steam boiled up into the crisp air as she stirred the soapy soup, and Peg O'Reilly managed a semblance of a smile when she caught sight of Dara Rose and Harriet.

Two of the O'Reilly children, both boys, ran whooping around their mother like Sioux braves on the warpath, both of them barefoot and coatless. Their older sister, Addie, must have been inside, where it was, Dara Rose devoutly hoped, comparatively warm.

"Mornin', Miz Nolan," Peg called, though she didn't smile. She was probably self-conscious about that missing tooth, Dara Rose figured, with a stab of well-hidden pity.

Dara Rose smiled, offered a wave and paused at the edge of the road, even though she'd meant to keep going. Lord knew, she had reason enough to be discouraged herself, after being turned away from all those doors, but she just couldn't bring herself to pass on by.

Harriet, no doubt weary from keeping up with Dara Rose all morning, tugged reluctantly at her mother's hand, wanting to go on.

"How's Addie?" Dara Rose asked.

"She's poorly," Peg replied. "Been abed since yesterday, so she's not much help with these little yahoos." Still tending to the wash, which was just coming to a simmer, she indicated the boys with a nod of her head.

They had both stopped their chasing game to stare at Harriet in abject wonder. Even in her poor clothes and the shoes she would outgrow all too soon, she probably looked as pretty to them as that doll over at the mercantile did to her.

"Mama," Harriet whispered, looking up at Dara Rose from beneath the drooping brim of her bonnet, "what's that smell?"

"Hush," Dara Rose whispered back, hoping Peg hadn't heard the little girl's voice over the crackling of the fire and the barking of a neighbor's dog.

Peg let go of the old broomstick she used to stir the shirts and trousers and small clothes as they soaked, and wiped a forearm across her brow. The sleeves of her calico dress were rolled up to her elbows, and her apron was little more than a rag.

"Could you use some eggs?" Dara Rose asked, in the manner of one asking a favor. "I've got plenty put by."

A flicker of yearning showed in Peg O'Reilly's care-worn face before she squared her shoulders and raised her chin a notch. "I'd say no, on grounds that I've got my pride and I know you're having a hard time of it, too, but for the young'uns," she replied. "The last of the oatmeal is used up, and we're almost out of pinto beans, but a nice fried egg might put some color in Addie's cheeks and that's for sure."

"I'll send Edrina over with a basket right after she gets home from school," Dara Rose said.

"You understand that I can't pay you nothin'," Peg warned, stiffening her backbone.

"I understand," Dara Rose confirmed lightly, though every egg her hens laid was precious, since it could be sold for cash money or traded for things she couldn't raise, like flour. "I've got too many, and I don't want them to go to waste."

"Mama," Harriet interjected, "we don't—"

This time, Dara Rose didn't hush her daughter out loud, but simply squeezed the child's hand a little more tightly than she might otherwise have done.

"Obliged, then," Peg said, and went back to her stirring.

Dara Rose nodded and started off toward home again, poor Harriet scrambling to keep up.

"Mama," the child insisted, half-breathless, "you already traded away all the eggs, remember? Over at the mercantile? And the hens probably haven't laid any new ones yet."

"There are nearly two dozen in the crock on the pantry shelf," Dara Rose reminded her daughter. Like the potatoes, carrots, turnips and onions she'd squirreled away down in the root cellar, along with a few bushels of apples from the tree in her yard, the eggs suspended in water glass were part of her skimpy reserves, something she and the girls could eat if the hens stopped laying or the hawks got them.

"Yes," Harriet reasoned, intrepidly logical, "but what if there's a hard winter and *we* need to eat them?"

"Harriet," Dara Rose replied, walking a little faster because it was almost time for Edrina to come home for the midday meal, "there are times when a person simply has to help somebody who needs a hand and hope the good Lord pays heed and makes recompense." Parting with a few eggs didn't trouble her nearly as much as the realization that her five-year-old daughter had obviously been worrying about whether or not there would be enough food to get them through.

"What's 'recompense'?" Harriet asked.

"Never mind," Dara Rose answered.

They reached the house, removed their bonnets and their wraps—Dara Rose's cloak and Harriet's coat—and Dara Rose ladled warm water out of the stove reservoir for the washing of hands.

In her mind, she heard Peg O'Reilly's words of brave despair. *The last of the oatmeal is used up, and we're almost out of pinto beans....*

Peg earned a pittance taking in laundry as it was, and what little money she earned probably went to pay for starvation rations and to meet the rent on that converted chicken coop of a house they all lived in.

As she reheated the canned venison leftover from last night's supper, then sliced and thinly buttered the last of the bread she'd made a few days before, Dara Rose silently reminded herself of something Parnell had often told her. "No matter how tough things get," he used to say, "you won't have to look far to find somebody else who'd be glad to trade places with you."

Her children were healthy, unlike Peg's eldest, and the three of them had a roof over their heads. And Parnell, at least, hadn't left them willingly, the way Jack O'Reilly had done.

Harriet, her mother's busy little helper, set three places

at the table and then dragged a chair over to the side window so she could stand on the seat and keep a lookout for her sister. Although they had their scuffles and tiffs, like all children, Harriet's admiration for Edrina knew no bounds.

"There she is!" Harriet shouted gleefully, after a few moments of peering through the glass. "There's Edrina!"

Dara Rose smiled and began ladling warm venison and broth into enamel-coated bowls. She'd just set the bread plate in the middle of the improvised table when Edrina dragged in, looking despondent.

"You might as well know straightaway that I'm in trouble again," she immediately confessed. "Thomas Phillips tried to steal my bonnet at recess, and near strangled me with the ties while he was at it, and I socked him in the stomach. Miss Krenshaw made me stand in the corner for a whole hour, and I have to stay after school to wash the blackboard every day this week."

Dara Rose sighed, shook her head in feigned dismay and placed her hands on her hips. "Edrina," she said, on a long breath, and shook her head again.

"Did Thomas have to stand in the corner, too?" Harriet inquired, already a great believer in fair play.

"Yes," Edrina answered, with precious little satisfaction. "He has to carry in the drinking water for the whole school."

"Wash your hands," Dara Rose said mildly, when her elder daughter would have sat down to her meal instead.

Edrina obeyed, with a sigh of her own, and pulled the stool out from under the sink to climb up and plunge her small hands into the basin of warm water Dara Rose had set there.

"Mr. McKettrick came by the schoolhouse today," the child announced. "That sure is a fine horse he rides."

Dara Rose felt an odd little catch at the mention of the new marshal and, to her shame, caught herself wondering if he'd found Alvira Krenshaw at all fetching. She was certainly eligible, Miss Krenshaw was, and while she wouldn't win any prizes for looks, most people agreed that she was a handsome woman with a good head on her shoulders.

"Was there some kind of trouble? Besides your disagreement with Thomas?"

Edrina had finished washing up, and she climbed deftly back down off the stool, drying her hands on her skirts as she approached the table. "No," she replied, "but he talked to Miss Krenshaw at the gate for a long time."

Dara Rose, who had long since learned to choose her battles, decided to let the hand-drying incident pass. She hoisted Harriet onto the stool, helped her lather to her elbows and then rinse and lifted her down again.

The three of them gathered at the table.

It was Harriet's turn to say grace. "Thank you for the venison and the bread," she said, in her direct way, her bright head bowed and her eyes squeezed shut. "And if there's any way I could get that pretty doll in the window of the mercantile for my very own, I would appreciate the kindness. Amen."

Dara Rose suppressed a smile even as she endured another pang to her heart. Much as she'd have loved to give her daughters toys for Christmas, she couldn't afford to do it. And even if she'd had any spare money at all, Edrina and Harriet needed shoes and warm clothes and nourishing food, like milk.

"What do you want St. Nicholas to bring you for Christmas?" Harriet asked Edrina, with companionable interest, as they all began to eat.

Edrina answered without hesitation, a note of gentle tolerance in her voice. "You know there isn't any St. Nicholas, Harriet," she reminded her sister. "He's just a story person, made up by that Mr. Moore."

"Couldn't we just *pretend* he's real?" Harriet wanted to know. "Just 'til lunch is over?" She sounded more like an adult than a little girl and Dara Rose, though proud of her bright daughters, hoped they weren't growing up too fast.

"It wouldn't hurt to pretend," she put in quietly.

Harriet's face lit up. "What do *you* want for Christmas, Mama?" she asked eagerly, forgetting all about her food.

Dara Rose pretended to think very hard for a few moments. "A cow, I think," she finally decided. "Then we'd have milk and butter of our own. Maybe even cheese."

Harriet looked nonplussed. "A cow?" she repeated.

Edrina glanced at Dara Rose, her expression almost conspiratorial, and considered the question under discussion. "I know what *I'd* want," she said presently. "Books. Exciting ones, with bears and outlaws and spooks in them."

Again, Dara Rose's heart pinched. She'd be lucky to afford peppermint sticks to drop into the girls' Christmas stockings this year, never mind dolls and books.

She cleared her throat. "Harriet and I stopped by the O'Reilly place today," she said. "Little Addie's under the weather again, and those boys looked hungry enough to dip spoons into the laundry kettle."

"And something smells bad there," Harriet added.

Dara Rose didn't scold her, but went right on. "I think they'd be grateful to have firewood and enough to eat, like we do," she said, hoping she'd made her point and wouldn't have to follow up with a sermon on Christian charity.

"Mama's giving them some of our eggs," Harriet said matter-of-factly. "She says sometimes a person just has to help somebody else and hope the good Lord pays heed and makes competition."

Edrina didn't say anything, since she had a mouthful of bread.

Dara Rose wondered if Harriet even knew what it meant to pay heed. "The two of you can take a basket over to the O'Reillys', as soon as school's out for the day," she said. "And furthermore, Harriet Nolan, you will *not* remark on the bad smell."

"It's probably the outhouse that stinks," Edrina said. "Ours might get that way, too, without Papa around to shovel lye into it once in a while."

"Edrina," Dara Rose said, "we are at the table."

A long pause ensued.

"I have to stay after to wash the blackboard," Edrina reminded her mother.

"Fine," Dara Rose answered, pushing back her chair and carrying her bowl and spoon to the sink. "I'll wash the eggs and put them in the basket and you can drop them off at the O'Reilly place on your way back to school."

"There will be hell to pay if I'm late for class," Edrina said frankly. "Don't forget, I'm already in trouble for slugging Thomas Phillips in the stomach."

Dara Rose bit the inside of her lower lip to keep from smiling. "I won't forget," she said, heading for the single shelf that served as a pantry, bowl in hand, and fishing eight perfect brown ovals out of the crock filled to the brim with water glass. "If you hurry, you can deliver the eggs and still get back to school before Miss Krenshaw rings the bell. *And* I will thank you not to swear, Edrina Nolan."

Harriet, who staunchly maintained that she was too

old to take naps, was already getting heavy-lidded, chin drooping, and yawning a little.

Dara Rose washed the eggs and put them into the basket, covering them with a flour-sack dish towel. She handed them to Edrina, who was already buttoning her coat. "Wear your bonnet," she instructed. "The sky may be blue as summer, but the wind has a bite to it."

Edrina nodded, resigned, and let herself out, taking the egg basket with her.

"Bring that basket home," Dara Rose called after her. "And the dish towel, too."

Edrina replied, but Dara Rose didn't hear what she said. She was already scooping up her sleepy child and carrying her to bed.

CLAY CHECKED THE BITTER Gulch Saloon and looked in at the bank, but there was no malfeasance afoot in either place.

Figuring it was indeed going to be a long winter, he walked back to the jailhouse, where he had a tiny office, a potbellied stove and a cot, and helped himself to a cup of the passable coffee he'd made earlier.

The stuff was stale and lukewarm, but stout enough to rouse a dead man from his eternal rest.

That, he supposed, was what this coming winter was going to feel like. Eternal rest.

He sighed, crossed to the single cell and peered through the bars, almost wishing he had a prisoner. That way, there would have been somebody to talk to, at least.

Alas, lawbreakers seemed to be pretty thin on the ground around those parts at the moment, a fact he supposed he should have been grateful to note.

Clay sat down in the creaky wooden chair behind the

scarred wooden table that served as a desk and reached for the dusty stack of wanted posters and old mail piled on one corner.

If anybody stopped by, he'd like to give the impression that he was working, even if he wasn't. It made him smile to imagine what his granddad would think if he could see him now, collecting seventy-five dollars a month for doing not much of anything except drinking bad coffee and flipping through somebody else's correspondence.

He set aside the older wanted posters and read the few missives that looked even remotely official—none of them were, it turned out—and he was thinking maybe he ought to meander over to the livery stable and brush old Outlaw down, when he came to the last two letters and realized they were addressed to Mrs. Parnell B. Nolan.

The first, from an outfit called the Wildflower Salve Company, was most likely a sales pitch of some kind, but the second looked personal and smelled faintly of lemon verbena. The envelope was fat, made of good vellum, and the handwriting on the front was flowing cursive, with all kinds of loops and swirls.

Clay looked at the postmark, but couldn't make out where the letter had been mailed, or when, and there wasn't any return address.

Not that any of this was his concern in the first place.

Clay frowned, wondering how long the letters had been moldering in that pile, and then he smiled, holding the envelopes in one hand and lightly slapping them against the opposite palm.

Maybe it wasn't his sworn duty to make sure the mail got delivered, but it was as good an excuse as any for calling on Dara Rose Nolan.

Clay rose from his chair, fetched his coat and hat and set out on foot.

THERE HE STOOD, on her front doorstep this time, looking affably handsome.

For the briefest fraction of a moment, Dara Rose feared that Clay McKettrick had changed his mind, decided he wanted the house, after all. Her stomach quivered in a peculiar way that didn't seem to have much to do with the fear of eviction.

"I found these letters over at the office," he said, and produced two envelopes from an inside pocket of his duster. "They're addressed to you."

Dara Rose's eyes rounded. Getting a letter was a rare thing indeed. Getting two at once was virtually unheard-of.

She opened the door a little wider, extended a hand for the envelopes and spoke very quietly because Harriet was napping. "Thank you," she said.

He let her take the envelopes, but he held on to them for a second longer than necessary, too.

Although her curiosity was great, Dara Rose wanted to savor the prospect of those letters for a little while. She'd read them later, by lamplight, when the girls were both down for the night and the house was quiet.

She tucked them into the pocket of her apron, blushing a little.

"Come in," she heard her own voice say, much to her surprise.

It simply wasn't proper for a widow to invite a man into her home, even in broad daylight, but she'd done just that and already stepped back so he could pass, and the marshal didn't hesitate to step over the threshold.

He stood in the middle of the front room, seeming to fill it to capacity with the width of his shoulders and the sheer unwieldy substance of his presence. His gaze went straight to the oversize daguerreotype of Parnell on one wall.

He seemed to consider her late husband's visage for a few moments, before turning to meet her eyes.

"He doesn't look like the kind of man who'd die in a brothel," he remarked.

Dara Rose was jangled, but not offended. Everyone knew what had happened to Parnell, and the scandal, though still alive, had long since died down to an occasional whisper, especially since Jack O'Reilly had left his wife and children for a sloe-eyed girl from the Bitter Gulch Saloon.

"He wasn't," she said, very softly, and then colored up again. "That kind of man, I mean. Not really."

Dara Rose had never confided the truth about her marriage to Parnell Nolan to a single living soul west of the Mississippi River, and she was confounded by a sudden urge to tell Marshal McKettrick everything.

Not a chance, she thought, running her hands down the front of her apron as if they'd been wet.

"It must have been hard for you and the children," Clay said quietly. His eyes, blue as cornflowers in high summer, took on a solemn expression. "Not just his dying, but being left on your own and all."

"We manage," Dara Rose said.

"I reckon you do," he agreed, and he looked more puzzled than solemn now.

She knew he was wondering why she hadn't found another husband, but she wasn't about to volunteer an explanation. Maybe she hadn't actually loved Parnell Nolan, but she'd liked him. Depended on him. Even respected him.

Parnell had been kind to her, cherished the girls like they were his daughters instead of his nieces, and married her.

She would have felt disloyal, discussing Parnell with

a relative stranger; though, oddly enough, in some ways she felt as if she'd always known Clay McKettrick, and known him well. He stirred vague memories in her, like dreams that left only an echo behind when the sun rose.

The silence was awkward.

Dara Rose didn't ask the marshal to sit down, and she couldn't offer him coffee because she didn't have any.

So the two of them just stood there, each one waiting for the other to speak.

Finally, Clay grinned ever so slightly and turned his hat decisively in his hands. He went to the door and opened it, pausing to look back at Dara Rose, his impressive form rimmed in wintry light.

"Good day to you, Mrs. Nolan," he said.

Dara Rose swallowed. "Good day, Mr. McKettrick," she replied formally. "And, once again, thank you."

"Anytime," he said, and then he left the house, closed the door behind him.

Dara Rose resisted the temptation to rush to the window and watch him heading down the walk.

Harriet appeared in the doorway to the bedroom, hair rumpled, rubbing her eyes with the backs of her hands. "I thought I heard Papa's voice," she said.

Dara Rose's heart cracked and then split down the middle. "Sweetheart," she said, bending her knees so she could look directly into the child's sleep-flushed face, "Papa's gone to heaven, remember?"

Harriet's lower lip wobbled, which further bruised Dara Rose's already injured heart. How could such a small child be expected to understand the permanence of death?

"Is heaven a real place?" Harriet asked. "Or is it just pretend, like St. Nicholas?"

"I believe it's a real place," Dara Rose said.

Harriet frowned, obviously puzzled. "Is it like here? Are there trees and kittens and trains to ride?"

Dara Rose blinked rapidly and rose back to her full height. "I don't know, sweetheart. One day, a long, long time from now, we'll find out for sure, but right now, we have to live in *this* world, and we might as well make the best of it."

"I think I would like this world better," Harriet told her, "if there was a St. Nicholas in it."

Dara Rose gave a small, strangled chuckle at that, and pulled her daughter close for a hug. "We don't need St. Nicholas, you and Edrina and me," she said. "We have one another."

Chapter 4

⟨⟨⟨ ⟩⟩⟩

AFTER THE CHICKENS WERE FED and had retreated into their coop to roost for the night, Dara Rose made a simple supper of baked potatoes and last summer's string beans, boiled with bits of salt pork and onion, for herself and the girls, and the three of them sat at the table in the kitchen, eating by the light of a kerosene lantern and chatting quietly.

The subject of St. Nicholas did not come up again, thankfully. In Dara Rose's humble opinion, Clement C. Moore had a lot to answer for. By writing that lengthy and admittedly charming poem, "'Twas the Night Before Christmas," he'd created expectations in children that many parents couldn't hope to meet.

Instead, Edrina recounted her visit to the O'Reillys' after lunch, and fretted that it wasn't fair that she had to wash the blackboard every single day for a week when all she'd done was defend herself against that wretched Thomas. Large flakes of snow drifted, like benevolent ghosts, past the darkened window next to the back door, and brought a sigh to hover in the back of Dara Rose's throat.

Winter. As a privileged only child, back in Massachusetts, she'd loved everything about that season, even the cold. It was a time to skate and sled and build castles out of snow and then drink hot chocolate by the fire while Nanny told stories or recited long, exciting poems about shipwrecks and ghosts and Paul Revere's ride.

Had she ever really lived such a life? Dara Rose wondered now, as she did whenever her childhood came to mind.

"Mama?" Edrina said, breaking the sudden spell the sight of snowflakes had cast over Dara Rose. "Did you hear what I said about Addie O'Reilly?"

Dara Rose gave herself an inward shake and sat up a little straighter in her chair. "I'm sorry," she said, because she was always truthful with the children. "I'm afraid I was woolgathering."

Edrina's perfect little face glowed, heart-shaped, in the light of love and a kerosene lantern. "She's really sick," she informed her mother, in a tone of good-natured patience, as though she were the parent and Dara Rose the child. "Mrs. O'Reilly told me she has romantic fever."

Dara Rose did not correct Edrina. She was too stricken by the tragedy of it, the patent unfairness. *Rheumatic fever.* Was there no end to the sorrows and hardships visited on that poor family?

"That's dreadful," she said.

"And Addie gets lonely, staying inside all the time," Edrina went on. "So I said Harriet and I would come to visit on Saturday morning. We can, can't we, Mama? Because I promised."

Dara Rose's heart swelled with affection for her daughter, and then sank a little. It was like her spirited Edrina to make such an offer, and follow through on it, too, whether or not she had her mother's permission. When Edrina made a promise, she kept it, which meant she was really asking if Harriet could go with her.

As far as Dara Rose knew, rheumatic fever wasn't contagious, but heaven only knew what other diseases her children might contract during a visit to the O'Reilly house—diphtheria, the dreaded influenza, perhaps even typhoid or cholera.

"You mustn't promise such things, in the future, without speaking to me first," Dara Rose told Edrina, hedging. "I feel as sorry for the O'Reillys as you do, Edrina, but there are other considerations."

"And it stinks over there," Harriet interjected solemnly, her nose twitching a little at the memory.

Dara Rose had lost her appetite, which was fine, because she'd had enough to eat, anyway. "Harriet," she said. "That will be enough of that sort of talk. It is not suitable for the supper table."

Harriet sighed. "It's *never* suitable," she lamented.

"Hush," Dara Rose told her, her attention focused, for the moment, on her elder daughter. "You may visit the O'Reillys on Saturday morning," she stated, rising to begin clearing the table. "But only because you gave your word and I would not ask you to break it."

"If I hadn't promised, you wouldn't let me go?" Edrina pressed. She'd never been one to quit while the quitting was good, a trait she came by honestly, Dara Rose had to admit. She had the same shortcoming herself.

"That's right," she replied, at some length. "I have to think about your safety, Edrina, and that of your sister."

"My safety? The O'Reillys wouldn't hurt us."

"Not deliberately," Dara Rose allowed, "but it isn't the most sanitary place in the world, and you might catch something."

Although she didn't mention it, she was thinking of the diphtheria outbreak two years before, during which four children had perished, all of them from one family.

"Is that suitable talk for the supper table?" Harriet asked sincerely.

"Never mind," Dara Rose said. "It's time you both got ready for bed. Shall I walk with you to the outhouse, or are you brave enough to go on your own?"

Edrina scraped back her chair, rose to fetch her coat and Harriet's from the pegs near the back door. Her expression said she was brave enough to do anything, and protect her little sister in the bargain.

"Maybe that's why Addie's so lonesome," Edrina said, opening the door to the chilly night, with its flurries of snow. "Because everybody is afraid of catching something if they visit."

Chagrin swept over Dara Rose—*out of the mouths of babes*—but she assumed a stern countenance. "Don't stand there with the door open," she said.

Later, when the children were in bed, and she'd read them a story from their one dog-eared book of fairy tales and heard their prayers—Harriet put in another request for the doll from the mercantile—kissed them good-night and tucked them in, Dara Rose returned to the kitchen.

There, she took the two letters Mr. McKettrick had delivered earlier from her apron pocket, and sat down.

The kerosene in the lamp was getting low, and the wick was smoking a little, but Dara Rose did not hurry.

She knew the plump missive was from her cousin, Piper, who taught school in a small town in Maine. She meant to save that one for last, and she took the time to weigh it in her hand, run her fingers over the vellum and examine the stamp before setting it carefully aside.

She opened the letter from the Wildflower Salve Company first, even though she knew it was an advertisement and nothing more, and carefully smoothed the single page on the tabletop.

Her eyes widened a little as she read, and her heart fluttered up into her throat as her excitement grew.

Bold print declared that Dara Rose was holding the key to financial security right there in her hand. She could win prizes, it fairly shouted. She could earn money. And all she had to do was introduce her friends and neighbors to the wonders of Wildflower Salve. Each colorfully decorated round tin—an elegant keepsake in its own right, according to the Wildflower Salve people—sold for a mere fifty cents. And she would get to keep a whopping twenty-five cents for her commission.

Dara Rose sat back, thinking.

Twenty-five cents was a lot of money.

And there were prizes. All sorts of prizes—toys, household goods, luxuries of all sorts—could be had in lieu of commissions, if the "independent business person" preferred.

Out of the goodness of their hearts, the folks at the Wildflower Salve Company, of Racine, Wisconsin, would be happy to send her a full twenty tins of this "medicinal miracle" in good faith. If for some incomprehensible reason her "friends and relations" didn't snap up the whole shipment practically as soon as she opened the parcel, she could return the merchandise and owe nothing.

Five dollars, Dara Rose thought. If she sold twenty

tins of Wildflower Salve, she would earn *five dollars*—a virtual fortune.

The kerosene lamp flickered, reminding her that she'd soon be sitting in the dark, and Dara Rose set aside "the opportunity of a lifetime" to open the letter from Piper.

A crisp ten-dollar bill fell out, nearly stopping Dara Rose's heart.

She set it carefully aside, and her hands trembled as she unfolded the clump of pages covered in Piper's lovely cursive. The date was nearly eight months in the past.

"Dearest Cousin," the missive began. "News of your tragic misfortune reached me yesterday, via the telegraph…"

Piper's letter, misplaced all this time, went on to say that she hoped Dara Rose could put the money enclosed to good use—that the weather was fine in Maine, with the spring coming, but she already dreaded the winter. How were the girls faring? Did Dara Rose intend to stay on in "that little Texas town," or would she and the children consider coming to live with her? The teacher's quarters were small, she wrote, bringing tears to Dara Rose's eyes, but they could make do, the four of them, couldn't they? There were crocuses and tulips and daffodils shooting up in people's flower beds, Piper went on to relate, and the days were distinctly longer. For all that, alas, she was lonesome when she wasn't teaching. She'd been briefly engaged, but the fellow had turned out to be a rascal and a rounder, and there didn't seem to be any likely prospects on the horizon.

Dara Rose read the whole letter and then immediately read it again. Besides Edrina and Harriet, Piper was the only blood relation she had left in all the world, and Dara Rose missed her sorely. Holding the letter, seeing the familiar handwriting spanning the pages, was the next best thing to having her cousin right there, in the flesh, sitting across the table from her.

But what must Piper think of her? Dara Rose fretted, after a third reading. She'd written this letter so long ago, and sent such a generous gift of money, only to receive silence in return.

The lantern guttered out.

Dara Rose sighed, folded the letter carefully and tucked it back into its envelope. She took the ten-dollar bill with her to the bedroom, where the girls were sound asleep, and placed it carefully between the pages in her Bible for safekeeping.

She undressed quickly, since the little room was cold, and donned her flannel nightgown, returned to the kitchen carrying a lighted candle stuck to a jar lid and dipped water from the stove reservoir to wash her face. When that was done, she brushed her teeth at the sink and steeled herself to make the trek to the outhouse, through the snowy cold.

When she got back, she locked the door, used the candle to light her way back to the bedroom, blew out the flame and climbed into bed with her daughters.

She was tired, but too excited to fall asleep right away.

She had ten precious dollars.

The Wildflower Salve Company had offered her honest work.

She'd as good as—well, *almost* as good as—spent an evening with her cousin and dearest friend, Piper.

And Marshal Clay McKettrick had the bluest eyes she'd ever seen.

THE JAILHOUSE, CLAY SOON discovered, was a lonely place at night.

He'd already had supper over at the hotel dining room—

chicken and dumplings almost as good as his ma's—and he'd paid a visit to Outlaw, over at the livery stable, too. He'd even sent a telegram north to Indian Rock, to let his family know he'd arrived and was settling in nicely.

That done, Clay had filled the water bucket and set up the coffeepot for morning, then filled the wood box next to the potbellied stove. There being no place to hang up his clothes, he left them folded in his travel trunk, there in the back room, where the bed was. Most of his books hadn't arrived yet—he had a passel of them and they had to be shipped down from Indian Rock in crates—and he couldn't seem to settle down to read the one favorite he'd brought along on the train, Jules Verne's *Around the World in Eighty Days*. He must have read that book a dozen times over the years, and he never got tired of it, but that night, it failed to hold his interest.

He kept thinking about Dara Rose Nolan, the gold of her hair and the fiery blue spirit in her eyes. He thought about her shapely breasts and small waist and smooth skin and that flash of pride that was so easy to arouse in her.

And the same old question plagued him: Why in the devil would a man with a wife like that squander his time in a whorehouse, the way her husband had done?

Nobody could help dying, of course, but they had at least some choice about *where* they died, didn't they? It was simple common sense—folks didn't turn up their toes in places they hadn't ventured into in the first place.

Knowing he wouldn't sleep, anyhow, Clay strapped on his gun belt, shrugged into his duster and reached for his hat.

He was the marshal, after all.

He'd just take a little stroll up and down Main Street and make sure any visiting cowpokes or drifters were minding their manners. If anybody needed arresting, he'd throw them in the hoosegow and start up a conversation.

What he really needed, he supposed, stepping out onto the dark sidewalk, was a woman. Someone like Dara Rose Nolan.

Maybe he'd get himself a dog—that would provide some companionship. He'd have to do all the talking, of course, but he liked critters. He'd grown up with all manner of them on the ranch.

Yes, sir, he needed a dog.

He hadn't even reached the corner when he heard the first yelp.

He frowned, stopped to pinpoint the direction.

"Dutch, you kick that dog again," he heard a male voice say, "and I'll shoot *you*, 'stead of him!"

Clay, having located the disturbance, pushed his coat back to uncover the handle of his .45 and stepped into the alley.

It was dark, and the snow veiled the moon, but light struggled through the filthy windows of the buildings on either side, and he could make out two men, one holding a pistol, standing over a shivering form huddled close to the ground.

"Hold it right there," Clay said, in deadly earnest, when the man with the pistol raised it to shoot. "What's going on here?"

The dog whimpered.

"Nothin', Marshal," one of the men answered, in a drunken whine. "The poor mutt's half-starved, just a bag of bones. We figured on putting it out of its misery, that's all. Meant it as a kindness."

"Get the hell out of here," Clay said. He could not abide a bully.

The two men responded by turning on their heels and running in the other direction.

Clay waited until they were out of sight before he put the .45 back in its holster and approached the dog. "You in a bad way there, fella?" he asked, crouching to offer a hand.

The animal sniffed cautiously at his fingers and whimpered again.

"Where'd you come from?" Clay asked, gently examining the critter for broken bones or open wounds. He seemed to be all right, though his ribs protruded and his belly was concave and he stunk like all get-out.

The dog whined, though this time there was less sorrow in the sound.

"You know," Clay told the animal companionably, "I was just thinking to myself that what I need is a dog to keep me company. Now, here you are. How'd you like to help me keep the peace in this sorry excuse for a town?"

The dog seemed amenable to the idea, and raised himself slowly, teetering a little, to his four fur-covered feet. He had burrs stuck in his coat, that poor cuss, and there was no telling what color he was, or if he leaned toward any particular breed.

"You come on with me, if you can walk," Clay said. "I brought home what was left of my supper, and it seems to me you could use a decent meal."

With that, he turned to head back toward the sidewalk. The dog limped after him, pausing every few moments, as though afraid he'd committed some transgression without knowing about it.

Back at the jailhouse, Clay got a better look at the dog, after lighting a lantern to see by, but seeing didn't help much. The creature was neither big nor little, and he had floppy ears, but that was the extent of what Clay could make out.

Glad to have something to do, not to mention some companionship, Clay poured the remains of his chicken and dumplings onto the one tin plate he possessed and set it on the floor, near the stove.

The dog sniffed at the food, looked up at Clay with the kind of uncertainty that breaks a decent person's heart and waited.

"You go ahead and have supper," Clay said gently. "I imagine you could use some water, too."

Slowly, cautiously, the dog lowered his muzzle and began to eat.

Clay walked softly, approaching the water bucket, and ladled up a dipperful.

The dog lapped thirstily from the well of the dipper, then returned to his supper, clearly ravenous, licking the plate clean as a whistle.

Clay carried in more water from the pump out back, heated it bucket by bucket on the potbellied stove and finally filled the washtub he'd found in one of the cells. He eased the dog into the warm water and sluiced him down before lathering his hide with his own bar of soap.

The animal didn't raise any fuss, he simply stood there, shivering and looking like nothing so much as a half-drowned rat. Gradually, it became clear that his coat was brown and white, speckled like a pinto horse.

Clay dried him off with one of the two towels he'd purchased earlier, over at the mercantile, hefted him out of the tub and set him gently on his feet, near the stove.

The dog looked up at him curiously, head tilted to one side.

Clay chuckled. "Now, then," he said. "You look a lot more presentable than you did before."

The dog gave a single, tentative *woof,* obviously unsure how the remark would be received in present company.

Clay leaned to pat the animal's damp head. "What you are," he said, "is a coincidence. Like I told you, I was thinking about how much I'd like to have a dog, and then you and I made our acquaintance. But since 'coincidence' would be too much trouble for a name, I figure I'll call you Chester."

"Woof," said Chester, with more confidence than before.

Clay laughed. "Chester it is, then," he agreed.

Using a rough blanket from the cot in the jail cell, Clay fashioned a bed for the dog, close to the stove. Chester sniffed the cloth, stepped gingerly onto it, made a circle and settled down with a sigh.

"Night," Clay said.

Chester closed his eyes, sighed again and slept.

THE HENS HAD ONLY LAID three eggs between the lot of them, Dara Rose discovered the next morning, when she visited the chicken coop, but she wasn't as disappointed by this as she normally would have been.

She had ten dollars tucked between the leaves of her Bible—a fortune.

And she had a future, a bright one, as Blue River, Texas's sole distributor of Wildflower Salve. All she had to do was fill out the coupon and mail it in, and before the New Year, she'd be in business.

Granted, there weren't a lot of people in Blue River, but there were plenty of surrounding farms and ranches, and those isolated women would be thrilled to purchase salve in a pretty tin, especially after she explained the benefits of regular use.

Not that she knew exactly what those benefits *were,* but the Wildflower Salve people had promised to send a training guide along with her first shipment.

As soon as she'd gotten Edrina off to school, she intended to write a long letter to Piper, explaining that *her* letter had been accidentally misplaced all this time, and she'd only received it the day before, and that was why her answer was so late in coming. Of course she'd thank her cousin profusely for the generous gift of ten dollars, and bring Piper up-to-date where she and the girls were concerned.

Her mind bumbled back and forth between the planned letter and her impending career in merchandising like a bee trapped inside a jar while she prepared oatmeal for breakfast, toasted bread in the oven and officiated over a debate between Edrina and Harriet, concerning whose turn it was to sleep in the middle of the bed that night.

Neither one wanted to, and Dara Rose finally said *she'd* take the middle, for heaven's sake, and what had she done to deserve two such argumentative daughters?

After breakfast, Dara Rose and Harriet bundled up to walk Edrina to school. Normally, Edrina managed the distance on her own, but today, Dara Rose wanted a word with Miss Krenshaw.

"I'm *already* being punished," Edrina fussed, as the three of them hurried along a road hoary with frost and hardened snow. "I *told* you I have to stay after and wash the blackboard. So why do you need to talk to Miss Krenshaw, when you know all that?"

Dara Rose hid a smile. She was holding Harriet's hand, and trying to pace herself to the child's much shorter strides. "I merely want to inquire about the Christmas pageant," she replied. There was always some sort of program at the schoolhouse, whether it was carol singing, a Nativity play or an evening of recitals, and everyone attended.

"Oh," said Edrina, still sounding not only mystified, but apparently a little nervous, too.

Dara Rose wondered if there was something her daughter should have told her, but hadn't.

"Do you think it will snow again, Mama?" Harriet asked, tilting her head way back to look up at the glowering sky. "Christmas is less than two weeks away, and St. Nicholas will need a lot of snow, since he travels in a sleigh."

"Goose," Edrina said, nudging her sister with one elbow. "There *isn't* any St. Nicholas, remember?"

"Edrina," Dara Rose interceded gently.

"I'm *pretending,* that's all," Harriet said, with a toss of her head. "You can't *stop* me, either."

"Pretending is *stupid,*" Edrina said. "It's for babies."

Dara Rose stopped, and both her children had to stop, too, since she was holding Harriet's hand at the time and it was easy to catch Edrina by the shoulder and halt her progress.

"Enough," Dara Rose said firmly.

They began to walk again.

THE SKY WAS HEAVY and gray that morning when Clay left Chester to digest the leftovers from his hotel dining room breakfast within the warm radius of the jailhouse stove and headed over to the livery stable to fetch Outlaw.

It was cold and getting colder, so Clay raised the collar of his duster as he led the saddled gelding out into the road. There had been snow during the night, leaving a hard crust on the ground, and there would be more, judging by the weighted clouds brooding overhead, but the ride was a short one and he'd be back in Blue River before any serious weather had a chance to set in.

Raised in the high country, where a soft, slow, feathery snowfall could turn into a raging blizzard within a span of ten minutes, he had a sense of what signs he ought to look out for, as well as those he could safely ignore.

Today, all the indications—the direction of wind, the foul promise of the darkening sky, the way the cold bit through the heavy canvas of his duster—inclined a man toward caution.

He let Outlaw have his head once they were out of town, let the horse run for the sheer joy of it, and they soon reached their destination, the flat acres where Clay intended to erect a house and a barn.

There, he dismounted and left Outlaw to catch his breath and graze on the scant remains of last summer's grass, paced off the perimeters of the house and marked the corners with piles of small rocks. He did the same for the barn, then stood a while, the wind slicing clear to his marrow, and imagined the place, finished.

The house, a kit he'd sent away to Sears, Roebuck and Company for, amounted to a sensible rectangle, the kind he could easily add on to as the years went by, with windows on all sides, white clapboard walls and a shingled roof. He'd have to hire some help to put the thing together, of course, but he planned to do a lot of the work with his own hands, and that included everything from laying floorboards to gathering rock for the fireplace and then mortaring the stones together.

With the McKettrick family expanding the way it had been for some years, Clay had helped build several houses, and put up additions, too. The kit wouldn't arrive until late April, but he'd need to have the foundation ready, and the well dug, too.

Of course, a lot depended on what kind of winter they were in for—Blue River was in the Hill Country, and therefore the climate wasn't as temperate as it was in some parts of Texas—but he could already feel the heft of a shovel in his hands, the steady strain in his muscles, and he was heartened.

Next year at this time, he promised himself, he'd be ranching, right here on this land. He'd have a wife and, if possible, a baby on the way. Christmas would be getting close, and he'd go out and cut a tree and bring it into the house to be hung with ornaments and paper garlands, and there would be a fire crackling on the hearth—

But that was next year, and this was now, Clay reminded himself, with a sigh. He assessed the sky again, then whistled, low, for Outlaw.

The horse trotted over, reins dangling, and Clay gathered them and swung up into the saddle.

"We've got our work cut out for us," he told the animal.

The snow began coming down, slowly at first and then in earnest, when they were still about a mile outside of town, and by the time he and Outlaw reached the livery, it was hard to see farther than a dozen feet in any direction.

Zeb Dooley, the old man who ran the stable and adjoining blacksmith's shop, came out to meet him. Taking Outlaw's reins as soon as Clay had stepped down from the saddle, Zeb shouted to be heard over the rising screech of the wind. "Best head on over to the jailhouse or the Bitter Gulch, Marshal, because this blow is bound to get worse before it gets better!"

Clay took the reins back. "I want to look in over at the

schoolhouse," he called in reply. "Make sure the children are all right."

Zeb, clad for the cold in dungarees and a heavy coat, shook his balding head. "Miss Krenshaw will keep them there 'til it's safe to leave. The town makes sure there's always a stash of firewood and grub, in case they need it."

Clay's worries were only partially allayed by Zeb's re-assurance. A storm like this sure as hell meant trouble for *somebody,* and he didn't feel right about heading for the jailhouse to hunker down with Chester and wait it out, not just yet, anyway.

Clay turned away, mounted up again, bent low over Outlaw's neck to speak to him and started for the far edge of town.

He rode slowly, Outlaw stalwartly shouldering his way through the thickening snow, up one street and down an-other, until he'd covered all of them. Nobody called out to him as he passed, and lantern light glowed in most of the windows so, after half an hour, he and the horse felt their way back to the livery.

There was no sign of Zeb, and the big double doors of the stables were latched and rattling under the assault of the wind.

Clay opened them, led Outlaw inside and into his stall, gave him hay and made sure his water trough was full. Then he retraced his steps, latched the doors again and walked, wind-battered, toward the jailhouse.

Chapter 5

─────── ⚭ ───────

DARA ROSE RUBBED THE GLASS in the door of the mercantile with one gloved hand, clearing a circle to look through and seeing nothing but dizzying flurries of angry white. She'd come here to mail her letter to Piper and send off the coupon to the Wildflower Salve Company, and now she wished she hadn't been in such a hurry to leave home.

Mr. Bickham doubled as Blue River's postmaster. Being in a position to know who wrote to whom, and who received letters from whom, he tended to mind everybody's business but his own.

"You might just as well sit down here by the stove as try to see any farther than the end of your nose in weather like this," Philo counseled, from behind his long counter. "That's about the tenth time you wiped off that window, and it just keeps fogging up again."

Dara Rose bit her lower lip, still fretful. She and Harriet were safe and warm, but what about Edrina? Suppose she tried to walk home from school in this storm? Miss Krenshaw could be depended upon to keep her students inside, of course, but Edrina was, as recent history proved, well able to get past her teacher when she chose.

Harriet, who considered the whole thing a marvelous lark, sat on top of a pickle barrel and gazed raptly at the exquisite doll in the display window. Dara Rose, noting this, felt another pinch to the heart.

She had the ten dollars Piper had sent; she could buy the doll for Harriet and several books for Edrina, set it all out for them after they went to bed on Christmas Eve, to find in the morning and rejoice over. But both children still needed warm coats, and sturdy shoes that fit properly, and for all the vegetables she'd stored in the root cellar and the chickens producing fresh eggs right along—until this morning, that was—there was barely enough food to see them through the winter.

This year, with Parnell gone and even the roof over their heads a precarious blessing, there would be no store-bought presents, no brightly decorated tree, no goose or turkey for Christmas dinner.

"I could let you have that doll for two dollars even," Philo whispered, suddenly standing beside Dara Rose and startling her half out of her skin. Because of the thick layers of sawdust covering the floor, she hadn't heard him approach. "Put a dollar down, and you can pay the rest over time, out of the egg money."

Dara Rose looked at him sharply, momentarily distracted from her worry over Edrina, who might at any moment take it into her head to strike out for home, blizzard or no blizzard, perhaps concerned about her mother and sister and the chickens.

That would be like Edrina.

"No, Mr. Bickham," Dara Rose whispered back, while

Harriet paid neither one of them a whit of notice, "I will not be purchasing the doll, and that's final."

"But look at your little girl," the storekeeper cajoled. "She wants that pretty thing in the worst way."

Dara Rose's cheeks throbbed, and her throat thickened. It was only by the sternest exercise of self-control that she did not burst into tears. "I can barely afford to give my children what they *need*," she told him pointedly, though in a very quiet voice. "What they *want* is out of the question just now. Please do not press the matter further."

Philo gave a deep sigh and, at the same moment, the door Dara Rose had been standing next to only moments before burst open on a gust of wind.

Snow blew in, along with a swift and bitter chill, and then Clay McKettrick stepped over the threshold, accompanied by a medium-size dog, coated in white. Even for a strong man like he was, shutting that door again was an effort.

Dara Rose stood looking at the marshal and the dog, feeling oddly stricken, a state this man seemed to inflict upon her at every encounter. *She* might have been the one braving the frigid weather outside, instead of Clay, the way her breath stalled in the back of her throat.

With a smile, Clay took off his hat, dusting off the snow with his other hand, and nodded. "Afternoon, Mrs. Nolan," he said.

His voice was deep and quiet, his manner unhurried.

Dara Rose didn't answer, merely inclined her head briefly in response.

Harriet, meanwhile, forgot the doll she'd been so fascinated by until now, leaped nimbly off the pickle barrel and slowly approached the newcomers.

"Does that dog bite?" she asked forthrightly, studying

the animal closely before tilting her head back to look up at Clay.

"I can't rightly say, one way or the other," Clay replied honestly. "He and I just took up with each other last night, so we're not all that well acquainted yet. Offhand, though, I'd say you oughtn't to pet old Chester until we know a little more about his nature."

Harriet smiled, enchanted. "Hullo, Chester," she said.

Chester looked her over, but stayed close to Clay's side.

"I don't normally allow dogs in my store," Philo said. Then, with a smile and a genial spreading of his hands, "But I'll make an exception for you, Marshal."

"I'm obliged," Clay said. "It's a fair hike back to the jailhouse and I'd rather not leave him alone there, anyhow."

Dara Rose opened her mouth, closed it again. When it came to Clay McKettrick, she was as bad as Harriet with the doll, prone to ogle and be struck dumb with awe.

As if to prove himself a gentleman, Chester ambled away from Clay to nestle down in the warm sawdust in front of the stove. With a sigh of grateful contentment, the dog closed his eyes and went to sleep.

Harriet giggled. "He must be tired," she said.

"I reckon he is at that," Clay agreed. "I think old Chester traveled a hard road before he found his way to me."

Dara Rose had never envied a dog before, but she did in that moment. She'd traveled a hard road, too, she and the girls, but it hadn't led to a handsome, steady-minded man who was probably able to handle just about anything.

She cleared her throat, fixing to make another attempt at speaking, but before a word came to her, Harriet had reached out and taken Clay's hand, tugging him in the direction of the display window.

"Look," she said reverently, pointing at the doll.

Dara Rose finally found her voice, but it didn't hold up for long. "Harriet—"

Clay lifted the child easily, holding her in one arm, so she was at eye level with the splendid toy.

"Isn't she pretty?" Harriet murmured, wonderstruck again.

"Not as pretty as you are," Clay told her. His gaze sought Dara Rose, found her, and brought yet another embarrassing blush to her cheeks. His expression was solemn, as if he wanted to ask some question but knew it would be improper to do so.

"If I sold my hair for two dollars and fifty cents," Harriet prattled on, wide-eyed, seemingly as at home in Clay's arms as she would have been in Parnell's, "I could take her home with me for good. Do you know of a place where folks buy hair?"

Dara Rose closed her eyes briefly, mortified.

"Can't say as I do," Clay replied affably. He was still looking at Dara Rose, though; she could feel it.

She opened her eyes, watched, tongue-tied with misery, as he gently set Harriet back on her feet.

"I'd name her Florence," Harriet continued. "Don't you think that's a pretty name? Florence?"

Clay allowed as how it was a very nice name.

Dara Rose realized she was staring and looked quickly away, only to have her gaze collide with Mr. Bickham's. A benevolent smirk wreathed the storekeeper's round face.

"Looks like the snow's letting up a little," Bickham said, with a glance at the window. "Maybe the marshal and his dog here could see you and little Harriet home safe while there's a lull."

Dara Rose needed to get back to her place, in case Edrina was there or on her way, but it wouldn't be wise for her and Harriet to attempt the journey, however short, on their own. So she swallowed her pride and turned back to Clay. "Would you mind?" she asked.

Clay cleared his throat before answering, but his words still came out sounding husky. "No, ma'am," he said, almost shyly. "I wouldn't mind."

So Dara Rose bundled Harriet up as warmly as she could, and then herself, and Clay lifted Harriet up again, simultaneously whistling for the dog.

Chester got up immediately, ready to go.

"You give some thought to what I said, Miz Nolan," Philo shouted after her, as she followed Clay out into the waning snowstorm. "Ain't no shame in buying on credit!"

Dara Rose ignored him.

The snow, having fallen hard and fast all morning, was nearly knee-deep and powdery. Clay and the dog seemed to navigate it with relative ease, Chester moving in a hopping way that might have been comical under more ordinary circumstances, and Dara Rose picked her way along in the tracks of the marshal's boots.

Harriet, snug against Clay's chest, with the front of his coat around her, looked back over his shoulder at Dara Rose, her eyes merry with adventure. The child was clearly reveling in *Mr. McKettrick's* attention—it was imprudent to think of him as "Clay," Dara Rose had decided—and no doubt pretending she had a papa again.

The thought made Dara Rose's throat ache like one big bruise, and her eyes scalded. She was glad Mr. McKettrick couldn't see her face.

They trooped on, Clay forging a way for all of them when the dog grew tired, and the snow was thickening again by the time they reached the house. The respite, it seemed, was nearly over.

The air was shiver-cold, and Chester needed to rest. Even though Dara Rose was mildly alarmed by the thought of the new marshal filling her house with his purely masculine presence, she had no choice but to ask him in.

There was no sign of Edrina, which was both a relief and a worry to Dara Rose. Once she had her elder daughter at home, safe and sound, she'd move on to the other concerns—how the chickens were faring, for a start, and the state of the woodpile stacked against the back of the house. Thanks to the town council, there was a good supply of firewood, but some of it would need drying out before it could be burned.

Clay—*Mr. McKettrick* suddenly seemed too unwieldy even in her thoughts—walked straight through to the kitchen, set Harriet on her feet and went about building up the dwindling fire in the cookstove.

Chester practically collapsed on the rug in front of the sink.

"I'll go on to the schoolhouse," Clay told Dara Rose, when he'd finished at the stove, "and see about bringing Edrina home. It would be a favor to me, Mrs. Nolan, if you'd let my dog stay here while I'm gone, since he's probably too tuckered out to go much farther."

This time, Dara Rose welcomed the heat that surged through her, pulsing in her face. They weren't without their blessings, she and the children. "Of course," she said awkwardly. "Harriet and I will look after Chester. And I don't mind admitting I'm worried that Edrina might try to make her way home on her own."

Clay nodded, grinned a little. "She might, at that," he said.

That grin *did* something to Dara Rose. She told herself

it was simple thankfulness. She needed help, and someone was there to give it and that was that.

"What about the other children?" she asked, as Clay started for the back door.

"If any of them are stranded at the schoolhouse," he answered, his hand on the knob, "I'll make sure they get where they're supposed to go—after I bring your girl home, that is." He turned toward Harriet, who was now on her knees next to Chester, all concern for his temperament evidently past, drying off his coat with a flour-sack dish towel, and tugged at the brim of his hat. "Thank you for minding my friend, there," he told the child. "Looks as though he likes you."

Harriet beamed. "I *knew* he wouldn't bite me," she said.

Clay smiled briefly then, opened the door, leaned into the wind that rushed to meet him and stepped outside. The door closed behind him.

CLAY FOUND HIS WAY to the schoolhouse more from memory than by use of his eyesight, and Miss Krenshaw met him at the door, took him firmly by the arm and pulled him inside, out of the cold and the wind and the blinding assault of the snow.

Except for Edrina, who was huddled close to the stove and bundled inside a faded quilt, the schoolmarm was alone. Evidently, the other kids had already been collected by kinfolks and taken home.

Edrina smiled at him. "I knew you'd come to fetch me, if Mama didn't," she said, with a certainty that warmed his heart.

"Sit down, Marshal," Miss Krenshaw all but commanded, indicating her desk chair, which was the only one in the schoolroom big enough for an adult. "I've got some coffee brewing in back."

Clay didn't plan to tarry long, since the storm was more likely to get worse than it was to get better, and he wanted to get Edrina back to her mother and sister while the getting was good. But hot coffee sounded mighty nice to him just then, and he wouldn't mind sitting for a few minutes, either. He was still a young man, and fit, but that cold made his bones ache.

"Thank you," he said, and took the offered chair.

Miss Krenshaw disappeared into the back, where she probably had private quarters, and returned promptly with the promised coffee.

"Thanks," Clay repeated, taking the steaming mug from her hand.

Not one to be idle, it would seem, Miss Alvira got busy erasing the day's lessons off the blackboard.

"You'll be all right here, on your own?" Clay asked presently, restored by the tasty brew. Miss Alvira had laced it with whiskey, which raised her a notch in his already high estimation. Too bad he couldn't work up an interest in courting the lady.

"I'll be just fine," Miss Alvira said, still busy. She sounded a mite affronted by the question, in fact. "I have everything I need, right here."

Edrina, still seated by the stove, took in the conversation, but offered no comment. She did look somewhat pensive, though, and Clay wondered briefly what was going through that busy little brain of hers.

He finished the coffee, got to his feet, glanced at one of the windows.

There was no letup to the snow, as far as he could tell.

Miss Alvira marched into the cloakroom, came out with

Edrina's coat and bonnet and briskly prepared the child for the journey home. For good measure, she wrapped the quilt around Edrina again, too.

"There," she said, with a slight smile.

Clay put his hat back on—he'd left it on a peg next to the door, coming in—and hoisted Edrina, quilt and all, into his arms. As he'd done with Harriet, leaving the mercantile, he tried to cover her with his coat, as well.

"You're sure there's nowhere you'd like to go?" he asked Miss Alvira, before opening the door. "To the hotel, maybe? There're bound to be some folks around, and I could walk you over—"

The schoolmarm gave a little sniff and hiked up her chin again. "Marshal," she said, putting a point on the word, "as I've already told you, I am quite capable of looking after myself, and besides, I wouldn't think of spending good money on a hotel room."

"All right, then," Clay said, with a slight smile and a nod of farewell.

He followed his own quickly disappearing boot prints back to Dara Rose's front door, shoulders braced against the wind, his arms tight around the little girl tucked in the folds of that old quilt.

A lamp burned in the center of Dara Rose's kitchen table, and the house was not only blessedly warm, but there was something savory simmering on the stove.

Her face lit up at their return, and even though Clay knew most of that joy was for Edrina, he basked in the welcome, anyway. And Chester was just about beside himself, he was so happy to see Clay.

"You'll stay for supper," Dara Rose informed Clay briskly, once he'd set Edrina down, and then she commenced to unwinding that now-damp quilt from around the little girl.

Clay just stood there for a long moment, in his snowy duster and his wet hat, waiting for his bones and sinews to thaw and just enjoying the sight of her. Dara Rose's aquamarine eyes were bright and her cheeks flushed, probably from the heat of the stove and happiness because Edrina was home.

"All right," he said, finally realizing that her statement called for some kind of response, however mundane. "Whatever you're cooking, it smells good."

She smiled at him, briefly, distractedly, and all but set him back on his heels by the doing of it.

"Edrina, you go in and change into dry clothes," she told the child.

Edrina hesitated, then left the room. Harriet, after trying in vain to get Chester to come along on the jaunt, followed her sister, chattering about the walk home from the mercantile.

It was a heady thing, being alone with Dara Rose in that steamy little room.

And Clay, a quiet man but not a shy one, couldn't come up with a single thing to say.

Dara Rose tightened the bands on her apron, a reach-back motion that made her shapely bosom rise and jut out a little. "If the chickens survive this," she said, with an anxious glance toward the room's one opaque window, "it will be a miracle, and I sure hope some of the men in town give a thought to the O'Reillys, like they generally do at times like this…."

Her voice fell away, and she gnawed fretfully at her lower lip, likely pondering the fate of the poultry, the family she'd just mentioned, or both.

"The O'Reillys?" Clay croaked out, grabbing hold of the rapidly sinking conversational lifeline with the first thing that jumped off his tongue.

Dara Rose sighed again, turned away from him to stir whatever was cooking in that pot. The scent of it made his stomach rumble, and it came to him that, except for Miss Krenshaw's whiskeyed-up coffee, he hadn't had anything since breakfast.

"Peg O'Reilly's no-good excuse for a husband," she said quietly, after a glance in the direction of the doorway the little girls had hurried through earlier, "ran off with some…some…*woman* he met at the Bitter Gulch Saloon, and left a wife and three children behind to fend for themselves!"

For a moment, Clay was taken aback—not by the story, which unfortunately was not an uncommon one, especially with the war in Europe picking up momentum—but by Dara Rose's apparent failure to draw any correlation between Mrs. O'Reilly's situation and her own. Except for one obvious variable—Parnell had had the bad fortune to die, while the long-gone Mr. O'Reilly was presumably still alive—the two women had essentially been dealt the same bad hand of cards.

Dara Rose seemed to sense that he was looking at her, and she turned to meet his gaze, colored up again and looked quickly away. The girls returned to the kitchen just then, before anything more could be said, Harriet going on about that doll she meant to name Florence, and Edrina replying in lofty, big-sister fashion that Harriet ought to wish in one hand and spit in the other and see which one got full faster.

Clay went to the sink, rolled up his shirtsleeves and commenced to washing his hands with the harsh yellow soap Dara Rose kept in an old saucer wedged behind the pump handle.

He felt a combination of things while he was at it, but mainly, he realized, he was glad. Glad just to be where he was, right there in that kitchen, out of the cold wind, with a lovely woman, two kids and a dog for company.

For the first time since he'd left Arizona, Clay didn't have to fight down a hankering for home, didn't second-guess his decision to strike out on his own instead of making a life on the ever-expanding Triple M with the rest of the family.

Be sure you're leaving because it's what you really want to do, Clay, his pa had counseled him, *and not because Annabel Carson broke your heart.*

It made Clay smile a little to remember that conversation, and others like it, with various members of the home outfit, and he reckoned now that Annabel hadn't broken his heart at all—she'd just sprained it a little.

The stuff in the pot on the stove turned out to be some kind of mixture of canned venison and leftover vegetable preserves, and it was better, in Clay's opinion, than a big steak at Delmonico's.

"Miss Krenshaw keeps a picture of a soldier in her top desk drawer," Edrina chimed, in the middle of the meal, pretty much out of nowhere.

Snow rasped at the windows and the small cookstove seemed to strain to put out more heat.

"And how would you know a thing like that, Edrina Nolan?" Dara Rose asked, arching one eyebrow, her spoon poised halfway between her mouth and the bowl of soup sitting in front of her.

"She takes it out and looks at it, when she thinks nobody's looking," Edrina explained nonchalantly. "Sometimes, she gets tears in her eyes, and her lips move like she's talking to somebody."

Clay's gaze connected with Dara Rose's.

"Are you going to fight in the war, Mr. McKettrick?" Edrina asked, without missing a beat.

"No," Clay answered. The armed forces would need beef, and plenty of it, and like his granddad said, somebody had to raise the critters. "But my cousin Gabriel thinks he might join up, if things don't simmer down some over the next year or two."

A sad expression flickered across Dara Rose's expressive face; he figured the war was a subject she tried not to think about, since there was nothing she could do to change it.

After supper, Edrina and Harriet cleared the table and set the dishes in the sink, without being told.

Dara Rose crossed the room to take her cloak and bonnet down from their peg near the door. She clearly dreaded whatever she was about to do, and Clay found himself beside her before he'd made a conscious decision to move, reaching for his hat and duster.

Dara Rose looked up at him, and he caught the briefest glimpse into the shimmering vastness of her heart and mind and spirit. There was so much more to her than just her flesh-and-blood person, he realized, with a start akin to waking up suddenly after a long, deep sleep.

"The chickens—" she began, and then went silent.

"I'll see to them," Clay said, very quietly. "You stay here, with the girls."

She considered the idea briefly, then shook her head no. She meant to go out to that chicken coop and that was that. He'd be wasting his breath to argue.

"I'll heat water to wash the dishes when I get back,"

she told the children. "Don't get too close to the stove, and no scuffling."

"Oh, Mama," Edrina said, with a roll of her eyes. "You've told us that a *thousand times* already."

A smile quirked at one corner of Dara Rose's mouth. Like the rest of her, visible and invisible, that mouth fascinated Clay out of all good sense and reason. "Well," she said, "now it's a thousand and *one*."

After a glance at Clay's face, she opened the door and stepped right out into that blizzard.

Clay followed, and the wind was so strong that it buffeted her back a step, so they collided, her back to his torso. He put his arms out to steady her, and a powerful jolt of... *something*...shot through him.

Since it was too cold to dally, they recovered quickly and advanced toward the rickety coop.

The chickens had taken refuge inside and, with the exception of the rooster, who squawked indignantly as he paced the floor of that shed, as though fussing over the pure injustice of a snowstorm, the birds huddled close to one another on the length of wood that served as a roost.

There was a visible easing in Dara Rose as she looked around. "At least none of them have frozen to death," she said, and she might have been addressing herself, not him, trundling over to lift the lid off a wooden bend and lean inside to scoop out feed. Judging by how *far* she had to lean—Lordy, she had a shapely backside—the supply was starting to run low.

Like a lot of other things in her life, probably.

Clay watched, offering no comment, as Dara Rose filled a shallow pan with feed and set it out for the hens to peck at. That done, she picked up a second pan, went to the doorway and shoveled up some snow. The stuff was already melting around the edges, cold as that chicken coop was, when Dara Rose waded back into the center of the noisy flock to set the second pan down beside the first.

They fought their way back to the house, side by side, heads down, shoulders braced. Clay wanted to put an arm around Dara Rose's waist, so she wouldn't fall or blow away, but every instinct warned against it.

The woman had a right to her pride, probably needed it just to press on from one day to the next.

By the time they got back inside the house, the girls had left the kitchen for the front room.

Their voices carried, a happy sound, like the chiming of bells somewhere off in the muffled distance.

Dara Rose moved to untie her bonnet laces, but Clay closed his hands over hers. "You've done a fine job raising those girls of yours," he said, though he hadn't actually planned the words ahead of time.

Those wonderful eyes of hers searched his face, almost warily. Then she smiled and went on to take off her bonnet, Clay's hands falling away from hers and back to his sides.

"Thank you, Mr. McKettrick," she said, stepping back to shed her snow-speckled cloak.

"Clay," he said, knowing she wanted him to step aside so she could get on with whatever it was she planned to do next but stubbornly holding his ground. "I don't generally answer to 'Mr. McKettrick,' as it happens. Usually, when folks use that moniker, they're talking to my granddad."

She blushed, but her eyes flashed. "When I say it," she told him, "I'm addressing *you*. We haven't known each other long enough to use first names."

He chuckled at that. Curved his finger sideways under her chin and lifted. "Have it your way…Dara Rose," he said, partly to get under her hide and partly because he just liked saying her name.

Still wearing his coat and hat, he summoned the dog with a soft whistle.

Edrina and Harriet immediately appeared in the inside doorway, squashed together as though there was barely enough room in the gap to contain both of them. Their eyes were wide with curiosity and something else—maybe worry.

"You're going?" Edrina asked.

"And taking Chester?" Harriet added.

Clay touched the brim of his hat, momentarily ignoring Dara Rose, who was probably still prickly over his impertinent use of her Christian name. "Yep," he said. "Chester and I ought to be getting over to the jailhouse, in case somebody comes looking for us."

"But it's getting dark," Edrina protested.

"And it's still snowing *really hard*," Harriet said. "What if you and Chester get lost?"

"We'll find our way," Clay promised, his voice a little huskier than normal. "Don't you worry about us."

Dara Rose surprised him by laying a hand on his arm. "Take the lantern," she said.

Clay was moved by the offer, but he didn't let it show, of course. He just shook his head and smiled a little. "It wouldn't do much good, hard as the wind's blowing," he said. "But I thank you kindly, just the same. And thanks for supper, too, and a right pleasant evening."

Dara Rose opened her mouth, closed it again and then sighed. "Be careful," she said.

"I will certainly do that, ma'am," he answered.

The winter night bit into him like teeth when he moved out into it, Chester struggling along at his side.

Before they got as far as the gate, the dog was practically sinking out of sight with every cautious step, so Clay picked him up, carrying him in the curve of his right arm.

With his free hand, Clay pulled his hat brim down low over his eyes and blinked a couple of times, until he could see. If it weren't for thin snatches of lamplight, spilling from various windows along the way, he and Chester might have been in some trouble.

As it was, Clay was half-frozen by the time he fumbled with the latch on his office door, stepped over the threshold and set the dog down to feel along the wall for the metal box that held the matches for the stove and the lanterns.

Chester gave a low growl as Clay struck the match.

There was a shuffling clatter over by the desk, followed by the sound of boot soles striking the plank floor and a grumbled curse.

"Damn it, Clay," growled his cousin Sawyer, "you oughtn't to sneak up on a man like that, especially when he's sleeping."

Chapter 6

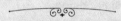

"I THOUGHT IT DIDN'T SNOW in Texas," Sawyer said, after stretching and letting go with a lusty yawn.

Clay patted the dog, reassured him with a few quiet words and lit one of the two lanterns he had on hand. "What are you doing here, Sawyer?" he countered gruffly.

"I *was* catching up on my shut-eye," Sawyer replied affably, grinning that cocky grin that sometimes made Clay want to backhand his cousin, "until you came banging through the door and disturbed me."

Clay lit the other lantern, the one that stood on the bookcase, and then went to the stove to build up the fire. The last time he'd seen his cousin and one-time best friend, they'd had words, not just about Annabel, but about a few other things, too.

"You're a long way from home, cousin," Clay finally remarked.

"So are you," Sawyer answered, perching on the edge of Clay's desk now, with his arms folded. The youngest son of Clay's uncle Kade, and aunt Mandy, Sawyer had the fair hair and dark blue eyes that ran in intergenerational streaks through the McKettrick bloodline.

Clay shut the stove door with a clang and rustled up some leftovers for Chester, who seemed to have decided that the surprise visitor made acceptable company.

Which just went to show what a dog knew about anything, Clay thought glumly. Most of them liked everybody, and Chester was no exception.

"I'm going to ask you once more," Clay said evenly, "*just once,* what you're doing here, and if I don't get a clear answer, I swear I'll toss you behind bars on a trespassing charge."

Sawyer chuckled. "I'm just passing through," he said. "Since I was in your neck of the woods, I decided to board my horse in San Antonio and take the train to Blue River, see how you're faring and all."

"I'm faring just fine," Clay responded, "so you can get on tomorrow's train, if it makes it through, and go right back to San Antonio."

Sawyer strolled to the window, in no evident hurry to get there. He had the born horseman's rolling, easy stride. "Good thing I didn't bring the horse," he said, as though Clay hadn't as good as told him, straight out, that he wasn't welcome. "We'd probably be out there in the blizzard someplace, freezing to death." A visible shudder moved through his lean, agile form, but he didn't turn around. "Like I said, nothing anybody ever told me about Texas prepared me for ass-deep snow."

Clay ladled water into the coffeepot, a dented metal receptacle coated with blue enamel, and set it on top of the potbellied stove. Then he commenced to spoon ground coffee beans into it, along with a pinch of salt to make the grounds settle after the stuff brewed. "That's the thing about weather," he said, at considerable length. "It's un-predictable."

Sawyer finally turned around, but he lingered at the window, frost-coated and all but opaque behind him. "Annabel Carson got married soon after you left," he said, gruffly and with care.

"Not to you, it appears," Clay said, turning his back to the stove and absorbing the heat.

Sawyer made a sound that might have been a chuckle, though it contained no noticeable amusement. "Not to me," he confirmed. "She got hitched to Whit Taggard, over near Stone Creek. You know, that banker in his fifties, with more money than one man ever ought to have? She swears it's a love match."

"You came all the way to Blue River to tell me that?" Clay asked, strangely unmoved by news that probably would have devastated him not so long ago. Chester had finished his meal of leftovers from the hotel dining room and gone to curl up on his blanket. The wind howled and hissed under the eaves, as if it were fixing to raise the roof right off that old jailhouse and carry it next door, if not farther.

"No," Sawyer said. "I came all the way to Blue River because your mama's been worried about you, and I love my aunt Chloe."

Clay sighed. "I already sent Ma and Pa a wire," he said, mildly exasperated. "They know I'm fine."

"Your saying it and their knowing it for sure are two different things, Clay," Sawyer went on, his tone reasonable and quiet, as if he were calming a jittery horse or a cow mired in deep mud and struggling against the ropes meant to pull it onto dry ground. "It's not every day a man picks up and leaves the place and the people he's known all his life."

Clay had no answer for that, had already done all the explaining he ever intended to do, where the decision to put home behind him for good—at least as far as living there—was concerned, anyhow. Much as he loved his granddad and his pa and his uncles, he didn't want to spend the rest of his life taking orders from them. He wanted to build and run his own outfit, marry and have sons and daughters, grandchildren and great-grandchildren.

"You hungry?" Clay asked, hoping to get the conversation going in another direction.

"I had fried chicken over at the hotel, soon as I'd checked in and stowed my gear," Sawyer answered, with a shake of his head. He looked around at the humble quarters Clay presently called home, sighed. "Nobody can accuse you of living high on the hog, I reckon," he finished, sounding weary now.

Clay shoved a hand through his hair, recalling the difficult trek back from Dara Rose's place. It had taken him and Chester the better part of half an hour to cover the five hundred yards or so between the jail and that snug little house.

Once he'd warmed up, had some coffee and put on long johns and an extra layer of clothes, he meant to venture out again, track down that family Dara Rose had mentioned—the O'Reillys—and see for himself that they were warm and had something to eat. He figured it was his duty, as marshal, to see that folks made it through when there was an emergency like that snowstorm, especially women and children.

"Finding your way back to the hotel in this blizzard

might be tricky," Clay told his cousin, in his own good time. "You can bunk in the cell there if you want."

One side of Sawyer's mouth quirked upward in a grin. "And give you a prime opportunity to lock me up, soon as I shut my eyes, and then drop the key down a deep well? Not likely, cousin."

"You sorely overestimate my ability to tolerate your company," Clay responded dryly. "The sooner you're on your way, the happier I'm going to be."

Sawyer didn't reply right away, which was a telling thing, because he was usually quick to shoot off his mouth. There *was* a whole other side to Sawyer, though—one nobody, including Clay, really knew much about.

"You must know I never laid a hand on your girl, Clay," Sawyer said, as a chunk of wood crackled and splintered to embers inside the stove. "So what exactly is it about me that sticks in your craw? We used to be as close as brothers."

Too warm now that he'd been standing near the stove for a while, Clay moved on to his desk, reclaimed the creaky wooden chair, sat back in it with his hands cupped behind his head. Chester, lying nearby on his blanket pile, gave a single, chortling snore, and another piece of wood collapsed in the fire, with a series of sharp snaps.

"You come here," Clay answered presently, "uninvited, I might add, and let on that I'm a grief to the family, like some prodigal son off squandering his birthright in a far country, and then you have the gall to ask what sticks in my craw? It's the hypocrisy of it. *You're a gunslinger,* Sawyer, a hired gun. Little better than an outlaw, most likely. It might even be that if I went through all these wanted posters on my desk, I'd come across a fair likeness of your face."

"I'm not an outlaw," Sawyer said flatly. "You know that."

"Do I?" Clay asked. "You blow through the Triple M every few years like a breeze—just long enough last time to turn my girl's head—and then, one fine day, a telegram comes in, and you're gone again, without a word to anybody. Like you know somebody's picked up your trail so you'd better be moving on, pronto."

Sawyer sighed again, and it came out raspy. "I don't reckon anything I say is going to get through that inch-thick layer of bone you call a skull," he said. "You made up your mind about me a long time ago, didn't you, cousin?"

There was no denying that. "I reckon I did," Clay replied quietly, feeling wrung out. "You can tell Ma and the rest of the family that you've seen me and I'm fine. Seems to me that your business here is finished."

Even as he spoke those words, Clay wondered what the *real* reason for Sawyer's visit might be. Blue River was too far out of his cousin's way for this to be about Annabel, or a favor to Clay's ma and pa.

Sawyer crossed to the door, took his hat and canvas duster down from their pegs and put them on. Then he hesitated, one hand on the old-fashioned iron latch. "You're right," he said, with more sadness than Clay had heard in his voice since they were ten years old and Sawyer's dog took sick and died. "I guess there's no getting back on your good side. I'll be on tomorrow's train, if it gets here, and you can get on with whatever the hell it is you think you're doing."

With that, Sawyer opened the door and went out, letting in a blast of snow-speckled cold that reached into the deepest parts of Clay and held on.

He almost relented, almost called Sawyer back—but in the end, he figured it was best to let him go.

THE SNOW LAY LIKE A THICK, glittering mantle over the countryside when Dara Rose went out to feed the chickens, carrying the egg basket and a jug to refill their water pan, but the sky was the purest blue, cloudless and benign. As quickly as it had arisen, the storm was over; water dripped rhythmically from the edges of the roof, and the path to the henhouse was slushy under the soles of her high-button shoes.

Hope stirred, springlike, in Dara Rose's heart, as she crossed the yard. She could hear the chickens clucking away in the coop, wanting their breakfast and their liberty from a long night of confinement.

Using the side of her foot, Dara Rose cleared a patch of ground for the birds and let them out while she ducked inside to fetch the water pan. Pleased to see that every member of her little flock had survived, she scattered their feed and then went on to collect the eggs.

There were six—a better count than the day before, though still less than she'd hoped for—and Dara Rose set each one carefully in the basket and returned to the house.

Edrina and Harriet were up and dressed, Edrina full of glee because she didn't have to go to school that day, and Harriet equally happy to have a playmate.

Dara Rose took off her bonnet and cloak, hung them up, washed her hands at the pump in the sink and put a pot of water on to boil, for oatmeal.

In the middle of the meal, a knock sounded at the front door.

Frowning, wondering who would be out and about so early, with the snow still deep enough to make traveling through it a trial, she pushed back her chair, told the children to finish eating and behave themselves and hurried through the small parlor. On some level, she realized, she'd hoped to find Clay McKettrick standing on her tiny porch, but this only came to her when she saw Mayor Wilson Ponder there instead.

Through the glass oval in the door, the older man's face looked purposeful, and a little grim.

Dara Rose opened the door. "Mayor Ponder," she said, not bothering to hide her surprise. He'd arrived, she saw now, looking past him to the street, in a sleigh drawn by two sturdy mules. "Come in."

"I won't tarry," Ponder said gravely, with a distracted tug at the brim of his bowler hat. He remained where he was, forcing Dara Rose to stand in the bright cold of the doorway and wait to hear what business he had with her. "I know this isn't a convenient time, what with the blizzard and all, but frankly, I'm not comfortable putting the task off any longer." He reddened slightly, though that might have been because of the weather, and not any sense of chagrin, and his muttonchop whiskers wobbled as he prepared to go on. "The town purchased this house for the use of the marshal, Mrs. Nolan, and if Clay McKettrick doesn't mean to use the place, well, we—the town council, that is—would prefer to sell it."

Dara Rose felt the floor shift under her feet, but she kept her shoulders squared and even managed not to shiver at the cold, and the news the mayor had just delivered.

"Oh," she said, hugging herself and wishing for her cloak, wishing for summer and better times. "Do you have a prospective buyer?"

"Ezra Maddox wants the property," Mayor Ponder said, after more whisker-wriggling. "He's offering two hundred and fifty dollars cash money and, what with bringing in electricity, the town could use the funds."

Ezra Maddox owned a farm, Dara Rose thought, dazed and frustrated and quite cornered. What did the man want with a run-down house miles from his crops and his dairy cows?

By now, everyone knew Clay had decided to live over at the jailhouse. Could it be that Mr. Maddox was simply trying to force her hand by buying the house out from under her? Was he hoping she would give in and accept his offer of a so-called housekeeping job, possibly followed by marriage, and send her children away in the bargain?

Dara Rose seethed, even as cold terror overtook her. "How long until we have to move?" she asked, amazed at how calm she sounded.

Mayor Ponder hesitated before he answered, perhaps ashamed of that morning's mission. On the other hand, he'd gone to all the bother of hitching mules to a sleigh to get there bright and early, which did not indicate any real degree of reluctance on his part. "Ezra's mighty anxious to take possession of the place," he finally said. "But since Christmas is just two weeks away, well, he's—*we're*—willing to let you stay until the first of the year."

Dara Rose gripped the door frame with one hand, thinking she might actually swoon. Behind her, in the kitchen, the girls' voices rang like chimes as they conducted some merry disagreement, laced with giggles.

"Well, then," Dara Rose managed, meeting the mayor's gaze, seeing both sympathy and resolve there, "that's that, isn't it? Thank you for letting me know."

With that, she shut the door in his face.

And stood trembling, there in the small parlor, until she heard his footsteps retreating on the porch.

"Mama?" Harriet, light-footed as ever and half again too perceptive for a five-year-old, was standing directly behind her. "Can we get a dog? Edrina says we don't need another mouth to feed, but a puppy wouldn't eat very much, would it?"

All of Dara Rose's considerable strength gave way then, like a dam under the strain of rising water. She uttered a small, choked sob, shook her head and fled to the bedroom.

Dara Rose seldom cried—even at Parnell's funeral service, she'd been dry-eyed—but she was only human, after all.

And she'd come to the end of her resources, at least for the moment.

So she sat on the edge of the bed she shared with her daughters—Parnell had slept on the settee in the parlor—covered her face with both hands and wept softly into her palms.

CLAY WAS HAVING BREAKFAST over at the hotel dining room—bacon and eggs and hotcakes, with plenty of hot, fresh coffee—when Sawyer wandered in, looking well-rested and clean-shaven, his manner at once affable and distant.

"Mind if I join you?" he said, pulling back a chair opposite Clay and sitting down before Clay could answer. He picked up the menu and studied it with the same grave concentration their illustrious granddad reserved for government beef contracts.

Politicians and pencil pushers, Angus had been known to remark, on the occasions he did business with such officials. *A man would have to be simpleminded to trust a one of them.*

"Make yourself at home," Clay said, dryly and long

after the fact. He hadn't slept much the night before, thanks to Dara Rose and Sawyer's unexpected presence and the long slog through the snow to the O'Reilly place.

He'd found them huddled around a poor fire like characters in a Dickens novel, wrapped in thin blankets. They'd had fried eggs for supper, Mrs. O'Reilly had told him, and those were all gone, and he was welcome to what was left of yesterday's pinto beans if he was hungry.

Clay had thanked her kindly and said he'd already had supper, which happened to be the truth, though he would have lied without a qualm if it hadn't been, and then he'd carried in most of their dwindling wood supply to dry beside the homemade stove. Before coming to the hotel for breakfast that morning, he'd stopped by the mercantile, pounded at the front door until the storekeeper let him in, and purchased a sackful of dried beans, along with flour, sugar, a pound of coffee and assorted canned goods for the O'Reillys. He'd paid extra to have the food delivered before the store was open for business.

Now, sitting across from his pensive cousin in a warm, clean, well-lighted place where good food could be had in plenty, he felt vaguely ashamed of his own prosperity. While the McKettricks didn't live grandly, they didn't lack for money, either. Clay had never missed a meal in his life, never had to go without shoes or wear clothes that had belonged to somebody else first. Unlike the O'Reilly children, and too many others like them, he'd had a strong, committed father, backed up by three uncles and a granddad.

The cook, a round-bellied man who doubled as a waiter, came over to the table to greet Sawyer and take his order.

Sawyer simply pointed toward Clay's plate and said, "That looks good."

The cook nodded and went away.

Sawyer sat there, easy in his hide, dressed like a prosperous gambler. Instead of his usual plain shirt and even plainer denim trousers, he sported a suit, complete with a white shirt, a string tie and a brocade vest. "You look miserable this morning, cousin," he said cheerfully, "but something tells me it isn't remorse over the uncharitable welcome you offered last night."

Clay gave a raw chuckle, void of mirth. His appetite was gone, all of a sudden, and he set down his knife and fork, pushed his plate away. "It definitely isn't remorse," he said.

Sawyer helped himself to a slice of toasted bread and bit into it, chewed appreciatively. Though his eyes twinkled, his voice was serious when he replied, "You could still go back to the Triple M, you know. They'd welcome you back into the fold with open arms and shouts of 'hurrah.'"

"I'll pay them a visit one of these days," he said. "There aren't any hard feelings on my side."

"Nor theirs, either." Sawyer shoved a hand through his unruly dark-gold hair, which was always a little too long. "You're lucky, Clay," he said, his gaze moving to the window next to their table. "Pa and Granddad can't seem to make up their minds whether to kill the fatted calf in my honor or take a horsewhip to me." He frowned, squinted at the foggy glass. "I think somebody's trying to get your attention," he observed.

Clay looked, and there, on the other side of that steamed-up window, was Edrina, practically pressing her nose to the glass. She waved one unmittened hand and retreated a step.

"I'll be damned," Clay muttered, gesturing for the child to come inside.

"Who's the kid?" Sawyer wanted to know.

"Friend of mine," Clay answered, as Edrina scampered toward the entrance to the dining room.

She hurried over to the table, face flushed with cold and purpose, and stood there like a little soldier.

"Mama's crying," she said. "Mama *never* cries."

Clay scraped back his chair, took Edrina's small hands into his own, trying to chafe some warmth into them. "Where's your bonnet?" he fussed, trying to process the idea of Dara Rose in tears. "You aren't wearing any mittens, and your coat is unbuttoned—"

"I was in a *hurry*," Edrina told him, with a little sigh of impatience. She spared Sawyer the briefest glance, then looked back at Clay with a proud plea in her eyes. "You'll come home with me, won't you? Right now? Because Mama is crying and Mama never, *ever* cries."

"Go on," Sawyer said to Clay. "I'll settle up for your breakfast."

Clay got up, retrieved his duster from the back of the chair beside his and his hat from the seat and put them on. "What's the matter with her?" he asked, more worried than he could ever remember being before. "Is she sick?"

Gravely, Edrina took his hand, tugged him in the direction of the door. "I don't know," she said fretfully. "Maybe. But she was fine while we were having our oatmeal. Then Mr. Ponder stopped by, and they talked, and when Harriet asked Mama if we could please get a dog, Mama commenced to blubbering and ran right out of the room."

Outside, the snow was melting under a steadily warming sky, but it was still deep. Clay curved an arm around Edrina's waist, much as he had done with Chester the night before, and set off for Dara Rose's place with long strides.

DARA ROSE MARCHED herself out into the kitchen, pumped cold water into the basin she kept on hand and splashed her face repeatedly while Harriet watched her solemnly from the doorway.

"Are you through crying, Mama?" the child asked, very softly.

Dara Rose felt ashamed. Now she'd upset Edrina and Harriet, and for what? A few moments of self-pity?

"I'm quite through," she said, drying her still-puffy face with a dish towel. "And I haven't the slightest idea what came over me." She hugged Harriet, then frowned, looking around. "Where is Edrina?"

Harriet bit her lower lip, clearly reluctant to answer.

"Harriet?" Dara Rose said, taking her little girl gently but firmly by the shoulders. *"Where is your sister?"*

Harriet's eyes were huge and luminous. "She went to fetch Mr. McKettrick," she finally replied.

Alarm rushed through Dara Rose, and not just because a glance at the row of hooks beside the back door revealed that Edrina had gone off through the deep snow without her bonnet or her mittens. She was just reaching for her own cloak when she heard footsteps on the front porch—boots, stomping off snow.

Clay knocked, but then he came right in, carrying Edrina. His gaze locked with Dara Rose's as he set the little girl down and pulled the door closed behind him.

She'd never seen a man look so worried before, not even when Parnell came to that settlement house in Bangor, Maine, to claim her and the children. They'd been mere babies then, Edrina and Harriet, and memories of their real father, Parnell's younger brother, Luke, soon faded.

"Are you sick?" Clay demanded, in the same tone he

might have employed to confront a drunk with disorderly conduct.

Dara Rose wasn't sick, except with mortification. "I'm quite all right," she said, but she didn't sound very convincing, even to herself. She shifted her attention to her elder daughter, letting her know with a look that she was in big trouble. "I apologize for any inconvenience—"

Clay's neck reddened, and his eyes narrowed. "I'd be obliged if you girls would wait in the kitchen," he said, though he never looked away from Dara Rose's face.

Edrina and Harriet, always ready with a protest when *she* made such a request, fled the room like rabbits with a fox on their trail.

"That little girl," Clay said, in a furious whisper, one index finger jabbing in the general direction of the kitchen a few times, "was so worried about you that she braved all that snow to find me and bring me here. So don't think for one minute that you're going to put me off with an apology for any *inconvenience*."

Dara Rose stared at him. "Why are you so angry?" she finally asked. *And why does it thrill me to see you like this?*

"I'm not angry," Clay rasped out, wrenching off his Wyatt Earp–style hat and flinging it so that it landed on the settee, teetered there and dropped to the floor. "Damn it, Dara Rose, whatever went on here this morning scared your daughter half to death, and since Edrina is the most courageous kid I've ever come across, *I* got scared, too."

The thrill didn't subside, and Dara Rose prayed her feelings didn't show. "I lost my composure for a moment," she confessed, as stiffly proud as a Puritan even as her heart raced and her breath threatened to catch in the back of her throat and never come loose. "Believe me, I regret it. I certainly didn't mean to frighten the children—"

"Well," Clay said, in earnest, "you *did*. And I'm not leaving here until you tell me what Ponder said to you that made you go to pieces the way you did."

Dara Rose swallowed, looked down at the floor. Right or wrong, Clay meant what he said—that much was obvious from his tone and his countenance. He wouldn't be going anywhere until she answered him.

"Dara Rose?" He was standing close to her now, his hands resting lightly on her shoulders. He smelled of fresh air, snow and something woodsy. "Tell me."

She knew she ought to pull away from him, ought to look anywhere but up into his face, but she couldn't manage either response. "Mayor Ponder stopped by to tell me that, since you don't want this house, the town council plans to sell it to Ezra Maddox for two hundred and fifty dollars," she said. It was remarkable how calm she sounded, she thought, when her insides were buzzing like a swarm of bees smoked out of their hive. "We have to be out by the first of the year."

"That son of a—" Clay ground out, before catching himself.

Dara Rose felt tears burning behind her eyes again, and she was determined not to disgrace herself by shedding them. "I have ten dollars," she said, like someone talking in their sleep. "And I've saved some of the egg money. It won't take us far, but it's enough to leave town."

"Where would you go?" Clay immediately asked.

"I don't know," Dara Rose replied honestly. "Somewhere."

"The town isn't going to sell this house," Clay said.

"Of course they are," Dara Rose argued, though not with any spirit.

"I'm the marshal," Clay told her, "and under the terms

of our agreement, I'm entitled to living quarters. It just so happens that I've decided I'd rather live here than in the jailhouse."

Dara Rose's jaw dropped, and it took her a moment to recover. A *long* moment. "But we couldn't... Where would the children and I—?"

Clay hooked a finger under her chin. "Right here," he said. "You and Edrina and Harriet could live right here, with me—if you and I were married."

Dara Rose nearly choked. *"Married?"*

"It wouldn't do for us to live under the same roof otherwise," Clay said reasonably.

"But we're nearly total strangers—"

"For now," Clay went on, when her words fell away, "it would be a private arrangement. All business. I won't press you to bed down with me, Dara Rose. This place is too small for such shenanigans, anyhow, with the girls around."

Dara Rose couldn't believe what she was hearing. It was Parnell, all over again. Clay was offering a marriage that *wasn't* a marriage, offering shelter and safety and respectability. But unless she wanted to send her children away and move in with Ezra Maddox, she couldn't afford to refuse.

"Why?" she asked, barely breathing the word. "Why would you want to do this, Clay McKettrick?"

He smiled at her. Tucked a tendril of hair behind her right ear, where it had escaped its pins. "I want a wife," he said, as though that explained everything, instead of raising dozens, if not hundreds, of new questions.

"But you said the marriage wouldn't be real."

"It won't be, at first," Clay told her. Where did he get all that certainty, all that confidence? All that *audacity?* "But maybe, with time..."

"What if nothing changes?" Dara Rose broke in, feeling

almost as though she needed to shout to be heard over the thrumming of her heartbeat, though of course she *didn't* shout, because the children would have heard.

"Then there'll be no harm done," Clay said. "We'll have the marriage annulled, I'll set you and the girls up in decent circumstances somewhere far from Blue River, and we'll go our separate ways."

No harm done? He spoke so blithely.

Was the man insane?

Possibly, Dara Rose decided. But he was also an infinitely better bet than Ezra Maddox.

Chapter 7

By THE FOLLOWING MORNING, Sawyer was long gone and the snow had turned to mud so deep that folks had had to lay weathered boards and old doors in the street, just to get from one side to the other without sinking to their knees in the muck. Hardly anybody rode a horse or drove a wagon through town or along the side roads, either, but the sun shone like the herald of an early spring, and the breezes were almost balmy.

Clay considered all this as he stood in his small room at the jailhouse, stooping a little to peer at himself in the cracked shaving mirror fixed to the wall. He'd washed up and shaved, and then shaken out and put on the only suit he'd brought to Blue River—the getup consisted of a black woolen coat fitted at the waist, matching trousers, his best white shirt, starched and pressed for him at the Chinese laundry before he left Indian Rock, a brown brocade vest and a string tie.

He hated ties.

Hated starched shirts, too, for that matter.

He'd worn this suit exactly three times since he bought

it—to one wedding and two funerals. Today, it was a wedding—his own—and even though it was his choice to get married, the occasion had its somber aspects, as well.

Up home, the ceremony would have been a community event, like a circus or a tent revival or the Independence Day fireworks, drawing crowds from miles around and working the womenfolk up into a frenzy of sewing and cooking and marking their calendars so they'd know how long the first baby took to show up. The men would complain about having to wear their Sunday duds, sip moonshine from a shared fruit jar out in the orchard behind the church after the "I do's" had been said and lament that another unwitting member of their sex had been roped in and hog-tied.

Clay smiled to think of all that nuptial chaos and was glad he'd managed to escape it, though he felt a twinge of nostalgia, too. He and Dara Rose would be married quietly and sensibly, in a civil ceremony performed by Mayor Ponder at her place, with Edrina and Harriet the only guests. There would be no cake, no photographs, no rings and no wedding night, let alone a honeymoon, because this was an arrangement, a transaction—not a love match.

Which wasn't to say that Clay didn't fully expect to bed Dara Rose when the time came, and if they got a baby started right away, too, so much the better. He figured the actual consummation of their union would probably have to wait until spring, though, when the ranch house was finished and he and Dara Rose had a room to themselves.

Fine as the weather was, spring seemed a long way off when he thought of it in terms of making love to his wife.

Resigned, and leaving his hat behind because it didn't look right with the suit, Clay bid his dog a temporary farewell—Chester had taken to curling up on the cot inside the jail's one cell whenever he wanted to sleep, which was often—and set out for Dara Rose's little house, following the sidewalk as far as he could and then crossing the street by way of the peculiar system of planks and discarded doors and the beds of old wagons.

Mayor Ponder arrived by the same means, followed single file by a thin woman in very prim garb and one of the town council members—they'd come along to serve as witnesses, Clay supposed. Clutching a copy of the Good Book and a rolled sheet of paper as he minced his way over the swamplike road, Ponder looked none too pleased at the prospect of joining the new marshal and the pretty widow in holy matrimony.

Clay disliked the mayor, mainly because of the remark Ponder had made about not minding if Dara Rose wound up working upstairs at the Bitter Gulch Saloon, but he could tolerate the man long enough to get hitched. The rest of the time, Wilson Ponder was fairly easy to ignore.

"There's still time to change your mind," Ponder boomed out, as if he wanted the whole town to hear, when he and Clay met at Dara Rose's front gate. "Charity is charity, but I think you might be taking it a little too far in this instance."

Charity is charity.

The front door of the house was open, probably to admit as much fresh air as possible before the winter weather returned, and Clay had to unlock his jawbones by an act of will. What if Dara Rose had heard what Ponder said? Or the children?

He didn't respond, but simply glowered at Ponder until the other man cleared his throat and muttered, "Well, let's get on with it, then."

Edrina and Harriet appeared in the doorway, beaming. They had ribbons in their hair, and they were wearing summer dresses, very nearly outgrown and obviously their best.

"Mama looks so pretty in her wedding dress!" Edrina enthused, as Clay moved ahead of the others, stepped onto the porch and immediately swept both children off their feet, one in the curve of each arm.

They giggled at that, and the sound heartened Clay. Reminded him that he'd put on that itchy suit because he was going to a *wedding,* not a funeral.

Behind him, the female witness made a sighlike sound, long-suffering and full of righteous indignation.

Once again, Clay tamped down his temper. He wanted to pin that old biddy's ears back, verbally, anyhow—he'd never struck a woman, a child or an animal, and never intended to, though he'd landed plenty of punches in the faces of his boy cousins growing up—but today was neither the time nor the place to hold forth on what he thought of nasty-natured gossips.

For one thing, he didn't want to spoil the day for Edrina and Harriet. They were clearly overjoyed at the prospect of a wedding, though with Edrina, it was partly about being allowed to miss a few hours of school.

"I'll bet your mama *does* look pretty," Clay agreed, in belated reply to Edrina's statement. "Almost as pretty as the pair of you, maybe."

That got them both giggling again, and Clay smiled as he set them on their feet.

And then nearly tripped over them when Dara Rose appeared, wearing an ivory silk gown with puffed-out sleeves and lace trim at the cuffs. Her cheeks were pink, her eyes bright with a combination of nervousness and hope, her hair done up in a soft knot at her nape and billowing cloud-like around her face.

The sight of her knocked the wind out of Clay as surely as if he'd been thrown from a horse and landed spread-eagle on hard ground.

Ponder cleared his throat again, and the wedding party assembled itself, with surprising grace, in the middle of that cramped front room.

Dara Rose's trim shoulder bumped Clay's arm as she took her place beside him, and he felt a jolt of sweet fire at her touch.

Ponder opened the book, and then his mouth, but before he could get a word said, a ruckus erupted out in the road.

Looking down at Dara Rose, Clay saw her shut her eyes, felt her stiffen next to him.

Outside, a mule brayed, and a drunken voice bellowed.

Clay took Dara Rose's hand and squeezed it lightly before turning to head for the doorway.

Edrina and Harriet were already there, staring out.

"Mama's not going to marry you, Ezra Maddox!" Edrina shouted to the stumbling man trying to free his feet from the deep mud. "She's taken, so you'd better just get your sorry self out of here before there's trouble!"

Clay had to choke back a laugh. He rested one hand on the top of Edrina's head and one on Harriet's, and said quietly, "Go stand with your mama. I'll handle this."

Maddox was a big man, broad-shouldered and clad in work clothes, and his hair and beard were grizzled, wiry. Once he'd gotten loose from the mud, he practically tore the gate off its rusty hinges, getting it open, and stormed in Clay's direction like a locomotive.

Clay stepped out onto the porch, waited.

Behind him, Ponder said, "Now, Ezra, don't be a sore

loser. You're out of the running where Dara Rose is concerned, and making a damn fool of yourself won't change that."

Ezra came to a shambling stop in the middle of the path, not because he'd taken Mayor Ponder's sage advice to heart, Clay reckoned, but because he was used to folks clearing the way between him and whatever it was he aimed to have.

Clay didn't move.

The two men studied each other, at a distance of a dozen yards or so, and Maddox swayed slightly, ran the back of one arm across his mouth. His gaze narrowed.

"Did you get to the part where the justice of the peace inquires as to whether or not anybody has reason to object to this marriage?" Maddox ranted. "Because that's when I mean to say my piece."

"Let's hear it," Clay said, in an affable drawl. He hoped the situation wouldn't disintegrate into a howling brawl in the mud, with him and Maddox rolling back and forth with their hands on each other's throats, because he didn't want that to be what Dara Rose, Edrina and Harriet remembered when they looked back on this day.

Another part of him relished the idea of a knock-down-drag-out fisticuff.

Maddox straightened, swayed again and spoke with alacrity. "I have already offered for you, Dara Rose Nolan, and you belong to me," he said, as she stepped up beside Clay and put her hand on his arm.

A thrill of something rushed through Clay, though he'd hoped Dara Rose would stay inside, out of harm's way, until he and Maddox had settled their differences.

"You belong to me," Maddox reiterated.

"I belong to myself," Dara Rose informed him. "And

no one else, except for my children. I want nothing to do with you, Mr. Maddox, and I'll count it as a favor if you leave, right now."

"All right," Maddox erupted, flinging his beefy arms out from his sides with such force that he nearly fell over sideways, "you can bring the girls along, and I'll marry you straight off—today, if that's what you want."

"You are too late, Mr. Maddox," Dara Rose said, in a clear and steady voice. "Please be on your way so we can get on with the wedding."

Clay wondered distractedly if Dara Rose had ever seriously considered taking up with a lug like Maddox. He couldn't imagine her parting with her children.

Maddox just stood there, evidently weighing his options, which were few, and broke the ensuing silence by spitting violently and barking out, "This feller might have a badge, Dara Rose, but he ain't Parnell come back to life."

He turned partially, as if to walk away, but he jabbed a finger in Dara Rose's direction and went right on running off at the mouth. "I'll tell you what he is, this man you're so dead set on marryin'—he's a *stranger,* a lying drifter, for all you know—and when he moves on, leavin' you with another babe in your belly and no way to feed your brood, don't you come cryin' to me!"

Clay's restraint snapped then, but before he could take more than a single step in Maddox's direction, Dara Rose tightened her grip on his arm and stopped him.

Maddox spat again, but then he whirled around and headed for the gate and the waiting mule, every step he took making a sucking sound because of the mud.

Dara Rose let go of Clay's arm and walked, with high-chinned dignity, back into the house, leaving Clay and Mayor Ponder standing on the porch.

Ponder's gaze followed Maddox as he mounted the mule to ride away. "I'd watch my back if I were you, Marshal," he said thoughtfully. "Ezra's the kind to hold a grudge, and he's got a sneaky side to him."

INSIDE, DARA ROSE was shaken, but she made sure it didn't show.

Mayor Ponder's wife, Heliotrope, was a scandalmonger with nothing better to do than spread gossip, heavily laced with her own interpretation of any given person or situation, of course, and thanks to Ezra Maddox's unexpected visit, she'd have plenty of fodder as it was.

Dara Rose wasn't about to give her more to work with.

Besides, the children were watching her, and they'd follow whatever example she set. She wanted them to see strength in their mother, and courage, and dignity.

So she straightened her spine, lifted her chin and once again took her place at Clay McKettrick's side.

Mayor Ponder opened his book again and began to read out the words that would bind her to this tall man standing next to her.

The mayor's voice turned to a drone, and the very atmosphere seemed to pulse and buzz around Dara Rose, making her light-headed.

She spoke when spoken to, answered by rote.

After three weddings, she could have gotten married in her sleep.

Questions plagued her, swooped down on her like raucous birds. *What if Ezra had been right? Suppose Clay was a liar and a drifter—or worse? Was she marrying him because some deluded part of her had him confused with Parnell?*

"I now pronounce you man and wife," Mayor Ponder

said, slamming the book closed between his pawlike hands. "Mr. McKettrick, you may kiss the bride."

Clay looked down at her, one eyebrow slightly raised, and a grin crooked at a corner of his mouth.

On impulse, and to get it over with, Dara Rose stood on tiptoe and kissed that mouth, very lightly, very quickly and very briefly.

"There," she said. "It's done."

Clay merely chuckled.

She could still back out, Dara Rose reminded herself fitfully. She could refuse to sign the marriage certificate, ask Mayor Ponder to reverse the declaration that they were now man and wife.

Was that legal?

For a moment, Dara Rose thought she might swoon, just faint dead away right there in her own front parlor. But Clay slipped a strong arm around her waist, effectively holding her up until she signaled, with a furtive glance his way, that she could stand without help.

Thoughts still clamored through her mind, though, and her hand shook slightly when she signed "Dara Rose McKettrick" on the line reserved for the bride.

What had she *done*?

Suppose Clay was really a rascal and a drunk, instead of the solid man he seemed to be? Suppose he already *had* a wife tucked away somewhere, and he'd just made them both bigamists? And what if this stranger had spoken falsely when he promised not to exercise his rights as a husband unless and until she declared herself ready and willing?

The room felt hot, even with a chinook breeze sweeping in through the open door.

Edrina tugged at Dara Rose's hand, bringing her back

into the present moment. "Now you're Mrs. McKettrick," the little girl crowed. "Can Harriet and I be McKettricks, too?"

Dara Rose had no idea how to answer.

Clay, who had clearly overheard, judging by that little smile resting on his mouth as he bent to scrawl his name on the marriage certificate, said nothing. He waited while Mayor Ponder and both witnesses added their signatures where appropriate. Then money changed hands, and the ordeal was over.

The official part of it, at least.

Mayor Ponder and his companions took their leave, and Dara Rose was alone with her new husband and her delighted children.

"We want to be McKettricks, too," Edrina insisted.

"You're Nolans," Dara Rose reasoned. "What would your papa think if you changed your names?"

"*You* changed *yours,*" Edrina pointed out. "And, anyhow, Papa's dead."

Harriet's eyes rounded. "Papa's dead?"

"Of course he is, dolt," Edrina snapped. "Why do you suppose we put flowers on a grave with his name on it?"

"Edrina," Dara Rose reprimanded. "Stop it."

"I can't read," Harriet lamented, looking up at Dara Rose now, with tears welling in her eyes. "You said Papa was *gone*—"

Dara Rose exchanged glances with a somber-faced Clay and then bent her knees so she was crouching before her daughter, in the dress she'd worn to marry Luke, and then Parnell, and now Clay.

"Sweetheart," she said softly, "that's what 'gone' means sometimes. I know it's hard for you to understand, but you have to try."

Harriet turned, much to Dara Rose's surprise, and buried her face in one side of Clay's fancy suit coat, wailing in despair. This was unusual behavior, especially for even-tempered Harriet, but Dara Rose put it down to all the excitement of a front-room wedding.

"There, now," Clay said gruffly, as Dara Rose straightened, hoisting Harriet up into his arms. "You go right ahead and cry 'til you feel like stopping."

Dara Rose sank onto the settee, close to tears herself.

She was *married,* and there was so much she didn't know about Clay.

So much he didn't know about her.

Harriet bawled like a banshee—Dara Rose realized the child was going for effect now—her face hidden in Clay's shoulder.

"Here's what I think we ought to do," Clay said, to all of them. "We ought to go out to my ranch—I'll rent a buckboard and a couple of stout mules—and find ourselves a Christmas tree."

Harriet immediately stopped wailing.

Edrina lit up like a lightbulb wired to a power pole.

"A Christmas tree?" Dara Rose repeated, confounded.

"The roads are pretty muddy," Edrina speculated, but she was obviously warming to the idea, and so was Harriet, who had reared back to look at Clay in wet-eyed wonder.

"That's why we need mules," Clay replied.

"Do you believe in St. Nicholas?" Harriet asked him, in a hushed voice.

Clay looked directly at Dara Rose, silently dared her to say otherwise and replied, "I do indeed. One Christmas Eve, when my cousin Sawyer and I were about your age, we caught a glimpse of him flying over the roof of our granddad's barn in that sleigh of his, with eight reindeer harnessed to the rig."

Edrina blinked, swallowed. *"Really?"* she breathed, wanting so much to believe, even at the advanced age of six, that she'd been wrong to think there was no magic in the world.

Dara Rose's heart ached.

"Can't think what else it could have been," Clay answered, as serious in tone and expression as a man bearing witness in a court of law, under oath. "A sleigh pulled by eight reindeer is a fairly distinctive sight."

"Thunderation," Edrina exclaimed softly, while Harriet favored her older sister with a smug I-told-you-so look.

Dara Rose glared up at her bridegroom. "Mr. McKettrick," she began, but he cut her off before she could go on.

"Call me Clay," he said mildly. "I'm your husband now, remember?"

Dara Rose got to her feet. *"Clay,* then," she said dangerously. "I will have you know—"

Again he interrupted, setting Harriet on her feet and saying, "You two go on and change your clothes. Get your bonnets and your coats, too."

Edrina and Harriet rushed to obey.

Dara Rose stood there in her sorry-luck wedding dress, trembling with frustration. "How dare you get their hopes up like that?" she whispered furiously, flushed and near tears again. "How *dare* you encourage them to believe in things that aren't even real?"

"Whoa," Clay said, cupping her chin gently in one hand. "Are you saying that St. Nicholas *isn't real?"*

"Of *course* that's what I'm saying," Dara Rose retorted, under her breath but with plenty of bluster. "He *isn't."*

Clay gave a long, low whistle of surprise, though his too-blue eyes danced with delighted mischief. "I got here just in time," he said.

Dara Rose was brought up short. *"What?"* she managed, with more effort than a single word should have required.

Clay shook his head, as though he couldn't believe another human being could be so deluded as Dara Rose clearly was. "They're only going to be little girls once," he said, "and for a very short time. If I hadn't shown up when I did, you might have ruined one of the best things about being a kid—believing."

Dara Rose's mouth fell open. Clay closed it for her by levering up on her chin with that work-roughened and yet extraordinarily gentle hand of his.

"Now," he went on decisively, "Edrina and Harriet and I are going out to find a Christmas tree. You can either come with us, Mrs. McKettrick, or you can stay right here with the chickens. Which is it going to be?"

Dara Rose wasn't about to send her children out into the countryside in a mule-drawn buckboard with a stranger, but neither did she have the heart to insist that they forget the whole crazy plan.

"Edrina and Harriet are *my* children," she said, hearing the girls laugh and scuffle in the small bedroom as they went about exchanging their wedding garb for warmer things, "and I will not have them misled."

"Fair enough," Clay said, letting his eyes drop. "Shouldn't you get out of that fancy dress before we head out?"

THE MUD WAS DEEP, but the mules that came with the hired buckboard were strong and sure-footed. Once Clay had arranged the transaction, changed his clothes and collected Chester from the jailhouse, they made the short journey to the ranch with no trouble at all—in fact, it seemed to Clay that those mules knew how to avoid the worst of the muck and plant their hooves on solid ground.

He pulled back on the brake lever and simultaneously reined in the mules right where the kit-house would go up, come spring.

He jumped down, smiling as Edrina and Harriet piled eagerly out of the back of the buckboard, Chester leaping after them and barking fit to split a man's eardrums, and went around to reach up a hand to Dara Rose.

She hadn't said two words to him since they'd left town, and her color was high, but she let Clay lift her down.

Gasped when he made sure their bodies collided in the process.

He laughed, though she'd roused an ache inside him.

She blushed and straightened her bonnet with both hands, which made her bosom rise in that tantalizing way he so enjoyed.

"You gave your word," she whispered, narrow-eyed.

"And I'll keep it," Clay assured her. This was what he got for putting his mouth in motion before his head was in gear, he figured. A wife to contradict everything he said and no wedding night to make up for the inevitable difficulties of an intimate alliance.

If Sawyer had been there, he'd surely have called Clay crazy, denying himself the pleasures of matrimony, especially when he was married to a woman like Dara Rose.

And Clay would have had to admit his cousin was right.

He *was* crazy.

But a promise was a promise.

"Let's go," he said, reaching into the wagon-bed for the

short-handled ax he'd borrowed when he rented the team and buckboard over at the livery stable. "It'll be dark in a few hours, and there's no telling when the snow will start up again, so we'd better get started."

Edrina and Harriet were practically beside themselves with excitement, and Chester trotted around them all in big, swoopy circles, livelier than Clay had yet seen him.

The "tree" they finally settled upon looked more like a tumbleweed to Clay, who was used to the lush, fragrant firs that grew in northern Arizona, but Edrina and Harriet were enchanted. So Clay chopped down that waist-high scrub pine and carried it in one hand back to the wagon.

Dara Rose bore silent witness to all this, cautiously enjoying her daughters' delight.

Edrina had noticed the stone markers Clay had set in place the last time he was there, and she squatted on her haunches to peer at one of them. Harriet and Chester stood nearby.

"What *is* this?" Edrina asked.

Clay smiled, tossed the tree into the bed of the wagon and walked back to stand over the little girl. He was aware of Dara Rose on the periphery of things, but he didn't look in her direction.

"This is where I plan to put up my—*our*—house, once it arrives, that is."

Edrina looked up at him, brow crinkling a little. "Houses don't *arrive*," she said.

"This one will," Clay replied, enjoying the exchange. "It's coming by rail, from Sears, Roebuck and Company, all the way out in Chicago, Illinois."

"A *house* can't ride on a train!" Harriet proclaimed gleefully. "Houses are too *big* to fit!"

Clay laughed, crouched between the two girls, to put

himself at eye level with them. Chester nuzzled his arm and then, quick as can be, licked Clay's face.

"I guess you'd say this house is kind of like a jigsaw puzzle," Clay told the children. "It's broken down into parts and packed in crates. When it gets here, I'll have to put it together."

Edrina frowned, absorbing his words. Then she whistled, through her teeth, and said, *"Thunderation and spit."*

"Speak in a ladylike fashion, Edrina Nolan," Dara Rose interceded coolly, "or do not speak at all."

Clay tossed a look in his wife's direction and stood tall again, resting one hand on each bonneted head. "I reckon we'll head back to town now," he said. "I don't like the looks of that cloud bank over there on the horizon."

The wind was beginning to pick up a little, too.

Dara Rose shooed the girls toward the hired buckboard, but they didn't need anybody's help to climb inside. They shinnied up the rear wheels, agile as a pair of monkeys, and planted themselves on either side of the scrub pine.

Clay hoisted Chester aboard and fastened the tailgate, but before he could get to Dara Rose and offer her a hand up, she was already in the front of the wagon, perched on the seat and looking straight ahead.

"Will there be room for us in your new house?" Harriet asked, just as Clay settled in to take the reins.

Clay looked down at Dara Rose, who didn't acknowledge him in any visible way. "Yes," he said. "You and Edrina will have to share a room at first, most likely, but after a year or two, I'll be building on, and you'll each have one of your own."

"Then where will Mama be?" Harriet wanted to know. "In my room, or in Edrina's?"

"Neither," Clay said.

A flush bloomed into Dara Rose's cheeks and, even though she hastened to adjust her bonnet, Clay had already seen. "Harriet," Dara Rose said, "please sit down immediately."

Harriet sat.

Clay bit the inside of his lip, so he wouldn't smile, turned the team and wagon in a wide semicircle and headed toward town.

The girls chattered behind him and Dara Rose, in the bed of the buckboard, Chester no doubt hanging on every word. The wagon wheels, in need of greasing, squealed as the mules pulled the rig overland, puffing clouds of white fog from their nostrils, and the harnesses creaked.

For all that, Clay would remember that trip home as a silent one, because, once again, Dara Rose didn't say a word.

When they drove on along Main Street, passing the road that fronted the house without turning in, Dara Rose nudged him lightly with one elbow but still didn't speak.

"Where are we going?" Edrina called, from the back.

"We're having supper at the hotel tonight," Clay said, with a sidelong glance at Dara Rose. "Call it a celebration," he added dryly.

"Don't be silly," Dara Rose muttered in protest, but the girls were cheering by then, causing Chester to bark, and all of those noises combined to drown her out.

What with all the planks and doors in the road, Clay had to weave the team and wagon in and out half the length of Main Street, but he finally reined in, in front of the Texas Arms Hotel and Dining Room, and set the brake.

"This is extravagant," Dara Rose whispered to Clay, when everybody except Chester was standing on the board sidewalk. "We have food at home...."

"Tonight is special," Clay replied, before shifting his

attention to Chester. "You stay put, dog, and I'll bring you out some supper."

Chester seemed to understand; he settled down next to the Christmas tree, resting his muzzle on his outstretched front legs, sighed once and closed his eyes.

Edrina and Harriet raced, giggling, toward the main entrance to the hotel.

Dara Rose hesitated, though, and took a light but firm hold on Clay's arm. "You mustn't spoil my children," she said. "I don't want Edrina and Harriet getting used to luxuries I cannot hope to provide for them myself."

Clay suppressed a sigh. "Food," he said reasonably, "is not a luxury."

"It is when it's paid for, and someone else cooked and served it," Dara Rose insisted.

Clay smiled down at his bride. "Try to enjoy it just the same," he advised, taking her elbow and gently steering her across the sidewalk.

Chapter 8

⟨◦⟩

THE SMALL RUSTIC DINING establishment serving the Texas Arms Hotel was full of savory smells, causing Dara Rose's stomach to rumble.

Someone had hung a wreath made of holly sprigs behind the cash register, and limp tinsel garlands drooped from the edges of a long counter lined with stools.

Only one of the six tables was in use. A man, a woman and a little girl, probably a year or two older than Edrina, dined in companionable silence, their clothes exceedingly fine, their manners impeccable. Since Dara Rose had never laid eyes on them before, she knew they must have arrived on the afternoon train.

She wondered if they were just passing through, or if they'd come to Blue River to spend Christmas with friends or family.

Clay nodded a taciturn greeting to the man and the man nodded back.

Edrina and Harriet, stealing glances at the little girl, scrambled onto chairs at a table in front of the window, sitting side by side and swinging their feet. It had been an exciting day for them—first, the wedding, then the expedition to find a Christmas tree, and now a restaurant meal.

By the time they tumbled into bed that night, Dara Rose thought fondly, her daughters would be so deliciously exhausted, so saturated with fresh air, that they'd sleep like stones settling deep into the silt of a quiet pond.

Clay was just pulling back a chair for Dara Rose when the cook-waiter appeared, smiling a welcome. "I hear this is a wedding supper!" the man thundered. "Congratulations, Marshal."

It wouldn't have been proper to congratulate Dara Rose, since there would inevitably be an implication that she'd somehow *captured* her new husband, rounded him up like a rogue steer, and not by pure feminine allure. While she appreciated the courtesy, she did wish the man hadn't spoken so loudly, because the woman at the other table turned in their direction, her expression impassive, her gaze flickering briefly over Dara Rose's faded cloak, with its frayed, mud-splattered hem.

"Thanks, Roy," Clay responded, addressing the cook, with whom he was obviously acquainted, and the two men shook hands.

Dara Rose was not a person to compare herself to others, but as Clay pulled back a chair for her and she sat down, she couldn't help thinking how shabby she and the children must seem, in the eyes of that elegantly dressed woman and her little girl.

"What's it going to be, ladies?" Clay asked the children, while Dara Rose perused the menu, nearly overwhelmed by all the choices. "I can definitely recommend the fried chicken dinner, and the meat loaf is good, too."

"What's meat loaf?" Harriet wanted to know.

"You'll have the chicken dinner," Dara Rose said, without looking away from the menu. "One will be plenty for both of you."

She thought she might have felt Clay stiffen beside her, but then, as though she hadn't spoken at all, he simply answered Harriet's inquiry about the nature of meat loaf.

"I want that," Harriet said, when he'd finished. "Please."

"And I'll have stew with dumplings," Edrina added, sounding like a small adult, "if I may, please."

"You may," Clay said, without looking at Dara Rose, though she *did* see his mouth quirk briefly at one corner. "This is a very special occasion," he added, after clearing his throat quietly. "And, anyhow, Chester will be pleased to accept any leftovers. He's still building up his strength, you know."

Dara Rose's cheeks flamed. She loved animals. Her rooster and hens all had names, and she went out of her way to take good care of them. But she'd been so poor for so long—since she'd "married" Luke Nolan, a few months before Edrina was born—that the idea of giving a dog restaurant food just wouldn't fit into any of the compartments in her mind.

"There are *people* in this town who could put anything extra to good use," she said, sounding way more prim than she'd intended.

"Like the O'Reillys," Edrina said, with a sigh.

"Among others," Dara Rose agreed.

Clay was watching her so directly, and with such intensity, that she was forced to meet his gaze. "Shall we just scrape it all into a pan," he began, "and set it on the floor of their shanty, the way we'd do with Chester?"

Dara Rose blushed even harder. If they hadn't been in a public place, and if she'd been given to violence, she'd have slapped him across the face.

Before she could speak, Clay summoned Roy, the cook, back to their table with a polite gesture of one hand.

The man hurried over, eager to please.

Clay placed everyone's order—except for Dara Rose's—and then asked the cook to pack up enough fried chicken, meat loaf and trimmings to feed four people. He'd pay for and collect the extra food at the end of the meal, he said, and then looked pointedly at Dara Rose.

Confounded, and a little stung, she asked for chicken.

Edrina and Harriet were watching Clay raptly—they might have expected a laurel wreath or a winged helmet to appear on his head, from their expressions—and, not surprisingly, it was Edrina who broke the pulsing silence.

"Are we taking supper to the O'Reillys?" she asked.

"Yes," Clay said.

"Harriet and I are planning to visit Addie tomorrow," Edrina said. She turned a vaguely challenging glance in Dara Rose's direction. "Mama said we could."

Dara Rose, still feeling as though she'd been put smartly in her place and none too happy about it, thank you very much, returned Edrina's look in spades. "I said *you* could visit," she reminded her child, "since you'd already promised. I did *not* give permission for Harriet to accompany you."

"What's the harm?" Clay asked mildly, though his eyes contained a challenge, just as Edrina's had before. "That little girl looked to me as though she could use some company. Especially somebody close to her own age."

"She has romantic fever," Edrina said solemnly.

"That's not catching," Clay replied, and though his tone was serious, there was a twinkle in his eyes now. "In fact, I'd say your mother is immune to it."

"Other things *are* catching," Dara Rose felt compelled

to say, though she knew there was some kind of battle being waged here, and she was losing ground. Fast.

"It's probably too cold for lice and fleas at this time of year," Clay said.

Dara Rose didn't get a chance to respond. The food arrived, heaped on steaming plates, the children's first, and then Clay's and Dara Rose's.

The family of strangers, meanwhile, had finished their meal, and the man was settling the bill. The mother and the child rose from their chairs, and then the little girl walked right over to Edrina and Harriet and put out one tiny, porcelain-white hand.

"My name is Madeline Howard," she said. With her long, shining brown hair, deep green eyes and fitted emerald velvet dress, she bore a striking resemblance to the doll in the mercantile window. "What's yours?"

"I'm Edrina," answered Dara Rose's elder daughter, barely able to see over the mountain of food before her. "And this is my sister, Harriet."

"We're going to live in Blue River from now on," Madeline said. "Mama and Papa and me, I mean. Papa's going to build an office, and we'll have rooms upstairs."

The woman approached, laid a hand on Madeline's shoulder, offered a pained smile to everyone in general and no one in particular. "You mustn't bother people when they're eating, darling," she said.

Clay stood, put out his hand, and the woman shook it, after the briefest hesitation. "Clay McKettrick," he said. "This is my wife, Dara Rose."

This is my wife, Dara Rose.

No words could have sounded stranger to Dara Rose, and she had to swallow a ridiculous urge to explain, all in a rush, that theirs was a marriage of convenience, not a real one.

She merely nodded, though, and the woman nodded back. Like her daughter, she wore velvet, though her gown and short cape were a rich shade of brown instead of green. Not only that, but the pile on that fabric was plush, not worn away in places like most of the velvet one saw in Blue River, Texas.

The man had reached the table by then, and smiled as he and Clay shook hands. "Glad to meet you, Marshal," he said. "I'm Jim Howard, and my wife is Eloise."

Another stiff smile from Eloise. "My husband is a dentist," she said. "Most people address him as 'Dr. Howard,' of course."

Dara Rose, who had been trying to decide whether or not good manners required that she stand, like Clay, decided to stay seated.

"We could use a dentist around here," Clay said, with a grin dancing in his eyes but not quite reaching his mouth.

Madeline smiled broadly at Edrina and Harriet. "You both have very good teeth," she said admiringly. Her own were like small, square pearls, perfectly strung.

Jim Howard—*Dr.* Howard—chuckled at that. "We'll let you finish your meal in peace," he said, steering his womenfolk gently away, toward the hotel's modest lobby and then the stairs beyond.

Clay sat down. "Nice people," he said.

Madeline, Dara Rose noticed, kept looking back, her expression one of friendly longing, as though she would have liked to stay and chat with Edrina and Harriet.

"The lady is snooty," Edrina announced, holding a dinner roll daintily between a thumb and index finger. "But I like Madeline, and her papa, too."

Dara Rose was keenly aware, in that moment, that Edrina was following her lead. Hadn't she disliked Mrs. Howard almost immediately, and returned coolness for coolness instead of making an effort to be neighborly, offer a welcome to the newcomers?

It was tremendously difficult sometimes, she thought glumly, to be the sort of person she wanted her *daughters* to be, when they grew up. And she'd fallen far short of that standard tonight.

Unexpectedly, Clay reached over and gently squeezed her hand, just once and very briefly, but the gesture raised Dara Rose's flagging spirits.

It also sent something sharp and hot racing through her, a fiery ache she had to work very hard to ignore.

"Perhaps when we get to know Mrs. Howard better," she told Edrina, somehow managing a normal tone of voice, "we'll discover that she's a very nice person."

"Perhaps," Edrina agreed doubtfully.

The girls were practically nodding off in their chairs by the time the meal ended.

Clay took the leftovers out to Chester on a borrowed plate, while Roy packed the O'Reillys' supper into a large wooden crate, carefully covered with a dish towel. The bill was paid—the cost of it would have kept Dara Rose and the girls in groceries for the better part of a month—and Clay carried the crate out to the wagon, stowed it under the seat, where Chester couldn't get at it, and returned with the empty plate.

By then, Dara Rose had put on her cloak, Edrina was wearing her outdoor garb and, together, they maneuvered a sleepy Harriet into her coat and bonnet. Clay whisked the child up into his arms and carried her to the wagon.

A light snowfall was just beginning, and the wind was

picking up, so Clay took Dara Rose, the children and Chester back to the house first, saw them inside, and announced quietly that he'd return as soon as he'd dropped off the food at the O'Reilly place and turned in the mules and wagon at the livery.

Dara Rose moved by rote, helping the girls prepare for bed, tucking them in, hearing their prayers.

Harriet asked for the doll again.

Edrina said she was glad to have a new papa, then promised not to forget the old one.

Dara Rose was glad she'd turned down the wick in the kerosene lantern, leaving the room mostly in shadow, because there were tears in her eyes as she told her children good-night and kissed their foreheads.

THE SETTEE IN DARA Rose's parlor was about a foot shorter than he was, by Clay's estimation, but he'd slept in less comfortable places in his time, just the same. And Dara Rose *had* been considerate enough to set out a blanket and a pillow for him.

He smiled just imagining the joshing he'd get if Sawyer and the rest of his McKettrick cousins knew he was spending his wedding night alone, with his feet hanging over one end of a short sofa. He'd be lucky if he didn't wake up with his spine in the shape of a horseshoe and his toes numb from lack of circulation.

Chester, who'd settled himself nearby on the blanket Clay had brought over from the jailhouse, watched as he sat down on the settee to kick off his boots.

"Believe it or not," he told the dog, low-voiced, "I got married today."

Chester offered no comment.

The tumbleweed Christmas tree stood undecorated in

a corner of the room, stuck in a bucket of water and looking about as festive as Clay felt, but it had a nice pine scent that reminded him of home.

Because the house was small and he was mindful of the children, Clay decided to sleep in his clothes. He was about to extinguish the lantern and stretch out, as best he could, on that blasted settee, when Dara Rose stepped out of the bedroom.

Her hair was down, tumbling well past her waist, and she wore a long nightgown, covered with a plain flannel wrapper, cinched tight at her middle.

Clay's heart skipped a couple of beats, though he knew full well she wasn't there to render an annulment legally and morally impossible.

She stopped, glanced over at the hopeful tumbleweed and then stood a little straighter. This raised her to her full and unremarkable height, but whatever her errand, she sure enough looked like she meant business.

"Either you are an irresponsible man," Dara Rose said, making it clear how Edrina came by her bold certainty about everything, "or you have more money than you let on. Which is it?"

Clay stood, though he suddenly felt bone-tired, because there was a lady in the room. "I never said I was broke, Mrs. McKettrick," he replied dryly.

"Don't call me 'Mrs. McKettrick'!" Dara Rose immediately responded. "We made an agreement. This is a marriage in name only."

"Oh, I'm well aware of that," Clay responded, thinking he'd wait forever for this woman, if that was what he had to do. "But you are legally my wife, and that makes you Mrs. McKettrick."

She pulled so tight on the cinches of her wrapper then

that it was a wonder she didn't split right in two, like one of those showgirls in a magician's act. "Why do you keep pointing out that we are married in the eyes of the law?"

Clay was enjoying her discomfort a lot more than was gentlemanly. "Aren't we?" he asked, raising one eyebrow.

"Yes," she retorted, setting her hands down hard on her hips now and jutting out her elbows, "but it was a matter of expediency on my part, and nothing more."

"Gosh," Clay said, playing the rube. "Thanks."

"I would do anything for my daughters!" she blurted out. "Including marry a virtual stranger. I agreed to this arrangement *because* of them, not out of any desire to be your…your wife…." She stammered to a halt and turned a glorious shade of primrose-pink.

Clay waited a few moments before he spoke again. "That was quite a scene Maddox made today."

Dara Rose hesitated, trembled once and hugged herself as if she thought she might suddenly scatter in every direction, and it was all Clay could do not to cross the room and take her into his arms. "I suppose he believed he had call to object to—to our getting married," she continued, after a few moments of miserable struggle, "and it's true enough that he proposed—sort of."

"Sort of?" He'd known about the situation between Dara Rose and Maddox from Ponder and the others, but he wanted to hear it directly from her.

It was a long time before she answered. "I was supposed to work as his housekeeper for a year, so he could be sure I'd make a suitable wife. Then, if I passed muster, he'd put a ring on my finger."

Clay felt a fresh surge of rage rise up within him, and he waited for it to subside before he said anything. "Where did Edrina and Harriet fit into all this?"

He knew the answer to that question, too, at least indirectly but, again, he wanted the first-hand truth from Dara Rose herself.

Her eyes welled, but she looked so proud and so vulnerable that Clay continued to keep his distance. He figured she *might* actually shatter into bits if he touched her.

"They didn't," she said, at long last. Then, speaking so softly that Clay barely heard her, she went on. "He wanted me to put my children in an orphanage, or send them out to work for their board and room."

That was when Clay took a chance. He held his arms out to her.

Dara Rose paused briefly, considering, and then moved slowly into his embrace.

Clay rested his chin on top of her head. "No matter how things turn out between you and me, Dara Rose," he told her, "you will never have to send your girls away, I promise you that."

She looked up at him, her eyes moist, though she still wouldn't allow tears to fall. "How can you make a promise like that, Clay?" she whispered brokenly. "How?"

At least she hadn't called him "Mr. McKettrick." Wasn't that progress?

"I just *did* make a promise like that," he replied, wanting to kiss her more than he'd ever wanted to kiss a woman before, and still unwilling to take the chance, "and you'll find that I'm a man of my word."

She blinked. "There's so much you don't know about me," she said.

He grinned, holding her loosely, with his hands clasped behind the small of her back. "There are, as it happens, a few things you don't know about me," he replied. "I didn't come to Blue River to work as the town marshal for the rest

of my life, for one. I mean to be a rancher, Dara Rose—
I come from a family of them. That's why I bought two
thousand acres of good grazing land, and that's why I plan
to build a house on the site we visited today."

"And that's why you wanted a wife," she said, almost
forlornly.

"Not just any wife," he pointed out.

"Parnell and I—" She looked at the large likeness on
the wall. And suddenly, she choked up again. Couldn't
seem to go on.

"It's all right, Dara Rose," Clay said, kissing her lightly
on her crown, where her silken hair parted. She smelled
sweetly of rainwater and flowery soap. "We've both got
stories to tell, but it doesn't have to happen tonight."

She sniffled, smiled bravely, but otherwise she gave
no response.

"Exactly why did you come out here in the first place?"
Clay asked.

Dara Rose looked flustered. "I forgot to feed the chickens," she said. "And I was hoping you'd be asleep so I
could sneak past."

Clay chuckled. "Well, I have to admit, that's something
of a disappointment."

"I *never* forget to feed the chickens," Dara Rose fretted, chagrined. "The poor things—"

"I fed them, Dara Rose," Clay said.

"When?"

"Before we went to find the Christmas tree," he said,
with a nod toward the tumbleweed.

She seemed to realize then that he was still holding her,
and she stepped back suddenly, as though startled. "About
Christmas," she began.

"What about Christmas?"

"I'd really rather you didn't encourage Edrina and Harriet to entertain fanciful notions."

"Such as?" Clay asked, feigning innocence.

Dara Rose bristled up again.

He loved it when she did that.

"Well," she huffed, "there *was* that tall tale about seeing St. Nicholas flying past your grandfather's barn roof in a sleigh drawn by reindeer—"

He smiled. "Why, Mrs. McKettrick—are you calling me a liar?"

"You and your cousin must have been inebriated."

"We were eight," Clay said.

"Then you were dreaming."

"The same dream, at the same time? Sawyer and I are blood kin, but we don't share a brain."

Dara Rose sighed again. It was plain that she didn't know what to say next, or what to do, either.

Both were encouraging signs, Clay figured.

"Get some sleep," he told her. "You've had a long day."

She glanced at the settee, then took his measure with her eyes. Drew the obvious conclusion. "You are in for an uncomfortable night," she said, without any discernible concern.

For more reasons than one, Clay thought. But what he said was, "I'll be just fine. See you in the morning."

Dara Rose nodded, turned around and went back into the bedroom.

Clay watched her go, rubbing his chin with one hand, calculating the number of settee nights he'd have to put in between now and spring, when the house would be ready.

In the end, he slept on the floor, next to Chester.

At least that way, he could stretch out.

WHEN HE OPENED HIS EYES again, it was morning, and Edrina and Harriet were standing over him, looking worried.

"We thought you might be dead," Edrina said, with a relieved and somewhat wobbly smile.

"But you're not," Harriet added emphatically.

"No," Clay said, with a laugh, as he sat up. "I do believe I'm still among the living."

Both children were dressed for daytime, with their curly hair brushed and held back at the sides of their heads by small combs. Their faces were rosy from a recent scrubbing and their eyes shone.

"Mama is taking us over to the O'Reillys' place to visit Addie," Edrina said, "as soon as she's finished feeding the chickens and gathering the eggs and making breakfast."

Clay yawned expansively and got to his feet. "Where's Chester?"

"He's outside with Mama," Harriet replied. "She said he needed to do his business."

"What time is it?" Clay wondered aloud. He owned a pocket watch but seldom carried it; there had been no real need for that, back on the Triple M. There, where there was always a full day's work to do, you started at sunrise and finished when you finished, whatever time it was.

Before either child replied, he caught sight of the timepiece hanging prominently on the wall. Eight o'clock.

"When we get back from the O'Reillys'," Harriet piped up, "can we decorate the Christmas tree?"

Clay hesitated to answer, realizing that he didn't even know if Dara Rose *owned* any decorations, or whether she'd take kindly to his buying some for her, over at the mercantile.

Reckon you should have thought about that before you

cut down that sorry sprig of sagebrush you're calling a Christmas tree, he told himself silently.

"That's up to your mama," he finally said.

Both children looked deflated.

"She'll just say it's a whole week 'til Christmas and St. Nicholas isn't coming, anyhow, so what do we need with a silly tree," Edrina said, in a rush of words.

Inwardly, Clay sighed. These were Dara Rose's children, and she had a perfect right to raise them as she saw fit, but he hoped she'd ease up on that rigid personal code of hers a little, and let them be kids while they could.

In the near distance, the back door opened, and Clay felt the rush of cool air where he stood. Dara Rose called out, "Girls? You're not bothering Mr. McKettrick, are you?"

Chester trotted through the inside doorway, came over to greet him.

Clay smiled and ruffled the dog's ears.

"We don't want to call you 'Mr. McKettrick,'" Edrina told Clay.

"We want to call you 'Papa,'" Harriet said.

The backs of Clay's eyes stung a little. "I'd like that," he said quietly, "but that's another thing that's got to be left up to your mama."

"What's to be left up to me?" Dara Rose asked, standing in the doorway. Her hair was pinned up, unlike last night, and like the girls', her cheeks were pink with well-being.

"Whether or not we can call Mr. McKettrick 'Papa,'" Harriet answered.

"And if we can put baubles on the Christmas tree," Edrina added.

Both of them stared expectantly at their mother.

"Oh," she finally said, shifting the handle of the egg basket from one wrist to the other. Her gaze flicked to

Clay's face and then back to the girls. "It's too soon to address Mr. McKettrick in such a familiar fashion," she said. "But I don't see why we couldn't get out the Christmas things."

So she *had* Christmas things, Clay thought. That was something, anyway.

Edrina and Harriet swapped glances and made what would seem to be a tacit agreement to take what they could get.

"Breakfast will be ready in a few minutes," Dara Rose said. "And there are plenty of eggs this morning. We can each have one—Mr. McKettrick may have two, if he wishes—and there will still be enough left to sell over at the mercantile."

"One egg will suit me fine," Clay said, gruff-voiced. Soon as he'd put in a few hours over at the jailhouse and walked through the town once or twice to make sure there wasn't any trouble brewing, he'd head over to the mercantile and stock up on foodstuffs. See if old Philo would agree to deliver what he bought.

Dara Rose wouldn't like it, he supposed, when the storekeeper turned up with sugar and coffee beans and a wagonload of other goods, but he already had an argument ready. He didn't expect her to feed him and Chester; therefore, he wanted to contribute to the grubstake.

Plus, he had to have coffee in the morning, to get himself going.

So they ate their simple breakfast, the girls so excited, between the promised outing and the tree waiting to be festooned with geegaws, that they could barely sit still.

Dara Rose cleared the table while Clay donned his duster and his hat and summoned the dog. He'd left his gun belt and pistol over at the jailhouse, because of Edrina and Harriet, but he'd strap on the long-barreled .45 before he set out on his rounds. It wasn't that he expected to need a firearm, but he wanted any potential troublemakers to know the new marshal was serious about upholding his duties.

"Thanks for breakfast," Clay said, with a tug at his hat brim.

Dara Rose nodded, then looked away.

THE VISIT TO LITTLE Addie O'Reilly was necessarily brief since the child was bedridden. Last night's snow hadn't stuck, thank heaven, but there was still a bitter chill in the air, and Addie's two younger brothers sat on the bare floor near the odd, cobbled-together stove, playing with half a dozen marbles.

Peg tried to put a good face on things, but Dara Rose could tell she was embarrassed. There was no place to sit, except on one of the two beds or an upended crate—undoubtedly the same one that had contained last night's donated supper.

The girls, meanwhile, chatted with Addie.

"Somebody left a box of hot food at my doorstep," Peg said, following Dara Rose's gaze to the crate. Four clean plates, plus utensils, were stacked beside it. "We sure did have ourselves a fine feast, and there's enough left to get us through today, too."

"That's…wonderful," Dara Rose said.

"I figure it had to come from the dining room over to the hotel," Peg went on, wiping her hands down the skirt of her calico dress. "I mean to take the plates and silverware back later."

Dara Rose merely nodded. Clay must have wanted to

keep his part in the enterprise a secret, so she didn't say anything.

Fortunately, neither did Edrina or Harriet. They were busy telling Addie all about the little girl, Madeline, whose papa was a dentist.

"You'll never guess who stopped by here yesterday," Peg said, taking Dara Rose by surprise.

"Who?" Dara Rose asked, simply to make conversation.

"Ezra Maddox," Peg said. "He's offered me housekeeping work, Mrs. Nolan. The job doesn't pay much, but at least there'll be plenty of good farm food for these kids, and if things work out, Mr. Maddox and me will be married come the spring." She paused. "You don't mind, do you? Now that you've married the marshal and all?"

Dara Rose smiled. "I don't mind," she was quick to say. Then, cautiously, afraid Peg O'Reilly might have misunderstood Maddox's offer, she asked, "He didn't object to your bringing the children along?"

"He did," Peg confided, in a whisper, "but I told him I wouldn't be parted from my little ones for anything or anybody, and he finally agreed to take them in."

The boys were still busy with their game of marbles, and Edrina was telling Addie that there wasn't going to be a Christmas program over at the schoolhouse this year because that last snowstorm threw everything out of whack.

"What about—?"

"My husband?" Peg asked. "Ezra knows about him, of course. Says we'll look into getting me a divorce if it comes to that."

Dara Rose's heart ached for Peg O'Reilly. "This is what you want to do?" she asked, very quietly.

"It's the answer to a prayer," Peg replied, looking a little surprised by Dara Rose's question.

Ezra Maddox, the answer to a prayer?

It just went to show, Dara Rose thought, that one woman's idea of hell was *another* woman's idea of heaven.

Chapter 9

❦

FULL OF CONSTERNATION, Dara Rose studied the Closed sign on the door at the mercantile, the handle of the egg basket looped over one wrist, and wondered what on earth could have prompted Mr. Bickham to close his establishment at midmorning. Edrina and Harriet, meanwhile, climbed onto the bench in front of the store and peered in through the display window.

"Mama!" Harriet suddenly cried, so startling Dara Rose that she almost dropped the egg basket. "She's gone! *Florence is gone!*"

Dara Rose caught her breath, the fingers of her free hand splayed across her breastbone to keep her heart from jumping right out of her chest.

Florence?

Harriet let out a despairing wail.

"Hush!" Edrina told her sister, speaking sternly but slipping an arm around the child's shoulders just the same. The two of them looked so small, standing there on the seat of that bench, like a pair of beautiful urchins.

The doll, Dara Rose realized belatedly.

Of course. Florence was the doll Harriet had been admiring—yearning after—ever since it first appeared in the mercantile window, the day after Thanksgiving. And now the doll was gone.

It would be set out for some other child to find on Christmas morning.

Although Dara Rose had never for one moment believed she could buy that doll for her little girl, Harriet's disappointment grieved her sorely. Like any mother, she longed to give her children nice things, but that was a pleasure she couldn't afford; they needed practical things, and some small measure of security, be it the egg money she squirreled away a penny at a time, or the ten dollars resting between the pages of her Bible.

Hurting as much as her child was—maybe more—and doing her best to hide it, Dara Rose set the egg basket down carefully and gathered Harriet into her arms, lifting her off the bench and holding her tightly. "There, now," she whispered, her throat so thick she could barely speak. Not that there was a great deal to say at a moment like that, anyway. "There, now."

"I should have sold my hair!" Harriet sobbed. "Then I would have had the money to buy Florence!"

Once again, Dara Rose thought of Piper's gift, safe at home, and ached.

Edrina jumped down from the bench, tomboylike, and tugged at Harriet's dangling foot. "Stop carrying on, goose," she commanded, but there was a slight quaver in her voice. "You'll have the whole town staring at us."

Harriet shuddered and buried her wet face in Dara Rose's neck. "I—really—thought—I—could—have—Florence—for—my—very—own," she said, punctuating her words with small but violent hiccups.

"Shh," Dara Rose said gently, still holding the child. "Everything will be all right, sweetheart. We'll go home now. Edrina, bring the egg basket."

By the time the three of them reached the end of Main Street and turned toward the house, Harriet had settled down to the occasional quivering sniffle.

A buckboard stood near Dara Rose's front gate, with two mules hitched to it.

Philo Bickham sat in the wagon box, reins in hand, beaming at Dara Rose as she approached with the children.

"I was just about to unload all this merchandise and leave it on the porch," he said. "The marshal said he'd be here to accept delivery, but there's been no sign of him so far."

Dara Rose frowned, at once wary and intrigued.

Edrina bolted forward and scrambled right up the side of that buckboard, skillful as a monkey, using the wheel spokes as footholds. "Thunderation!" she whooped.

Mr. Bickham jumped to the ground, nimble for a man of his age and bulk. He strode around to the back of the wagon and lowered the tailgate. "He darned near bought the place out, your new husband," the storekeeper crowed, no doubt pleased to make such a sale. Blue River was not a wealthy community, which meant the owner of the mercantile scraped by like most everyone else.

"Mama," Edrina spouted, "there's a tin of tea…and a big ham…and *peaches*…and all sorts of things wrapped in brown paper—"

"Edrina Nolan," Dara Rose said, setting Harriet on her feet, "get down from there this instant."

"Don't go poking around in those packages," Mr. Bickham said good-naturedly, shaking a finger at Edrina and then Harriet. "The marshal made himself mighty clear on that score. After all, it's almost Christmas, and there's a secret or two afoot."

Dara Rose was still trying to think what to say when Clay rode around the corner on Outlaw, Chester trotting in their wake.

Mr. Bickham hailed him, and Dara Rose sent the girls inside, over their protests.

"Sorry if I held you up any, Philo," Clay told Mr. Bickham, barely glancing at Dara Rose as he swung down from the saddle. "A telegram came in from Sears, Roebuck and Company. They've shipped the makings of my house out by rail, and the whole works will be arriving here in about ten days."

"You'd better get that foundation dug and that well put in, then," Mr. Bickham said, giving Clay a congratulatory slap on one shoulder. "Reckon you can round up some hired help down at the Bitter Gulch, and if this weather holds, since you've got a put-together house coming, you'll be out there on your own place in no time."

Clay nodded and, once again, his gaze touched on Dara Rose's face.

"What is all this?" she asked evenly, as soon as Mr. Bickham had hoisted the first box from the back of the wagon and started toward the house with it.

Clay gave her a wry look and lifted out a second box. "Chester and I," he said, with a twinkle, "don't believe in freeloading. We always pay our own way."

Dara Rose opened her mouth, closed it again. "But all those packages, and the tea, and that enormous ham—"

"You like tea, don't you?" Clay teased, starting toward the house.

Dara Rose scurried to keep up with his long strides. "Of

course I like tea," she said, flustered, "but it's a luxury, and we don't need it—"

"Sure you do," Clay replied, climbing the porch steps now. "What do you plan on serving all the ladies of Blue River when they start dropping by to see for themselves just what kind of mischief we're up to over here?"

Harriet and Edrina, huddled in the doorway, scattered to let them through.

Mr. Bickham was coming from the other direction, and Clay sidestepped him.

"Mr. McKettrick," Dara Rose persisted, when the two of them were alone in the kitchen, "I do have my pride."

"Yes, Mrs. McKettrick," Clay agreed. "I have taken note of that fact." He took a large tin from the box he'd carried in. "Would you mind putting some coffee on to brew while Bickham and I finish unloading that wagon? I've got a hankering for the stuff, and I like it strong and black."

Dara Rose couldn't seem to untangle her tongue.

"You do own a coffeepot, don't you?" Clay asked offhandedly.

"Yes," she managed, blushing. "Parnell drank coffee every morning."

Clay merely nodded, as though she'd confirmed something he already knew, and went out again.

Dara Rose got out Parnell's coffeepot, rinsed it at the sink and pumped fresh water into it. Then she had to ferret out the grinder, with its black wrought-iron handle.

She was wiping the dust out of the contraption with one corner of a flour-sack dish towel when Clay and Mr. Bickham came in again, both of them carrying boxes.

Edrina and Harriet were, of course, consumed with curiosity.

Harriet, though puffy-eyed, had long since stopped crying.

"Sugar," Edrina cataloged, joyfully examining each item. "And flour. And lard. And *raisins*. Mama, you could bake a pie."

"Perhaps," Dara Rose agreed, afraid to say too much because she wasn't sure she could control all the contradictory emotions welling up inside her. Her pride stung like a snakebite, but in some ways, she was as jubilant as the children.

Tea. Sugar. Flour.

A whole ham, big enough to feed half the town of Blue River.

They'd been doing without such things for so long that it was impossible not to rejoice, at least inwardly.

Firmly, Dara Rose brought herself up short. She squared her shoulders and poured coffee beans into the grinder and began turning the handle, enjoying the rich aroma. "Mr. McKettrick has been very generous," she said, not looking at Edrina and Harriet. "But we mustn't come to expect such things—"

"Why not?" The voice was Clay's.

Dara Rose kept her back to him, spooning freshly ground coffee beans into the well of her dented pot, setting it on to boil. "Because we mustn't, that's all," she said. She bent and opened the stove door and pitched in more wood. Jabbed at the embers with the poker.

"There's some stuff for the Christmas tree in the box I left on the settee," Clay said quietly, sending the girls scampering with chimelike hurrahs into the front room.

Dara Rose, thinking Mr. Bickham must be within earshot, taking it all in, turned to look for him. He was as big a gossip as Heliotrope Ponder and, running the only general store in town, he got plenty of chances to tell everything he knew and then some.

But there was only Clay, filling the doorway, watching her. Philo Bickham must have been outside, fetching another box from the buckboard.

"It's almost Christmas," Clay said gruffly. "Just this once, Dara Rose, let yourself be happy. Let your *daughters* be happy."

Her face burned, and she couldn't help remembering all the times Parnell had splurged on some little treat for the girls, running up an account at the mercantile that had taken her months to pay off.

"Did you go into debt for all this?" she asked, keeping her voice down so the girls and Mr. Bickham wouldn't hear. Nobody knew better than she did how little the marshal of Blue River actually earned.

Clay smiled, though his eyes remained solemn, and then he shook his head, not in reply, but in disbelief. "I paid cash money," he said, turning to walk away.

By the time the coffee was ready, the kitchen and part of the front room were jammed with boxes and crates and brown parcels, tied shut with twine.

"Where's Mr. Bickham?" Dara Rose asked, when Clay returned to the kitchen, squeezed past her to wash his hands at the sink pump. "I thought he'd stay for coffee."

"He has a store to run," Clay said quietly.

In the next room, the girls giggled and Chester barked and the noise was pleasant to hear, even though Dara Rose was uncommon jittery.

She put away the cup she'd set out for Mr. Bickham and filled the remaining one, returned the pot to the stove.

"Mr. McKettrick?"

"What, Mrs. McKettrick?" Clay countered wearily, as

he drew back a chair, sat down and reached for the steaming cup of coffee.

Dara Rose brought out the sugar bowl, long unused, filled it from the newly purchased bag and set it on the table, along with a teaspoon.

"Thank you," she said meekly, not looking at him. "For all these groceries, I mean—"

That was when he pulled her onto his lap. His thighs felt hard as a wagon seat under her backside, and *that* realization started all sorts of untoward things rioting inside her.

"You're welcome," he said, in a throaty drawl.

Dara Rose's heart pounded, and she felt dizzy. "Clay—the *children*—"

He sighed. "They're busy squeezing parcels," he said.

Dara Rose sat very still, afraid to move.

Clay watched her mouth for a few moments, and managed to leave Dara Rose as breathless as if he'd actually kissed her, and soundly. Then he said, very quietly, "Just so we understand each other, Mrs. McKettrick, I do mean to bed you, right and proper, one day soon."

Dara Rose gulped, knowing she ought to pull free and get back on her own two feet but strangely unable to do so. "But you said—"

He rested an index finger on her mouth, and a hot shiver went through her. "I know what I said, Dara Rose, and I'll keep my word. But it's only fair to tell you that I'm fixing to do everything I can to bring you around to my way of thinking."

Dara Rose absolutely could not speak. She was full of indignation and longing and searing heat.

That was when he kissed her—softly at first, and then in a deep way that made everything inside her melt, including her very bones.

When their mouths finally parted, it was Clay's doing, not Dara Rose's.

She'd have been content to let that kiss go on forever, it felt so good.

"I believe I'm making progress," he said, with a certain satisfaction.

He was indeed, Dara Rose thought. If Edrina and Harriet hadn't been in the house, never mind the very next room, she might have taken Marshal Clay McKettrick by the hand and led him straight to her bed. She sighed wistfully.

It had been so long since she'd been held in a strong man's arms, reveled in the sweet responses lovemaking roused in her.

She glanced at the doorway, but her children were still in the front room, playing some game with the dog, filling that little house with barks and giggles. "Parnell and I—we weren't...we didn't..."

Clay simply listened, looking thoughtful.

"What I mean is, we were never...*intimate,*" Dara Rose confessed. Even saying that much—telling such a small part of her story—was a tremendous relief. "He married me to give my children a name."

"Go on," Clay said.

Dara Rose checked the doorway again. "I was married— or I *thought* I was married—to Parnell's younger brother, Luke." She swallowed hard. "Edrina was born, and then Harriet, and then—"

Clay didn't prompt her. He was a patient man.

"And then Luke was thrown from a horse and killed, and I learned—I learned that he'd had another wife all along. A *real* wife, and several children. I'd been a—a kept woman from the first, without even knowing it, and our—*my*—children had been born out of wedlock."

Something moved in Clay's handsome face.

Pain? Fury? Pity, perhaps? She couldn't tell.

Afraid she'd lose her courage if she didn't finish the story right now, Dara Rose went on. "I had no money, and no place to go, and after his brother's funeral, Parnell came to me and offered marriage. He was such a good man, Clay." She realized she was crying. When had the tears begun? "When he died upstairs at the Bitter Gulch, everyone felt so sorry for the children and me, and there was this huge scandal, and I couldn't—I couldn't explain that I wasn't a true wife to him. He must have been so lonely...."

When she didn't go on, Clay set her on her feet, and try though she did, Dara Rose couldn't read his expression.

He got up from his chair, his coffee forgotten on the table, and whistled for his dog.

Chester came to him eagerly, without hesitation, as Clay was putting on his duster and his distinctive round-brimmed hat.

"This calls for some thinking about, Dara Rose," he said. "And I need to get Outlaw back to the livery stable, see that he's put up proper for the night."

With that, Clay opened the back door, and he and Chester went out.

Edrina and Harriet appeared in the inside doorway the instant he'd closed the door behind him.

"Aren't we going to decorate the Christmas tree?" Edrina asked plaintively.

Dara Rose didn't answer. She hurried across the kitchen and through the front room to watch through the window as Clay rounded a corner of the house, passed through the gate, gathered his horse's reins and mounted up.

"What about the Christmas tree?" Harriet trilled, from somewhere behind Dara Rose.

"After supper," she heard herself say, as her heart climbed into her throat. "We'll tend to it after supper."

And Clay McKettrick rode away, Chester following, leaving Dara Rose to wonder if he meant to come back.

WHEN HE REACHED the jailhouse, Clay let himself in, started a fire in the potbellied stove and nearly fell over the large crate waiting by his desk.

He approached the box, apparently delivered while he was away, peering down at the return address: *The Triple M. Indian Rock, Arizona.*

He felt a twinge of homesickness, but it passed quickly.

Much as he loved the ranch, and his family, the Triple M wasn't home anymore. Home, for better or for worse, was wherever Dara Rose happened to be.

When had he fallen in love with her?

He wasn't sure. It might have been today, when she sat on his lap in her tiny kitchen and poured out her heart to him.

Or it might have been when he first laid eyes on her, just a few days before.

All he could say for sure was that it felt a lot like being kicked in the belly by a mule, this falling in love.

He was exultant.

He was crushed.

Dara Rose had loved another man, and that man had betrayed her, and if Luke Nolan hadn't already been dead, Clay would have cheerfully killed him.

His deepest regret? That he hadn't been there to step in and make things right for her and for the kids, as illogical as that was. Parnell had been the one to rescue her, give his two-timing brother's family a legal right to the Nolan name.

Clay McKettrick was jealous of a dead man and, at the same time, he knew he could never have settled for the kind of empty marriage Dara Rose and Parnell had had together. He was a young man, and red-blooded, and he needed more.

He wanted everything—wanted Dara Rose's heart, as well as her body. Wanted to adopt Edrina and Harriet, change their last name for good, raise them as McKettricks.

And he surely wanted to make more babies with Dara Rose.

Oh, yes, he wanted it all.

He drew in a deep breath. *Slow down, cowboy,* he thought. *Get a grip.*

There was no telling what Dara Rose thought when he'd walked out on her that way, but he needed to sort things through, needed to *think*.

That was the kind of man he was.

He fetched a knife, pried up the lid on the crate his mother had sent from the Triple M. She must have paid a hefty freight charge to get it there before Christmas, even by train.

Inside, carefully nestled in straw, he found a dozen succulent oranges, a tin full of exotic nuts and a number of his favorite books, some of which he'd owned since he first learned to read. There was more, but Clay's eyes were so blurred by then that he was lucky to be able to read his mother's letter and, even then, he only got this word and that.

"Sawyer wired that you're married…two stepdaughters…bring them home when you can…we're all so anxious to welcome your wife and your children to the family—"

Clay closed his eyes, drew a deep breath. That was Chloe McKettrick for you. If he loved a woman, and that woman's children, then his mother was ready to enfold them in the warmth of her heart, receive them as her own.

It was the McKettrick way. Babies were born into the family, or they arrived by marriage, and it made no difference either way. Once a McKettrick, always a McKettrick.

No matter what happened between him and Dara Rose, Edrina and Harriet were part of the fold, now and forever. If he died tomorrow, or Dara Rose did, his pa and ma, his aunts and uncles and sisters and brothers and cousins—even old Angus and his wife, Concepcion—would take them in and love them like their own flesh and blood.

The knowledge made Clay's throat tighten and his eyes scald.

He wanted to go back to Dara Rose right then, wanted that more than anything, but he didn't give in to the desire.

Yes, she was his wife.

And yes, it was a safe bet that she wanted him as much as he wanted her, after that episode in her kitchen.

But what mattered now was the children.

And that was why Clay McKettrick decided to spend his second night as a married man in the spare room behind the jailhouse. If he'd gone back to Dara Rose's place, he wasn't at all sure he could have resisted her.

He needed her.

He *loved* her.

And that was precisely why he couldn't go home to that little house, with its tiny rooms and its thin walls.

Clay McKettrick knew his limits.

And, where Dara Rose was concerned, he'd reached them.

DARA ROSE LISTENED for Clay's footstep on the back porch as she peeled potatoes to fry up for supper with some of the salt pork he'd bought at the store. When the meal was over and the dishes had been washed and put away and he still wasn't back, she declared that it was time to decorate the Christmas tree.

"We'd rather wait for Mr. McKettrick," Edrina said, looking glum.

"Where did he go?" Harriet asked.

Dara Rose sighed. She'd been a fool to go against her own better judgment and marry Clay McKettrick. Men couldn't be depended upon to stick around. They lied and cheated and got themselves thrown from horses and killed, they died in the arms of prostitutes above some saloon or, like Mr. O'Reilly, they simply decided they'd rather be elsewhere and took to their heels.

Devil take the hindmost.

"To the livery stable, I think," Dara Rose finally replied.

"He left a long time ago," Edrina reasoned. "It's getting dark outside."

Harriet's lower lip wobbled. "Maybe he's not coming back," she said.

Dara Rose pretended not to hear. "I'll fetch the Christmas box from the cedar chest," she told the children, marching into the front room. "And then we'll see what we can do with this tree."

The girls didn't speak, so she turned her head to look at them.

They stood side by side, arms folded, expressions recalcitrant.

"That wouldn't be right," Edrina said staunchly. "Mr. McKettrick cut that tree down himself. We wouldn't even have it if it weren't for him."

Harriet nodded in grim agreement.

Dara Rose thought fast. "Wouldn't it be a nice surprise, though, if he came home to find it all sparkling and merry?"

Edrina, self-appointed spokeswoman for her little sister as well as for herself, stood her ground. "We'd rather wait," she reiterated.

Dara Rose shook her head, proceeded into the bedroom to give the children a chance to change their minds and lifted the lid of the cedar chest at the foot of the bed. She kept the few simple ornaments they owned, most of them homemade, tucked away there, inside an old boot box of Parnell's.

There was a shining paper chain, made of salvaged foils of all sorts.

There were stars, cut from tin, with the sharp edges hammered down to a child-safe smoothness, and ribbons, and Parnell's broken pocket watch.

And there were two tiny angels, sewn up from scraps of calico and embroidered with Edrina's and Harriet's names, their wings improvised out of layers of old newspapers, cut out and pasted together.

Dara Rose had always treasured these humble decorations, as had the girls, but now, in the dim light of the rising moon, falling softly through the window, they looked humble indeed. Nearly pitiful, in fact.

She swallowed, straightened her spine, and returned to the front room with the dog-eared carton, only to find Edrina and Harriet busy with the one Clay had spoken of earlier.

There's some stuff for the Christmas tree in the box I left on the settee, he'd said.

The children looked wonder-struck as they lifted one

glistening item after another out of the box—a porcelain angel, with feathers for wings and a golden halo fashioned of thin wire; shimmering baubles of blown glass, in bright shades of red and blue and gold and silver; a package of glittering tinsel that flashed in the lamplight like a tiny waterfall.

Dara Rose spoke in a normal tone, but it was a struggle. "Shall we decorate the tree after all, then?" she asked.

But Edrina and Harriet shook their heads.

Slowly, carefully, they put all the exquisite ornaments Clay had purchased back into the box from the mercantile.

"We'll wait," Edrina said.

And that was that.

The girls went off to get ready for bed, without being told.

Dara Rose, not quite sure *what* she was feeling exactly, put on her cloak and went outside to make sure the chickens were safe in their coop, with their feed and water pans full.

When that was done, she tarried, looking up at the silvery stars popping out all over the black-velvet sky, hoping Clay would step through the backyard gate.

He didn't, of course.

So Dara Rose went back into the house, to her children, to oversee the washing of faces and the brushing of teeth and the saying of prayers.

Edrina, hands clenched together and one eye slightly open, asked God to make sure Mr. McKettrick and Chester found their way back home, please, and soon.

Harriet said she hoped whatever little girl had Florence would take good care of her and not lose the doll's shoes or break her head.

Dara Rose offered no comment on either prayer.

She simply kissed her precocious children good-night, tucked them in and left the room.

In the kitchen, she brewed tea, and sat savoring it at the table, with the kerosene lantern burning low on the narrow counter.

After Luke, and again after Parnell, Dara Rose had solemnly promised herself she would never wait up for another man as long as she lived.

And here she was, waiting for Clay McKettrick.

HAVING MADE HIS DECISION, Clay locked up the street door and banked the dwindling fire, and he collapsed onto the bed in the back room of the jailhouse, not expecting to sleep.

He must have been more tired than he thought, because he awakened with sunlight streaming into his face through the one grimy window, and Chester snoring away in the nearby cell.

Clay got up, made his way into the office, made a fire in the stove and put on a pot of coffee. He let Chester out the rear door and stood on what passed for a porch, studying the sky.

It was bluer than blue, that sky, and the day promised to be unseasonably warm.

Even with half his mind down the road, following Dara Rose around that little house of hers, there was room in Clay's brain for all the things that needed to be done before the kit-house arrived.

He heated water on the stove top, once the coffee had come to a good boil, and washed up as best he could, but his shaving gear and his spare clothes were stashed behind the settee at Dara Rose's.

In the near distance, church bells rang, and Clay realized it was Sunday.

The good folks of the town would be settling themselves in pews right about now, waiting for the sermon to start—and then waiting for it to end.

The ones who wouldn't mind working on the Sabbath Day, on the other hand, were probably gathered down at the Bitter Gulch Saloon, defiant in their state of sin.

Since he needed a well dug, and a foundation, too, Clay figured he'd better get to the latter bunch before they got a real good start on the day's drinking.

An hour later, Chester stuck to his heels the whole time, he'd hired seven men, roused a blinking and grimacing Philo Bickham to open the mercantile and sell him picks and shovels, a pair of trousers and a plain shirt, and rented two mules and a wagon from the livery to haul the workers and the tools out to the ranch.

For a pack of habitual drunks, those men got a lot of digging done.

Clay worked right alongside them, while Chester roamed the range, probably hunting for rabbits. He'd make a fine cattle-dog when there was a herd to tend.

At noon, Clay drove the team and wagon back to town, Chester along for the ride, bought food enough for an army at the hotel dining room and returned to the work site and his hungry crew.

He'd felt a pang passing the turn to Dara Rose's place, having finally remembered that he'd promised Edrina and Harriet that they'd decorate the Christmas tree the night before, but he'd make that up to them later.

Somehow.

Just about supper time, Clay called a halt to the work, satisfied that the foundation was dug and they'd made good progress on the well. The crew climbed into the back of the wagon, as did Chester, and the marshal of Blue River, Texas, turned the mules townward.

He paid the men generously, turned the team and wagon in at the livery and took his time tending to Outlaw, lest the horse feel neglected after being left to stand idle in his stall all day.

Too tired to bother with supper, and too dirty to stand himself for much longer, Clay returned to the lonely jailhouse, lit a lantern, fed Chester some leftovers from the midday meal and commenced carrying and heating water to fill the round washtub he'd found hanging from a nail just outside the back door.

The new clothes he'd bought that morning were stiff with newness and smelled of starch.

Once there was enough hot water in the washtub to suit him, Clay stripped off his filthy clothes, climbed in and sat down, cross-legged like an Apache at a campfire, sighing as the strain eased out of his muscles. He was no stranger to hard physical work, coming from a family of ranchers, but it had been a while since he'd swung a pick or wielded a shovel.

He was sore.

As the water cooled, Clay scoured off a couple of layers of grime and sweat and planned what he'd say to Dara Rose, later tonight, when he intended to knock at her kitchen door and ask if he and Chester could bunk in her front room again. In the morning, they could talk things through.

Only it didn't happen that way.

Clay was just coming to grips with the fact that he didn't have a towel handy when the jailhouse door flew open and

Dara Rose stormed in, wearing her cloak but no bonnet and, temper-wise, loaded for bear.

Seeing Clay sitting there in the washtub in the altogether, she stopped in her tracks and gasped.

"You're just in time, Mrs. McKettrick," he said. "It seems I'm in something of a predicament here."

Dara Rose blinked and looked quickly away, keeping her head turned and not asking what the predicament might happen to be.

"My children," she said, "refuse to decorate the Christmas tree unless you're there."

"If you'll fetch me a towel, Mrs. McKettrick," Clay drawled, enjoying her discomfort more than he'd enjoyed much of anything since yesterday's kiss at her kitchen table, "I'll make myself decent, and we'll attend to that Christmas tree."

Dara Rose kept her face averted. "Where…?"

"The towel? It's hanging from a hook next to my shaving mirror, in the back room."

"I meant to say," Dara Rose sputtered, still not looking in his direction, *where have you been* since last night?" She gave him a wide berth as she went in search of the towel.

"I'm glad you asked," Clay said, smiling to himself as he waited for her to come back, so he could dry off and get dressed in his new duds. "It shows you care."

She returned, flung the towel at him and turned her back. "Nonsense," she said. "Edrina and Harriet were very disappointed when you left—that's the only reason I'm here."

Clay rose out of the tub, the towel around his middle, and sloshed his way into the spare room, where he hastily wiped himself dry and put on the other set of clothes.

Dara Rose had her eyes covered with both hands when he came back. "Are you dressed?" she asked pettishly.

"Yes, Mrs. McKettrick," he said easily. "I am properly attired."

She lowered her hands, looked at him with enough female fury to sear off some of his hide and repeated her original question, dead set on an answer.

"Where *were* you, Clay McKettrick?"

Chapter 10

꧁✦꧂

WHERE WERE YOU, Clay McKettrick? Clay crossed to Dara Rose, laid his hands gently on her shoulders and felt a tremor go through her slight but sumptuous body. "First," he began, his voice low, "I'll tell you where I *wasn't,* Mrs. McKettrick. I wasn't with a secret wife, and I wasn't upstairs at the Bitter Gulch Saloon, enjoying the favors of a dance-hall girl. I'm not Luke, and I'm not Parnell. I'm *Clay McKettrick,* and it would behoove you to get that straight in your mind. As for where I was, I slept right here last night, and this morning I hired a crew and went out to the ranch to start digging a foundation and a well. The makings of our house will be here right after the first of the year, as I told Philo Bickham yesterday, in your presence and hearing. And as long as the weather cooperates, I plan to spend as much time as I can out there, making the necessary preparations, because the sooner we can move into a place of our own, the better."

She looked up at him, confused and probably startled by the uncommon length of the speech he'd just given. He could see that she was still afraid to hope, afraid to trust, when it came to any personal dealings with a man. She bit down on her lower lip but didn't speak.

Clay smiled, kissed the top of her head. She wasn't wearing her bonnet, and her hair was coming loose from the knot at her nape, tendrils falling around her cheeks and across her forehead.

I love you, he thought. He was ready to say it right out loud, but he wasn't sure Dara Rose was ready to *hear* it, so he put the declaration by for later.

"I think we'd better get over to the house and decorate the Christmas tree," Clay drawled, enjoying the soft, pliant warmth of her, standing there in his arms, innately uncertain and, at the same time, one of the strongest women he'd ever encountered. "You see, Mrs. McKettrick, if we stay here much longer, I'm liable to seduce you, and I surely do not want our first time together to happen in a jailhouse."

She pinkened in that delightful way that only made him ache to see the rest of her, bare of all that calico, and mischief danced in her upturned eyes. Every signal she was sending out, however subtle, said she was a woman who enjoyed the intimate attentions of a man, who wasn't afraid or ashamed to uncover herself, body, mind and spirit, and then lose herself in the pleasures of making love.

Glory be.

"You seem to have a great deal of confidence in your powers of seduction, *Mr.* McKettrick," she remarked, after twinkling up at him for a few spicy moments. "What makes you think you could persuade me to give in?"

He cupped her chin in his hand, bent to nibble briefly at her mouth. Another shiver went through her at his touch. "Trust me," he said gruffly, after drawing back. "I am a persuasive man."

She sighed. "Yes," she admitted. "I believe you are."

He steered her in the direction of the door, whistled for Chester, took his hat and coat from their pegs. "For instance," he teased, as they stepped out onto the blustery sidewalk, the dog following, "I talked you into marrying me, when we'd only known each other for a few days. And I didn't even ask you to work as my housekeeper for a year before I decided whether to keep you or throw you back."

Dara Rose elbowed him, walked a little faster. "I agreed to your proposal," she whispered, though there was no one on the street to overhear, "*only* because I was desperate to keep my family together, with a roof over our heads."

"Speaking of your children," Clay drawled, "did you leave them home alone to come over here to the jail and hector me?"

She stopped, right there on the sidewalk, with Clay between her and the empty street. "Of *course* not," she said, as indignant as a little hen with her feathers ruffled. "Alvira Krenshaw is with them."

"The schoolmarm?"

Dara Rose nodded pertly. "The woman you probably considered courting before you turned your charms on me," she said.

Clay slipped an arm around Dara Rose's small waist and got her moving again, in the direction of the house where he'd be spending another night on the front room floor, with his dog. "Miss Krenshaw," he said, "was never in the running. And how did you manage to wrangle a woman who herds kids for a living into looking after those two little Apaches of yours?"

"Alvira dropped by with a book she wanted to lend to Edrina. A thick one, with lots of pictures, likely to keep that child busy until school takes up again, after New Year's. Anyhow, I made tea." Dara Rose continued to walk, but she'd turned thoughtful. "Alvira sat down to talk and, well, there's something *about* tea, it seems, that causes a person to drop her guard, at least a little. The whole story—most of it, anyway—just poured out of me."

Clay suppressed a chuckle, knowing it would not be well-received. *Remind me to dose you up with tea first chance I get,* he thought. But, "Go on," was what he said, as they started across the street, his hand resting lightly at the small of her back now, barely touching, but still protective.

"I didn't tell Alvira about Luke, or even how it really was between Parnell and me," Dara Rose confided. "But I *did* say that you and I had had a disagreement and I couldn't stop thinking about where you might be or what you might be doing."

Even in the near darkness, Clay saw her blush. It had cost her, pride-wise, to make that admission, even to a good friend, and it was costing her still.

"I see," he said.

They'd rounded the corner now, and Dara Rose's house was just ahead, so she hastened to finish. "Alvira said I'd better come and find you, then, to settle my mind, while she looked after Edrina and Harriet."

"Is it?" Clay asked.

"Is *what?*" Dara Rose retorted, sounding a mite testy.

"Is your mind settled, where I'm concerned?"

They stood in front of her gate by then, light spilling out of the windows into the darkened yard. The apple tree was a spare shadow, etched into the night.

"Where you are concerned, Mr. McKettrick," Dara Rose finally replied, "*nothing* is settled. I don't know what to think, what to believe—"

He kissed her then, deeply, the way he would have done

if they'd had the whole world to themselves. Adam and Eve, in Texas instead of the Garden.

"Believe *that*," he said, when he'd caught his breath. "And the rest will take care of itself."

Dara Rose just stood there, looking dazed. Even in the poor light, he could see that her lips were swollen, still moist from his kiss.

Calmly, Clay opened the gate, held it for her and shut it after they'd gone through, Dara Rose and Chester and, finally, himself.

At the base of the porch steps, Dara Rose stopped and sort of bristled, about to make some delayed response to being kissed, Clay supposed, but she didn't get the chance, because the front door sprang open and Edrina and Harriet burst out, barely able to contain their glee.

"*Now* can we decorate the Christmas tree?" Harriet demanded.

Miss Krenshaw stood, smiling, on the threshold behind them, already buttoning her practical woolen coat, ready to leave.

"Yes," Dara Rose confirmed, fondly weary in her tone. "We can decorate the Christmas tree." Her gaze shifted to Miss Krenshaw. "You're not leaving, are you?"

"I have a few letters to write, back at the teacherage," Miss Krenshaw replied, sparing a polite nod of greeting for Clay. And with that, she was past them, down the steps, striding along the walk toward the gate. There, she turned back. "Don't forget about the party at the schoolhouse," she called, most likely addressing Dara Rose.

"WHAT PARTY AT THE schoolhouse?" Clay asked, as Edrina and Harriet beset him with hugs, in their joy at his return. Without missing a beat, he scooped them up, one in each arm, and the sight struck a deep and resonant chord in-side Dara Rose.

She led the way into the kitchen, where she'd stowed a plate of supper in the warming oven, in hopes that Clay would be around to eat it.

"After the blizzard," Dara Rose explained, wadding up a dish towel to use as a pot holder and taking Clay's meal from the heat, "Miss Krenshaw decided to call off the Christmas program at school. Now, with all this spring-like weather and Pastor Jacobs called away because of an illness in his family, so there won't be a church service, she's had second thoughts. There's no time for the children to memorize recitations and the like, but we can still have some sort of informal gathering on Christmas Day, for the community—sing a few hymns and carols...."

She paused, glanced back at him, felt a thrill as he set the girls down, then removed and hung up his hat and coat. His movements were easy and deliberate, and he looked from her face to the plate in her hands and back again.

"You must be hungry, after a hard day's work at the ranch," she said, suddenly and desperately shy.

"I am indeed hungry, Mrs. McKettrick," he said, in a throaty voice, letting his eyes move over her once before heading to the sink to wash his hands. Everything about him was so masculine—his stance, the movement of his powerful shoulders, the back of his head where his dark hair curled against the neck band of his collarless shirt. He turned, damp and handsome, his sleeves rolled up to his elbows, water spiking his eyelashes. "I am indeed."

"Eat fast!" Edrina urged Clay, as he sat down at the table. "We've been waiting *forever* to decorate the Christ-mas tree!"

"Forever," Harriet testified.

"For that," he said, "I do apologize." Clay looked down at the simple but plentiful meal Dara Rose had prepared—boiled potatoes, the last of the preserved venison and green beans she had grown in her own garden the summer before and subsequently put up in jars for the winter. He favored her with a slight, appreciative smile, and then spoke again to the children, who were fairly electrified with energy. "Settle down now," he said quietly. "We'll get to that tree, I promise."

They subsided, dragged themselves melodramatically out of the kitchen, portraying despondency, Chester tagging along, his ears perked up in anticipation of some new and wonderful game the three of them might play.

Clay ate at his own pace, the way he did everything, and seemed to savor the food Dara Rose had put aside for him, with no real conviction that he'd be around to eat it.

Once he'd finished, Dara Rose offered coffee, but Clay shook his head, said, "No thank you," and started for the front room. When Dara Rose lingered to clear the table, Clay shook his head a second time and beckoned politely for her to follow.

Edrina and Harriet had been busy, Dara Rose discovered. They'd taken every single ornament out of the boxes and laid them in neat rows on the settee.

Later, out in the woodshed behind the house, working by lantern light and supervised by two very lively little girls and an eager dog—Dara Rose spent the time fussing over her chickens—Clay cobbled together a stand to support the small tree and they all went back inside.

To Dara Rose, the thing looked more like a shrub than a tree, but both Edrina's and Harriet's eyes glowed with awe as one decoration after another was reverently added to this bough or that one. The homemade ornaments held

their own against the store-bought ones, in Dara Rose's
opinion, and she had to admit that, when finished, the effect was very nearly magical—especially when the porcelain angel with the wire halo and the feather wings seemed
to hover over the whole of it, offering a blessing.

"Thunderation," Edrina breathed, reflected light from
the colorful blown-glass ornaments shining on her face.

"It's bee-you-tee-ful," Harriet pronounced.

Even Chester, sitting between the children and gazing
at the shining display, seemed spellbound.

"It's enough to make a person believe in St. Nicholas,"
Clay said quietly, for Dara Rose alone to hear. "Isn't it?"

"No," she said promptly, but without her usual conviction.

Only days ago, Dara Rose reflected dizzily, she'd been
alone in the world, with two children to support, winter
coming on and the threat of eviction hanging over her
head. She might well have lost Edrina and Harriet forever,
the way things were going.

But then Clay McKettrick had arrived by train, with his
handsome horse, and pinned on the marshal's badge, and
turned her entire life upside down.

The man had even managed to turn a scrub pine into a
more-than-respectable Christmas tree.

It was hard, under such circumstances, *not* to believe
in magic.

Christmas Eve

THE CLOCK ON THE FRONT room wall chimed ten times, and
the lantern light wavered as Clay came out of the bedroom,
shaking his head.

"Not yet," he said to Dara Rose, who was waiting to fill

the pair of small stockings she'd allowed the girls to hang from the knobs on the side table. She'd sent him in to see if Edrina and Harriet were really asleep, or just pretending. "Those two are playing possum, for sure."

Dara Rose had an orange to drop into the toe of each stocking, thanks to the box from Clay's people up north, along with a bright copper penny and the new mittens she'd bought at the mercantile a few days before.

These things alone would delight the children, she knew, but there was so much more; she'd splurged on shoes and ready-made coats for her daughters, and Clay's packages—still wrapped in their brown paper and tucked beneath the lowest boughs of the tree—contained numerous mysteries.

They retreated into the kitchen, Clay drinking lukewarm coffee left over from supper, and Dara Rose sipping tea. She'd felt downright reckless, spending Piper's ten dollars so freely, and it still made her breath lurch to think how she'd spent some of it.

Idly, Clay took a small package from the pocket of his shirt, and set it down next to Dara Rose's teacup.

She looked up at him, but she didn't—couldn't—speak.

"Open it," he urged, with that crooked grin tilting his mouth upward at one side, in the way she'd come to love.

Dara Rose hesitated, drew a folded sheet of paper from her skirt pocket and handed it to Clay. "This is for you," she said, so softly that he cocked his head slightly in her direction to catch the words.

"You go first," he said, holding the paper between fingers calloused from working practically every spare moment to prepare for the arrival of the Sears, Roebuck and Company house, all while tending to his duties as town marshal.

Dara Rose's fingers trembled as she opened the little packet, folding back its edges.

A golden wedding band gleamed inside, sturdy and full of promise.

"Will you wear my wedding band, Dara Rose?" Clay asked.

In some ways, it would always seem to both of them that *that* was the moment they were truly married, there at the kitchen table, in the light of a single lantern, on Christmas Eve.

She nodded, murmured, "Yes," all the while blinking back tears, and allowed him to slip the ring onto her finger. It was a perfect fit.

Clay sat watching her for a few moments, his gaze like a caress, and then, very slowly, he opened the sheet of paper she'd given him.

His eyebrows rose slightly as he read, and then a grin spread across his face, lighting him up from within.

She'd given him a receipt for a night's lodging at the Texas Arms Hotel—for two.

"Does this mean what I hope it does?" Clay asked.

Dara Rose had been blushing a lot since she met Clay McKettrick, but at that moment, she outdid herself. Her whole face caught fire as she nodded.

Clay still didn't seem convinced. "You're giving me a wedding night for a Christmas gift?"

She blushed even harder. As her legal husband, he was *entitled* to a wedding night, their bargain notwithstanding. Maybe she should have waited, given him socks or a book or perhaps a fishing pole....

Meanwhile, his golden band gleamed on her left ring finger, simple but heavy.

"Yes," she forced herself to say.

"Hallelujah!" Clay replied, and then he got up from his chair and pulled her into his arms—clear off her feet, in fact—and kissed her so thoroughly that she was gasping when he let her go.

Dara Rose dashed out of the kitchen, afraid of her own scandalous tendencies, and went to look in on the children.

Certain that Edrina and Harriet were at last asleep, she returned to the front room just in time to see Clay set the exquisite doll from the mercantile window squarely in front of the Christmas tree, next to a stack of storybooks that must have been meant for Edrina.

Dara Rose drew in her breath.

"Oh, Clay," she whispered. She hadn't dared think, or hope, that he'd been the one to buy Florence.

But he had.

He waggled an index finger at her and spoke gruffly. "Don't you dare tell me I shouldn't have done this, Mrs. McKettrick. I might not be Edrina and Harriet's real father, but I couldn't love them more if I were, and besides, after all they've been through in their short lives, they deserve a special Christmas."

Dara Rose was fresh out of arguments. She simply went to Clay, slipped her arms around his lean waist and let her head rest against his chest. She could feel his steady, regular heartbeat under her cheekbone.

"I love you, Clay McKettrick," she heard herself say.

Clay drew back just far enough to tilt her face upward with one curved finger. "Do you mean it, Dara Rose?"

"I never say anything I don't mean," she replied, quite truthfully.

He grinned. "I meant to be the first one to say 'I love you,'" he told her, "and darned if you didn't beat me to it."

"Hold me," Dara Rose said. "Hold me tightly, so I know this isn't a dream."

"It isn't a dream," he told her. His breath was warm in her hair. "I love you, Dara Rose. I think I have since I first laid eyes on you that first day, when I brought Edrina home on Outlaw and you were so riled up, you were practically standing next to yourself."

She clung to him, with both arms, and her body ached to receive his, but that would have to wait.

Still, it was Christmas Eve, and Clay was holding her, and in a few weeks, they'd be settled in their new house, with a room to themselves and all the privacy a married couple could want.

She'd waited a long time for Clay McKettrick, and she could wait a little longer.

ON CHRISTMAS DAY, in the early afternoon, members of the community began arriving at Blue River's one-room schoolhouse, some on foot, some on horseback, others riding in wagons or buggies.

Miss Alvira Krenshaw had done a fine job decorating the place with paper chains and the like, and everyone who could afford to brought food to share with their neighbors. Clay carefully carried in the huge ham, arranged on a scrubbed slab of wood and draped in clean dish towels, and set it on top of one of the bookcases, with the mounds of fried chicken and the beef roasts and various other dishes already provided by earlier arrivals.

Edrina, preening a little in her new coat and shoes, carried another of her gifts, a game of checkers in a sturdy wooden box, under one arm, hoping, Dara Rose supposed, to find some unsuspecting child to challenge to a game.

Harriet, also sporting a new coat and lace-up shoes—

the first pair she'd ever owned that hadn't belonged to Edrina first—held Florence tightly against her side. The doll came with a small wardrobe, neatly folded inside a travel trunk, and Harriet had changed its clothes three times before they left home.

Everyone was there, including Dr. Howard, his wife, Eloise, and little Madeline, the newcomers.

People laughed and talked, often-lonely country folks crowded together in small quarters, and eventually Miss Krenshaw sat down at the out-of-tune piano and launched into a lively version of "God Rest Ye Merry Gentlemen."

Just about everybody sang along; though, of course, some voices were better than others. Some hearty, some thin and wavering.

"Hark, the Herald Angels Sing" followed, and then "Silent Night."

Snow began drifting past the windows, and Ezra Maddox showed up, along with Peg O'Reilly, her two boys and little Addie, bundled warmly in a quilt.

Holding the child in his strong farmer's arms, Mr. Maddox looked around at the assemblage, as though daring anyone to question his presence.

"Come in, come in," Miss Krenshaw sang out, from the piano seat, "we're just about to start supper."

Dara Rose immediately approached Peg, though she gave Mr. Maddox a wide berth, and hugged her friend warmly. Peg had obviously made an effort to dress up, and the children looked clean and eager to share in festivities.

"Happy Christmas, Peg," Dara Rose said, smiling.

"Ezra didn't say we ought to bring food," Peg whispered, looking fretful, as though she might be poised to flee.

"Never mind that," Dara Rose assured the other woman.

"There's plenty to go around. In fact, I wouldn't be surprised if we wound up with as many leftovers as the Lord's disciples gathered up after the feast of the loaves and fishes."

Peg managed a tentative smile. "Addie shouldn't be out—she's been running a fever. But the little ones were so pleased to have some kind of Christmas..."

Dara Rose couldn't help seeing some of herself in Peg O'Reilly. After her husband's desertion, and all the struggles to keep body and soul together, for her children and herself, Peg barely believed in good fortune anymore, or human generosity. If, indeed, she'd *ever* believed.

Putting a hand on the small of Peg's bony back, she steered her friend toward the part of the schoolhouse where the food awaited, helped her to fill plates for Addie and the little boys and find places for them to sit.

After that, everyone sort of stampeded forward, and there was much merriment and laughter as the people of Blue River, Texas, shared a simple Christmas.

Although she made sure Edrina and Harriet had supper, Dara Rose barely saw her husband for the rest of the evening. He was always on the other side of the crowded schoolhouse, it seemed, but each time she found him with her eyes, he smiled and winked and made her blush.

They finally converged at the cloakroom—Clay and Dara Rose, Edrina and Harriet—and the girls, probably exhausted, seemed unusually reticent.

Harriet tugged at Dara Rose's skirt and said, "Mama, bend down so I can speak to you."

Smiling, Dara Rose leaned to look directly into her youngest daughter's face.

"We have lots of presents at home," Harriet said, with

a rueful glance at her lovely doll, which was now looking a bit rumpled from being clenched so tightly in her arms.

"And the O'Reillys didn't get anything at all," Edrina added, shifting her checkers game from one arm to the other. "They didn't even have a *tree*."

Clay had joined them by then, and he'd managed to collect their coats from the conglomeration in the cloakroom, but he didn't say anything.

"Do you think St. Nicholas would be sad if I gave Florence to Addie?" Harriet asked, her eyes luminous as she searched Dara Rose's face.

"And her brothers would probably like this checkers game," Edrina added.

Dara Rose's vision blurred.

She looked helplessly up at Clay.

He laid a hand on Edrina's shoulder, smiled down at Harriet. "I think a thing like that would make St. Nicholas mighty happy," he said.

Both girls shifted their gazes to Dara Rose.

She could only nod, since her throat had tightened around any words she might have said, cinching them inside her.

Edrina and Harriet raced off, beaming, to give away their Christmas presents.

Epilogue

꧁꧂

December 26, 1914

CLAY GAVE DARA ROSE PLENTY of time to settle into their room at the Texas Arms Hotel that evening, making his usual rounds as marshal, tending to Outlaw in his stall at the livery stable and the chickens in the backyard at home. The children were spending the night with Miss Krenshaw, in the teacher's quarters behind the schoolhouse, and the thought made her smile every time it came to her. After all the times Edrina had played hooky, it was ironic, her being so pleased by the idea of sleeping there.

At her leisure, Dara Rose unpacked her tattered carpetbag, took a long, luxurious bath in the gleaming copper tub carried in, set down in front of the room's simple fireplace, the hearth blazing with a crackling and fragrant fire, and filled with steaming, fragrant water. She soaked and scrubbed and dreamed, and when she heard Clay's light knock at the door, she started.

She'd lost track of time. Meant to be properly clad in the lovely lace-trimmed nightgown and wrapper Clay had given her for a private Christmas gift, presented when the children were asleep and they were alone. Instead, though, here she was, stark naked, her skin slick with moisture, her hair still pinned up in a knot at the back of her neck. She stood, trembling, not with fear, but with anticipation, and reached for her towel.

"It's me, Mrs. McKettrick," Clay said, from the other side of the door. "May I come in?"

Dara Rose gulped hard. "Yes," she said.

His key turned in the lock, and the door opened, and Clay stepped inside. His eyes drank her in even as he shut the door again. Slowly, he took off his hat and then his coat, with its star-shaped badge, unbuckled the ominous gun belt he wore when he was working, set it aside.

"Do you really need that towel?" he asked, with a hint of mischief in his eyes, as he ran a hand through his dark hair.

Dara Rose, feeling deliciously reckless, let the towel drop.

Clay looked at her frankly, his gaze touching her bare breasts, rousing her nipples to peaks, gliding like reverent hands down the sides of her waist and over her hips and even to the silk thatch at the juncture of her thighs.

He swallowed visibly. "Mrs. McKettrick," he said, in a rumbling drawl, "you are unreasonably beautiful."

What did one say to that? Dara Rose didn't know, didn't try.

She simply waited to be touched.

Clay approached her then, lifted her out of the tub by her waist and set her in front of him. Kissed her until she felt drunk with the sensation of his mouth on hers, the radiant heat and hard substance of his body promising so much to her soft one.

"You have me at a disadvantage, Mr. McKettrick," Dara

Rose managed, free to be the temptress she was at long last, and exulting in that.

"How's that?" he asked, arching one dark eyebrow and running his hands lightly up and down, along her ribs.

"You, sir," she replied, breathless at his touch, wanting more, so much more, "are fully dressed, while I am quite naked."

"Indeed you are," he agreed huskily, using one hand to loosen her chignon and send her heavy hair spilling down her back.

In the next moment, Clay lifted her again and, secret vixen that she was, Dara Rose locked her bare legs around his hips, tilted her head back with a slight groan when she felt the length of his shaft against her. That made him chuckle, and find her mouth with his, and kiss her into another, even deeper daze of jubilant need.

Suddenly, she landed, with a soft but decisive bounce, on the hotel bed, looked up at Clay as he unbuttoned his shirt, tossed it aside. Instead of stretching out beside her, though, he knelt at the side of the bed, gently parted her legs and kissed his way, very lightly, up the inside of her right thigh.

She gasped and arched her back when he conquered that most intimate place, and took her fully into his mouth.

Suckled, lightly at first, and then with increasing hunger.

Dara Rose, twice married, had never been so deliciously ravished, never felt so beautiful or so womanly, never known such a wild and frantic greed for pleasure.

Instinctively, she arched her back, and Clay slipped his hands under her buttocks, now quivering with the strain of making an offering of her entire self, and feasted on her until her body buckled and undulated in fierce spasms of celebration and she cried out.

The sound was low and long and husky, part howl and full of triumph that must have sounded, instead, like agony.

"That—" Clay chuckled against her still-tingling flesh "—is why we need our own bedroom, Mrs. McKettrick. One with thick walls."

Dara Rose laughed, or sobbed, or both. She couldn't tell which, didn't care.

All that mattered, for the moment, was that she loved this man, and he loved her, and she could, at last, abandon herself completely to this one someone, leave behind her practicality and her fears and simply *be*.

How odd, she thought, that there could be such freedom in surrender.

Still soaring from that first shattering release, Dara Rose was only dimly aware of Clay rising, removing the rest of his clothes. But when he lay down with her, on the turned-back sheets, the deepest satisfaction she'd ever known instantly gave way to the deepest *need*.

It was primitive, urgent, that need. It rocked her.

Desperate, she tried to pull Clay on top of her, feverish to take him inside her. Hold him there, to please him and be pleased *by* him.

Her body, one with his.

Her soul, one with his.

But Clay was as deliberate about making love as he was about everything else he did. He moved with slow confidence, every kiss, every caress, backed with certainty.

He enjoyed her breasts freely, and for a long time.

She moaned, her nipples pebble-hard and wet from his tongue, his lips.

He teased her. He whispered in her ears, and nibbled at

her lobes, and traced the length of her neck with the tip o
his tongue, leaving a line of sweet fire behind.

And when he finally lay down flat on the bed, his hand
strong, he set her astraddle of his mouth and devoured he
all over again, until she was rocking on him, clenching th
rails in the headboard of the bed, damp with perspiration
her head tipped back in a low, guttural cry of relief as h
finally allowed her to crest the pinnacle and let go.

As she descended, he told her quietly that he had not ye
begun to make love to her, that they'd be at it for a lifetime

He told her all the places he would have her, all th
times and ways. She reveled in the knowledge.

"Suppose someone hears?" she fretted, when Clay lai
her down again and, at last, poised himself above her.

"Suppose they do?" Clay countered hoarsely, with
grin. And then, in one long, fiery thrust, he was finall
inside her, deep, deep inside her.

Part of her.

And all the flexing and needing and carrying on starte
all over again.

Just as Dara Rose's *life* had started all over again, wit
the arrival of this man, with his quiet, steady ways and hi
strength, so at home in his own skin.

It was the beginning of forever, for both of them.

And a fine forever it would be.

* * * * *

DARING MOVES

For Melba. Your friendship was a gift from H.P.

Chapter 1

❦

THE LINE OF PEOPLE WAITING for an autograph reached from the bookstore down the length of the mall to the specialty luggage shop. With a sigh, Amanda Scott bought a cup of coffee from a nearby French bakery, bravely forgoing the delicate, flaky pastries inside the glass counter, and took her place behind a man in an expensive tweed overcoat.

Distractedly he turned and glanced at her, as though somehow finding her to blame for the delay. Then he pushed up his sleeve and consulted a slim gold watch. He was a couple of inches taller than Amanda, with brown hair that was only slightly too long and hazel eyes flecked with green, and he needed a shave.

Never one to pass the time in silence if an excuse to chat presented itself, Amanda took a steadying sip of her coffee and announced, "I'm buying Dr. Marshall's book for my sister, Eunice. She's going through a nasty divorce." The runaway bestseller was called *Gathering Up the Pieces,* and it was meant for people who had suffered some personal loss or setback.

The stranger turned to look back at her. The pleasantly mingled scents of new snow and English Leather seemed to surround him. "Are you talking to me?" he inquired, drawing his brows together in puzzlement.

Amanda fortified herself with another sip of coffee. She hadn't meant to flirt; it was just that waiting could be so tedious. "Actually, I was," she admitted.

He surprised her with a brief but brilliant smile that practically set her back on the heels of her snow boots. In the next second his expression turned grave, but he extended a gloved hand.

"Jordan Richards," he said formally.

Gulping down the mouthful of coffee she'd just taken, Amanda returned the gesture. "Amanda Scott," she managed. "I don't usually strike up conversations with strange men in shopping malls, you understand. It's just that I was bored."

Again that blinding grin, as bright as sunlight on water.

"I see," said Jordan Richards.

The line moved a little, and they both stepped forward. Amanda suddenly felt shy, and wished she hadn't gotten off the bus at the mall. Maybe she should have gone straight home to her cozy apartment and her cat.

She reminded herself that Eunice would benefit by reading the book and that, with this purchase, her Christmas shopping would be finished. After today she could hide in her work, like a soldier crouching in a foxhole, until the holidays and all their painful associations were past.

"Too bad about Eunice," Jordan Richards remarked.

"I'll give her your condolences," Amanda promised, a smile lighting her aquamarine eyes.

The line advanced, and so did Amanda and Jordan.

"Good," he said.

Amanda finished her coffee, crumpled the cup and tossed it into a nearby trash bin. Beside the bin there was a sign that read Is Therapy For You? Attend A Free Minises-

sion With Dr. Marshall After The Book Signing. Beneath
was a diagram of the mall, with the public auditorium
colored in.

"So," she ventured, "are you buying *Gathering Up the
Pieces* for yourself or somebody else?"

"I'm sending it to my grandmother," Jordan answered,
consulting his watch again.

Amanda wondered if he had to be somewhere else later,
or if he was just an impatient person.

"What happened to her?" she asked sympathetically.

Jordan looked reluctant, but after a few moments and
another step forward as the line progressed, he said, "She
had some pretty heavy-duty surgery a while back."

"Oh," Amanda said, and without thinking, she reached
out and patted his arm so as not to let the mention of the
unknown grandmother's misfortune pass without some
response from her.

Something softened in Jordan Richards's manner at the
small demonstration. "Are you attending the 'free minisession'?" he asked, gesturing toward the sign. The expression in his eyes said he fully expected her to answer no.

Amanda smiled and lifted one shoulder in a shrug.
"Why not? I've got the rest of the afternoon to blow, and
I could learn something."

Jordan looked thoughtful. "I suppose nobody has to talk
if they don't want to."

"Of course not," Amanda replied confidently, even
though she had no idea what would be required. Some of
the self-help groups could get pretty wild; she'd heard of
people walking across burning coals in their bare feet, or
letting themselves be dunked in hot tubs.

"I'll go if you'll sit beside me," Jordan said.

Amanda considered the suggestion only briefly. The
mall was a well-lit place, crowded with Christmas shop-

pers. If Jordan Richards were some kind of weirdo—and that seemed unlikely, unless crackpots were dressing like models in *Gentlemen's Quarterly* these days—she would be perfectly safe. "Okay," she said with another shrug.

After the decision was made, they lapsed into a companionable silence. Nearly fifteen minutes had passed by the time Jordan reached the author's table.

Dr. Eugene Marshall, the famous psychology guru, signed his name in a confident scrawl and handed Jordan a book. Amanda had her volume autographed and followed her new acquaintance to the cash register.

Once they'd both paid, they left the store together.

There was already a mob gathered at the double doors of the mall's community auditorium, and according to a sign on an easel, the minisession would start in another ten minutes.

Jordan glanced at the line of fast-food places across the concourse. "Would you like some coffee or something?"

Amanda shook her head, then reached up to pull her light, shoulder-length hair from under the collar of her coat. "No, thanks. What kind of work do you do, Mr. Richards?"

"Jordan," he corrected. He took off his overcoat and draped it over one arm, then loosened his tie and collar slightly. "What kind of work do you think I do?"

Amanda assessed him, narrowing her blue eyes. Jordan looked fit, and he even had a bit of a suntan, but she doubted he worked with his hands. His clothes marked him as an upper-management type, and so did that gold watch he kept checking. "You're a stockbroker," she guessed.

He chuckled. "Close. I'm a partner in an investment firm. What do you do?"

People were starting to move into the auditorium and take seats, and Amanda and Jordan moved along with them. With a half smile, she answered, "Guess."

He considered her thoughtfully. "You're a flight attendant for a major airline," he decided after several moments had passed.

Amanda took his conjecture as a compliment, even though it was wrong. "I'm the assistant manager of the Evergreen Hotel." They found seats near the middle of the auditorium, and Jordan took the one on the aisle. Amanda was just daring to hope she was making a favorable impression, when her stomach rumbled.

"And you haven't had lunch yet," Jordan stated with another of those lethal, quicksilver grins. "It just so happens that I'm a little hungry myself. How about something from that Chinese fast-food place I saw out there—after we're done with the minisession, I mean?"

Again Amanda smiled. She seemed to be smiling a lot, which was odd, because she hadn't felt truly happy since before James Brockman had swept into her life, turned it upside down and swept out again. "I'd like that," she heard herself say.

Just then Dr. Marshall walked out onto the auditorium stage. At his appearance, Jordan became noticeably uncomfortable, shifting in his seat and drawing one Italian-leather-shod foot up to rest on the opposite knee.

The famous author introduced himself, just in case someone who had never watched a TV talk show might have wandered in, and announced that he wanted the audience to break up into groups of twelve.

Jordan looked even more discomfited, and probably wouldn't have participated if a group hadn't formed around him and Amanda. To make things even more interesting, at least to Amanda's way of thinking, the handsome, silver-haired Dr. Marshall chose their group to work with, while his assistants took the others.

"All right, people," he began in a tone of pleasant authority, "let's get started." His knowing gray eyes swept the small gathering. "Why does everybody look so worried? This will be relatively painless—all we're going to do is talk about ourselves a little." He looked at Amanda. "What's your name?" he asked directly. "And what's the worst thing that's happened to you in the past year?"

She swallowed. "Amanda Scott. And—the worst thing?"

Dr. Marshall nodded with kindly amusement.

All of the sudden Amanda wished she'd gone to a matinee or stayed home to clean her apartment. She didn't want to talk about James, especially not in front of strangers, but she was basically an honest person and *James* was the worst thing that had happened to her in a very long time. Not looking at Jordan, she answered, "I fell in love with a man and he turned out to be married."

"What did you do when you found out?" the doctor asked reasonably.

"I cried a lot," Amanda answered, forgetting for the moment that there were twelve other people listening in, including Jordan.

"Did you break off the relationship?" Dr. Marshall pressed.

Amanda still felt the pain and humiliation she'd known when James's wife had stormed into her office and made a scene. Before that, Amanda hadn't even suspected the terrible truth. "Yes," she replied softly with a miserable nod.

"Is this experience still affecting your life?"

Amanda wished she dared to glance at Jordan to see how he was reacting, but she didn't have the courage. She lowered her eyes. "I guess it is."

"Did you stop trusting men?"

Considering all the dates she'd refused in the months since she'd disentangled herself from James, Amanda supposed she had stopped trusting men. Even worse, she'd stopped trusting her own instincts. "Yes," she answered very softly.

Dr. Marshall reached out to touch her shoulder. "I'm not going to pretend you can solve your problems just by sitting in on a minisession, or even by reading my book, but I think it's time for you to stop hiding and take some risks. Agreed?"

Amanda was surprised at the man's insight. "Agreed," she said, and right then and there she made up her mind to read Eunice's copy of *Gathering Up the Pieces* before she wrapped it.

The doctor's attention shifted to the man sitting on Amanda's left. He said he'd lost his job, and the fact that Christmas was coming up made things harder. A woman in the row behind Amanda talked about her child's serious illness. Finally, after about twenty minutes had passed, everyone had spoken except Jordan.

He rubbed his chin, which was already showing a five o'clock shadow, and cleared his throat. Amanda, feeling his tension and reluctance as though they were her own, laid her hand gently on his arm.

"The worst thing that ever happened to me," he said in a low, almost inaudible voice, "was losing my wife."

"How did it happen?" the doctor asked.

Jordan looked as though he wanted to bolt out of his chair and stride up the aisle to the doors, but he answered the question. "A motorcycle accident."

"Were you driving?" Dr. Marshall's expression was sympathetic.

"Yes," Jordan replied after a long silence.

"And you're still not ready to talk about it," the doctor deduced.

"That's right," Jordan said. And he got up and walked slowly up the aisle and out of the auditorium.

Amanda followed, catching up just outside. She didn't quite dare to touch his arm again, yet he slowed down at the sound of her footsteps. "How about that Chinese food you promised me?" she asked gently.

Jordan met her eyes, and for just a moment, she saw straight through to his soul. What pain he'd suffered.

"Sure," he replied, and his voice was hoarse.

"I'm all through with my Christmas shopping," Amanda announced once they were seated at a table, Number Three Regulars in front of them from the Chinese fast-food place. "How about you?"

"My secretary does mine," Jordan responded. He looked relieved at her choice of topic.

"That's above and beyond the call of duty," Amanda remarked lightly. "I hope you're giving her something terrific."

Jordan smiled at that. "She gets a sizable bonus."

"Good."

It was obvious Jordan was feeling better. His eyes twinkled, and some of the strain had left his face.

"I'm glad company policy meets with your approval."

It was surprising, considering her unfortunate and all-too-recent experiences with James, but it wasn't until that moment that Amanda realized that she hadn't checked Jordan's hand for a wedding band. She glanced at the appropriate finger, even though she knew it would be bare, and saw a white strip where the ring had been.

"Like I said, I'm a widower," he told her with a slight smile, obviously having read her glance accurately.

"I'm sorry," Amanda told him.

He speared a piece of sweet-and-sour chicken. "It's been three years."

It seemed to Amanda that the white space on his ring finger should have filled in after three years. "That's quite a while," she said, wondering if she should just get up from her chair, collect her book and her coat and leave. In the end she didn't, because a glance at her watch told her it was still forty minutes until the next bus left. Besides, she was hungry.

Jordan sighed. "Sometimes it seems like three centuries."

Amanda bit her lower lip, then burst out, "You aren't one of those creeps who goes around saying he doesn't have a wife when he really does, are you? I mean, you could have remarried."

He looked very tired all of a sudden, and pale beneath his tan. Amanda wondered why he hadn't gotten around to shaving.

"No," he said. "I'm not married."

Amanda dropped her eyes to her food, ashamed that she'd asked the question, even though she wouldn't have taken it back. The experience with James had taught her that a woman couldn't be too careful about such things.

"Amanda?"

She lifted her gaze to see him studying her. "What?"

"What was his name?"

"What was whose name?"

"The guy who told you he wasn't married."

Amanda cleared her throat and shifted nervously in her chair. The thought of James didn't cause her pain anymore, but she didn't know Jordan Richards well enough to tell him just how badly she'd been hoodwinked. A sudden, crazy panic seized her. "Gosh, look at the time," she said, pulling back her sleeve to check her watch a split second after she'd spoken. "I'd better get home." She bolted out of her chair and put her coat back on, then reached for her purse and the bag from the bookstore. She laid a five-dollar bill on the table to pay for her dinner. "It was nice meeting you."

Jordan frowned and slowly pushed back his chair, then stood. "Wait a minute, Amanda. You're not playing fair."

He was right. Jordan hadn't run away, however much he had probably wanted to, and she wouldn't, either.

She sank back into her seat, all too aware that people at surrounding tables were looking on with interest.

"You're not ready to talk about him," Jordan said, sitting down again, "and I'm not ready to talk about her. Deal?"

"Deal," Amanda said.

They discussed the Seattle Seahawks after that, and the Chinese artifacts on display at one of the museums. Then Jordan walked with her to the nearest corner and waited until the bus pulled up.

"Goodbye, Amanda," he said as she climbed the steps.

She dropped her change into the slot and smiled over one shoulder. "Thanks for the company."

He waved as the bus pulled away, and Amanda ached with a bittersweet loneliness she'd never known before, not even in the awful days after her breakup with James.

When Amanda arrived at her apartment building on Seattle's Queen Anne Hill, she was still thinking about Jordan. He'd wanted to offer to drive her home, she knew, but he'd had the good grace not to, and Amanda liked him for that.

In her mailbox she found a sheaf of bills waiting for her. "I'll never save enough to start a bed and breakfast at this rate," she complained to her black-and-white long-haired cat, Gershwin, when he met her at the door.

Gershwin was unsympathetic. As usual, he was interested only in his dinner.

After flipping on the lights, dropping her purse and the

book onto the hall table and hanging her coat on the brass-plated tree that was really too large for that little space, Amanda went into the kitchenette.

Gershwin purred and wound himself around her ankles as she opened a can of cat food, but when she scraped it out onto his dish, he abandoned her without compunction.

While Gershwin gobbled, Amanda went back to the mail she'd picked up in the lobby and flipped through it again. Three bills, a you-may-have-already-won and a letter from Eunice.

Amanda set the other envelopes down and opened the crisp blue one with her sister's return address printed in italics in one corner. She was disappointed when she realized that the letter was just another litany of Eunice's soon-to-be-ex-husband's sins, and she set it aside to finish later.

In the bathroom she started water running into her huge claw-footed tub, then stripped off the skirt and sweater she'd worn to the mall. After disposing of her underthings and panty hose, Amanda climbed into the soothing water.

Gershwin pushed the door open in that officious way cats have and bounded up to stand on the tub's edge with perfect balance. Like a tightrope walker, he strolled back and forth along the chipped porcelain, telling Amanda about his day in a series of companionable meows.

Amanda listened politely as she bathed, but her mind was wandering. She was thinking about Jordan Richards and that recently removed wedding band of his.

She sighed. All her instincts told her he was telling the truth about his marital status, but those same instincts had once insisted that James was all right, too.

AMANDA WAS WAITING when the bus pulled up at her corner the next morning. The weather was a little warmer, and the snow, so unusual in Seattle, was already melting.

Fifteen minutes later Amanda walked through the huge revolving door of the Evergreen Hotel. Its lush Oriental carpets were soft beneath the soles of her shoes, and crystal chandeliers winked overhead, their multicolored reflections blazing in the floor-to-ceiling mirrors.

Amanda took the elevator to the third floor, where the hotel's business offices were. As she was passing through the small reception area, Mindy Simmons hailed her from her desk.

"Mr. Mansfield is sick today," she said in an undertone. Mindy was small and pretty, with long brown hair and expressive green eyes. "Your desk is buried in messages."

Amanda went into her office and started dealing with problems. The plumbing in the presidential suite was on the fritz, so she called to make sure Maintenance was on top of the situation. A Mrs. Edman in 1203 suspected one of the maids of stealing her pearl earring, and someone had mixed up some dates at the reception desk—two couples were expecting to occupy the bridal suite on the same night.

It was noon when Amanda finished straightening everything out—Mrs. Edman's pearl earring had fallen behind the television set, the plumbing in the presidential suite was back in working order and each of the newlywed couples would have rooms to themselves. At Mindy's suggestion, she and Amanda went to the busy Westlake Mall for lunch, buying salads at one of the fast-food restaurants and taking a table near a window.

"Two more weeks and I start my vacation," Mindy stated enthusiastically, pouring dressing from a little carton over her salad. "Christmas at Big Mountain. I can hardly wait."

Amanda would just as soon have skipped Christmas altogether if she could have gotten the rest of the world to go along with the idea, but of course she didn't say that. "You and Pete will have a great time at the ski resort."

Mindy was chewing, and she swallowed before answering. "It's just great of his parents to take us along—we could never have afforded it on our own."

With a nod, Amanda poked her fork into a cherry tomato.

"What are you doing over the holidays?" Mindy asked.

Amanda forced a smile. "I'm going to be working," she reminded her friend.

"I know that, but what about a tree and presents and a turkey?"

"I'll have all those things at my mom and stepdad's place."

Mindy, who knew about James and all the dashed hopes he'd left in his wake, looked sympathetic. "You need to meet a new man."

Amanda bristled a little. "It just so happens that a woman can have a perfectly happy life without a man hanging around."

Mindy looked doubtful. "Sure," she said.

"Besides, I met someone just yesterday."

"Who?"

Amanda concentrated on her salad for several long moments. "His name is Jordan Richards, and—"

"Jordan Richards?" Mindy interrupted excitedly. "Wow! How did you ever manage to meet him?"

A little insulted that Mindy seemed to think Jordan was so far out of her orbit that even meeting him was a feat to get excited about, Amanda frowned. "We were in line together at a bookstore. Do you know him?"

"Not exactly," Mindy admitted, subsiding a little. "But my father-in-law does. Jordan Richards practically doubled his retirement fund for him, and they're always writing about him in the financial section of the Sunday paper."

"I didn't know you read that section," Amanda remarked.

"I don't," Mindy admitted readily, unwrapping a bread stick. "But we have dinner with my in-laws practically every Sunday, and that's all Pete and his dad ever talk about. Did he ask you out?"

"Who?"

"Jordan Richards, silly."

Amanda shook her head. "No, we just had Chinese food together and talked a little." She deliberately left out the part about how they'd gone to the minitherapy session and the way she'd reacted when Jordan had asked her about James.

Mindy looked disappointed. "Well, he did ask for your number, didn't he?"

"No. But he knows where I work. If he wants to call, I suppose he will."

A delighted smile lit Mindy's face. Positive thinking was an art form with her. "He'll call. I just know it."

Amanda grinned. "If he does, I won't be able to accept the glory—I owe it all to an article I read in *Cosmo*. I think it was called 'Big Girls Should Talk to Strangers,' or something like that."

Mindy lifted her diet cola in a rousing roast. "Here's to Jordan Richards and a red-hot romance!"

With a chuckle, Amanda touched her cup to Mindy's and drank a toast to something that would probably never happen.

Back at the hotel more crises were waiting to be solved, and there was a message on Amanda's desk, scrawled by the typist who'd filled in for Mindy during lunch. Jordan Richards had called.

A peculiar tightness constricted Amanda's throat, and a flutter started in the pit of her stomach. Mindy's toast echoed in her ears: *"Here's to Jordan Richards and a red-hot romance."*

Amanda laid down the message, telling herself she didn't have time to return the call, then picked it up again. Before she knew it, her finger was punching out the numbers.

"Striner, Striner and Richards," sang a receptionist's voice at the other end of the line.

Amanda drew a deep breath, squared her shoulders and exhaled. "This is Amanda Scott," she said in her most professional voice. "I'm returning a call from Jordan Richards."

"One moment, please."

After a series of clicks and buzzes another female voice came on the line. "Jordan Richards's office. May I help you?"

Again Amanda gave her name. And again she was careful to say she was returning a call that had originated with Jordan.

There was another buzz, then Jordan's deep, crisp voice saying, "Richards."

Amanda hadn't expected a simple thing like the man saying his name to affect her the way it did. It was the strangest sensation to feel dizzy over something like that. She dropped into the swivel chair behind her desk. "Hi. It's Amanda."

"Amanda."

Coming from him, her own name had the same strange impact as his had had.

"How are you?" he asked.

Amanda swallowed. She was a professional with a very responsible job. It was ridiculous to be overwhelmed by something so simple and ordinary as the timbre of a man's voice. "I'm fine," she answered. Nothing more imaginative came to her, and she sat there behind her broad desk, blushing like an eighth-grade schoolgirl trying to work up the courage to ask a boy to a sock hop.

His low, masculine chuckle came over the wire to surround her like a mystical caress. "If I promise not to ask any more questions about you know who, will you go out with me? Some friends of mine are having an informal dinner tonight on their houseboat."

Amanda still felt foolish for talking about James in the therapy session, then practically bolting when Jordan brought him up again over Chinese food. Lately she just seemed to be a mass of contradictions, feeling one way one minute, another the next. What it all came down to was the fact that Dr. Marshall was right—she needed to start taking chances again. "Sounds like fun," she said after drawing a deep breath.

"Pick you up at seven?"

"Yes." And she gave him her address. A little thrill went through her as she laid the receiver back on its cradle, but there was no more time to think about Jordan. The telephone immediately rang again.

"Amanda Scott."

The chef's assistant was calling. A pipe had broken, and the kitchen was flooding fast.

"Just another manic day," Amanda muttered as she hurried off to investigate.

Chapter 2

⟡

IT WAS TEN MINUTES AFTER SIX when Amanda got off the bus
in front of her apartment building and dashed inside. After
collecting her mail, she hurried up the stairs and jammed
her key into the lock. Jordan was picking her up in less than
an hour, and she had a hundred things to do to get ready.

Since he'd told her the evening would be a casual one,
she selected gray woolen slacks and a cobalt-blue blouse.
After a hasty shower, she put on fresh makeup and quickly
wove her hair into a French braid.

Gershwin stood on the back of the toilet the whole time
she was getting ready, lamenting the treatment of house
cats in contemporary America. She had just given him his
dinner when a knock sounded at the door.

Amanda's heart lurched like a dizzy ballet dancer, and
she wondered why she was being such a ninny. Jordan
Richards was just a man, nothing more. And so what if
he was successful? She met a lot of men like him in her
line of work.

She opened the door and knew a moment of pure exalta-
tion at the look of approval in Jordan's eyes.

"Hi," he said. He wore jeans and a sport shirt, and his

hands rested comfortably in the pockets of his brown leather jacket. "You look fantastic."

Amanda thought he looked pretty fantastic himself, but she didn't say so because she'd used up that week's quota of bold moves by talking about James in front of people she didn't know. "Thanks," she said, stepping back to admit him.

Gershwin did a couple of turns around Jordan's ankles and meowed his approval. With a chuckle, Jordan bent to pick him up. "Look at the size of this guy. Is he on steroids or what?"

Amanda laughed. "No, but I suspect him of throwing wild parties and sending out for pizza when I'm not around."

After scratching the cat once behind the ears, Jordan set him down again with a chuckle, but his eyes were serious when he looked at Amanda.

Something in his expression made her breasts grow heavy and her nipples tighten beneath the smooth silk of her blouse. "I suppose we'd better go," she said, sounding somewhat lame even to her own ears.

"Right," Jordan agreed. His voice had the same effect on Amanda it had had earlier. She felt the starch go out of her knees and she was breathless, as though she'd accidentally stepped onto a runaway skateboard.

She took her blue cloth coat from the coat tree, and Jordan helped her into it. She felt his fingertips brush her nape as he lifted her braid from beneath the collar, and hoped he didn't notice that she trembled ever so slightly at his touch.

His car, a sleek black Porsche—Amanda decided then and there that he didn't have kids of his own—was parked at the curb. Jordan opened the passenger door and walked around to get behind the wheel after Amanda was settled.

Soon they were streaking toward Lake Union. It was

only when he switched on the windshield wipers that Amanda realized it was raining.

"Have you lived in Seattle long?" she asked, uncomfortable with a silence Jordan hadn't seemed to mind.

"I live on Vashon Island now—I've been somewhere in the vicinity all my life," he answered. "What about you?"

"Seattle's home," Amanda replied.

"Have you ever wanted to live anywhere else?"

She smiled. "Sure. Paris, London, Rome. But after I graduated from college, I was hired to work at the Evergreen, so I settled down here."

"You know what they say—life is what happens while we're making other plans. I always intended to work on Wall Street myself."

"Do you regret staying here?"

Amanda had expected a quick, light denial. Instead she received a sober glance and a low, "Sometimes, yes. Things might have been very different if I'd gone to New York."

For some reason Amanda's gaze was drawn to the pale line across Jordan's left-hand ring finger. Although the windows were closed and the heater was going, Amanda suppressed a shiver. She didn't say anything until Lake Union, with its diamondlike trim of lit houseboats, came into sight. Since the holidays were approaching, the place was even more of a spectacle than usual.

"It looks like a tangle of Christmas tree lights."

Jordan surprised her with one of his fleeting, devastating grins.

"You have a colorful way of putting things, Amanda Scott."

She smiled. "Do your friends like living on a houseboat?"

"I think so," he answered, "but they're planning to move in the spring. They're expecting a baby."

Although lots of children were growing up on Lake Union, Amanda could understand why Jordan's friends would want to bring their little one up on dry land. Her thoughts turned bittersweet as she wondered whether she would ever have a child of her own. She was already twenty-eight—time was running out.

As he pulled the car into a parking lot near the wharves and shut the engine off, she sat up a little straighter, realizing that she'd left his remark dangling. "I'm sorry…I… How nice for them that they're having a baby."

Unexpectedly Jordan reached out and closed his hand over Amanda's. "Did I say something wrong?" he asked with a gentleness that almost brought tears to her eyes.

Amanda shook her head. "Of course not. Let's go in— I'm anxious to meet your friends."

David and Claudia Chamberlin were an attractive couple in their early thirties, he with dark hair and eyes, she with very fair coloring and green eyes. They were both architects, and framed drawings and photographs of their work graced the walls of the small but elegantly furnished houseboat.

Amanda thought of her own humble apartment with Gershwin as its outstanding feature, and wondered if Jordan thought she was dull.

Claudia seemed genuinely interested in her, though, and her greeting was warm. "It's good to see Jordan back in circulation—finally," she confided in a whisper when she and Amanda were alone beside the table where an array of wonderful food was being set out by the caterer's helpers.

Amanda didn't reply to the comment right away, but her gaze strayed to Jordan, who was standing only a few feet away, talking with David. "I guess it's been pretty hard for him," she ventured, pretending to know more than she did.

"The worst," Claudia agreed. She pulled Amanda a little distance farther from the men. "We thought he'd never get over losing Becky."

Uneasily Amanda recalled the pale stripe Jordan's wedding band had left on his finger. Perhaps, she reflected warily, there was a corresponding mark on his soul.

Later, when Amanda had met everyone in the room and mingled accordingly, Jordan laid her coat gently over her shoulders. "How about going out on deck with me for a few minutes?" he asked quietly. "I need some air."

Once again Amanda felt that peculiar lurching sensation deep inside. "Sure," she said with a wary glance at the rain-beaded windows.

"The rain stopped a little while ago," Jordan assured her with a slight grin.

The way he seemed to know what she was thinking was disconcerting.

They left the main cabin through a door on the side, and because the deck was slippery, Jordan put a strong arm around Amanda's waist. She was fully independent, but she still liked the feeling of being looked after.

The lights of the harbor twinkled on the dark waters of the lake, and Jordan studied them for a while before asking, "So, what do you think of Claudia and David?"

Amanda smiled. "They're pretty interesting," she replied. "I suppose you know they were married in India when they were there with the Peace Corps."

Jordan propped an elbow on the railing and nodded. "David and Claudia are nothing if not unconventional. That's one of the reasons I like them so much."

Amanda was slightly deflated, though she tried hard not to reveal the fact. With her ordinary job, cat and apartment, she knew she must seem prosaic compared to the Chamberlins. Perhaps it was the strange sense of hopelessness she felt that made her reckless enough to ask, "What about your wife? Was she unconventional?"

He turned away from her to stare out at the water, and for a long moment she was sure he didn't intend to answer. Finally, however, he said in a low voice, "She had a degree in marine biology, but she didn't work after the kids were born."

It was the first mention he'd made of any children— Amanda had been convinced, in fact, that he had none. "Kids?" she asked in a small and puzzled voice.

Jordan looked at her in a way that was almost, but not quite, defensive. "There are two—Jessica's five and Lisa's four."

Amanda knew a peculiar joy, as though she'd stumbled upon an unexpected treasure. She couldn't help the quick, eager smile that curved her lips. "I thought—well, when you were driving a Porsche—"

He smiled back at her in an oddly somber way. "Jessie and Lisa live with my sister over in Port Townsend."

Amanda's jubilation deflated. "They live with your sister? I don't understand."

Jordan sighed. "Becky died two weeks after the accident, and I was in the hospital for close to three months. Karen—my sister—and her husband, Paul, took the kids. By the time I got back on my feet, the four of them had become a family. I couldn't see breaking it up."

An overwhelming sadness caused Amanda to grip the railing for a moment to keep from being swept away by the sheer power of the emotion.

Reading her expression, Jordan gently touched the tip of her nose. "Ready to call it a night? You look tired."

Amanda nodded, too close to tears to speak. She had

a tendency to empathize with other people's joys and sorrows, and she was momentarily crushed by the weight of what Jordan had been through.

"I see my daughters often," he assured her, tenderness glinting in his eyes. He kissed her lightly on the mouth, then took her elbow and escorted her back inside the cabin.

They said their goodbyes to David and Claudia Chamberlin, then walked up the wharf to Jordan's car. He was a perfect gentleman, opening the door for Amanda, and she settled wearily into the suede passenger seat.

Back at Amanda's building, Jordan again helped her out of the car, and he walked her to her door. Amanda waited until the last possible second to decide whether she was going to invite him in, breaking her own suspense by blurting out, "Would you like a cup of coffee or something?"

Jordan's hazel eyes twinkled as he placed one hand on either side of the doorjamb, effectively trapping Amanda between his arms. "Not tonight," he said softly.

Amanda's blue eyes widened in confusion. "Don't look now," she replied in a burst of daring cowardice, "but you're sending out conflicting messages."

He chuckled, and his lips touched hers, very tenderly.

Amanda felt a jolt of spiritual electricity spark through her system, burning away every memory of James's touch. Surprise made her draw back from Jordan so suddenly that her head bumped hard against the door.

Jordan lowered one hand to caress her crown, and she felt the French braid coming undone beneath his fingers.

"Careful," he murmured, and then he kissed her again.

This time there was hunger in his touch, and a sweet, frightening power that made Amanda's knees unsteady.

She laid her hands lightly on his chest, trying to ground this second mystical shock, but he interpreted the contact differently and drew back.

"Good night, Amanda," he said quietly. He waited until she'd unlocked her door with a trembling hand, and then he walked away.

Inside the apartment Amanda flipped on the living room light, crossed to the sofa and sagged onto it. She felt as though she were leaning over the edge of a great canyon and the rocks were slipping away beneath her feet.

Gershwin hurled himself into her lap with a loud meow, and she ran one hand distractedly along his silky back. Dr. Marshall had said it was time she started taking chances, and she had an awful feeling she was on the brink of the biggest risk of her life.

THE MASSIVE REDWOOD-AND-GLASS house overlooking Puget Sound was dark and unwelcoming that night when Jordan pulled into the driveway and reached for the small remote control device lying on his dashboard. He'd barely made the last ferry to the island, and he was tired.

As the garage door rolled upward, he thought of Amanda, and shifted uncomfortably on the seat. He would have given half his stock portfolio to have her sitting beside him now, to talk with her over coffee in the kitchen or wine in front of the fireplace...

To take her to his bed.

Jordan got out of the car and slammed the door behind him. The garage was dark, but he didn't flip on a light until he reached the kitchen. Becky had always said he had the night vision of a vampire.

Becky. He clung to the memory of her smile, her laughter, her perfume. She'd been tiny and spirited, with dark hair and eyes, and it seemed to Jordan that she'd never been far from his side, even after her death. He'd loved her to an excruciating degree, but for the past few months she'd been steadily receding from his mind and heart. Now, with the coming of Amanda, her image seemed to be growing more indistinct with every passing moment.

Jordan glanced into the laundry room, needing something real and mundane to focus on. A pile of jeans, sweatshirts and towels lay on the floor, so he crammed as much as he could into the washing machine, then added soap and turned the dial. A comforting, ordinary sound resulted.

Returning to the kitchen, Jordan shrugged out of his leather jacket and laid it over one of the bar stools at the counter. He opened the refrigerator, studied its contents without actually focusing on a single item, then closed it again. He wasn't hungry for anything except Amanda, and it was too soon for that.

Too soon, he reflected with a rueful grin as he walked through the dining room to the front entryway and the stairs. He hadn't bothered with such niceties as timing with the women he'd dated over the past two years—in truth, their feelings just hadn't mattered much to him, though he'd never been deliberately unkind.

He trailed his hand over the top of the polished oak banister as he climbed the stairs. With Amanda, things were different. Timing was crucial, and so were her feelings.

The empty house yawned around Jordan as he opened his bedroom door and went inside. In the adjoining bathroom he took off his clothes and dropped them neatly into the hamper, then stepped into the shower.

Thinking of Amanda again, he turned on the cold water and endured its biting chill until some of the intolerable heat had abated. But while he was brushing his teeth, Amanda sneaked back into his mind.

He saw her standing on the deck of the Chamberlins' boat, looking up at him with that curious vulnerability showing in her blue-green eyes. It was as though she didn't know how beautiful she was, or how strong, and yet she had to, because she was out there making a life for herself.

Rubbing his now-stubbled chin, Jordan wandered into the bedroom, threw back the covers and slid between the sheets. He felt the first stirrings of rage as he thought about the mysterious James and the damage he'd done to Amanda's soul. Jordan had seen the bruises in her eyes every time she'd looked at him, and the memory made him want to find the bastard who'd hurt her and systematically tear him apart.

Jordan turned onto his stomach and tried to put the scattered images of the past two days out of his thoughts. This time, just before he dropped off to sleep, was reserved for thoughts of Becky, as always.

He waited, but his late wife's face didn't form in his mind. He could only see Amanda, with her wide, trusting blue eyes, her soft, spun-honey hair, her shapely and inviting body. He wanted her with a desperation that made his loins ache.

Furious, Jordan slammed one fist into the mattress and flipped onto his back, training all his considerable energy on remembering Becky's face.

He couldn't.

After several minutes of concentrated effort, all of it fruitless, panic seized him, and he bolted upright, switched on the lamp and reached for the picture on his nightstand.

Becky smiled back at him from the photograph as if to say, *Don't worry, sweetheart. Everything will be okay.*

With a raspy sigh, Jordan set the picture back on the table and turned out the light. Becky's favorite reassurance didn't work that night. Maybe things would be okay in the long run, but there was a lot of emotional white water between him and any kind of happy ending.

It was Saturday morning, and Amanda luxuriated in the fact that she didn't have to put on makeup, style her hair, or even get dressed if she didn't want to. She really tried to be lazy, but she felt strangely ambitious, and there was no getting around it.

She climbed out of bed and padded barefoot into the kitchen, where she got the coffee maker going and fed Gershwin. Then she had a quick shower and dressed in battered jeans, a Seahawks T-shirt and sneakers.

She was industriously vacuuming the living room rug, when the telephone rang.

The sound was certainly nothing unusual, but it fairly stopped Amanda's heart. She kicked the switch on the vacuum cleaner with her toe and lunged for the telephone, hoping to hear Jordan's voice since she hadn't seen or heard from him in nearly a week.

Instead it was her mother. "Hello, darling," said Marion Whitfield. "You sound breathless. Were you just coming in from the store or something?"

Amanda sank onto the couch. "No, I was only doing housework," she replied, feeling deflated even though she loved and admired this woman who had made a life for herself and both her daughters after the man of the house had walked out on them all.

"That's nice," Marion commented, for she was a great believer in positive reinforcement. "Listen, I called to ask if you'd like to go Christmas shopping with me. We could have lunch, too, and maybe even take in a movie."

Amanda sighed. She still didn't feel great about Christmas, and the stores and restaurants would be jam-packed. The theaters, of course, would be full of screaming children left there by harried mothers trying to complete their shopping. "I think I'll just stay home, if you don't mind."

She stated the refusal in a kindly tone, not wanting to hurt her mother's feelings.

"Is everything all right?"

Amanda caught one fingernail between her teeth for a moment before answering, "Mostly, yes."

"It's time you put that nasty experience with James Brockman behind you," Marion said forthrightly.

The two women were friends, as well as mother and daughter, and Amanda was not normally secretive with Marion. However, the thing with Jordan was too new and too fragile to be discussed; after all, he might never call again. "I'm trying, Mom," she replied.

"Well, Bob and I want you to come over for dinner soon. Like tomorrow, for instance."

"I'll let you know," Amanda promised quickly as the doorbell made its irritating buzz. "And stop worrying about me, okay?"

"Okay," Marion answered without conviction just before Amanda hung up.

Amanda expected one of the neighbor children, or maybe the postman with a package, so when she opened the door and found Jordan standing in the hallway, she felt as though she'd just run into a wall at full tilt.

For his part, Jordan looked a little bewildered, as though he might be surprised to find himself at Amanda's door. "I should have called," he said.

Amanda recovered herself. "Come in," she replied with a smile.

He hesitated for a moment, then stepped into the apartment, his hands tucked into the pockets of his jacket. He was wearing jeans and a green turtleneck, and his brown hair was damp from the Seattle drizzle. "I was wondering if you'd like to go out to lunch or something."

Amanda glanced at the clock on the mantel and was

amazed to see that it was nearly noon. The morning had flown by in a flurry of housecleaning. "Sure," she said. "I'll just clean up a little—"

He reached out and caught hold of her hand when she would have disappeared into her bedroom. "You look fine," he told her, and his voice was very low, like the rumble of an earthquake deep down in the ground.

By sheer force of will, Amanda shored up her knees, only to have him pull her close and lock his hands lightly behind the small of her back. A hot flush made her cheeks ache, and she had to force herself to meet his eyes.

Jordan chuckled. "Do I really scare you so much?" he asked.

Amanda wet her lips with the tip of her tongue in an unconscious display of nervousness. "Yes."

"Why?"

The question was reasonable, but Amanda didn't know the answer. "I'm not sure."

He grinned. "Where would you like to go for lunch?"

She would have been content not to go out at all, preferring just to stand there in his arms all afternoon, breathing in his scent and enjoying the lean, hard feel of his body against hers. She gave herself an inward shake. "You know, I just refused a similar invitation from my mother, and she would have thrown in a movie."

Jordan laughed and smoothed Amanda's bangs back from her forehead. "All right, so will I."

But Amanda shook her head. "Too many munchkins screaming and throwing popcorn."

His expression changed almost imperceptibly. "Don't you like kids?"

"I love them," Amanda answered, "except when they're traveling in herds."

Jordan chuckled again and gave her another light kiss.

"Okay, we'll go to something R-rated. Nobody under seventeen admitted without a parent."

"You've got a deal," Amanda replied.

Just as he was helping her get into her coat, the telephone rang. Praying there wasn't a disaster at the Evergreen to be taken care of, Amanda answered, "Hello?"

"Hello, Amanda." She hadn't heard that voice in six long months, and the sound of it stunned her. It was James.

Grimacing at Jordan, she spoke into the receiver. "I don't want to talk to you, now or ever."

"Please don't hang up," James said quickly.

Amanda bit down on her lip and lowered her eyes. "What is it?"

"Madge is divorcing me."

She drew a deep breath and let it out again. "Congratulations, James," she said, not with cruelty but with resignation. After all, it was no great surprise, and she had no idea why he felt compelled to share the news with her.

"I'd like for you and me to get back together," he said in that familiar tone that had once rendered her pliant and gullible.

"There's absolutely no chance of that," Amanda replied, forcing herself to meet Jordan's gaze again. He was standing at the door, his hand on the knob, watching her with concern but not condemnation. "Goodbye, James." With that, she placed the receiver back in its cradle.

Jordan remained where he was for a long moment, then he crossed the room to where Amanda stood, bundled in her coat, and gently lifted her hair out from under her collar. "Still want to go out?" he asked quietly.

Amanda was oddly shaken, but she nodded, and they left the apartment together. The phone began ringing again when they reached the top of the stairs, but this time Amanda made no effort to answer it.

"I guess I can't blame him for being persistent," Jordan remarked when they were seated in the Porsche. "You're a beautiful woman, Amanda."

She sighed, ignoring the compliment because it didn't register. "I'll never forgive James for lying to me the way he did," she got out. Tears stung her eyes as she remembered the blinding pain of his deceit.

Jordan pulled out into the rainy-day traffic and kept his eyes on the road. "He wants you back," he guessed.

Amanda noticed that his hands tensed slightly around the steering wheel.

"That's what he said," she confessed, staring out at the decorated streets but not really seeing them.

"Do you believe him?"

Amanda shrugged. "It doesn't matter whether I do or not. I've made my decision and I'm not going to change my mind." She found some tissue in her purse and resolutely dried her eyes, trying in vain to convince herself that Jordan hadn't noticed she was crying.

He drove to a pizza joint across the street from a mall north of the city. "This okay?" he asked, bringing the sleek car to a stop in one of the few parking spaces available. "We could order takeout if you'd rather not go in."

Amanda drew a deep breath, composing herself. The time with James was behind her, and she wanted to keep it there, to enjoy the here and now with Jordan. Christmas crowds or none. "Let's eat here," she said.

He favored her with a half grin and came around to open her door for her. As she stood, she accidentally brushed against him, and felt that familiar twisting ache deep inside herself. She was going to end up making love with Jordan Richards, she just knew it. It was inevitable.

The realization that he was reading her thoughts once more made Amanda blush, and she drew back when he took her hand. His grip only became firmer, however, and she didn't try to pull away again. She was in the mood to follow where Jordan might lead—which, to Amanda's way of thinking, made it a darned good thing they were approaching the door of a pizza parlor instead of a bedroom.

Chapter 3

⟨᠊⟩

THE PIZZA WAS UNCOMMONLY good, it seemed to Amanda, but memories of the R-rated movie they saw afterward made her fidget in the passenger seat of Jordan's Porsche. "I've never heard of anybody doing that with an ice cube," she remarked with a slight frown.

Jordan laughed. "That was interesting, all right."

"Do you think it was symbolic?"

He was still grinning. "No. It was definitely hormones, pure and simple."

Amanda finally relaxed a little and managed to smile. "You're probably right."

Since there were a lot of cars parked in front of Amanda's building, a sleek silver Mercedes among them, Jordan parked almost a block away. It seemed natural to hold hands as they walked back to the entrance.

Amanda was stunned to see James sitting on the bottom step of the stairway leading up to the second floor. He was wearing his usual three-piece tailor-made suit, a necessity for a corporate chief executive officer like himself, and his silver gray hair looked as dashing as ever. His tanned face showed signs of strain, however, and the once-over he gave Jordan was one of cordial contempt.

Amanda's first instinct was to let go of Jordan's hand, but he tightened his grip when she tried.

Meanwhile James had risen from his seat on the stairs. "We have to talk," he said to Amanda.

She shook her head, grateful now for Jordan's presence and his grasp on her hand. "There's nothing to say."

The man she had once loved arched an eyebrow. "Isn't there? You could start by introducing me to the new man in your life."

It was Jordan who spoke. "Jordan Richards," he said evenly, without offering his hand.

James studied him with new interest flickering in his shrewd eyes. "Brockman," he answered. "James Brockman."

A glance at Jordan revealed that he recognized the name—anyone active in the business world would have—but he clearly wasn't the least bit intimidated. He simply nodded an acknowledgment.

Amanda ran her tongue over her lips. "Let us pass, James," she said. She'd never spoken so authoritatively to him before, but she took no pleasure in the achievement because she knew she wouldn't have managed it if Jordan hadn't been there.

James did not look at Amanda, but at Jordan. Some challenge passed between them, and the air was charged with static electricity for several moments. Then James stepped aside to lean against the banister, leaving barely enough room for Jordan and Amanda to walk by.

"Richards."

Jordan stopped, still holding Amanda's hand, and looked back at James over one shoulder in inquiry.

"I'll call your office Monday morning. I'd be interested

to know what we have in common—where investments are concerned, naturally."

Amanda felt her face heat. Again she tried to pull away from Jordan; again he restrained her. "Naturally," Jordan responded coldly, and then he continued up the stairway, bringing Amanda with him.

"I'm sorry," she said the moment they were alone in her apartment. She was leaning against the closed door.

"Why?" Jordan asked, reaching out to unbutton her coat. He helped her out of it, then hung it on the brass tree. Amanda watched him with injury in her eyes as he removed his jacket and put it with her coat.

She had been leaning against the door again, and she thrust herself away. "Because of James, of course."

"It wasn't your fault he came here."

She sighed and stopped in the tiny entryway, her back to Jordan, the fingers of one hand pressed to her right temple. She knew he was right, but she was slightly nauseous all the same. "That remark he made about what the two of you might have in common…"

Jordan reached out and took her shoulders in his hands, turning her gently to face him. "Your past is your own business, Amanda. I'm interested in the woman you are now, not the woman you were six months or six years ago."

Amanda blinked, then bit her upper lip for a moment. "But he meant—"

He touched her lip with an index finger. "I know what he meant," he said with hoarse gentleness. "When and if it happens for us, Amanda, you won't be the first woman I've been with. I'm not going to condemn you because I'm not the first man."

With that, the subject of that aspect of Amanda's relationship with James was closed forever. In fact, it was almost as though the subject hadn't been broached. "Would you like some coffee or something?" she asked, feeling better.

Jordan grinned. "Sure."

When Amanda came out of the kitchenette minutes later, carrying two mugs of instant coffee, Jordan was studying the blue-and-white patchwork quilt hanging on the wall behind her couch. Gershwin seemed to have become an appendage to his right ankle.

"Did you make this?"

Amanda nodded proudly. "I designed it, too."

Jordan looked impressed. "So there's more to you than the mild-mannered assistant hotel manager who gets her Christmas shopping done early," he teased.

She smiled. "A little, yes." She extended one mug of coffee and he took it, lifting it to his lips. "I had a good time today, Jordan."

When Amanda sat down on the couch, Jordan did, too. His nearness brought images from the movie they'd seen back to her mind. "So did I," he answered, putting his coffee down on the rickety cocktail table.

Damn that guy with the ice cube, Amanda fretted to herself as Jordan put his hands on her shoulders again and slowly drew her close. It seemed to her that a small eternity passed before their lips touched, igniting the soft suspense Amanda felt into a flame of awareness.

The tip of his tongue encircled her lips, and when they parted at his silent bidding, he took immediate advantage. Somehow Amanda found herself lying down on the sofa instead of sitting up, and when Jordan finally pulled away from her mouth, she arched her neck. He kissed the pulse point at the base of her throat, then progressed to the one beneath her right ear. In the meantime, Amanda could feel her T-shirt being worked slowly up her rib cage.

When he unsnapped her bra and laid it aside, revealing

her ripe breasts, Amanda closed her eyes and lifted her back slightly in a silent offering.

He encircled one taut nipple with feather-light kisses, and Amanda moaned softly when he captured the morsel between his lips and began to suckle. She entangled her hands in his hair and spread her legs, one foot high on the sofa back, the other on the floor, to accommodate him.

The eloquent pressure of his desire made Amanda ache to be taken, but she was too breathless to speak, too swept up in the gentle incursion to ask for conquering. When she felt the snap on her jeans give way, followed soon after by the zipper, she only lifted her hips so the jeans could be peeled away. They vanished, along with her panties and her sneakers, and Jordan began to caress her intimately with one hand while he enjoyed her other breast.

The ordinary light in the living room turned colors and made strange patterns in front of Amanda's eyes as Jordan kissed his way down over her satiny, quivering belly to her thighs.

She whimpered when he burrowed into her deepest secret, gave a lusty cry when he plundered that secret with his mouth. Her hips shot upward, and Jordan cupped his hands beneath her bottom, holding her in his hands as he would sparkling water from a stream. "Jordan," she gasped, turning her head from side to side in a fever of passion when he showed her absolutely no mercy.

He flung her over the savage brink, leaving her to convulse repeatedly at the top of an invisible geyser. When the last trace of response had been wrung from her, he lowered her gently back to the sofa.

She lay there watching him, the back of one hand resting against her mouth, her body covered in a fine mist of perspiration. Jordan was sitting up, one of her bare legs draped across his lap, his eyes gentle as he laid a hand on Amanda's trembling belly as if to soothe it.

"I want you," she said brazenly when she could speak.

Jordan smiled and traced the outline of her jaw with one finger, then the circumferences of both her nipples. "Not this time, Mandy," he answered, his voice hardly more than a ragged whisper.

Amanda was both surprised and insulted. "What the hell do you mean, 'not this time'? Were you just trying to prove—"

Jordan interrupted her tirade by bending to kiss her lips. "I wasn't trying to prove anything. I just don't want you hating my guts when you wake up tomorrow."

Amanda's body, so long untouched by a man, was primed for a loving it wasn't going to receive. "You're too late," she spat, bolting to an upright position and righting her bra and T-shirt. "I *already* hate your guts!"

Jordan obligingly fetched her jeans and panties from the floor where he'd tossed them earlier. "Probably, but you'll forgive me when the time is right."

She squirmed back into the rest of her clothes, then stood looking down at Jordan, one finger waggling. "No, I won't!" she argued hotly.

He clasped her hips in his hands and brought her forward, then softly nipped the place he'd just pillaged so sweetly. Even through her jeans, Amanda felt a piercing response to the contact; a shock went through her, and she gave a soft cry of mingled protest and surrender.

Jordan drew back and gave her a swat on the bottom. "See? You'll forgive me."

Amanda would have whirled away then, but Jordan caught her by the hand and wrenched her onto his lap. When she would have risen, he restricted her by catching hold of her hands and imprisoning them behind her back.

With his free hand, he pushed her T-shirt up in front again, then boldly cupped a lace-covered breast that throbbed to be bared to him once more. "It's going to be very good when we make love," he said firmly, "but that isn't going to happen yet."

Amanda squirmed, infuriated and confused. "Then why don't you let me go?" she breathed.

He chuckled. "Because I want to make damn sure you don't forget that preview of how it's going to be."

"Of all the arrogance—"

Jordan pulled down one side of her bra, causing the breast to spring triumphantly to freedom. "I've got plenty of that," he breathed against a peak that strained toward him.

Amanda moaned despite herself when he took her into his mouth again.

"Umm," he murmured, blatant in his enjoyment.

Utter and complete surprise possessed Amanda when she realized she was being propelled to another release, with Jordan merely gripping her hands behind her and feasting on her breast. She didn't want him to know, and yet her body was already betraying her with feverish jerks and twists.

She bit down hard on her lower lip and tried to keep herself still, but she couldn't. She was moving at lightning speed toward a collision with a comet.

Jordan lifted his mouth from her breast just long enough to mutter, "So it's like that, is it?" before driving her hard up against her own nature as a woman.

She surrendered in a burst of surprised gasps and sagged against Jordan, resting her head on his shoulder when it was finally over. "H-how did that happen?"

Still caressing her breast, Jordan spoke against her ear.

"No idea," he answered, "but it damned near made me change my mind about waiting."

Amanda lay against his chest until she'd recovered the ability to stand and to breathe properly, then she rose from his lap, snapped her bra and pulled down her T-shirt. In a vain effort to regain her dignity, she squared her shoulders and plunged the splayed fingers of both hands through her hair. "You don't find me attractive—that's it, isn't it?"

"That's the most ridiculous question I've ever been asked," Jordan answered, rising a little awkwardly— and painfully, it seemed to Amanda—from the sofa. "I wouldn't have done the things I just did if I didn't."

"Then why don't you want me?"

"Believe me, I do want you. Too badly to risk lousing things up so soon."

Amanda wasn't satisfied with that answer, so she turned on one heel and fled into the bathroom, where she splashed cold water on her face and brushed her love-tousled hair. When she came out, half fearing that Jordan would be gone, she found him standing at the window, gazing out at the city.

Calmer, she stood behind him, slipped her arms around his lean waist and kissed his nape. "Stay for supper?"

He turned in her embrace to smile down into her eyes. "That depends on what's on the menu."

Amanda was mildly affronted, remembering his rejection. "It isn't me," she stated with a small pout, "so you can relax."

He laughed and gave her another playful swat on the bottom. "Take it from me, Mandy—I'm not relaxed."

She grinned, glad to know he was suffering justly, and kissed his chin, which was already darkening with the shadow of a beard. "Nobody has called me 'Mandy' since first grade," she said.

"Good."

"Why is that good?" Amanda inquired, snuggling close.

"Because it saves me the trouble of thinking up some cutesy nickname like 'babycakes' or 'buttercup.'"

She laughed. "I can't imagine you calling me 'buttercup' with a straight face."

"I don't think I could," he replied, bending his head to kiss her thoroughly. Amanda's knees were weak when he finally drew back.

"You delight in tormenting me," she protested.

His eyes twinkled. "What's for supper?"

"Grilled cheese sandwiches, unless we go to the market," Amanda answered.

"The market it is," Jordan replied. Once again, in the entryway he helped Amanda into her coat.

"You have good manners for a rascal," Amanda remarked quite seriously.

Jordan laughed. "Thank you—I think."

They walked to a small store on the corner, where food was overpriced but fresh and plentiful. Amanda selected two steaks, vegetables for a salad and potatoes for baking.

"Does your fireplace work?" Jordan asked, lingering in front of a display of synthetic logs.

Amanda nodded, wondering if she could stand the romance of a crackling fire when Jordan was so determined not to make love to her. "Are you trying to drive me crazy, or what?" she countered, her eyes snapping with irritation.

He gave her one of his nuclear grins, then picked up two of the logs and carried them to the checkout counter, where he threw down a twenty-dollar bill. He would have paid for the food, too, except that Amanda wouldn't let him.

She did permit him to carry everything back to the apartment, however, thinking it might drain off some of his excess energy.

When they were back in Amanda's apartment, he moved the screen from in front of the fireplace as Gershwin meowed curiously at his elbow. After opening the damper, he laid one of the logs he'd bought in the grate. Amanda glanced at the label on the other log and saw it was meant to last a full three hours.

She grinned as she got her favorite skillet out of the drawer underneath the stove. Two logs totaled six hours. Maybe Jordan would change his mind about waiting before that much time slipped past.

Dusting his hands together, he came into the kitchenette, and Amanda could see the flicker of the fire reflected on the shiny front of her refrigerator door. Without being asked, he took the vegetables out of the bag and began washing them at the sink.

Amanda went to his side, handing him both the potatoes. "You're pretty handy in a kitchen, fella," she remarked in a teasing, sultry voice.

Jordan's eyes danced when he looked at her, and his expression said he was pretty handy in a few other rooms, too. "Thanks." He scrubbed the potatoes and handed them back to Amanda, who put a little swing in her hips as she walked away because she knew he was watching.

He laughed. "You need a spanking."

Amanda poked the potatoes with a fork and set them in the tiny microwave oven her mother and stepfather had given her the Christmas before. "Very kinky, Mr. Richards."

Jordan chuckled as he went back to chopping vegetables, and Amanda found the wooden salad bowl she'd bought in Hawaii and set it on the counter beside him.

They ate at the glass table in Amanda's living room, the fire dancing on the hearth and casting its image on their wineglasses. Darkness had long since settled over the city, and Amanda wondered why she hadn't noticed when the daylight fled.

"Tell me about your daughters," she said when the meal was nearly over.

Jordan pushed his plate away and took a sip of his wine before replying. "They're normal kids, I guess. They like to watch *Sesame Street,* have me read the funny papers to them, things like that."

Amanda felt sad, but if someone had asked, she would have had to admit she wasn't thinking about Jordan's children at all. She was remembering how it felt when her dad had gone away that long-ago Christmas Day, swearing never to come back. And he hadn't. "Do you miss them?" she asked.

"Yes," he admitted frankly. "But I know they're better off with Karen and Paul."

"Why?" Amanda dared to ask.

Jordan lifted his shoulders in a slight shrug. "I told you—my sister and her husband took them in when I was in the hospital. I'm more like an uncle to them than a father. They wouldn't understand if I uprooted them now."

Amanda wasn't so sure, but she didn't say that because she knew she'd already overstepped her bounds in some ways. If Jordan didn't want to raise his own children, that was his business, but it made Amanda wonder what would happen if the two of them were ever married and had babies. If she died, would he just send the kids to live with someone else?

She refilled her wineglass and took a healthy sip.

There was a look of quiet understanding in Jordan's eyes as he watched her. "What have I done now?" he asked.

"Nothing," Amanda lied, setting her glass down and jumping up to begin clearing the table.

Jordan rose from his chair and elbowed her aside. "Go and sit by the fire. I'll take care of this."

Apparently giving orders had become a habit with Jordan over the course of his successful career. "I'll help," she insisted, following him into the kitchen with the salad bowl in her hands.

Jordan scraped and rinsed the plates, and Amanda put them, along with the silverware and glasses, into the dishwasher.

"Somebody trained you rather well," she commented grudgingly.

He gave her a meltdown grin. "Thanks for noticing," he said with a slight leer.

Amanda's face turned pink. "I was talking about cooking and doing dishes!"

Jordan smiled at her discomfiture. "Oh," he said, but he sounded patently unconvinced.

Amanda put what remained of the salad in a smaller bowl, covered that tightly with plastic wrap, then stuck it into the refrigerator. She longed to ask him what kind of wife Becky had been, but she didn't dare. She knew he'd say she'd been wonderful, and Amanda wasn't feeling grown-up enough to deal with that.

He was leaning against the sink, watching her, his arms folded in front of his chest. "James is a lot older than you are," he said.

The remark was so out of left field that Amanda was momentarily stunned by it. "I know," she finally managed, standing in the doorway that led to the living room.

"Where did you meet him?"

Amanda couldn't think why she was answering, since they had agreed not to talk about James, but answer she did. "At the hotel," she replied with a sigh. "He taught a management seminar there a year and a half ago."

"And you went?"

She couldn't read Jordan's mood either in his eyes or his voice, and she was unsettled by the question. "Yes. He asked me out to dinner the first night, and after that I saw him whenever he was in Seattle on business."

Jordan crossed the room and enfolded Amanda in his arms, and the relief she felt was totally out of proportion to the circumstances.

"I have to know one thing, Mandy. Do you love him?"

She shook her head. "No." She tasted wine on Jordan's lips when he kissed her. And she tasted wanting. *Do you still love Becky?* she longed to ask, but she was too afraid of the answer to voice the question.

Slipping his arm around her waist, Jordan ushered Amanda into the living room, where they sat on a hooked rug in front of the fireplace. He gripped her hand and stared into the flames in the silence for a long time, then he turned, looked into her fire-lit eyes and said, "I'm sorry, Mandy. I didn't have any right to ask about James."

She let her head rest against the place where his arm and shoulder met. "It's okay. I made a fool of myself, and I can admit that now."

Jordan caught her chin in his hand and wouldn't let her look away. "Let's get one thing straight here," he said in gentle reproach. "The only mistake you made was trusting the bastard. He's the fool."

Amanda sighed. "That's a refreshing opinion. Most people either say or imply that I should have known better."

"Not this people," Jordan answered, tasting her lips.

Although it seemed impossible, Amanda wanted Jordan more now than she had on the couch earlier when he'd brought her face-to-face with her own womanhood. She longed to take him by the hand and lead him to her bed, but the thought of a second rebuff stopped her. In fact, she supposed it was about time she started taking the advice her mother had given her in ninth grade and play hard to get.

She moved a little apart from Jordan, stiffened her shoulders and raised her chin. "Maybe you should go," she said.

Jordan showed no signs of leaving. Instead he put his hands on Amanda's shoulders and lowered her to the hooked rug, stretching out beside her and laying one hand brazenly on her breast. The nipple tightened obediently beneath his palm.

Amanda moved to rise, but Jordan pressed her back down again, this time with a consuming kiss. "Don't you dare start anything you don't intend to finish," she ordered in a raspy whisper when at last he'd drawn away from her mouth. Having obtained the response he wanted from her right breast, he was now working on her left.

"I'll finish it," he vowed in a husky murmur, "when the time is right."

He lowered his hand to her belly, covering it with splayed fingers, and Amanda's heart pounded beneath her T-shirt. She pulled on his nape until his mouth again joined with hers, and the punishment for this audacious act was the unsnapping of her jeans.

"Damn it, Jordan, I don't like being teased."

He pulled at the zipper, and then his hand was in between her jeans and her panties, just resting there, soaking up her warmth, making her grow moist. That part of her body was like an exotic orchid flowering in a hothouse.

"Tough," he replied with a cocky grin just before he bent and scraped one hidden nipple lightly with his teeth, causing it to leap to attention.

Amanda's formidable pride was almost gone, and she had to grasp the rug and bite down on her lower lip to keep from begging him to make love to her.

"This night is just for you," he told her, his hand making a fiery circle at the junction of her thighs. "Why can't you accept that?"

"Because it isn't normal, that's why," Amanda gasped, trying to hold her hips still but finding it impossible. "You're a man. You're supposed to have just one thing on your mind. You're supposed to be trying to jump my bones."

He laughed at that. "What a chauvinistic thing to say."

Amanda groaned as he continued his sweet devilment. "I've never seen anything in *Cosmopolitan* that told what to d-do when this happens," she complained.

Again Jordan laughed. "I can tell you what to do," he said when he'd recovered himself a little. "Enjoy it."

Amanda was beginning to breathe hard. "Damn you, Jordan—I'll make you pay for this!"

"I'm counting on that," he said against her mouth.

Moments later Amanda was soaring again. She dug her fingers into Jordan's shoulders while she plunged her heels into the rug, and everyone in the apartment building would have known how well he'd loved her if he hadn't clamped his mouth over hers and swallowed her cries.

"IF THIS IS some kind of power game," Amanda sputtered five minutes later when she could manage to speak, fastening her jeans and sitting up again, "I don't want to play."

"You could have fooled me," Jordan responded.

Amanda gave a strangled cry of frustration and anger. "I can't imagine why I keep letting you get away with this."

"I can," he replied. "It feels good, and it's been a long time. Right?"

Amanda let her forehead rest against his shoulder, embarrassed. "Yes," she confessed.

He kissed the top of her head. "I should have dessert before dinner more often," he teased.

Amanda groaned, unable to look at him, and he chuckled and lifted her chin for a light kiss. "You're impossible," she murmured.

"And I'm leaving," he added with a glance at his watch. "It's time you were in bed."

Bleakness filled Amanda at the thought of climbing into bed alone, and she was just about to protest, when Jordan laid a finger to her nose and asked, "Will you go Christmas shopping with me tomorrow?"

Amanda would have gone to Zanzibar. "Yes," she answered like a hypnotized person.

Jordan kissed her again, leaving her lips warm and slightly swollen. "Good night," he said. And then, after a backward look and a wave, he was gone.

Chapter 4

❧

THE TELEPHONE JANGLED JUST as Amanda finished with her makeup the next morning. She'd managed to camouflage the shadows under her eyes—the result of sleeping only a few hours—with a cover stick.

"Hello?" she blurted into the receiver of her bedside telephone, hoping Jordan wasn't calling to back out of their shopping trip.

"If I remember correctly," her mother began dryly without returning the customary greeting, "you were supposed to call last night and let us know whether you were coming over for supper."

Amanda stretched the phone cord as far as her closet, where she took out black wool slacks. "Sorry, Mom," she answered contritely. "I forgot, but you'll be glad to know it was because of a man." She went to the dresser for her pink cashmere sweater while waiting for her mother to digest her last remark.

"A man?" Marion echoed, unable to hide the pleasure in her voice.

"And James was here yesterday," Amanda went on after pulling the sweater on over her head.

Marion drew in her breath. "Don't tell me you're seeing him again—"

"Of course not, Mom," Amanda scolded, propping the receiver between her shoulder and her ear while she wriggled into the sleek black pants.

"You're deliberately confusing me," Marion accused.

Amanda sighed. "Listen, I'll tell you everything tomorrow, okay? I'll stop by after work and catch you up on all the latest developments."

"So there is somebody besides James?" Marion pressed, sounding pleased.

"Yep," Amanda answered just as the door buzzer sounded. "Gotta go—he's here."

"Bye," Marion said cooperatively, and promptly hung up.

Amanda was brushing her hair as she hurried through the apartment to open the door. She was smiling, since she expected Jordan, but she found a delivery man from one of the more posh department stores in the hallway, instead. He was holding two silver gift boxes, one large and one fairly small. "Ms. A. Scott?" he asked.

Amanda nodded, mystified.

"These are for you—special express delivery," the man said, holding on to the packages while he shoved a clipboard at Amanda. "Sign on line twenty-seven."

She found the appropriate line and scrawled her name there, and the man gave her the packages in return for the clipboard.

After depositing the boxes on the couch and rummaging through her purse for a tip, she closed the door and lifted the lid off the smaller box. A skimpy aqua bikini lay inside, but there was no card or note to explain.

She opened the large box and gasped, faced with the rich, unmistakable splendor of sable. A small envelope lay on top, but Amanda didn't need to read it to know the gifts were from James.

As a matter of curiosity, she looked at the card: "Honeymoon in Hawaii, then on to Copenhagen? Call me. James."

With a sigh, Amanda tossed down the card. She was just about to call the store and ask to return the two boxes, when there was a knock at the door.

She rushed to open it and found Jordan standing in the hallway, looking spectacular in blue jeans, a lightweight yellow sweater and a tweed sport jacket.

"Hi," he said, his bright hazel eyes registering approval as he looked at her.

"Come in," Amanda replied, stepping back and holding the door open wide. "I'm just about finished with my hair. Pour yourself a cup of coffee and I'll be right out."

He stopped her when she would have turned away from him, and lightly entangled the fingers of one hand in her hair. "Don't change it," he said hoarsely. "It looks great."

Amanda's heart was beating a little faster just because he was close and because he was touching her. Since she didn't know what to say, she didn't speak.

Jordan kissed her lightly on the lips. "Good morning, Mandy," he said, and his voice was still husky. Amanda had a vision of him carrying her off to bed, and heat flooded her entire body, a blush rising in her cheeks.

"Good morning," she replied, her voice barely more than a squeak. "How about that coffee?"

His gaze had shifted to the boxes on the couch. "What's this?" There was a teasing reproach in his eyes when they returned to her face. "Opening your presents before Christmas, Mandy? For shame."

Amanda had completely forgotten the unwanted gifts, and the reminder deflated her spirits a little. "I'm sending them back," she said, hoping Jordan wouldn't pursue the subject.

His expression sobered. "James?"

Amanda licked her lips, then nodded nervously. She wasn't entirely displeased to see a muscle in Jordan's cheek grow taut, then relax again.

"Persistent, isn't he?"

"Yes," Amanda admitted. "He is." And after that there seemed to be nothing more to say—about James, anyway.

"Let's go," Jordan told her, kissing her forehead. "We'll get some breakfast on the way."

Amanda disappeared into the bedroom to put on her shoes, and when she came out, Jordan was studying the quilt over her couch again, his hands in his hip pockets.

"You know, you have a real talent for this," he said.

Amanda smiled. James had always been impatient with her quilting, saying she ought to save the needlework for when she was old and had nothing better to do. "Thanks."

Jordan followed her out of the apartment and waited patiently while she locked the door. He held her elbow lightly as they went down the stairs, once again giving her the wonderful sensation of being protected.

The sun was shining, which was cause for rejoicing in Seattle at that time of year, and Amanda felt happy as Jordan closed the car door after her.

When he slid behind the wheel, he just sat there for a few minutes and looked at her. Then he put a hand in her hair again. "Excuse me, lady," he said, his voice low, "but has anybody told you this morning that you're beautiful?"

Amanda flushed, but her eyes were sparkling. "No, sir," she answered, playing the game. "They haven't."

He leaned toward her and gave her a lingering kiss that made a sweet languor blossom inside her.

"There's an oversight that needs correcting," he murmured afterward. "You're beautiful."

Amanda was trembling when he finally turned to start the ignition, fasten his seat belt and steer the car out into the light Sunday morning traffic. Something was terribly wrong in this relationship, she reflected. It was supposed to be the man who wanted to head straight for the bedroom, while the woman held out for knowing each other better.

And yet it was all Amanda could do not to drag Jordan out of the car and back up the stairs to her apartment.

"What's the matter?" Jordan asked, tossing a mischievous glance her way that said he well knew the answer to that question.

Amanda folded her arms and looked straight ahead as they sped up a freeway ramp. The familiar green-and-white signs slipped by overhead. "Nothing," she said.

He sighed. "I hate it when women do that. You ask them what's wrong and they say 'nothing,' and all the while you know they're ready to burst into tears or clout you with the nearest blunt object."

Amanda turned in her seat and studied his profile for a few moments, one fingernail caught between her teeth. "I wasn't about to do either of those things," she finally said. She didn't quite have the fortitude to go the rest of the way and admit she was wondering why he didn't seem to want her.

Jordan reached out and laid a hand gently on her knee, once again sending all her vital organs into a state of alarm.

"What's the problem, then?"

She drew in a deep breath for courage and let it out slowly. "If we sleep together, you'll be the second man I've ever been with in my life, so it's not like I'm hot to trot or anything. But I usually have to fight guys off, not wait for them to decide the time is right."

He was clearly suppressing a smile, which didn't help.

"'Hot to trot'? I didn't think anybody said that anymore."

"Jordan."

He favored her with a high-potency grin. "Believe me, Mandy, I'm a normal man and I want you. But you're going to have to wait, because I've got no intention of—forgive me—screwing this up."

Amanda sighed and folded her arms. "Exactly what is it you're waiting for?"

His wonderful eyes were crinkled with laughter, even though his mouth was unsmiling.

"Exactly what is it you want me to do?" he countered. "Pull the car over to the side of the freeway and, as you put it last night, 'jump your bones'?"

Amanda blushed. "You make me sound like some kind of loose woman," she accused.

He took her hand and squeezed it reassuringly. "I can't even imagine that," he said in a soothing voice. "Now what do you say we change the subject for a while?"

That seemed like the only solution. "Okay," Amanda agreed. "Remember how you admired the quilt I made?"

Jordan nodded, switching lanes to be in position for an upcoming exit. "It's great."

"Well, I've been designing and making quilts for years. Someday I hope to open a bed and breakfast somewhere, with a little craft shop on the premises."

He grinned as he took the exit. "I'm surprised. Given your job and the fact that you live in the city, I thought you were inclined toward more sophisticated dreams."

"I was," Amanda said, recalling some of the glamorous, exciting adventures she had had with James. "But life changes a person. And I've always liked making quilts. I've been selling them at craft shows for a long time, and saving as much money as I could for the bed and break-fast."

Jordan was undoubtedly thinking of her humble apartment when he said, "You must have a pretty solid nest egg."

Amanda sighed, feeling discouraged all over again. "Not really. The real estate market is hot around here, what with so many people moving up from California, and the prices are high."

They had left the freeway, and Jordan pulled the car into the parking lot of a family-style restaurant near the mall. "Working capital is one of my specialties, Mandy. Maybe I can help you."

Amanda surprised even herself when she shook her head so fast. She guessed it was partly pride that made her do that, and partly disappointment that he wasn't trying to talk her out of establishing a business in favor of something else. Like getting married and starting a family.

"Did we just hit another tricky subject?" Jordan asked good-naturedly, when he and Amanda were walking toward the restaurant.

She shrugged. "I want the bed and breakfast to be all my own."

Jordan opened the door for her. "What if you decide to get married or something?"

Amanda felt a little thrill, even though she knew Jordan wasn't on the verge of proposing. She would have refused even if he had. "I guess I'll cross that bridge when I come to it."

A few minutes later they were seated at a small table and given menus. They made their selections and sipped the coffee the waitress had brought while they waited for the food.

"Who are we shopping for today?" Amanda asked, to get the conversation going again. Jordan was sitting across from her, systematically making love to her with his eyes, and she was desperate to distract him.

"Jessie and Lisa mostly, though I still need to get something for Karen and Paul."

Something made Amanda ask, "What about your parents?"

Sadness flickered in the depths of Jordan's eyes, but only for a moment. "They were killed in a car accident when I was in college," he replied.

Amanda reached out on impulse and took his hand. It seemed to her that Jordan had had more than his share of tragedy in his life, and she suddenly wanted to share her mother and stepfather with him. "I'm sorry."

He changed the subject so abruptly his remark was almost a rebuff. "What do you think Karen would like?"

Amanda was annoyed and a little hurt. "How would I know? I've never even met the woman."

The waitress returned with their breakfast, setting bacon and eggs in front of Jordan and giving Amanda wheat toast and a fruit compote. When they were alone again, Jordan replied, "Karen's thirty-five, a little on the chubby side—and totally devoted to Paul and the girls."

Amanda tried to picture the woman and failed. "Do she and Paul have children of their own?"

Jordan was mashing his eggs into his hash browns. "No."

She speared a melon ball and chewed it distractedly. "That's sad," she said after swallowing.

"These things happen," Jordan replied.

Amanda looked straight into his eyes. "I guess Karen would be pretty upset if she ever had to give Jessica and Lisa back to you," she ventured to say.

He returned her bold, assessing stare. "I wouldn't do

that to her or to the girls," he said, and there was no hint of mischief about him this time. He was completely serious.

Things were a little strained between them throughout the rest of the meal, but as soon as they reached the toy store at the mall, they were both caught up in the spirit of the season. They bought games for the girls, and dolls, and little china tea sets.

Amanda couldn't remember the last time she'd had so much fun, and her eyes were sparkling as they stuffed everything into the back of the Porsche.

From the toy store they headed to a big-name department store where, after great deliberation, they chose expensive perfume and bath powder for Karen and a sweater for her husband.

They had lunch in a fast-food hamburger place jammed to the rafters with excited kids, and by the time they returned to Amanda's apartment, she was exhausted.

"Coming in?" she asked at the door because, in spite of everything he'd said about waiting, she'd been entertaining a discreet fantasy all morning.

Jordan shook his head. "Not today," he said. "I've got to drive up to Port Townsend and look in on the kids."

Amanda was hurt that he didn't want to take her along, but she hid it well. After all, she didn't have the right to any injured feelings. "Say hello for me," she said softly.

He kissed her, lightly at first, then with an authority that brought the fantasy to the forefront of her mind. Amanda surreptitiously gripped the doorknob to keep from sliding to the floor.

"I'll be out of town most of next week," he said when the kiss was over. "Is it okay if I call?"

Is it okay? She would be shattered if he didn't. "Sure," she answered in a tone that said it wouldn't matter one way or the other because she'd be busy with her glamorous, sophisticated life.

Jordan waited until she'd unlocked the door and stepped safely inside, then she heard him walking away.

She tossed aside her purse, kicked off her shoes and hung up her coat. The coming week yawned before her like an abyss.

Ignoring the boxes still sitting on her couch, she bent distractedly to pet a meowing Gershwin, then stumbled into her bedroom, stripped off her clothes and crawled back into the unmade bed. All those hours she hadn't slept the night before were catching up with her.

Later she awoke to full darkness, the weight of Gershwin curled up on her stomach and the ringing of the phone.

Groping with one hand, she found the receiver, brought it to her ear and yawned, "Hello?"

"It's Mom," Marion announced. "How are you, dear?"

Amanda yawned again. "Tired. And hungry."

"Perfect," Marion responded with her customary good cheer and indefatigable energy. "Drag yourself over here, and I'll serve you a home-cooked meal that will put hair on your chest."

Amanda giggled, rubbing her eyes and stretching. The movement made Gershwin jump down from her stomach and land with a solid *thump* on the floor. "There's one flaw in your proposal, Mom. Who needs hair on their chest?"

Marion laughed. "Just get in your car and drive over here. Or should I send Bob, so you don't have to go wandering around in that dark parking lot behind your building?"

"There's an attendant," Amanda said, sitting up. "I'll drive over as soon as I've had a quick shower to revive myself."

Marion agreed, and the conversation came to an amicable end.

With her hair pulled back into a ponytail, Amanda was wearing jeans, a football jersey and sneakers when she arrived at her parents' house in another part of the city. And she was making a determined effort not to think about Jordan and the fact that he hadn't asked her to go to Port Townsend with him.

Her mother, a slender, attractive woman with shoulder-length hennaed hair and skillfully applied makeup, met her at the front door. Marion looked wonderful in her trim green jumpsuit, and her smile and hug were both warm.

"Bob's in the living room, cussing that string of Christmas tree lights that always goes on the blink," the older woman confided in a merry whisper.

Amanda laughed and wandered into the front room. There were cards everywhere—they lined the top of the piano, the mantel and were arranged into the shape of a Christmas tree on one wall. Amanda had been putting hers in a desk drawer that year.

"Hi, Bob," she said, giving her stepfather a hug. He was a tall man, with thinning blond hair and kindly blue eyes, and he'd been very good to Marion. Amanda loved him for that reason, if for no other.

He was standing beside a fresh-smelling, undecorated pine tree, which was, as usual, set up in front of the bay window facing the street. The infamous string of lights was in his hands. "I don't know why she won't let me throw these darned things out and buy new ones," he fussed in a conspiratorial whisper. "It's not as if we couldn't afford to."

Amanda chuckled. "Mom's sentimental about those lights," she reminded him. "They've been on the tree since Eunice and I were babies."

"Speaking of your sister," Marion remarked from the

kitchen doorway, wiping her hands on her white apron, "we had a call from her today. She's coming home for Christmas."

Amanda was pleased. This was a hard time in Eunice's life; she needed to get away from the wreckage of her marriage, if only for a week or two. "What about her job at the university?"

Marion shrugged. "I guess she's taking time off. Bob and I are picking her up at the airport late next Friday night."

Amanda left Bob to his Christmas tree light quandary and followed her mother into the bright, fragrant kitchen, where they had had so many talks before. "Seattle will be a shock to Eunice after Southern California," she remarked.

Marion gave her a playful flick with a dish towel. "Forget the harmless chitchat," she said with a grin. "What's going on in your life these days? Who's the new man, and what the devil was James doing, dropping by?"

Drawing up a battered metal stool, Amanda sat down at the breakfast counter Bob had built when he remodeled the kitchen, and started cutting up the salad vegetables her mother indicated. "James is getting divorced," she said, avoiding Marion's gaze. "Evidently he has some idea that we can get back together."

"I presume you set him straight on that."

"I did." Amanda sighed. "But I'm not sure he's getting the message. He sent me a sable jacket and a silk bikini today, along with an invitation to Hawaii and Copenhagen."

The oven door slammed a touch too hard after Marion pulled a pan of fragrant lasagna from it. "You'd never guess he was such a scumbag, would you?"

Amanda grinned and tossed a handful of chopped celery into the salad bowl. "You've got to stop watching all those cop shows, Mom. It's affecting your vocabulary."

"No way," replied Marion, who had a minor crush on Don Johnson. "So, who's the other guy?"

"Did I say there was another guy?"

"I think so," Marion replied airily, "but you wouldn't have had to. There's a sparkle in your eyes and your cheeks are pink."

"His name is Jordan Richards," Amanda said. Personally she attributed any sparkle in her eyes or color in her cheeks to the nap she'd taken.

Marion stopped slicing the lasagna to look directly at her daughter. "And?"

"And he makes me crazy, that's what."

Marion beamed. "That's a good sign."

Amanda wondered if her mother would still be of the same opinion if she knew just how hard her daughter had fallen. And how bold she'd been. "I guess so."

"What does he do for a living?" Bob asked from the kitchen doorway. Since it was a classic parental question, Amanda didn't take offense.

"He's a partner in an investment firm—Striner, Striner and Richards."

Bob whistled and tucked his hands in his pockets. "That's the big time, all right."

"Amanda doesn't care how much money he makes," Marion said with mock haughtiness. "She just wants his body."

At this, both Amanda and Bob laughed.

"Mom!" Amanda protested.

"It's true," Marion insisted. "I'd know that look anywhere. Now let's all sit down and eat."

They trooped into the dining room, where Marion had set a festive table using the special Christmas dishes that always came out of storage, along with the nativity set, on the first of December. Despite the good food and the conversation, Amanda's mind was on Jordan.

"About those presents James sent you," Marion began when she and Amanda were alone in the kitchen again, washing dishes while Bob fought it out with the Christmas tree lights. "You are sending them back, aren't you?"

Amanda favored her mother with a rueful smile. "Of course I am. First thing tomorrow."

"Some women would have their heads turned, you know, by such expensive things."

"Expensive is right. All James wants in return for his presents is my soul. What a bargain."

Marion finished washing the last pot, drained the sink and washed her hands. "I'm glad you're wise enough to see that."

Amanda shrugged. "I don't know how smart I am," she replied. "The only reason I'm so sure about everything where James is concerned is that I don't love him anymore. I'm not sure what I'd do if I still cared."

"I am," Marion said confidently. "You've always had a good head on your shoulders. That's why I think this new man must really be something."

Amanda indulged in a smile as she shook out the dish towel and hung it on the rack to dry. "He is." But her smile faded as she thought of those two little girls living far away from their father with an aunt and uncle, and of Becky, cut down before she'd even had a chance to live.

"What is it?" Marion wanted to know. She had already poured two cups full of coffee, and she carried them to the kitchen table while waiting for Amanda to answer.

Amanda sank dejectedly into one of the chairs and cupped her hands around a steaming mug. "He's a widower, and I think—well, I think he might have some problems with commitment."

"Don't they all?" Marion asked, stirring artificial sweetener into her coffee.

"Bob didn't," Amanda pointed out, her voice solemn. "He loved you enough to marry you, even though he knew you had two teenage daughters and a pile of debts."

Marion looked thoughtful. "How long have you known this man?"

"Not very long," Amanda confessed. "About ten days, I guess."

Marion chuckled and shook her head. "And you're already bandying words like 'commitment' about?"

"No. I'm only *thinking* words like 'commitment.'"

"I see. Well, this is serious. Why do you think he wouldn't want to settle down?"

Amanda ran the tip of her index finger around the rim of her coffee mug. "He has two little girls, and they don't live with him—his sister and brother-in-law are raising them. He sort of bristled when I asked him about it."

Marion laid a hand on her daughter's arm. "You're a little gun-shy, dear, and that's natural after what happened with James. Just give yourself some time."

Time. Jordan was asking the same thing of her. Didn't anyone act on impulse anymore?

Marion smiled at her daughter's frustrated expression. "Just take life one day at a time, Amanda, and everything will work out."

Amanda nodded, and after chatting briefly with her mother about Eunice's upcoming visit, she put on her coat, kissed both her parents goodbye and went out to her nondescript car.

"You be careful to park where the attendant can see

you," Bob instructed her just before she pulled away from the curb.

The attendant was on duty, and Amanda parked where there was plenty of light.

It turned out, however, that it was the inside of her building that she should have looked out for, not the parking lot.

James was sitting on the stairs again, and this time she didn't have Jordan along to act as a buffer.

"I'm glad you're here," Amanda said in a cold voice. "You can take back the fur and the bikini."

James's handsome, distinguished face fell. "You still haven't forgiven me, have you?" he asked in a pained voice, spreading his hands wide for emphasis. "Baby, how many times do I have to tell you? Madge and I haven't been in love for years."

Amanda ached as she remembered Madge Brockman's raging agony during the confrontation. "Maybe *you* haven't been," she muttered sadly.

James either didn't hear the remark or chose to ignore it. "Just let me talk to you. Please."

Having summoned up the courage she needed, Amanda passed him on the narrow stairway. "Nothing you can say will change my mind, James." She reached her door and unlocked it as he made to follow her. "So just take your presents and give them to some other fool."

Suddenly James caught her elbow in a hard grasp and wrenched her around to face him. "You're in love with Richards, aren't you? The boy wonder! You think he's pretty hot stuff, I'll bet! Well, let me tell you something— I could buy and sell him ten times over!"

Amanda pulled free of James, stormed over to the couch, picked up the boxes and shoved them at him. "Take these and get out!"

He stared at her as though she'd lost her mind.

"And while you're at it, you can just take everything *else* you've ever given me, too!"

With that, she strode into the bedroom and yanked open her jewelry box, intending to return the gold bracelet and pearl earrings she'd forgotten about. She only became aware that James had followed her when he cried out.

Turning, Amanda saw him clasp his chest with one hand and topple to the floor.

Chapter 5

⊙✦⊙

JAMES'S FACE WAS CONTORTED with pain, and he was only partially conscious. "Help—me—" he groaned.

Amanda lunged for the phone on her bedside table, punched 911 and barked out her address when someone came on the line. She followed that with a brief description of the problem.

"Someone will be there in a few minutes," the woman on the telephone assured her. "Is the patient conscious?"

James was clearly in agony, but he was awake. "Yes."

"Then just cover him up and make him as comfortable as you can—and try to reassure him. The paramedics will take care of everything else when they get there."

Amanda hung up and draped James with a quilt dragged from her bed. When it was in place, she knelt beside him and grasped his hand.

"It's going to be okay, James," she said, her eyes stinging with tears. "Everything is going to be okay."

His free hand was clenched against his chest. "Hurts—so much…crushing…"

"I know," Amanda whispered, holding his knuckles to

her lips. She could hear sirens in the distance. "Help will be here soon."

A loud knock sounded at the door just a few minutes later.

"In here!" Amanda called, and soon two paramedics burst into the bedroom, bringing a stretcher and some other equipment. She scrambled out of the way and perched on the end of her bed, still unmade from her nap earlier, watching as James was examined, loaded onto the stretcher and given oxygen and an IV.

"Any history of heart disease?" one of the men asked Amanda as he and his partner lifted the stretcher.

"I—I don't know," Amanda whispered.

"We'll be taking him to Harborview Hospital, if you'd like to come along," the other volunteered.

Amanda only sat there, gripping the edge of the mattress and shaking her head, unable to tell them she wasn't James's wife.

When the telephone rang a full hour later, she was still sitting in the exact same place.

"H-hello?"

Jordan's voice was warm and low. "Hello, Mandy. Is something wrong?"

Amanda dragged her forearm across her face, wiping away tears that had long since dried. *James had a heart attack in my bedroom,* she imagined herself answering.

She couldn't explain the situation to Jordan over the phone, she decided, sinking her teeth into her lower lip.

"Mandy?" Jordan prompted when the silence had stretched on too long.

"I thought you were in Port Townsend," she managed in a small voice that was hoarse from crying.

"I just got back," he answered. "As a matter of fact, I'm

spending the night in a hotel out by the airport, since my plane leaves so early tomorrow."

Amanda swallowed hard and did her best to sound ordinary. There would be time enough to tell Jordan what had happened when he got back from his business trip. "Wh-where are you going?"

"Chicago. Mandy, what's the matter?"

She closed her eyes. "We can talk about it when you get home."

There was a long pause while he digested that. "Is this something I should know about?"

Amanda nodded, even though he wasn't there to see her. "Yes," she admitted, "but I can't talk about it like this. I have to be with you."

"I could get in the car and be there in half an hour."

Amanda would have given anything short of her very soul to have Jordan there in the room with her, to be held and comforted by him. But she'd only known him a little while, and she had no right to make demands. "I'll be okay," she said softly.

After that, there didn't seem to be much to say. Jordan promised to phone her from Chicago the first chance he got and Amanda wished him well, then the call was over.

Amanda had barely replaced the receiver, when the bell jangled again, startling her. If it had been Jordan she would have relented and asked him to come over, but the voice on the other end of the line was a woman's.

"Well, I must say, I half expected you to be at the hospital, clutching James's hand and swearing your undying love."

Amanda closed her eyes again, feeling as though she'd been struck. The caller was Madge Brockman, James's estranged wife. "Mrs. Brockman, I—"

"Don't lie to me, please. I just spoke to someone on the

hospital staff, and they told me James had suffered a heart attack 'at the home of a friend.' It didn't take a genius to figure out just who that 'friend' might be."

Deciding to let the innuendos pass unchallenged, Amanda asked, "Is James going to be all right?"

"He's in critical condition. I'm flying in tonight to sit with him."

It was a relief to know James wouldn't be going through this difficult time alone. "Mrs. Brockman, I'm very sorry—for everything."

The woman hung up with a slam, leaving Amanda holding the receiver in one trembling hand and listening to a dial tone. Slowly she put down the phone, then crouched to unplug it from the outlet. After disconnecting the living room phone, as well, she took a long, hot shower and crawled into bed.

The sound of her alarm and faceful of bright sunshine woke her early the next morning. The memory of James lying on her bedroom floor in terrible pain was still all too fresh in her mind.

But Amanda had a job, so, even though she would have preferred to stay in bed with her face turned to the wall, she fed the cat, showered, dressed and put on makeup. Once she'd pinned her hair up in a businesslike chignon, she reconnected the telephones and called the hospital.

James was in stable condition.

Longing for Jordan, who might have been able to put the situation into some kind of perspective, Amanda pulled on her coat and gloves and left her apartment.

Late that afternoon, just as she was preparing to go home for the day, Jordan called. He was getting ready to have dinner with some clients, and there was something clipped about his voice. Something distant.

"Feeling better?" he asked.

Amanda heard a whole glacier of emotion shifting beneath the tip of the iceberg. "Not a whole lot," she admitted, "but it's nothing for you to worry about."

She could almost see him hooking his cuff links. "I read about James in the afternoon edition of the paper, Amanda."

So he knew about the heart attack, and she was no longer 'Mandy.' "Word gets around," she managed, propping one elbow on her desk and sinking her forehead into her palm.

"Is that what you didn't want to talk about last night?"

There was no point in trying to evade the question further. "Yes. It happened in my bedroom, Jordan."

He was quiet for a long time. Much too long.

"Jordan?"

"I'm here. What was he doing in your bedroom, or don't I have the right to ask?"

Tears were brimming in Amanda's eyes, and she prayed no one would step into her office and catch her displaying such unprofessional emotions. "Of course you have the right. He came over because he wanted to persuade me to start seeing him again. I told him to take back the things he gave me, and then I remembered some jewelry he'd given me a long time ago. I went to get them, and he followed me." She drew in a shaky breath, then let it out again. "He got very angry, and he was yelling at me. He just—just fell to the floor."

"My God," Jordan rasped. "What kind of shape is he in now?"

"When I called the hospital this morning, he was stable."

Jordan's voice was husky. "Mandy, I'm sorry."

Amanda didn't know whether he meant he was sorry

for doubting her, or he was sorry about James's misfortune. "I wish you were here," she said, testing the water. Everything would ride on his reply.

"So do I," he answered.

Relief flooded over Amanda. "You're not angry?"

He sighed. "No. I guess I just lost my head for a little while there. Do you want me to come back tonight, Mandy? There's a flight at midnight."

"No." She shook her head. "Stay there and set the financial world on its ear. I'll be okay."

"Promise?"

For the first time since before James's collapse, Amanda smiled. "I promise."

"In that case, I'll be back sometime on Friday night. How about penciling me into your busy schedule, Ms. Scott?"

Amanda chuckled. "Consider yourself penciled."

"In fact," he went on, "have a bag packed. I'll stop and pick you up on my way home from the airport."

"Have a bag packed?" Amanda echoed. "Wait a minute, Jordan. What are you proposing here?"

He hesitated only a moment before answering, "I want you to spend the weekend at my place."

Amanda's throat tightened. "Is this the Jordan I know—the one who insists on taking things slow and easy?"

"The same," Jordan replied, his words husky. "I need to have you under the same roof with me, Mandy. Whether we sleep together is entirely up to you."

She plucked some tissue from the box on her desk and began wiping away the mascara stains on her cheeks. "That's mighty mannerly of you, Mr. Richards," she drawled.

"See you Friday," he replied.

And after just a few more words, Amanda hung up.

It was some time before she got out of her chair, though. She'd had some violent ups and downs in the past twenty-four hours, and her emotional equilibrium was not what it might have been.

After taking a few minutes to sit with her head resting on her folded arms, Amanda finished up a report she'd been working on, then slipped into the ladies' room to repair her makeup. Leaving the elevator on the first floor of the hotel, she encountered Madge Brockman.

Mrs. Brockman was a slender, attractive brunette, expensively dressed and clearly well educated. There were huge shadows under her eyes.

"Hello, Amanda," she said.

At first Amanda thought it was just extraordinarily bad luck that she'd run into Mrs. Brockman, but moments later she realized the woman had been waiting in the lobby for her. "Hello, Mrs. Brockman. How is James?"

James's wife reached for Amanda's arm, then let her hand fall back to her side. "I was wondering if you wouldn't have a drink with me or something," she said awkwardly. "So we could talk."

Amanda took a deep breath. "If there's going to be a scene—"

Madge shook her head quickly. "There won't be, I promise."

Hoping Mrs. Brockman meant what she'd said, Amanda followed her into the cocktail lounge, where they took a quiet table in a corner. When the waiter came, Amanda asked for a diet cola and Mrs. Brockman ordered a gin and tonic.

"The doctor tells me James is going to live," Mrs. Brockman said when the drinks had arrived and the waiter was gone again.

Amanda dared a slight smile. "That's wonderful."

Madge looked at her with tormented eyes. "James admitted he went to your apartment on his own last night, and not because you'd invited him. He—he's a proud man, my James, so it wasn't easy for him to say that you'd rejected him."

Not knowing what to say, Amanda simply waited, her hands folded in her lap, her diet cola untouched.

"He's agreed to come back home to California with me when he gets out of the hospital," Mrs. Brockman went on. "I don't know if that's a new start or what, but I do know this much—I love James. If there's any way we can begin again, well, I want a fighting chance."

"It's over between James and me," Amanda said gently. "It has been for months and months."

Mrs. Brockman's eyes held a flicker of hope. "You were telling the truth six months ago when I confronted you in your office, weren't you? You honestly didn't know James was married."

Amanda sighed. "That's right. As soon as I found out, I broke it off."

"But you loved him, didn't you?"

Amanda felt a twinge of the pain that time and hard work and Jordan had finally healed. "Yes."

"Then why didn't you hold on? Why didn't you fight for him?"

"If he'd been my husband instead of yours, I would have," Amanda answered, reaching for her purse. She wasn't going to be able to choke down so much as a sip of that cola. "I'm not cut out to be the Other Woman, Mrs. Brockman. I want a man I don't have to share."

Madge Brockman smiled sadly as Amanda stood up. "Have you found one?"

"I hope so," Amanda answered. Then she laid a hand lightly on Mrs. Brockman's shoulder, just for a moment, before walking away.

JORDAN ARRIVED AT seven o'clock on Friday night, looking slightly wan, his expensive suit wrinkled from the trip. "Hi, Mandy," he said, reaching out to gather her close.

Dressed for the island in blue jeans, walking boots and a heavy beige cable-knit sweater, Amanda went into his arms without hesitation. "Hi," she answered, tilting her head back for his kiss.

He tasted her mouth before moving on to possess it entirely. "I don't suppose you're going to be merciful enough to tell me what you've decided," he said, sounding a little breathless, when the long kiss was over.

"About what?" Amanda asked with feigned innocence, and kissed the beard-stubbled underside of his chin. Of course she knew he wanted to know what the sleeping arrangements would be on the island that night.

Jordan laughed hoarsely and gave her a swat. "You know damn well 'about what'!" he lectured.

Despite the weariness she felt, Amanda grinned at him. "If you guess right, I'll tell you," she teased.

He studied her with tired, laughing, hungry eyes. "Okay, here's my guess. You're going to say you want to sleep in the guest room."

Amanda rocked back on her heels, resting against his hands, which were interwoven behind her, and said nothing.

"Well?" Jordan prodded.

"You guessed wrong," Amanda told him.

"Thank God," he groaned.

Amanda laughed. "Let's go—we'll miss the ferry."

Jordan's lips, warm and moist, touched hers. "We could just stay here—"

"No way, Mr. Richards," Amanda protested, pulling back. "You invited me to go away for the weekend and I want to *go away.*"

"What about the cat?" Jordan reasoned as Gershwin jumped onto the back of an easy chair and meowed plaintively.

"My landlady is going to take care of him," Amanda said, pulling out of Jordan's embrace and picking up her suitcase and overnight case. "Here," she said, shoving the suitcase at him.

"I like a subtle woman," Jordan muttered, accepting it.

Soon they were leaving the heart of the city behind for West Seattle, where they caught the Southworth ferry. Once they were on board the enormous white boat, however, they remained in the car instead of going upstairs to the snack bar with most of the other passengers.

"I've missed you," Jordan said, leaning back in the seat, resting his hand on Amanda's upper thigh and gripping her fingers.

"And I've missed you," Amanda answered. They'd already run through all the small talk; Jordan had told her about his business trip and she'd detailed her hectic week. By tacit agreement, they hadn't discussed James's heart attack.

Jordan splayed the fingers of his left hand and ran them through his rumpled hair, then gave a heavy sigh. He moved his thumb soothingly over Amanda's knuckles. "Do you have any idea how much I want you?"

She lifted his hand to her mouth and kissed it. "How much?"

He chuckled. "Enough to wish this were a van instead of a sports car." Jordan turned in the seat and cupped Amanda's chin in his hand. "You're sure you're ready for this?" he asked gently.

Amanda nodded. "I'm sure. How about you?"

Jordan grinned. "I've been ready since I turned around and saw you standing in line behind me."

"You have not."

"Okay," he admitted, "it started after that, when you threw five bucks on the table to pay for your Chinese food. For just a moment, when you thought I was going to refuse it, you had blue fire in your eyes."

"And?"

"And I had this fantasy about the whole mall being deserted—except for us, of course. I made love to you right there on the table."

Amanda felt a hot shiver go through her. "Jordan?"

His lips were moving against hers. "Yes?"

"We're fogging up the windows. People will notice that."

He chuckled and drew back. "Maybe we should go upstairs and have some coffee or something, then."

She felt the rough texture of his cheek against her palm. "Then what kind of fantasies would you be having?"

"I'd probably start imagining that we were right here, alone in a dark car, with nobody around." Slowly he unbuttoned the front of her coat. "I suppose I'd picture myself touching you like this." He curved his fingers around her breast.

Even through the weight of her sweater and the lacy barrier of her bra, Amanda could feel his caress in every nerve. "Jordan."

He moved his hand beneath the sweater and then, to the accompaniment of a little gasp of surprised pleasure from Amanda, beneath the bra. Cupping her warm breast, he rolled the nipple gently between his fingers. "I'd be thinking about doing this, no doubt."

Amanda was squirming a little, and her breath was quickening. "Damn it, Jordan—this isn't funny. Someone could walk by!"

"Not likely," he murmured, touching his mouth to hers as he continued to fondle her.

Although she knew she should, Amanda couldn't bring herself to push his hand away. What he was doing felt too good. "S-someone might see—they'd think…"

Jordan bent his head to kiss the pulse point at the base of her throat. "They'd think we were necking. And they'd be right." Satisfied that he'd set one nipple to throbbing, he proceeded to attend the other. "Ummm. Where were you on prom night, lady?"

"Out with somebody like you," Amanda gasped breathlessly.

Jordan chuckled and continued nibbling at her throat. She felt the snap on her jeans pop, heard the faint whisper of the zipper. "Did he do this?"

The windows were definitely fogging up. "No…" Amanda moaned as he slid his fingers down her warm abdomen to find what they sought.

"Lift up your sweater," Jordan said. "I want to taste you."

Amanda whimpered a halfhearted protest even as she obeyed, but when she felt his mouth close over a distended nipple, she groaned out loud and entangled her fingers in his hair. In the meantime he continued the other delicious mischief, causing Amanda to fidget on the seat.

She ran her hands down his back, then up to his hair again in a frantic search for a place to touch him and make him feel what she was feeling. His name fell repeatedly from her lips in a breathless, senseless litany of passion.

Just as the ferry horn sounded, Amanda arched her back and cried out in release. Her body buckled over and over again against Jordan's hand before she sagged into the seat, temporarily soothed. Gradually her breathing steadied.

"Rat," she said when her good sense returned. She righted her bra and pulled her sweater down while Jordan zipped and snapped her jeans. Not two seconds after that, the first of the passengers returning from the upper deck walked past the car and waved.

Amanda's cheeks glowed as Jordan drove off the ferry minutes later.

"Relax, Mandy," he said, shoving a tape into the slot on the dashboard. The car filled with soft music. "I'm on your side, remember?"

She ran her tongue over her lips and turned in the seat to look at him. Her body was still quivering like a resonating string on some exotic instrument. "I'm not angry—just surprised. Nobody's ever been able to make me forget where I was."

"Good," Jordan replied, turning the Porsche onto a paved road lined with towering pine trees. "I'd be something less than thrilled if that was a regular thing with you."

Amanda gazed out the window for a moment, then looked back at Jordan. "Is it a regular thing with you?" she asked, almost in a whisper.

He looked at her, but she couldn't read his expression in the darkness. "There have been women since Becky, if that's what you mean. But if it'll make you feel better, none of them has ever had quite the same effect on me that you do. And I've never taken any of them to the island."

Amanda didn't know whether she felt better or not. She peered at his towering house as they pulled into the driveway, but all she could see was a shadowy shape and a lot of dark windows.

The garage door opened at the push of a button, and Jordan pulled in and got out, then turned on the lights before coming around to open Amanda's door for her. Gripping the handle of her suitcase in one hand, the other hand pressed to the small of her back, he escorted her through a side door and into a spacious, well-designed kitchen.

Amanda stopped when he set the suitcase down on the floor. "Did you live here with Becky?" she blurted. She'd known she wouldn't have the courage to ask if she waited too long.

"No," Jordan answered, taking the overnight case from her hand and setting it on the counter.

She shrugged out of her coat, avoiding his eyes. "Oh."

"Are you hungry or anything?" Jordan asked, glancing around the kitchen as though he expected it to be changed somehow from the last time he'd seen it.

"I could use a cup of coffee," Amanda admitted. "Maybe with a little brandy in it."

Jordan chuckled and disappeared with her coat. When he came back, he was minus his suit jacket and one hand was at his throat, loosening his tie. "The coffee maker's there on the counter," he said, pointing. "The other stuff is in the cupboard above it. Why don't you start the coffee brewing while I bring my stuff in from the car?"

It sounded like a reasonable idea to Amanda, and she was thankful for something to occupy her. What she and Jordan were about to do was as old as time, but she felt like the first virgin ever to be deflowered. She nodded and busily set about making coffee.

Jordan made one trip to the garage and then went upstairs. When he returned, he stood behind Amanda and put his arms around her. "Are you sure you want coffee? It's late, and that's the regular stuff."

His lips moved against her nape, and she couldn't help the tremor that went through her. "I guess not," she managed to say.

Without another word, Jordan lifted her into his arms and carried her through the dark house and up a set of stairs. The light was on in his spacious bedroom, and Amanda murmured an exclamation at the low-key luxury of the place.

The bed was enormous, and it faced a big-screen TV equipped with a VCR and heaven-only-knows-what other kinds of high-tech electronic equipment. One wall was made entirely of windows, while another was lined with mirrors, and the gray carpet was deep and plush.

Amanda glanced nervously at the mirrors and saw her own wide eyes looking back at her.

Jordan kicked off his shoes, flung his tie aside and vanished into the bathroom, whistling and unbuttoning his shirt as he went. A few moments later Amanda heard the sound of a shower running.

Quickly she scrambled off the bed and found her suitcase, still feeling like a shy virgin. Suddenly the skimpy black nightgown she'd brought along didn't look sturdy enough, so she helped herself to a heavy terry-cloth robe from Jordan's closet. After hastily stripping, she wrapped herself in the robe and tied the belt with a double knot.

When Jordan came out sometime later, he was wearing nothing but a towel around his waist. His hair was blow-dried and combed back from his face, and his eyes twinkled at Amanda when he saw her sitting fitfully on the edge of the chair farthest from the bed.

"Scared?" he asked, approaching her and pulling her gently to her feet.

"Of course not," Amanda lied. The truth was, she was terrified.

Jordan undid the double knot at her waist as though it were nothing. "I guess I should have invited you to share my shower," he said, his voice a leisurely rumble.

"I had one at home," Amanda was quick to point out.

He opened the robe, laid it aside and looked at her, slowly and thoroughly, before meeting her eyes again. His lips quirked. "You're awfully nervous, considering how mad you were when I wouldn't make love to you last week."

Amanda moved to close the robe, but Jordan grasped her wrists and stopped her. He subjected her to another lingering assessment before pushing the garment off her shoulders with warm, gentle hands. It fell silently to the floor.

"We—we could turn the light out," she dared to suggest as Jordan lifted her again and carried her back to the bed.

"We could," he agreed, stretching out beside her, "but we're not going to."

He'd shaved, and his face was smooth and fragrant. He took her mouth and mastered it skillfully, leaving Amanda dizzy and disoriented when he drew away.

Tenderly he turned Amanda's head so that she was facing the mirrors, and a moan lodged in her throat when she saw him move his hand toward her breast.

"Jordan," she whispered.

"Shhh," he murmured against the tingling flesh of her neck, and Amanda was quiet, her eyes widening as she watched her conquering begin.

Chapter 6

⟡

THE DARK BLUE VELOUR bedspread felt incredibly soft against Amanda's bare skin, and she forgot the mirrored wall and even the lights as Jordan kissed and caressed her. Although she tried, she couldn't hold back the soft moans that escaped her, or the whispered pleas for release.

But Jordan would not be hurried. "All in good time, Mandy," he assured her, his mouth at her throat. "All in good time. Just relax."

"Relax?" Amanda gave a rueful semihysterical chuckle at the word. "Now? Are you crazy?"

He trailed his lips down over her collarbone, over the plump rounding of one breast. "Ummm-hmm," he said just before he took her nipple into his mouth. In the meantime he was stroking the tender skin on the insides of Amanda's thighs.

"Stop teasing me," she whimpered, moving her hands through his hair and over the muscular sleekness of his back.

"Never," he paused long enough to say. He left off tormenting Amanda to reach for a pillow, which he deftly tucked underneath her bottom. And then he caressed her in earnest.

Amanda was frantic. Jordan had been subjecting her to various kinds of foreplay for a week, and she simply couldn't wait any longer for gratification. Her body demanded it.

"Jordan," she pleaded, half-blind with the need of him, "*now*. Oh, please—"

She felt him part her legs, then come to rest between them. "Mandy," he rasped like a man being consumed by invisible fire. In one fierce, beautiful thrust, he was a part of her, but then he lay very still. "Mandy, open your eyes and look at me."

She obeyed, but she could barely focus on his features because she was caught up in a whirlwind of sensation. The pillow raised her to him like a pagan offering, and her body was still reacting to the single stroke he'd allowed her. "Jordan," she pleaded, and all her desperation, all her need, echoed in the name.

He kissed her thoroughly, his tongue staking the same claim that the other part of his body was making on her. Finally he began to move upon her, slowly at first, making her ask for every motion of his powerful hips, but as Amanda's passion heated, so did his own. Soon they were parting and coming together again in a wild, primitive rhythm.

Amanda was the first to scale the peak, and the splintering explosion in her senses was everything she'd hoped it would be. Her body arched like a bow with the string drawn tight, and her cries of surrender echoed off the walls.

Jordan was more restrained, but Amanda saw a panorama of emotions cross his face as he gave himself up to her in a series of short, frenzied thrusts.

They lay on their sides, facing each other, legs still entwined, for long minutes after their lovemaking had ended.

Jordan gave a raspy chuckle.

"What's funny?" Amanda asked softly, winding a tendril of his rich brown hair around one finger.

"I was just thinking of the first time I saw you. You were bored with waiting in line, so you struck up a conversation. I wondered if you were a member of some weird religious sect."

Amanda gave him a playful punch in the chest.

He laughed and leaned over to kiss her. "Let's go down to the kitchen," he said when it was over. "I'm starving."

Jordan rose off the bed and retrieved the yellow bathrobe from the floor, tossing it to Amanda. He took a hooded one of striped silk from the closet and put that on. Together, they went downstairs.

Jordan plundered the cupboards, while Amanda perched on a stool, watching him and sipping a cup of the coffee she'd made earlier. He finally decided on popcorn and thrust a bag into the microwave.

"This is a great house," Amanda said as the oven's motor began to whir. "What I've seen of it, anyway."

Jordan was busy digging through another cupboard for a serving bowl that suited him. "Thanks."

"And it's pretty big." Saying those words gave Amanda the same sense of breathless anticipation she would have felt if she'd walked outside with the intention of plunging a toe into the frigid sound.

He set a red bowl on the counter with a thump, and the grin he gave her was tinged with exasperation. "Big enough for a couple of kids, I suppose," he said.

Amanda shrugged and lifted her eyebrows. "Seems like you could fit Jessica and Lisa in here somewhere."

The popcorn was snapping like muted gunfire inside

its colorful paper bag. For just a moment, Jordan's eyes snapped, too. "We've been over that, Amanda," he said.

She took another sip of her coffee. "Okay. I was just wondering why you'd want a house like this when you live all alone."

The bell on the microwave chimed, and Jordan took the popcorn out, carefully opened the bag and dumped the contents into the bowl. The fragrance filled the kitchen, causing Amanda to decide she was hungry, after all.

"Jordan?" she prompted when he didn't reply.

He picked up a kernel and tossed it at her. "How about cooling it with the questions I can't answer?"

Amanda sighed and wriggled off the stool. "I'm sorry," she said. "Your living arrangements are none of my business, anyway."

Jordan didn't counter that statement. He simply took up the bowl and started back through the house and up the stairs. Amanda had no choice but to follow.

Returning to the bed, they settled themselves under the covers, with pillows at their backs, the popcorn between them, and Jordan switched on the gigantic TV screen.

The news was on. "I'm not in the mood to be depressed," Jordan said, working the remote control device with his thumb until a cable channel came on.

Amanda settled against his shoulder and crunched thoughtfully on a mouthful of popcorn. "I've seen this movie before," she said. "It's good."

Jordan slipped an arm around her and plunged the opposite hand into the bowl. "I'll take your word for it."

Images flickered across the screen, the popcorn diminished until there were only yellow kernels in the bottom of the bowl and the moon rose high and beautiful beyond the wall of windows. Amanda sighed and closed her eyes, feeling warm and contented.

THE NEXT THING she knew, it was morning, and Jordan was lying beside her, propped up on one elbow, smiling. "Hi," he said. He'd showered, and his breath smelled of mint toothpaste.

Amanda was well aware she hadn't and hers didn't. "Hi," she responded, speaking into the covers.

Jordan laughed and kissed her forehead. "Breakfast in twenty minutes," he said, and then he rose off the bed and walked away, wearing only a pair of jeans.

The moment he was gone, Amanda dashed to the bathroom. When he returned in the prescribed twenty minutes, he was carrying a tray and Amanda was sitting cross-legged in the middle of the bed. She'd exchanged Jordan's robe for a short nightgown of turquoise silk, and she grinned when she saw the tray in his hands.

"Room service! I'm impressed, Mr. Richards."

He set the food tray carefully in her lap, and Amanda's stomach rumbled in anticipation as she looked under various lids, finding sliced banana, toast, orange juice and two slices of crisp bacon. "Our services are *très* expensive, *madame*," he teased in a very good French accent.

"Put it on my credit card," Amanda bantered back, and picked up a slice of bacon and bit into it.

Jordan chuckled, still playing the Frenchman. "Oh, but *madame*, this we cannot do." He reached out to touch the tip of her right breast with his index finger, making the nipple turn button-hard beneath its covering of silk. "Zee policy is strictly cash and carry."

Amanda's eyes were sparkling as she widened them in mock horror. "We have a terrible problem then, *monsieur*, for I haven't a franc to my name. Not a single, solitary one!"

"This is a true pity," Jordan continued, laying a light, exploratory finger to Amanda's knee and drawing it slowly down to her ankle. "I am afraid you cannot leave this room until you have made proper restitution."

Amanda ate in silence for a time, while Jordan lingered, watching her with mischievous expectancy in his eyes. "Aren't you going to eat?" she asked, forgetting the game for a moment, and she went red the instant the words were out of her mouth.

Jordan chuckled, took the tray from her lap and set it aside. "About the price of your room, *madame*. Some agreement must be reached."

Recovered from her earlier embarrassment, Amanda slipped her arms around Jordan's neck and kissed him softly on the lips. "I'm sure we can work out something to our mutual satisfaction, *monsieur*."

He drew the silk nightgown gently over her head and tossed it away. *"Oui,"* he answered, laying a hand to her bare thigh even as he pressed her back onto the pillows.

Amanda groaned as he moved his hand from her thigh to her stomach, and when instinct caused her to draw up her knees, he claimed her with a finger in a sudden motion of his hand.

The sensation was exquisite, and Amanda arched her neck, her eyes drifting closed as Jordan choreographed a dance for her eager body. She groaned as Jordan's tongue tamed a pulsing nipple.

"Of course," he told her in that same accented English, "the customer, she must always have satisfaction first."

Only moments later, Amanda was caught in the throes of a climax that caused her to thrash on the bed and call Jordan's name even as she clutched blindly at his shoulders.

"Easy," he told her, moving his warm lips against her neck. "Nice and easy."

Amanda sagged back to the mattress, her breath coming in fevered gasps, her eyes smoldering as she watched

Jordan slip out of his jeans and poise himself above her. "No more waiting," she said. "I want you, Jordan."

He gave her only a portion of his magnificence at first, but then, when she traced the circumference of each of his nipples with a fingertip, he gave a low growl and plunged into her in earnest. And the whole splendid rite began all over again.

"A CHRISTMAS TREE?" Amanda echoed, standing in the middle of Jordan's living room with its high, beamed ceilings and breathtaking view of the mountains and Puget Sound. She was wearing jeans, sneakers and a sweatshirt, like Jordan, and there was a cozy fire snapping on the raised hearth.

"Is that so strange?" Jordan asked. "After all, it is December."

Amanda assessed the towering tinted glass window that let in the view. "It would be a shame to cover that up," she said.

Jordan pinched her cheek. "Thank you, Ebenezer Scrooge," he teased. Then he widened his eyes at her. "What is it with you and Christmas, anyway?"

With a sigh, Amanda collapsed into a cushy chair upholstered in dark blue brushed cotton, her arms folded. "I guess I'd like to let it just sort of slip past unnoticed."

"Fat chance," Jordan replied, perching on the arm of her chair. "It's everywhere."

"Yeah," Amanda said, lowering her eyes.

He put a finger under her chin and lifted. "What is it, Mandy?"

She tried to smile. "My dad left at Christmas," she admitted, her voice small as she momentarily became a little girl again.

"Ouch," Jordan whispered, pulling her to her feet. Then

he sank into the chair and drew Amanda onto his lap. "That was a dirty trick."

"You don't know the half of it," Amanda reflected, staring out at mountains she didn't really see. "We never heard another word from him, ever. He didn't even take his presents."

Jordan pressed Amanda's head against his shoulder. "Know what?" he asked softly. "Hating Christmas isn't going to change what happened."

She lifted her head so that she could look into Jordan's eyes. "It's the hardest time of the year when you've lost somebody you loved."

He kissed her forehead. "Believe me, Mandy, I know that. The first year after Becky died, Jessie asked me to write a letter to Santa Claus for her. She wanted him to bring her mother back."

Amanda smoothed the hair at Jordan's temple, even though it wasn't rumpled. "What did you do?"

"My first impulse was to get falling-down drunk and stay that way until spring." He sighed. "I didn't, of course. With some help from my sister, I explained to Jessie that even Santa couldn't pull off anything that big. It was tough, but we all got through it."

"Don't you miss them?" Amanda dared to ask, her voice barely more than a breath. "Jessica and Lisa, I mean?"

"Every day of my life," Jordan replied, "but I've got to think about what's best for them." His tone said the conversation was over, and so did his action. He got out of the chair, propelling Amanda to her feet in the process. "Let's go cut a Christmas tree."

Amanda smiled. "I haven't done that since I was still at home. My stepdad used to take my sister and me along every year—we drove all the way to Issaquah."

"So," Jordan teased with a light in his eyes, "your memories of Christmas aren't all bad."

Recalling how hard Bob had tried to make up not only for Marion's loss, but the girls', as well, Amanda had a warm feeling. "You're right," she admitted.

Jordan squinted at her and twisted the end of an imaginary mustache. This time his accent was Viennese, and he was, according to Amanda's best guess, Sigmund Freud. "Absolutely of course I am right," he said.

And then he pulled Amanda close and kissed her soundly, and she found herself wanting to go back upstairs.

That wasn't in the cards, however. Jordan had decided to cut down a Christmas tree, and his purpose was evidently unshakable. They put on coats, climbed into the small, late-model pickup truck parked beside the Porsche and sped off toward the tree farm.

Slogging up and down the rows of Christmas trees while the attendant walked behind them with a chain saw at the ready, Amanda actually felt festive. The piney smell was pungent, the air crisp, the sky painfully blue.

"How about this one?" Jordan said, pausing to inspect a twelve-footer.

Amanda looked at him in bewilderment. "What about it?"

Jordan gave her a wry glance. "Do you like it?" he asked patiently.

Amanda couldn't think why it mattered whether she liked the tree or not, but she nodded. "It's beautiful."

"We'll take this one," Jordan told the attendant.

They stood back while the man in the plaid woolen coat and blue overalls felled the tree, and followed when he dragged it off toward the truck.

By the time the tree had been paid for and tied down

in the back of Jordan's truck, it was noon and Amanda was famished.

Jordan favored her with a sidelong grin when they were seated in the cab. "Hungry?"

"How do you always know?" Amanda demanded, half surprised and half exasperated. A person couldn't have a private thought around this man.

"I'm psychic," Jordan teased, starting the engine. "Of course, the fact that you haven't eaten in four hours and your stomach is rumbling helped me come to the conclusion. How does seafood sound?"

"Wonderful," Amanda replied. The scent of the tree was on her clothes and Jordan's, and she loved its pungency.

They drove to a café overlooking the water and took a table next to a window, where they could see a ferry passing, along with the occasional intrepid sailboat and a number of other small vessels. Jordan flirted with the middle-aged waitress, who obviously knew him and gave Amanda a kindly assessment with heavily made-up eyes.

"So, Jordan Richards," the older woman teased, "you've been stepping out on me."

Jordan grinned. "Sorry, Wanda."

Wanda swatted him on the shoulder with a plastic-covered menu. "I'm always the last to know," she said. Her eyes came back to Amanda again. "Since Jordan doesn't have enough manners to introduce us, we'll just have to handle the job ourselves. My name's Wanda Carson."

Amanda smiled and held out her hand. "Amanda Scott," she replied.

After shaking Amanda's hand, Wanda laid the menus down and said, "We got a real good special today. It's baked chicken with rice."

Jordan ordered the special, perhaps to atone for "stepping out on" Wanda, but Amanda had her heart set on sea-food, so she ordered deep-fried prawns and French fries.

Amanda couldn't remember ever enjoying a meal more than she did that one, but honesty would have forced her to admit it was not the food but the company that made it special.

On the way back to Jordan's house, they stopped at a variety store, which was crowded with shopping carts and people, and bought an enormous tree stand, strings of lights, colorful glass ornaments and tinsel. "I gave away the stuff Becky and I had," he admitted offhandedly while they waited in line to pay.

A bittersweet pang squeezed Amanda's heart at the thought, but she only smiled.

They spent a good hour just dragging the massive tree inside the house and setting it up. It fell over repeatedly, and Jordan finally had to put hooks in the wall and tie it in place. It towered to the ceiling, every needle of its fresh, green branches filling the room with perfume.

"It's beautiful," Amanda vowed, resting her hands on her hips.

Jordan was bringing a high stepladder in from the garage. "So are you," he told her, setting the ladder up beside the tree. "In fact, why don't you come over here?"

Amanda laughed and shook her head. "No thanks. This fly knows a spider when she sees one."

Assuming a pretend glower, Jordan stomped over to Amanda, put his fingers against her ribs and tickled her until she toppled onto the couch, shrieking with laughter.

Then he pinned her down with his body and stretched her arms far above her head. "Hello, fly," he said, his eyes twinkling as he placed his mouth on hers.

"Hello, spider," Amanda responded, her lips touching

his. Just as the piney scent of the tree pervaded the house, Jordan's closeness permeated her senses.

Things might have progressed from there if the telephone hadn't rung, but it did, and Jordan reached over Amanda's head to grasp the receiver. There was a note of impatience in his voice when he answered, but his expression changed completely when the caller spoke.

He sat up on the edge of the couch, Amanda apparently forgotten. "Hi, Jessie. I'm fine, honey. How are you?"

Amanda suddenly felt like an eavesdropper. She got up from the couch and tiptoed out of the living room and up the stairs. She was pacing back and forth across the bedroom, when she noticed an overturned photograph on the bedside table.

An ache twisted in the pit of her stomach as she walked over, grasped the photograph and set it upright. A beautiful dark-haired woman smiled at her from the picture, her eyes full of love and laughter.

"Hello, Becky," Amanda whispered sadly, recalling the white stripe on Jordan's finger where his wedding band had been.

Becky seemed to regard her with kind understanding.

Amanda set the photo carefully back on the bedside table and stood up. A fathomless sorrow filled her; she felt as though she'd made love to another woman's husband. But this time she'd known what she was doing.

Turning her back on the picture, Amanda found her suitcase and her overnighter and packed them both. She was just snapping the catches on the suitcase, when the door opened and Jordan came in.

His gaze shifted from Amanda to the photograph and back again. "Is this about the picture?" he asked quietly.

Amanda lowered her head. "I'm not sure."

"Not good enough, Mandy." Jordan's voice was husky. "Until ten minutes ago when my daughters called, everything was okay. Then you came up here and saw the picture, and you packed your clothes."

She made herself look at him, and it hurt that he lingered in the doorway instead of crossing the room to take her into his arms. "I guess I feel like this is her house and you're her husband. It's kind of like being the other woman all over again."

"That's crazy."

Amanda shook her head. "No, it isn't. Look at your left hand, Jordan. You can still see where the wedding band was. When did you take it off? Two weeks ago? Last month?"

Jordan folded his arms. "What does it matter when I took it off? The point is, I'm not wearing it anymore. And as for the picture, I just forgot to put it away, that's all."

"The night we had dinner at my place, you told me I wasn't ready for a relationship. I think maybe *you're* the one who isn't ready, Jordan."

He sprang away from the door frame, strode across the room and took the suitcase and overnighter from Amanda's hands, tossing them aside with a clatter. "Remember me? I'm the guy whose mind you blew in that bed over there," he bit out. "Damn it, have you forgotten the way it was with us?"

"That isn't the issue!" Amanda cried, frustrated and confused.

"Isn't it?" Jordan asked, clasping her wrists in his hands and wrenching her close to him. "You're scared, Amanda, so you're looking for an excuse to make a quick exit. That way you won't have to face what's really happening here."

Amanda swallowed hard. "What *is* happening here?" she asked miserably.

Jordan withdrew from her, albeit reluctantly, except for the grip he'd taken on her hand. "I don't know exactly," he confessed, calmer now. "But I think we'd damn well better find out, don't you?"

At Amanda's nod, he led her out of the bedroom and down the stairs again. She sank despondently into an easy chair while he built up the fire on the hearth.

"I don't want to be the other woman, Jordan," she said when he turned to face her.

He crossed the room, knelt in front of her and placed one of her blue-jeaned legs over each arm of the chair, setting her afire all over again as he stroked the insides of her thighs. "You're the *only* woman," he answered, and he nipped at one of her nipples through the bra and sweatshirt that covered it. "Show me your breasts, Mandy."

It was a measure of her obsession with him that she pulled up her sweatshirt and unfastened the front catch on her bra so that she spilled out into full view. He grasped her knees, holding them up on the arms of the chair as he leaned forward to tease one nipple with his tongue.

Amanda remembered that there was somebody else in Jordan's life, but she couldn't remember a face or a name. Perspiration glowed on her upper lip as Jordan took his pleasure at her breasts, moving his right hand from one knee to the other, slowly following an erotic path.

Finally, when Amanda was half-delirious with wanting, he kissed his way down over her belly and lightly bit her through the denim at the crossroads of her thighs.

Amanda moaned helplessly and moved to close her legs, and Jordan allowed that, but only long enough to unsnap her jeans and dispose of them, along with her panties and shoes. Then he put her knees back into their original position, opened his own jeans and took her in a powerful, possessive thrust so pleasurable that she nearly fainted.

She longed to embrace Jordan with her legs, as well as her arms, but he didn't permit it. It was a battle of sorts, but Amanda couldn't be sure who was the loser, since every lunge Jordan made wrung a cry of delight from her throat.

Her climax made her give a long, low scream as she pressed her head into the chair's back. Jordan, both hands still holding her knees, uttered a desolate groan as his body convulsed and he spilled himself into Amanda.

Once the gasping aftermath was over and Amanda's breathing and heart rate had gone back to normal, she was angry. Jordan hadn't forced her, but he had turned her own body against her, and that was a power no one had ever had over Amanda before.

She moved to fasten her bra, but Jordan, still breathing hard, his eyes flashing with challenge, interrupted the action and took her tingling breasts gently but firmly into his hands. "We're not through, Amanda," he ground out.

"The hell we aren't!" she sputtered.

Keeping his hands where they were, he turned his head and lightly kissed the back of her knee.

Amanda trembled. "Damn it, Jordan…"

He moved his lips along her inner thigh, leaving a trail of fire behind them, and slid one of his hands down to rest on her lower abdomen, finding the hidden plum and making a small circle around it with the pad of his thumb. "Yes?" he answered at his leisure.

A whimper escaped Amanda, and Jordan chuckled at the sound, still working his lethal magic. "You were saying?" he prompted huskily.

Amanda reached backward to grasp the top of the chair, fearing she would fly away like a rocket if she didn't. "We're n-not through," she concluded.

Her reward was another baptism in sweet fire, and it made a believer out of her through and through.

THE NEXT DAY was cold and pristinely beautiful, and Jordan and Amanda decided to leave the tree undecorated and take a drive around the island. That was when Amanda saw the house.

It stood between Jordan's place and the ferry terminal, and she couldn't imagine why she hadn't noticed it before. It was white with green shutters, and very Victorian, and there was even a lighthouse within walking distance. Best of all a For Sale sign stood in the yard, swinging slowly in the salty breeze.

"Jordan, stop!" Amanda cried, barely able to restrain herself from reaching out and grasping the steering wheel.

After giving her one half-amused, half-bewildered look, Jordan steered the truck onto the rocky, rutted driveway leading past a tumbledown mailbox and a few discarded tires and empty rabbit pens.

Amanda was out of the truck a moment after they came to a jolting halt.

Chapter 7

⟨०⟩

THE GRASS IN THE YARD was overgrown, and the outside of the building needed paint, but neither of these facts dampened Amanda's enthusiasm. She hurried around the back of the house and found a screened porch that ran the full length of the place. On the upper floor there were lots of windows, providing an unobstructed view of the water and the mountains.

It was the perfect place for a bed and breakfast, and Amanda felt a thrill of excitement race through her blood.

A moment later, though, as Jordan caught up to her, her spirits plummeted. The place had obviously been neglected for a long time and would cost far more than she had to spend. People were willing to pay a premium price for waterfront property.

"I could help you," Jordan suggested, reading her mind.

Amanda quickly shook her head. A personal loan could poison their relationship if things went wrong later on, and besides, she wanted the accomplishment to be her own.

After they'd walked around the house and looked into the windows, Amanda wrote down the name of the real estate company and the phone number, tucking the information into her purse.

She could hardly wait to get to a telephone, and Jordan, discerning this, headed straight for the café where Wanda worked. While he chatted with the waitress and ordered clubhouse sandwiches, Amanda dialed the real estate agency's number and got an answering machine. She left her name and her numbers for home and work in Seattle and returned to the table.

"No luck?" Jordan asked as she sat down across from him in the booth and reached for the cup of coffee he'd ordered for her.

"They'll get in touch," Amanda answered with a little shrug. "I don't know why I'm so excited. I probably won't be able to afford the place, anyway."

Jordan's eyes twinkled as he looked at her. "That was a negative thing to say," he scolded. "You're not going to get anywhere in life if you don't believe in yourself."

"Thank you, Norman Vincent Peale," Amanda said somewhat irritably as she wriggled out of her coat and set it aside. "Just because you could probably write a check for the place on the spot doesn't mean I'd be able to."

The clubhouse sandwiches arrived, and Jordan picked up a potato chip and crunched it between his teeth. "Okay, so I have a knack with money. I should have—it's my business. And I don't understand why you won't let me help."

"I have my reasons, Jordan."

"Like what?"

Amanda shrugged. "Suppose in two days or two weeks we decide we don't want to see each other anymore. If I owed you a big chunk of money, things could get pretty sticky."

Jordan shook his head. "That's just an excuse, Mandy.

People borrow money to start businesses every day of the week."

In the short time they'd known each other, Amanda had to admit that Jordan had learned to read her well. "I want it to be mine," she confessed. "Is that too much to ask?"

"Nope," Jordan replied good-naturedly, and after that they dropped the subject and talked of other things.

They spent the rest of the afternoon exploring the beach fronting the property Amanda wanted to buy, and the time sped by. Too soon the weekend was over and Jordan was putting her suitcase and overnighter in the back of the Porsche.

Even the prospect of separation was difficult for Amanda. "How about having dinner at my place before you come back?" she asked somewhat shyly as Jordan pushed the button to turn on the answering machine in his study.

He smiled at her. "Smooth talker," he teased.

Amanda barely stopped herself from suggesting that he bring fresh clothes and a toothbrush, as well. All her life she'd been a patient, methodical person, but where this man was concerned, she had a dangerous tendency to be impulsive. She trembled a little when Jordan kissed her, and devoutly hoped he hadn't noticed.

During the ferry ride back to Seattle, they drank coffee in the snack bar, and when they reached the city, Amanda asked Jordan to stop at a supermarket. She bought chicken, fresh corn and potatoes.

Gershwin greeted them with a mournful meow when they entered Amanda's apartment. Appeasing his pique was easy, though; Jordan simply opened a can of cat food and set it on the floor for him.

Amanda was busy cutting up the chicken and washing the corn, so Jordan wandered back into the living room and used the log left from his last visit to start a fire on the hearth.

"We forgot to decorate your tree," Amanda said when he returned to the kitchenette to lean against the counter, watching her put floured chicken pieces into a hot skillet.

"It'll keep," Jordan answered. When she'd finished putting the chicken on to brown, he took her into his arms. "Mandy, Karen's bringing the girls to Seattle Friday night. They're going to spend two weeks with me."

Amanda was pleased, but a little puzzled that he'd waited until now to mention it. "That's great. I guess you found that out when the kids called."

He nodded.

"Why didn't you tell me?"

Jordan shrugged. "If you recall, we were a little busy after that phone call," he pointed out. "And then I was trying to work out how to ask you to spend next weekend on the island with us."

Amanda broke away long enough to turn the chicken pieces and put the corn on to boil. "I don't think that would be a very good idea, Jordan," she finally said, looking back at him over her shoulder. "After all, we aren't married, and we don't want to confuse the kids."

"How could we confuse them? They're not teenagers, Amanda. They're too small to understand about sex."

Amanda shook her head. "Kids know something is going on, whether they understand what it is or not. They sense emotional undercurrents, Jordan, and I don't want to get off on the wrong foot with them." She turned down the heat under the chicken and covered it with a lid. "Now how about a glass of wine?"

Jordan nodded his assent, but he looked distracted. After uncorking the bottle and pouring a glass for himself and for Amanda, he wandered into the living room.

Amanda followed, perching on the arm of the sofa while he stood at the window, watching the city lights.

"Come on, Jordan," she urged gently. "'Fess up. You're scared, aren't you? When was the last time you were responsible for your kids for two weeks straight?"

There was a hint of anger in his eyes when he turned to look at her. "I've been 'responsible' for them since they were born, Amanda."

"Maybe so," she retorted quietly, "but somebody else did the nitty-gritty stuff—first Becky, then your sister. You don't have any idea how to really take care of your daughters, do you?"

Jordan was offended initially, but then his ire gave way to a sort of indignant resignation. "Okay," he admitted, "you've got me. I wanted you to spend next weekend with us because I need moral support."

Amanda went back to the kitchen for plates and silverware, then began to set the small, round table in the living room. "You know my phone number," she said. "If you want moral support, you can call me. But you don't need somebody else in the way when you're bonding with your kids, Jordan."

"Bonding? Hell, you've been reading too many pop psychology books."

"You have a right to your opinion," Amanda responded, "but I'm not going to be there to act as a buffer. You're on your own with this one, buddy."

Jordan gave her an irate look, but then his expression softened and he took her in his arms. "Maybe I can't change your mind," he told her huskily, "but I can sure as hell let you know what you'll be missing."

Amanda pushed him away. "The chicken will burn."

Jordan chuckled. "Okay, Mandy, you win. For now."

Twenty minutes later they sat down to a dinner of fried

chicken, corn on the cob, mashed potatoes and gravy. Amanda's portable TV set was turned to the evening news, and the ambience of the evening was quietly domestic.

When they were through eating, Amanda began clearing the table, only to have Jordan stop her by slipping his arms around her waist from behind. "Aren't you forgetting something?" he asked, his voice a low rumble as he bent his head to kiss her nape and sent a jagged thrill swirling through her system.

"W-what?" Amanda asked, already a little breathless.

Jordan slid his hands up beneath her shirt to cup the undersides of her breasts. "Dessert," he answered.

Amanda was trembling. "Jordan, the food—"

"The food will still be here when we're through."

"No, it won't," Amanda argued, following her protest with a little moan as Jordan unfastened her bra and rubbed her nipples to attention with the sides of his thumbs. "G-Gershwin will eat it."

His lips were on her nape again. "Who cares?"

Amanda realized that she didn't. She turned in Jordan's embrace and tilted her head back for his kiss.

While taming her mouth, he grasped her hips in his hands and pressed her close, making her feel his size and power.

She was dazed when he drew back, pliant when he steered her toward the bedroom and closed the door behind them.

The small room was shadowy, the bed neatly made. Jordan set Amanda on the edge of the mattress and knelt to slowly untie her shoes and roll down her socks. For a time he caressed her feet, one by one, and Amanda was surprised at the sensual pleasure such a simple act could evoke.

When she was tingling from head to foot, he rose and

pulled her shirt off over her head, then smoothed away the bra he'd already opened. He pressed Amanda onto her back to unsnap her jeans and remove them and her panties, and she didn't make a move to stop him. All she could do was sigh.

After the last of her garments was tossed away, Jordan began removing his own clothes. They joined Amanda's in a pile on the floor.

"Jordan," Amanda whispered, entwining her fingers in his hair as he stretched out beside her, "don't make me wait. Please."

He gave her a nibbling kiss. "So impatient," he scolded sleepily, trailing his lips down over her chin to her neck. "Lovemaking takes time, Mandy. Especially if it's good."

Amanda remembered their session in Jordan's living room the day before. It had been fast and ferocious, and if it had been any better, it would have killed her. She moaned as Jordan made a slow, silken circle on her belly with his hand. "I can only stand so much pleasure!" she whimpered in a lame protest.

Jordan chuckled. "We're going to have to raise your tolerance," he said.

TWO HOURS LATER, when both Jordan and Amanda were showered and dressed and the table had been cleared, he reached for his jacket and shrugged into it. Amanda had to fight back tears when he kissed her, as well as pleas for him to spend the night. On a practical, rational level, she knew they both needed to let things cool down a little so they could get some perspective.

But when she'd closed the door behind Jordan, Amanda rested her forehead against it for a long moment and bit down hard on her lower lip. It was all she could do not to run out into the hallway and call him back.

Slowly she turned from the door and went about her usual Sunday night routine, choosing the outfits she would wear to work during the coming week, manicuring her nails and watching a mystery program on TV.

The bed was rumpled, and it still smelled of Jordan's cologne and their fevered lovemaking. Forlornly Amanda remade it and crawled under the covers, the small TV she kept in her room turned to her favorite show.

Two minutes after that week's victim had been done in, the telephone rang. Hoping for a call from the real estate agent or from Jordan, Amanda reached for the receiver on her bedside table and answered on the second ring.

"Amanda?"

The voice was Eunice's, and she sounded as though she'd been crying for a week.

Amanda spoke gently to her sister, because they'd always been close. "Hi, kid," she said, for she was the older of the two and Eunice had been "kid" since she was born. "What's the problem?"

"It's Jim," Eunice sobbed.

Now there's a real surprise, Amanda thought ruefully while she waited for her sister to recover herself.

"There's been someone else the whole time," Eunice wept, making a valiant, sniffling attempt to get a hold on herself.

Amanda was painfully reminded of what Madge Brockman had gone through because of her. "Are you sure?" she asked gently.

"She called this afternoon," Eunice said. "She said if Jim wouldn't tell me, she would. He's moved in with her!"

For a moment Amanda knew a pure, white-hot rage entirely directed at her soon-to-be ex-brother-in-law. Since her anger wouldn't help Eunice in any way, she counted to herself until the worst of it had passed. "Honey, this doesn't look like something you can change. And that means you have to accept it."

Eunice was quiet for almost a minute. "I guess you're right," she admitted softly. "I'll try, Amanda."

"I know you will," Amanda replied, wishing she could be nearer to her sister to lend moral support.

"Mom tells me you've met a guy." Eunice snuffled. "That's really great, Mand. What's he like?"

Amanda remembered making love with Jordan on the very bed she was lying in, and a wave of heat rolled over her. She also remembered the photograph of Becky and the white strip of skin on Jordan's left hand ring finger. "He's moderately terrific," she answered demurely.

Eunice laughed, and it was a good sound to hear. "Maybe I can meet him when I come home next week."

"I'd like that," Amanda replied. "And I'm glad you're coming home. How long can you stay?"

"Perhaps forever," Eunice replied, sounding blue again. "Everywhere I turn here, there's another reminder of Jim staring me in the face."

Amanda spoke gently. "Don't misunderstand me, sis, because I'd love for you to live in Seattle again, but I hope you realize you can't run away from your problems. You'll still have to find a way to work them out."

"That might be easier with you and Mom and Bob nearby," Eunice said quietly.

"You know we'll help in any way we can," Amanda assured her.

"Yeah, I know. It means the world to know you're there for me, Mand—you and Mom and Daddy Bob. But listen, I'll get off the line now because I know you're probably trying to watch that murder show you like so much. See you next week."

Amanda smiled. "You just try and avoid it, kid."

After that, the two sisters said their goodbyes and hung up. Amanda, having lost track of her TV show, switched off the set and the lamp on her bedside table and wriggled down between the covers.

How empty the bed seemed without Jordan sprawled out beside her, taking more than his share of the space.

Two DAYS PASSED before Amanda saw Jordan again; they met for lunch in a hotel restaurant.

"Did you ever hear from the real estate agent?" Jordan asked, drawing back Amanda's chair for her.

She sank into it, inordinately relieved just to be with him again. She wondered, with a chill, if she wasn't letting herself in for a major bruise to the soul somewhere down the line. "She called me at work yesterday. The down payment is five times what I have in the bank."

Jordan sat down across from her and reached out for her hand, which she willingly gave. "Mandy, I can lend you the money with no problem."

"You must be loaded," Amanda teased, having no intention of accepting, "if you can make an offer like that without even knowing how much is involved."

He grinned one of his melting grins. "I confess—I called the agency and asked."

Amanda shook out her napkin and placed it neatly on her lap. It was time to change the subject. "Who's going to take care of the kids while you're working?" she asked.

"Much to the consternation of Striner and Striner," said Jordan, "I'm taking two weeks off. I figure I'm going to need all my wits about me."

Amanda laughed. "No doubt about that."

Jordan leaned forward in his chair with a look of mock reprimand on his face. "I'll thank you to extend a little sympathy, here, Ms. Scott. You're looking at a man who has no idea how to take care of two little girls."

"They need to eat three times a day, Jordan," Amanda pointed out with teasing patience, "and it's a good idea if they have a bath at night, followed by about eight hours of sleep. Beyond that, they mainly just need to know they're loved."

Jordan was turning his table knife from end to end. "You're sure you won't come out for the weekend?"

"My sister is arriving on Friday night—in pieces, from the sounds of things."

"Ah," Jordan answered as a waiter brought menus and filled their water glasses. "The recipient of *Gathering Up the Pieces,* the pop psychology book of the decade. I'm sorry to hear things haven't improved for her."

Amanda sighed. "They've gone from bad to worse, actually," she replied. "But there's hope. Eunice is intelligent, and she's attractive, too. She'll work through this."

"Maybe she could work through the first part of it—say next Saturday and Sunday—without you?"

Amanda shook her head as she opened her menu. "Don't you ever give up?"

"Never," Jordan replied. "It's my credo—keep bugging them until they give in to shut you up."

Amanda laughed. "Such sage advice."

They made their selections and placed their orders before the conversation continued. Jordan reached out and took Amanda's hand again when the waiter was gone.

"I've missed you a whole lot."

"Then how come you didn't call?"

"I've been in meetings day and night, Amanda. Besides, I figured if I heard your voice, I wouldn't be able to stop myself from walking into your office and taking you on your desk."

Amanda's cheeks burned, but she knew her eyes were sparkling. "Jordan," she protested in a whisper, "this is a public place."

"That's why you're not lying on the table with your skirt up around your waist," Jordan answered with a perfectly straight face.

"You have to be the most arrogant man I've ever met," Amanda told him, but a smile hovered around her mouth. She couldn't very well deny that Jordan could make her do extraordinary things.

The waiter returned with their seafood salads, sparing Jordan from having to answer. His reply probably would have been cocky, anyway, Amanda figured.

The conversation had turned to more conventional subjects, when Madge Brockman suddenly appeared beside the table. There was a look of infinite strain in her face as she assessed Amanda, then Jordan.

Amanda braced herself, having no idea whether to expect a civil greeting or violent recriminations. "Hello, Mrs. Brockman," she said as Jordan pushed back his chair to stand. "I'd like you to meet Jordan Richards."

"Do sit down," Madge Brockman said when she and Jordan had shaken hands.

Jordan remained standing. "How is your husband?" he asked, knowing Amanda wouldn't dare ask.

"He's recovering," Madge replied with a sigh. "And he's adamant about wanting a divorce."

"I'm sorry," Amanda said softly.

The older woman managed a faulty smile. "I'll get over it, I guess. Well, if you'll excuse me, I'm supposed to meet my attorney, and I see him sitting right over there."

Jordan dropped back into his chair when Mrs. Brockman had walked away. "Are you okay?" he asked.

Amanda pushed her salad away. Even though she'd done

it inadvertently, she was partly responsible for destroying Mrs. Brockman's marriage, and the knowledge was shattering. "No," she answered. "I'm not okay."

"It wasn't your fault, Amanda."

There it was again, that strange clairvoyance of his.

"Yes, it was—part of it, at least. I didn't even bother to ask if James was married. And now look what's happening."

Jordan gave a ragged sigh. Apparently his appetite had fled, too, for he set down his fork and sank back in his chair, one hand to his chin.

"The man's marital status wouldn't have made a difference to a lot of women, you know," he remarked. "For instance, you're the first one I've dated who's asked me whether I was married."

"Okay, so infidelity is widespread. So is cocaine addiction. That doesn't make either of them right."

Jordan raised his eyebrows. "I wasn't saying it did, Mandy. My point is, you're being too damn hard on yourself. So you made a mistake. Welcome to the human race."

Amanda met Jordan's gaze. "Were you faithful to Becky?" she asked, having no idea why it was suddenly so important to know. But it was.

"That's none of your damn business," Jordan retorted politely, making a steeple under his chin with his hands, "but I'll answer, anyway. I was true to my wife, and she was true to me."

Amanda had known, in some corner of her heart, that Jordan was a man of his word, and she believed him. "Were you ever tempted?"

"About a thousand times," he replied. "But there's a difference between thinking about something and doing it, Mandy. Now, do you want to ask me about my bank balance or my tax return? Or maybe how I voted in the last election?"

Amanda smiled. "You've made your point, Mr. Richards. I'm being nosy. But I'm glad you were faithful to Becky."

"So am I," Jordan said, as by tacit agreement they rose to go. "When am I going to see you again, Mandy?"

Amanda held off answering until the bill was paid and they were walking down the sidewalk, wending their way through hordes of Christmas shoppers. "When do you want to see me?"

"As soon as possible."

"You could come to dinner tonight."

"Amanda Scott, you have a silver tongue. I'll bring the wine and the food, so don't cook."

Amanda's smile was born deep inside her, and it took its time reaching her mouth. "Seven?"

"Eight," Jordan said as they stopped in front of the Evergreen Hotel. "I have a meeting, and it might run late."

She stood on tiptoe to kiss him briefly. "I'll be waiting, Mr. Richards."

He grinned as he rubbed a tendril of her hair between his fingers. "Good," he answered.

His voice made Amanda's knees quiver beneath her green suede skirt.

WHEN AMANDA REACHED her desk, there was a message waiting for her. In a flash, work—and Jordan—fled her uppermost thoughts. The hospital had called about James, and the matter was urgent.

Amanda's fingers trembled as she reached for the panel of buttons on her telephone. She punched out the numbers written on the message slip and, when an operator answered, asked for the designated extension.

"Intensive Care," a sunny voice said when the call was put through. "This is Betsy Andrews."

Amanda sank into her desk chair, a terrible headache throbbing beneath her temples. "My name is Amanda Scott," she said in a voice that sounded surprisingly crisp and professional. "I received a message asking me to call about Mr. Brockman."

There was a short silence while the nurse checked her records. "Yes. Mr. Brockman isn't doing very well, Ms. Scott. And he's constantly asking for you."

Amanda closed her eyes and rubbed one temple with her fingertips. She'd broken up with James long ago, and had refused his gifts and his requests for a reconciliation. When was it going to be over? "I see."

"His wife has explained the—er—situation to us," the nurse went on, "but Mr. Brockman still insists on see-ing you."

"What is his doctor's recommendation?"

"It was his idea that we call you. We all feel that, well, maybe Mr. Brockman would calm down if he could just have a short visit from you."

Amanda glanced at her watch. Her headache was so intense that the numbers blurred. "I could stop by briefly after work." James had won this round. Under the circum-stances, there was no way she could refuse to visit him. "That would be about six o'clock."

Betsy Andrews sounded relieved. "I'll be off duty then, but I'll make a note in the record and tell Mr. Brockman you'll be coming in."

"Thank you," Amanda said with a defeated sigh. Once she'd hung up, she reached for the phone again, planning to call Jordan, but her hand fell back to the desk. She was a grown woman, and this was her problem, not Jordan's.

She couldn't go running to him every time some difficulty came up.

Pulling open her desk drawer, Amanda took out a bottle of aspirin, shook two tablets into her palm and swallowed them with water from the tap in her bathroom. Then she rolled up her sleeves and did her best to concentrate on her work.

At six-fifteen she approached James's door in the Intensive Care Unit, having gotten directions from a nurse.

He was lying in a room banked with flowers. Tubes led into his nose and the veins in both his hands. He seemed to sense Amanda's arrival and turned to look at her.

She approached the bed. "Hello, James," she said.

"You came," he managed, his voice hoarse and broken.

She nodded, unable for the moment to speak. And not knowing what to say.

"I'm going to die," he told her.

Amanda shook her head, her eyes filling with tears. She didn't love James anymore, but she had once, and it was hard to see him suffer. "No."

His eyes half-closed, he pleaded with her, "Just tell me there's a chance for us, and I'll have a reason not to give up."

Amanda started to tell him there was someone else, that there could never be anything between the two of them again, but something stopped her in the last instant. Some instinct that he really meant to die if she didn't give him hope, and she couldn't just abandon him to death. She bit down on her lower lip, then whispered, "All right, James. Maybe we could—start again."

Chapter 8

JORDAN WAS DUE TO ARRIVE a little more than twenty minutes after Amanda reached her apartment. Gershwin was hungry and petulant, and the boxes containing the fur jacket and the skimpy bikini James had sent were still sitting on the hallway table. Amanda had intended to return them to the department store and ask the clerk to credit James's account, but she hadn't gotten around to it.

Now, without stopping to analyze her motives—certainly she meant to tell Jordan about her promise to James—she stuffed the boxes into the back of her bedroom closet and hastily changed into a silky beige jumpsuit. She had just misted herself with cologne, when the door buzzer sounded.

After drawing a deep breath to steady herself, Amanda dashed through the apartment and opened the door. Jordan was standing in the hallway, a tired grin on his face, a bottle of wine and several bags from a Chinese take-out place in his arms.

Looking at him, Amanda thought of how it would be to have him walk out of her life forever, and promptly lost her courage. She told herself it wasn't the right time to tell him about James.

Smiling shakily, she took the wine and fragrant bags from him and stood on tiptoe to kiss his cheek.

He shrugged out of his overcoat and hung it on the coat tree while Amanda carried the food to the table. She hadn't put out place settings yet, so she hurried back to the kitchenette for plates, silverware, wineglasses and a cork screw.

Jordan looked at her strangely when she returned. "Is something wrong, Mandy?"

Amanda swallowed. *Tell him,* ordered the voice of reason. *Just come right out and tell him you're planning to visit James in the hospital until he's out of danger.* "Wr-wrong?" she echoed.

"You seem nervous."

Amanda imagined the scenario: herself telling Jordan that she meant to pretend she was still in love with James just until he was stronger, Jordan saying the idea was stupid, getting angry, walking out. Maybe forever. "I'm okay," she lied.

Jordan popped the cork on the wine bottle. "If you say so," he said with a sigh, and they both sat down at the table to consume prawns, fried noodles and chow mein. Their conversation, usually so free and easy, was guarded.

When they were through with dinner, Jordan made Amanda stay at the table, nursing a second glass of wine, while he cleared away the debris of their meal. Returning, he put gentle hands on Amanda's shoulders and began massaging her tense muscles.

"Will you stay tonight?" she asked, holding her breath after the words were out. She needed Jordan desperately, but at the same time she knew guilt would prevent her from enjoying their lovemaking.

Jordan sighed. "You've been through a lot lately, Mandy. I think it would be better if we let things cool off a little."

She turned to look up at him with worried eyes. "Is this the brush-off, Mr. Richards?"

He smiled and bent to kiss her forehead. "No. I just think you need some extra rest." With that, he turned and crossed the room to the entryway. He reached for his overcoat and put it on.

Amanda stood up quickly and went to him. Even though Jordan didn't know what was going on, he sensed something, and he was already distancing himself from her. She had to tell him. "Jordan—"

He interrupted her with a kiss. "Good night, Mandy. I'll talk to you tomorrow."

Amanda tried to call out to him, but the words stopped in her throat. In the end she simply closed the door, locked it and stood there leaning against the panel, wondering how she'd gotten herself into such a mess.

TRUE TO HIS word, Jordan called her the next morning at work, but their conversation was brief because he was busy and so was Amanda. She threw her mind into her job in order to distract herself from the fact that she had, in effect, lied to him. And a chilling instinct told her that deceit was one thing Jordan wouldn't tolerate.

At six-thirty that evening, Amanda walked into James's room in Intensive Care, after first making sure Madge wasn't there. She was wearing jeans and a sweater, and was carrying a bouquet of flowers from the gift shop downstairs.

He smiled thinly when he saw her and extended one hand. "Hello, Amanda."

She took his hand and bent to kiss his forehead. "Hi. How are you feeling today?"

"They're moving me out of the ICU tomorrow," he answered.

But he looked very sick to Amanda. He was gaunt, and his skin still had a ghastly pallor to it.

"That's good."

"You look wonderful."

Amanda averted her eyes for a moment, feeling like a highly paid call girl. What she was doing was all wrong, but how could she turn her back on another human being, allowing him to give up and die? That would be heartless. "Thanks."

James's grip on her hand was remarkably firm. "You're better off without that Richards character," he confided. "He might have made his mark in the business world, but he's really nothing more than an overgrown kid. Killed his own wife with his recklessness, you know."

Amanda was willing to go only so far with this charade, and listening to James bad-mouth Jordan was beyond the boundary. Somewhat abruptly she changed the subject. "Is there anything you'd like me to bring you? Magazines or books?"

He shook his head. "All I want is to know I'm going to get well and see you wear—and not wear—that blue bikini."

Feeling slightly ill, Amanda nonetheless managed a smile. "You shouldn't be thinking thoughts like that," she scolded. She had to get out of that room or soon she'd be smothered. "Listen, the nurses made me promise not to stay too long, so I'm going now. But I'll be back after work tomorrow."

When she would have walked away, James held her fast by the hand. "I want a kiss first," he said, a shrewd expression in his eyes.

Amanda shook her head, unable to grant his request.

She smiled brittlely and said in a too-bright voice, "You're too ill for that." Ignoring his obvious disappointment, she squeezed his hand once and then dashed out of the room, calling a hasty farewell over her shoulder.

Only when Amanda was outside in the crisp December air was she able to breathe properly again. She went home, flung her coat onto the couch and took a long, scalding hot shower. No matter how she tried, though, she couldn't wash away the awful feeling that she was selling herself.

In an effort to escape, Amanda telephoned the real estate agency on Vashon Island the next morning to see if the Victorian house had been sold. It hadn't, and even though she had no means of buying it herself, the news lifted her flagging spirits.

She visited James that night, and the next, and he seemed to be improving steadily. He told her repeatedly that she was his only reason for holding on.

By Friday, when Eunice was due to arrive, Amanda was practically a wreck. She had been avoiding Jordan's calls for several days, and she could barely concentrate on her job.

Marion noticed her elder daughter's general dishevelment when they met at the airport in front of the gate assigned to Eunice's flight. "What on earth is the matter with you?" she demanded. "You have bags under your eyes and you must have lost five pounds since I saw you last week!"

Amanda would have given anything to be able to confide in her mother, but she didn't want to spoil Eunice's homecoming—her sister would need all of Marion's and Bob's support. She shrugged and managed a halfhearted smile. "You know how it is. Falling in love takes a lot out of a person."

Marion's gaze was slightly narrowed and alarmingly shrewd. "You're not fooling me, you know," she said. "But just because I don't have time to drag it out of you now doesn't mean I won't."

Bob was just returning from parking the car, and he smiled and gave Amanda a hug. "You're looking a little peaky," he pointed out good-naturedly.

"She's up to something," Marion informed him just before the passengers from Eunice's flight began pouring out of the gate.

Amanda was the first to reach her brown-eyed, dark-haired sister, and they embraced. Tears stung both their eyes.

After the usual hassles of getting the luggage from the baggage carousel and fighting the traffic out of the airport, they drove back to the family home. Eunice chattered the whole time about how glad she was to be in Seattle again, how miserable she'd been in California, how she wished she'd never met Jim, let alone married him. By the time they reached the quiet residential area where Bob and Marion lived, Eunice had exhausted herself.

She stumbled into the room she and Amanda had once shared and collapsed on one of the twin beds.

Amanda took a seat on the other one. "I'm glad you're back," she said.

Her sister sat up on the bed and began unbuttoning her coat. "I didn't exactly return in triumph, like I thought I would," Eunice observed sadly. "Oh, Amanda, my life is a disaster area."

"I know what you mean," Amanda answered sadly, thinking of the deception she hadn't had the courage to straighten out.

Eunice yawned. "Maybe tomorrow we can put our heads together and figure out how to get ourselves back on track."

With a smile, Amanda opened her sister's suitcase and

found a nightgown for her. "Here," she said, tossing the billow of pink chiffon into Eunice's lap. "Get some sleep."

When Eunice had disappeared into the adjoining bathroom, Amanda returned to the kitchen. Her mother was sitting at the table, sipping decaffeinated coffee, and Bob was in the living room, listening to the news.

"How's Eunice?" Marion asked.

Amanda wedged her hands into the front pockets of her worn brown corduroy pants. "She'll be okay once she gets a perspective on things."

"And what about you?"

"I'm in a fix, Mom," Amanda admitted, staring at the darkened window over the kitchen sink. "And I don't know how to get out of it."

Marion went to the counter, poured a cup of coffee from the percolator and brought it back to the table for Amanda. "Sit down and tell me about it."

Amanda sank into the chair. "Some very good things have been happening between Jordan and me," she said, closing her fingers around the cup to warm them. "I never thought I'd meet anybody like him."

Marion smiled. "I feel the same way about Bob."

Amanda touched her mother's hand fondly. "I know."

"So what's the problem?"

"About a week ago," Amanda began reluctantly, "someone from the hospital called and said James was asking for me. He was in the ICU at the time, so I didn't feel I could ignore the whole thing. I went to see him, and while I was there, he told me he'd given up, that he was going to die."

Marion's lips thinned in irritation, but she seemed to know how hard it was for Amanda to keep up her momentum, so she didn't interrupt.

"Essentially, he said I was the only reason he had to go on living, and if I didn't want him, he was just going to give up. So I've been visiting him and pretending we'll be getting back together again once he's well."

Marion sighed heavily. "Amanda."

"I know it sounds crazy, but I feel guilty enough without being the reason somebody died!"

Marion reached out and covered Amanda's hand with her own. "I suppose you haven't told Jordan any of this."

"I'm afraid to. Maybe it would have been all right if I'd mentioned it that very first night after I spoke to James, when Jordan and I were together for dinner, but I couldn't bring myself to do it. I was too afraid he'd make me choose between him and James."

"I didn't think there was any question of a choice," Marion said. "You're in love with Jordan Richards, whether you know it or not."

Amanda bit her lower lip for a moment. "I guess I am."

"Tell him the truth, Amanda," Marion urged. "Don't put it off for another second. March right over to that phone and call him."

"I can't," Amanda said with a shake of her head. "It's not something I can say over the telephone, and besides, his little girls will be there. This is their first night together, and I don't want to spoil it."

"You're going to regret it if you don't straighten this out," Marion warned.

"I think it might already be too late," Amanda said brokenly, and then she rose from her chair, emptied her coffee into the sink and set the cup down. "You just concentrate on Eunice, Mom, and don't worry about me."

Marion shook her head as she got up to see her daughter to the door. "Talk to Jordan," she insisted as Amanda put on her coat and wrapped a colorful knitted scarf around her neck.

Amanda nodded and hurried through the cold night to her car.

The light on her answering machine was blinking when she arrived home, and after brewing herself a cup of tea, she pushed the Play button and sat down at the little table in her living room to listen.

The first call was from James. He'd missed her that night and hoped she'd come to visit in the morning.

Amanda closed her eyes against the prospect, though she knew she would have to do as he asked. Maybe if she used Eunice's visit as an excuse, she could get away after only a half hour or so.

The next message nearly made her spill her tea. "This is Madge Brockman," an angry female voice said, "and I just wanted to tell you that you're not going to get away with this. You took my husband, and I'm going to take something from you." After those bitter words, the woman had hung up with a crash.

Amanda was struggling to compose herself, when yet another voice came on. "Mandy, this is Jordan. I've survived supper, and the kids' baths and story time. I have a new respect for mothers. Call me, will you?" There was a click, and then the machine rewound itself.

Despite the fact that Madge Brockman's call had shaken her to her soul, Amanda reached for the phone and dialed Jordan's number at the island house.

He answered on the second ring.

"Hi, Jordan. It's Amanda."

"Thank God," he replied with a lilt to his voice.

"How are the girls?" She dabbed at her eyes with her sleeve and resisted an impulse to sniffle.

"They're fine. Mandy, are you all right?"

"I—I need to see you. Could I c-come out there?"

Jordan hesitated, then said, "Sure. If you hurry, you can still make the last ferry. Mandy—"

"I'll be there as soon as I can," Amanda broke in, and then she hung up the phone and dashed into her bedroom. She pulled her suitcase out from under the bed and tossed in two pairs of jeans, two sets of clean underwear and two sweaters. Then, after snatching up her toothbrush and makeup bag, she made sure Gershwin had plenty of food and water and hurried out of the apartment.

Several times on the way to West Seattle Amanda's eyes were so full of tears that she nearly had to pull over to the side of the road. But finally she drove on board the ferry and parked.

Safe in the bottom of the enormous boat, she let her forehead rest against the steering wheel and sobbed.

By the time she'd reached Vashon Island and driven to Jordan's house, however, she was beginning to feel a little foolish. She wasn't a child, she told herself sternly, and she couldn't expect Jordan to solve her problems. She might have backed out of the driveway and raced back to the ferry dock if Jordan hadn't come outside to greet her.

He was wearing sneakers, jeans and a Seahawks sweatshirt, and he looked so good to Amanda that she nearly burst into tears again.

Without a word, he opened the door and helped her out, then fetched her suitcase and overnighter from the backseat. Amanda preceded him into the house, wondering what she was going to say.

There was a fire snapping on the hearth, and after setting her luggage down in the entryway, Jordan helped Amanda out of her coat. "Sit down and I'll get you some brandy," he said hoarsely after kissing her on the cheek.

Amanda took a seat on the raised stone hearth of the

fireplace, hoping the warmth would take the numb chill out of her soul.

When Jordan sat down next to her and handed her a crystal snifter with brandy glowing golden in the bottom, her heart turned over. She knew she'd waited too long to explain things; she was going to lose him.

"Talk to me, Mandy," he said when she was silent, studying him with miserable eyes.

"I can't," she replied, setting the brandy aside untouched. "Will you just hold me, Jordan? Just for a few minutes?"

Gently he pulled her into his arms and pressed her head to his shoulder. He moved his hand soothingly up and down her back, but he didn't ask any questions or make any demands, and Amanda loved him more than ever for that.

Amanda had just about worked up her courage to tell him about her promise to James, when a small, curious voice asked, "Who's that, Daddy?"

Amanda started in Jordan's arms, but he held her fast. She turned her head and saw a little dark-haired girl standing a few feet away. She was wearing a pink quilted robe and tiny fluffy slippers to match.

"This is Amanda, Jess. Amanda, my daughter, Jessica."

"Hi," Amanda managed.

"How come you're hugging her?" Jessica wanted to know. "Did she fall down and hurt herself?"

"Sort of," Jordan answered. "Why don't you go back to bed now, honey? You can get to know Amanda better in the morning."

Jessica's smile was so like Becky's that Amanda was shaken by it. "Okay. Good night, Daddy. Good night, Amanda."

When the little girl was gone, Amanda sat there in Jordan's arms, sorely wishing she hadn't intruded. She didn't belong here.

"I shouldn't have come," she said, bolting to her feet.

Jordan pulled her back so that she landed on his lap. "You've missed the last ferry, Mandy," he pointed out. "Besides, I'm not letting you go anywhere in the shape you're in."

Amanda swallowed hard. "I can't sleep with you—not with your daughters in the house."

"I understand that," Jordan replied. "I have a guest room."

Why did he have to be so damned reasonable? Amanda fretted. She didn't deserve his patience or his kindness. "Okay," she said lamely, reaching for her brandy and downing the whole thing practically in one gulp. Maybe that would give her the courage to say what she needed to say.

But it only made her woozy and very nauseous. Jordan lifted her into his arms and carried her to the guest room, where he undressed her like a weary child, put her into one of his pajama tops because she'd forgotten to bring a nightgown and tucked her in.

"Jordan, I made a terrible mistake."

He kissed her forehead. "We'll talk tomorrow," he said. "Go to sleep."

Exhaustion immediately conquered Amanda, and when she awakened, it was morning. Jordan had brought her things to her room. There was a small bathroom adjoining, so she showered, brushed her teeth and put on makeup. When she arrived in the kitchen, wearing jeans and a blue sweater, she felt a hundred percent better than she had the night before.

Jordan was making pancakes on an electric griddle and cooking bacon in the microwave, while his daughters sat at the table, drinking their orange juice and watching him with amusing consternation. While Jessica resembled Becky, the smaller child, Lisa, looked like Jordan. She had his maple-brown hair and hazel eyes, and she smiled broadly when she saw Amanda.

Again, despite her improved mood, Amanda felt like an imposter shoving herself in where she didn't belong. She would have fled to her car if she hadn't known it would only compound her problems.

"Hungry?" Jordan asked, his eyes gentle as he studied Amanda's face.

She nodded, and, seeing that there were four places set at the table, took a chair beside Lisa.

"That's Daddy's chair," Jessica pointed out.

Amanda started to move, but Jordan slapped his hand down on her shoulder and pushed her back.

"It doesn't matter where Amanda sits," he said.

Jessica didn't take offense at the correction, and Amanda reached for the orange juice carton with a trembling hand. She was more than ready to tell Jordan the truth now, but it didn't look as though she was going to get the opportunity. After all, she couldn't just drop an emotional bombshell in front of his daughters.

Jordan's cooking was good, and Amanda managed to put away three pancakes and a couple of strips of bacon even though she couldn't remember the last time she'd been so nervous.

"I think it's about time we decorated that Christmas tree, don't you?" Jordan asked when the meal was over.

The girls gave a rousing cheer and bounded out of their chairs and into the living room.

"You'll have to get dressed first," Jordan called after them. Despite his lack of experience, he seemed to be picking up the fundamentals of active fatherhood rather easily.

"Lisa can't tie her shoes," Jessica confided from the kitchen doorway.

"Then you can do it for her," Jordan replied, beginning to clear the table.

Amanda insisted on helping, and the moment Jordan heard the kids' feet pounding up the stairway, he took her into his arms and gave her a thorough kiss. She melted against him, overpowered, as always, by his strange magic.

"It's very good to have you here, lady," he said in a rumbling whisper. "I just wish I could take you upstairs and spend about two hours making love to you."

Amanda shivered at the prospect. She wished that, too, with all her heart, but once she told Jordan about her visits to James's hospital room and her pretense of rekindling their affair, he probably wouldn't ever want to touch her again.

The idea of never lying in Jordan's arms another night, never feeling the weight of his body or going crazy under the touch of his hands or his mouth, made a hard lump form in her throat.

"Still not ready to talk?" he asked, touching the tip of her nose with a gentle finger.

Amanda shook her head.

"There's time," Jordan said, and he kissed her again, making her throw her arms around his neck in an instinctive plea for more.

"Daddy!" a little voice shouted from upstairs. "I can't find my red shoes!"

Amanda pushed away from Jordan as though he'd struck her, and lifted the back of one hand to her mouth when he turned away to go and help his daughter.

While he was gone, Amanda's bravery completely deserted her. She found her purse and dashed for her car, leaving her luggage behind in Jordan's guest room. He ran outside just as she pulled out of the driveway, but Amanda didn't stop. She put her foot down hard on the accelerator and drove away.

A glance at her watch told her the ferry wouldn't leave for another twenty minutes, and Amanda was half-afraid Jordan would toss the kids in the car and come chasing after her. Since she couldn't face him, she drove to the café where they'd eaten on a couple of occasions.

After parking her car behind a delivery truck, Amanda went into the restaurant, took a chair as far from the front door as she could and hid behind her menu until Wanda arrived.

"Well, hello there," the pleasant woman boomed. "Where's Jordan?"

"He's—busy. Could I get a cup of coffee?"

Wanda arched one artfully plucked eyebrow, but she didn't ask any more questions. She just brought a cup to Amanda's table and filled it from the pot in her other hand.

"Thanks," Amanda said, wishing she didn't have to give up the menu.

Jordan didn't show up, and Amanda was half disappointed and half relieved. She finished her coffee and went back to the ferry terminal just in time to board the boat.

Because she hoped there would be a message on the answering machine from Jordan and feared there would not, she went to the hospital first, instead of her apartment.

"You're late," James fussed when she walked into his room.

"I'm sorry—" Amanda began.

She'd forgotten what a master James was of the quick-silver change, and the brightness of his smile stunned her. "That's okay," he said generously. "I'm just glad you're here."

Amanda lowered her eyes. She would have given anything to be with Jordan and his children at that moment, helping to decorate the Christmas tree or even listening to a lecture. She regretted giving in to her impulse and running away. "Me, too," she lied.

"Tell me you love me," James said.

Amanda's heart stopped beating. She would have choked on the words if she'd tried to utter them.

For better or worse, Madge Brockman spared her the trouble. "Isn't this sweet?" she asked, sweeping like a storm into the room in a black full-length mink with a matching hat. Her eyes, full of poison, swung to Amanda. "To think I believed you when you said you and James were through."

"Amanda and I are going to be married," James protested, and he raised one hand to his chest.

Amanda was terrified.

"You idiot," Madge growled at him, gesturing wildly with one mink-swathed arm. "She's two-timing you with Jordan Richards!"

"That's a lie!" James shouted.

A nurse burst into the room. "Mr. Brockman, you must be calm!"

Terrified, Amanda backed blindly out into the hallway and ran to the elevator. It seemed to be her day for running away, she thought to herself as she got into her car and sped out of the parking lot.

For a time she just drove around Seattle, following an aimless path, trying to gather her composure. She considered visiting her mother, or one of her friends, but she couldn't, because she knew she'd break down and cry if she tried to explain things to anyone.

Finally Amanda drove back to her apartment building and went in through the rear entrance.

In the bathroom she splashed cold water on her face,

washing away the tearstains, but her eyes were still puffy afterward, and her nose was an unglamorous red. It was no real surprise when the door buzzer sounded.

"Jordan or the tiger?" she asked herself with a sort of wounded fancy as she made her way determinedly across the living room and reached for the doorknob.

Chapter 9

〜✤〜

JORDAN STOOD IN THE HALLWAY, holding Amanda's suitcase. He was alone, and his expression was quietly contemptuous.

For the moment Amanda couldn't speak, so she stepped back to let him pass. He set the luggage down with a clatter just inside the entryway and jammed his hands into the pockets of his leather jacket.

"Why the hell did you run off like that?" he demanded.

For a second or so, Amanda swung wildly between relief and dread. She turned away from Jordan, walked to the sofa and sank onto it. "You haven't had a call from Mrs. Brockman?" she asked in a small voice.

Without bothering to take off his jacket—he obviously didn't intend to stay long—Jordan perched on the arm of an easy chair. "James's wife? Why would she call me?"

Amanda swallowed. "I've been visiting James in the hospital," she blurted out. "I told him we could t-take up where we left off."

The color drained from Jordan's face. "What?"

"He said he was going to give up and die—that I was

all he had to live for. So I decided to pretend I still loved him, just until he was strong enough to go on his own."

"And you believed that?" His voice was low, lethal.

"Of course I believed it!" Amanda flared.

"Well, you've been had," Jordan replied coldly.

Amanda stared at him, wounded, her worst suspicions confirmed. "I knew you wouldn't understand, Jordan," she said. "That's why I was afraid to tell you."

"Damn it," he rasped, "don't make excuses. A lie is a lie, Amanda, and there's no room in my life for games like this!"

"It wasn't a game! You didn't see him, hear him…"

Jordan was on his feet again, his hands back in his pockets. "I didn't have to." He walked to the door and stood there for a moment with his back to Amanda. "I could understand your wanting to help," he said in parting. "But I'll never understand why you didn't tell me about it." With that, he opened the door and walked out.

Amanda jumped off the couch and raced to the entryway—she couldn't lose him, she *couldn't*—but at the door she stopped. Jordan had judged her and found her guilty, and he wasn't going to change his mind.

It was over.

Slowly Amanda closed the door. With a concerned meow, Gershwin circled her ankles. "He's gone," she said to the cat, and then she went into the bedroom, found the fur jacket and the skimpy bikini, and returned to her car.

With every mile she drove, Amanda became more certain that Jordan had been right: James had used emotional blackmail to get her to come back to him. She could see now that he'd given a performance every time she'd visited his room; she recalled the shrewd expression in his eyes, the things he'd said about Jordan.

"Fool!" Amanda muttered to herself, flipping on her windshield wipers as a light rain began to fall.

When she reached the hospital, Amanda marched inside, carrying the fur coat over her arm and the bikini in her purse. Some of her resolution faded as she got into the elevator, though. James had a serious heart condition, and for a time he'd been in real danger. Suppose what she meant to say caused him to suffer another attack? Suppose he died and it was her fault?

Amanda approached James's room reluctantly, then stopped when she heard him laughing. "Face it, Richards," he said. "You lose. In another week or two I'll be out of this place. And believe me, Amanda will be more than happy to fly off to Hawaii with me and make sure I recuperate properly."

Her first instinct was to flee, but Amanda couldn't move. She stood frozen in the hallway, resting one hand against the wall.

Jordan said something in response, but Amanda didn't hear what it was—maybe because the thundering of her heart drowned it out.

The scraping of a chair broke Amanda's spell, and she didn't know whether to stay and face Jordan or dodge into the little nook across the hall where a coffee machine stood. In the end she decided she'd done enough running away for a lifetime, and stayed where she was.

When Jordan walked out of James's room, he stopped cold for a moment, but then a weary expression of resignation came over his face.

"I'm going to tell him the truth," she said, her voice hardly more than a whisper.

Jordan shrugged. "It's a little late for that, isn't it?" His eyes dropped to the rich sable jacket draped over her arm. "Merry Christmas, Amanda."

Amanda saw all her hopes going down the drain, and something inside drove her to fight to save them. "Jordan, be reasonable. You know I never meant for things to turn out this way!"

He looked at her for a moment, then walked around her, as he would something objectionable lying on the sidewalk, and strode off down the hall.

Amanda watched him go into the elevator. He looked straight through her as the doors closed.

It was a few moments before she could bring herself to walk into James's room and face him. She no longer feared that her news would cause him another heart attack; now it was her anger she struggled to control.

Finally she was able to force herself through the doorway. She laid the coat at the foot of James's bed without meeting his eyes, then took the bikini from her purse and put it with the coat. When she thought she could manage it without hysterics, she turned to him and said, "You had no right to manipulate me that way."

"Amanda." His voice was a scolding drawl, and he stretched out his hand to her.

She evaded his grasp. "It's over, James. I can't see you anymore."

Surprisingly James smiled at her and let his hand fall to his side. "You might as well come back to me, baby. It's plain enough that Richards is through with you."

Hot rage made Amanda's backbone ramrod straight, but she didn't allow her anger to erupt in a flow of nasty retorts. Clinging to the last of her dignity, she whispered, "Maybe the time I had with Jordan will have to last me a lifetime. But he's the only man I'll ever love." With that, she turned and walked out.

"You'll be back!" James shouted after her. "You'll come

begging for my forgiveness! Damn it, Amanda, nobody walks out on me...."

While a nurse rushed into James's room, Amanda went straight on until she got to the elevator. She pushed the button and waited circumspectly for a ride to the main floor, even though her emotions were howling in her spirit like a storm. She wanted to be anywhere but there, anybody besides herself.

She'd hoped Jordan might be lingering somewhere downstairs, or maybe in her section of the parking lot, but there was no sign of him.

Beyond tears, she climbed behind the wheel of her car and started toward the house where she and Eunice had grown up.

She knocked at the door and called out "It's me!" and her mother instantly replied with a cheerful "Come in!"

Bob, it turned out, was putting in some overtime at the aircraft plant where he worked, but Marion and Eunice were wrapping festive presents on the dining room table. Eunice looked a little tired, but other than that she seemed to be in good spirits. Marion was taking her usual delight in the yuletide season, but her face fell when she got a look at her elder daughter.

"Merciful heavens," she sputtered, rushing over and forcing Amanda into a chair. "You're as pale as Marley's ghost! What on earth is the matter?"

Just minutes before, Amanda had been convinced she had no tears left to cry, but now a despondent wail escaped her and tears streamed down her face.

Eunice immediately rushed to her side. "Sis, what is it?" she whispered, near tears herself. She had always cried whenever Amanda did, even if she didn't know what was bothering her sister.

"It's Jordan!" Amanda sobbed. "He's gone—he never wants to see me again...."

"Get her a glass of water," Marion said to Eunice. She rested her hands on Amanda's shoulders, much as Jordan once had, trying to soothe away the terrible tension.

Eunice reappeared moments later, looking stricken, a glass of water in one hand.

"You told him," Marion said as Amanda sipped the cold water.

Eunice dragged up a chair beside her. "Told him what?"

Setting the water down with a thump, Amanda blurted out the whole story—how she'd fallen hopelessly in love with Jordan, how James had hoodwinked her into ruining everything. She ended with an account of the scene in James's hospital room when she'd given back his gifts once and for all.

"What kind of lunkhead is this Jordan," Eunice demanded, "that he doesn't understand something so simple?"

Amanda dragged her sleeve across her eyes, feeling like a five-year-old with both knees skinned raw. Only it was her heart that was hurting. "He's angry because I didn't tell him about it from the first." She paused to sniffle, and her mother produced a handful of tissues in that magical way mothers have. "I tried, I honestly did, but I was so scared of losing him."

"Men," muttered Eunice. "Who needs them?"

"I do," chorused Amanda and Marion. And at that, all three women laughed.

Eunice patted Amanda's shoulder. "Don't worry. After he thinks about it for a while, he'll forgive you."

Amanda shook her head, dabbing at her puffy eyes with a wad of damp tissue. "You don't know Jordan. He's probably never told a lie in his life. He just flat out doesn't understand deception."

"Maybe he's never lied," Marion said briskly, "but he's made mistakes, just like the rest of us. When he calms down, Amanda, he'll call."

Amanda prayed her mother was right, but the hollow feeling in the center of her heart made that seem unlikely.

An hour later, when Amanda announced that she was going home, Eunice grabbed her coat and insisted on riding along. She'd make supper, she said, and the two of them could just hang around the way they had in high school.

"I wasn't planning to stick my head in the oven or anything, if that's what you're worried about," Amanda said with a sad smile as she backed her car out of her parents' driveway.

Eunice grinned. "And singe those gorgeous, golden tresses? I should hope not."

Amanda laughed at the image. "You know what, kid? It's good to have you back."

Her younger sister patted her arm. "I'll be around awhile, I think," she replied. "There's an opening for a computer programmer at the university. I have an interview the day after Christmas."

"There's really no hope of getting back together with Jim, then?" Amanda asked as they wended their way through rainy streets, the windshield wipers beating out a rhythmic accompaniment to their conversation.

Eunice shook her head. "Not when there's somebody else involved," she said.

Amanda nodded. Just the idea of Jordan seeing another woman was more than she could tolerate, even with the relationship in ruins.

After parking the car, Amanda and Eunice dashed through the rain to the store on the corner and bought popcorn, a log for the fireplace, a pound of fresh shrimp and the makings for a salad.

Back at Amanda's apartment, Eunice prepared and cooked the succulent shrimp while Amanda washed and cut up the vegetables.

"You don't even have a Christmas tree," Eunice complained later when she was kneeling on the hearth, lighting the paper-wrapped log.

Amanda shrugged. "I was just planning to skip the whole holiday," she said.

"Knowing Jordan didn't change that?"

"When I was with him, he was all I thought about," Amanda explained. "Same thing when I wasn't with him."

Eunice grinned and got to her feet, dusting her hands off on the legs of her jeans as if she'd just carried wood in from the wilderness like a pioneer. "You could always throw yourself at his feet and beg for forgiveness."

Amanda lifted her chin stubbornly and went to the living room window. "I explained everything to him, and he wouldn't listen."

Rain pattered at the glass and made the people on the sidewalks below hurry along under their colorful umbrellas. Amanda wondered how many of them were happy and how many had broken hearts.

"You shouldn't give up if you really care about the guy," Eunice said softly.

Amanda sighed. "I didn't give up, Eunice," she said. "He did."

At that, the two sisters dropped the subject of Jordan and talked about other Christmases.

JORDAN HAD HIS own reasons for welcoming the rain, and after he drove on board the ferry to Vashon Island, he stayed in the car, staring bleakly at the empty van ahead

of him. He felt hollow and numb, as though all his vitals
had shriveled up and disappeared, but he knew the pain
would come eventually, and he dreaded it.

After losing Becky, Jordan had made up his mind never
to really care about another woman again. That way, he'd
reasoned in his naïveté, he'd never have to suffer the way
he had after his wife's death.

The trouble was, he'd reckoned without Amanda Scott.

He'd fallen hard for her without ever really being aware
of what was happening. Had he told her that he loved her?
He couldn't remember.

Maybe things would have been different if he had.

Jordan shook his head. He was being stupid. Telling
her he cared wouldn't have prevented her from deceiving
him. He drifted into a restless sleep, haunted by dreams
of things that might have been, and when the ferry's horn
blasted, he was startled. He hadn't been aware of the passing time.

Once the boat docked and his turn came, Jordan drove
down the ramp, just as he had a million times before. Rain
danced on the pavement, and wet gulls hid out beneath
the picnic tables in the park he passed. The world was the
same, and yet it was different.

He was alone again.

When he entered the kitchen through the garage door
minutes later, he heard the stereo blasting. Taking off his
jacket and running a hand through his rumpled hair, he
went into the living room.

Jessie and Lisa had dragged their presents out from
under the mammoth Christmas tree he and Amanda had
chosen together, and piled them up in two teetering stacks.
The babysitter, a teenage girl from down the road, was
curled up on the couch, chattering into the telephone receiver.

Sighting Jordan, his daughters flung themselves at him with shrieks of glee, and he lifted one in each arm, making the growling sound they loved and pretending to be bent on chewing off their ears.

The babysitter, a plain little thing with thick glasses, hung up the telephone and tiptoed over to the stereo to turn it off.

Jordan let the girls down to the floor, took out his wallet and paid the sitter. The moment she was gone, Jessie folded her arms and announced, "Lisa has more presents than I do."

Jordan pretended to be horrified. "No!"

"Count them for yourself," Jessie challenged.

He knelt and began to count. The red-and-silver striped package on the top of Lisa's stack turned out to be the culprit. "This one is for both of you," Jordan said, tapping at the gift tag with his finger. "See? It says 'Lisa *and* Jessie.'"

Jessie examined the tag studiously and was then satisfied that it was still a just world. "Where did Amanda go?" she asked, looking at him with Becky's eyes. "Why did she run away?"

Jordan had no idea how to explain Amanda's abrupt disappearance. He still didn't understand it completely himself. "She's at her apartment, I guess," he finally answered.

"But why did she runned away?" Lisa asked, rubbing her eye with the back of one dimpled hand.

"She probably went to heaven, like Mommy," Jessie said importantly.

Her innocent words went through Jordan like a lance. Young as they were, these kids were developing a strategy for being left—Mommy went to heaven; Daddy doesn't have time for us; Amanda was just passing through.

Jordan kissed both his girls resoundingly on the forehead. "Amanda's not in heaven," he said, sounding hoarse even to himself. "She's in Seattle. Now put these presents back under the tree before Santa finds out you've been messing around with them and fills your stockings with clam shells."

The telephone rang just as Jordan was rising to his feet, but he didn't lunge for it, even though that was his first instinct. He answered in a leisurely, offhand way, but his heart was pounding.

"Hi, little brother. It's Karen," his sister said warmly. "How are the monkeys getting along?"

Jordan forced himself to chuckle; he felt like weeping with disappointment. So it wasn't Amanda. What would he have said to her if it had been? "Do they always pile their presents in the middle of the living room?" he countered, trying to sound lighthearted.

Karen laughed. "No, that's a new one," she said. "How are you doing, Jord?"

He ran a hand through his hair. "Me? I'm doing great." *For somebody who's just had his insides torn out, that is.*

"No problems with memories?"

Jordan sighed and watched his children as they put their colorful gifts back underneath the tree. It seemed hard to believe there had ever been a time when he found it difficult even to look at them because they reminded him so much of Becky. "I guess I'm over that," he said huskily.

"Sounds to me like things are a little rocky."

Karen had always been perceptive. "It's something else," he said. The pain he'd been expecting was just starting to set in. "Listen, Karen, you and Paul and I have to have a talk about the girls. I want to spend more time with them."

"Took you long enough," Karen responded, her voice gentle.

Jordan remembered how she'd helped him through those dark days after Becky had died; she'd been there for him while he was in the hospital, and later, too. If she'd been in his living room instead of miles away on the peninsula, he'd have told her about Amanda.

"Better late than never," he finally replied.

"Paul and I will be down on Christmas Eve, as planned," Karen went on, probably sensing that Jordan wasn't going to confide anything important over the phone. "Save some room under that tree, because we're bringing a carload of loot, and Becky's parents will send boxes of stuff."

Jordan chuckled and shook his head. "Just what they need," he said, watching the greedy munchkins playing tug-of-war with a box wrapped in shiny blue paper. "See you Christmas Eve, sis."

Karen said a few more words, then hung up.

"I'm hungry," said Lisa as a stain spread slowly through the fabric of her plaid jeans.

"She peed her pants," Jessie pointed out quite unnecessarily.

With a grin, Jordan swept his younger daughter up in his arms and carried her off to the bathroom.

'TWAS THE NIGHT before Christmas, and Amanda Scott was feeling sorry for herself. She sat with her feet up in front of the fire while her mother, stepfather and sister bundled up to go to the midnight service at church.

"No fair peeking in the stockings while we're gone," said Bob with a smile and a shake of his finger.

Marion and Eunice were less understanding. They both looked as though they wanted to shake her.

"Moping around this house won't change anything," Marion scolded.

"Yeah," Eunice agreed, gesturing. "Put on your coat and come with us."

"I'm wearing jeans and a sweatshirt, in case you haven't noticed," Amanda pointed out archly. Bob had on his best suit, and Marion and Eunice were both in new dresses.

"Nobody's going to notice," Marion fussed, and she looked so hopeful that Amanda would change her mind that Amanda relented and pushed herself out of the chair.

Soon, she was settled beside Eunice in the backseat of her parents' car. It was so much like the old days that for a while Amanda was able to pretend her life wasn't in ruins.

"Maybe a little angel will whisper in Jordan's ear and he'll call you," Eunice said in a low voice as Marion and Bob sang carols exuberantly in the front seat.

Amanda gave her sister a look. "And maybe Saint Nicholas will land on our roof tonight in a sleigh drawn by eight tiny reindeer."

"Okay, then," Eunice responded, bristling, "why don't you call him?"

The truth was that Amanda had dialed Jordan's number a hundred times since they'd parted. Once she'd even waited to hear him say hello before hanging up. "Gee, why don't I?" she retorted. "Or better yet, I could plunge head-first off an overpass. I just *love* pain."

Eunice folded her arms. "Don't be such a poop, Amanda. I'm only trying to help."

"It isn't working," Amanda responded, turning her head to look out at the festive lights trimming roofs and windows and shrubbery.

The church service was soothing, as family traditions often are, and Amanda was feeling a little better when they drove back home. They all sat around the tree, sipping eggnog and listening to carols, and when Bob and

Marion finally retired for the night, Eunice dug a package out from under a mountain of gifts and extended it.

Amanda accepted the present, but refused to open it until she had found her gift to Eunice. It was another tradition; as girls, the sisters had always made their exchange just before going to bed.

When Amanda opened her gift, she laughed. It was a copy of *Gathering Up the Pieces,* the same book she'd bought for Eunice.

Eunice was amazed when she opened her package. "I don't believe this," she whispered, a wide smile on her face. She turned back the flyleaf. "And it's autographed. Wow."

"I waited in line for hours to get it signed," Amanda exaggerated. She was remembering meeting Jordan that day, and feeling all the resultant pain.

"Let's go to bed and read ourselves to sleep," Eunice suggested, standing up and switching off the Christmas tree. Its veil of tinsel seemed to whisper a silvery song in the darkness.

"Good idea," Amanda answered.

She was all the way up to chapter three before she finally closed her eyes.

THE KIDS WERE asleep and so, as far as Jordan knew, were Paul and Karen. He sat up in bed, switched on the lamp and reached for the telephone on the nightstand. The picture of Becky had been moved to a shelf in his study, but he looked at the place where it had stood and said, "Know what, Becky? I've got it bad."

A glance at his watch told him it was after two in the morning. If he called Amanda now, he would be sure to wake her up, but he didn't care. Whatever happened, he had to hear her voice and wish her a merry Christmas.

He punched out the number and waited, nervous as

a high school kid. While the call went through, a number of scenarios came to mind—such as James answering with a sleepy "Hello." Or Amanda telling him to go straight to hell.

Instead he got a recorded voice. "Hi. This is Amanda Scott, and I can't come to the phone right now...."

Jordan hung up without leaving a message, switched off the light and lay back on his pillows. She was probably at her parents' place, he told himself.

Or maybe she was in Hawaii, helping James recuperate.

Jordan turned onto his stomach and slammed one fist into the pillow. He knew the lush plains and contours of Amanda's body, and he begrudged them to every other man on earth. They were his to touch, and no one else's.

His groin knotted as he recalled how it was to bury himself in Amanda's depths, to feel her hands moving on his back and the insides of her thighs against his hips. She'd lain beneath him like a temptress, her eyes smoldering, her body rising to meet his, stroke for stroke, her hands curled on the sides of the pillow.

But then, as release approached, she would bite down hard on her lower lip and roll her eyes back, focusing dreamily on nothing at all. A low, keening whimper would escape her as she surrendered completely, breaking past her clamped teeth to become a shameless groan...

Jordan sat bolt upright in bed and switched on the lamp again. He couldn't quite face the prospect of a cold shower, but he was too uncomfortable to stay where he was. He tossed back the covers, reached for his robe and tied it tightly around his waist. The cloth stood out like canvas stretched over a tent pole.

Feeling reasonably certain he wouldn't meet anybody, Jordan slipped out of his room and down the darkened stairs. In the kitchen he poured himself a glass of chocolate milk and carried it back to the living room. There he sat, staring at the silent glimmer of the dark Christmas tree, the bulging shapes of the stockings. The thin light of a winter moon poured in through the smoked-glass windows, making everything look unfamiliar.

"Jordan?" It was Karen's voice, and seconds before she switched on the lights, he grabbed a sofa pillow and laid it on his lap. His plump, pretty sister, bundled in her practical blue chenille robe, looked at him with concern. "Are you all right?"

"No," Jordan answered, tossing back the last of his chocolate milk as though it could give him the same solace as brandy or good whiskey. Since it was safe to set aside the pillow, he did. "Don't ever let anybody tell you it's 'better to have loved and lost, than never to have loved at all,'" he advised, sounding for all the world like a melancholy drunk. "I've done it twice, and I wish to God I'd joined the foreign legion, instead."

Karen sat down next to him. "So you're just going to give up, huh?"

"Yeah," Jordan answered obstinately. He had to change the subject, or risk being smothered in images of Amanda lying in somebody else's bed. "About the kids—"

"You want them back," Karen guessed with a gentle smile.

Jordan nodded.

Chapter 10

❦

AMANDA SAT STARING AT THE bank draft in amazement that dreary Saturday morning in February while a gray rain drizzled at the kitchen windows. "I don't understand," she muttered, glancing from Marion's smiling face to Bob's to Eunice's. "What's this for?"

Bob reached across the table to cover her hand with his. "I guess you could say it's an investment. You've been walking around here for two months looking as though you've lost your last friend, so your mother and I decided you needed a lift. It's enough for the down payment on that old house you wanted, isn't it?"

Amanda swallowed, reading the numbers on the check in disbelief. It was five times the down payment the owner demanded—Amanda still called once a week to see if the house had sold, and had gone to see it twice—and must have represented a major chunk of her parents' savings account. "I can't take this," she said. "You've worked so hard and budgeted so carefully...."

But Bob and Marion presented a united front, and they were backed up by a beaming Eunice, who was now working full-time at the university and living in her own apartment.

"You have to accept it," Marion said firmly. "We won't take no for an answer."

"But suppose I fail?" Since the breakup with Jordan, Amanda's confidence had taken a decided dip, and everything was more difficult than it should have been.

"You won't," Bob said with certainty. "Now call that real estate woman and make an offer before the place is snapped up by some doctor or lawyer looking for a summer house."

Amanda hesitated only a moment. Hope was fluttering in her heart like a bird rising skyward; for the first time in two months she could see herself as a happy woman. With a shriek of delight, she bolted out of her chair and dashed for the telephone, and Bob and Marion laughed until they had tears in their eyes.

The real estate agent was delighted at Amanda's offer, and offered to bring the papers over to Seattle for her to sign. They agreed to meet Monday morning at Amanda's office in the Evergreen Hotel.

When Amanda was off the phone, she turned to her parents. "I can't believe you're doing this for me—taking such a chance—"

"A person can't expect to win in life if they're afraid to take a risk," Bob said quietly.

Amanda went back to the table and bent to hug each of her parents. "You'll be proud of me," she promised.

"We already are," Marion assured her.

ON MONDAY MORNING Amanda arrived at work with a carefully typed letter of resignation tucked into her briefcase. In another two weeks she would be rolling up her sleeves and making a start on her dream—or, at least, part of it.

She flipped through the messages on her desk, sorting them in order of importance, and at the same time looked into the future. The house she was buying was hardly more than a mile from Jordan's place. She was bound to meet him on the highway or run into him in the supermarket, and she wondered if she could deal with that.

Even after two months Amanda ached every time she thought of Jordan. Actually encountering him face-to-face might really set her back.

There was a rap at the door, and Mindy stepped in, smiling. "You look pretty cheerful today. What's going on? Did you and Jordan get back together or something?"

Amanda opened her briefcase and took out the letter of resignation, keeping her eyes down to hide the sudden pain the mention of Jordan had caused her. "No," she answered, "but I'll be leaving the Evergreen in a couple of weeks—I'm buying that house I wanted on Vashon Island."

"Wow," Mindy responded. "That's great!"

Amanda lifted her eyes to meet her friend's gaze. "Thanks, Mindy."

Mindy's brow puckered in a frown. "I'll miss you a lot, though."

"And I'll miss you." At that moment the intercom on Amanda's telephone buzzed, and she picked up the receiver as Mindy left the office. "Amanda Scott."

"Ms. Scott, this is Betty Prestwood, Prestwood Real Estate. I'm afraid I've been delayed, so I won't be arriving in the city until around noon. Could we possibly meet at Ivar's for lunch at twelve-fifteen? I'll have the proper papers with me, of course."

Amanda automatically glanced at her calendar, even though she already knew she was free for lunch that day. She probably would have eaten yogurt in her office or gone to the mall with Mindy for fast food. "That will be fine."

After ending that phone call, Amanda went to the executive manager's office suite and handed in her resignation. Mr. Mansfield, a middle-aged man with a bald head and an ulcer, was not pleased that his trusty assistant manager was leaving.

He instructed her to start preliminary interviews for a replacement as soon as possible.

Amanda spent the rest of the morning on the telephone with various employment agencies in the city, and when it came time to meet Mrs. Prestwood for lunch, she was relieved. It wasn't the food that attracted her, but the prospect of a break.

After exchanging her high heels for sneakers, Amanda walked the six blocks from the hotel to the seafood restaurant on the waterfront. The sun was shining, and the harbor was its usual noisy, busy self.

Mrs. Prestwood, a small, trim woman with carefully coiffed blond hair and tasteful makeup, was waiting by the reservations desk.

She and Amanda shook hands, then followed the hostess to a table by a window.

Just as Amanda was sitting down, she spotted Jordan—it was as though her eyes were magnetized to him. He looked very Wall Street in his three-piece suit as he lunched with two other men and a woman.

Evidently he'd sensed Amanda's stare, for his eyes shifted to her almost instantly.

For a moment the whole restaurant seemed to fall into eerie silence for Amanda; she had the odd sensation of standing on the bottom of the ocean. It was only with enormous effort that she surfaced and forced her gaze to the menu the waitress had handed her. *Don't let him come over here,* she prayed silently. *If he does, I'll fall apart right in front of everybody.*

"Is something wrong?" Betty Prestwood asked pleasantly.

Amanda swallowed and shook her head, but out of the corner of her eye she was watching Jordan.

He had turned his attention back to his companions, especially the woman, who was attractive, in a tweedy sort of way, with her trim suit and her dark hair pulled back into a French twist. She was laughing at something Jordan had said.

Amanda made herself study the menu, even though she couldn't have eaten if her life depended on it. She finally decided on the spinach salad and iced tea, just for show.

Mrs. Prestwood brought out the contracts as soon as the waitress had taken their orders, and Amanda read them through carefully. Lunch had arrived by the time she was done, and in a glance she saw that Jordan and his party were leaving. He was resting his hand lightly on the small of the woman's back, and Amanda felt for all the world like a betrayed wife.

Forcing her eyes back to the contracts, she signed them and handed Mrs. Prestwood a check. Since the owner was financing the sale himself, it was now just a matter of waiting for closing. Amanda could rent the house in the interim if she wished.

She wrote another check, then stabbed a leaf of spinach with her fork. Try as she might, she couldn't lift it to her mouth. Her stomach was roiling angrily, unwilling to accept anything.

She laid the fork down.

"Is everything all right?" Mrs. Prestwood asked, seeming genuinely concerned.

Amanda lied by nodding her head.

"You don't seem very hungry."

Amanda managed a smile. Was Jordan sleeping with

that woman? Did she visit him on the island on weekends? "I'm just getting over the flu," she said, which was at least a partial truth. She was probably coming down with it, not getting over it.

Mrs. Prestwood accepted that excuse and finished her lunch in good time. The two women parted outside the restaurant with another handshake, then Amanda started back up the hill to the hotel. By the time she arrived, her head was pounding and there were two people waiting to be interviewed for her job.

She talked to both of them and didn't pass either application on to Mr. Mansfield for his consideration. One had obviously considered herself too good for such a menial position, and the other had an offensive personal manner.

Amanda's headache got progressively worse as the afternoon passed, but she was too busy interviewing to go home to bed, and besides, she couldn't be sure the malady wasn't psychosomatic. She hadn't started feeling really sick until after she'd seen Jordan with that woman in the dress-for-success clothes.

At the end of the day Amanda dragged herself home, fed Gershwin, made herself a bowl of chicken noodle soup and watched the evening news in her favorite bathrobe. By the time she'd been apprised of all the shootings, rapes, drug deals and political scandals of the day, she was thoroughly depressed. She put her empty soup bowl in the sink, took two aspirin and fell into bed.

The next morning she felt really terrible. Her head seemed thick and heavy as a medicine ball, and her chest ached.

Reluctantly she called in sick, took more aspirin and went back to sleep.

A loud knocking at the door awakened her around eleven-thirty, and Amanda rolled out of bed, stumbled into the living room with one hand pressed to her aching head and called, "Who is it?"

"It's me," a feminine voice replied. "Mindy. Let me in—I come bearing gifts."

With a sigh, Amanda undid the chains, twisted the lock and opened the door. "You're taking your life in your hands, coming in here," she warned in a thick voice. "This place is infested with germs."

Mindy's pretty hair was sprinkled with raindrops, and her smile was warm. "I'll risk it," she said, stepping past Amanda with a stack of magazines and a box of something that smelled good. She grimaced as she assessed Amanda's rumpled nightgown and unbrushed hair. "You look like the victim in a horror movie," she observed cheerfully. "Sit down before you fall down."

Amanda dropped into a chair. "What's going on at the office?"

"It's bedlam," Mindy answered, setting the magazines and food down on the table to shrug out of her coat. "Mr. Mansfield is finding out just how valuable you really are." Her voice trailed back from the kitchenette, where she was opening cupboards and drawers. "He's been interviewing all morning, and he's such a bear today, he'll be lucky if anybody wants to work for him."

Amanda sighed. "I should be there."

Mindy returned from the kitchenette and handed Amanda a plate of the fried Chinese noodles she knew she loved. "And spread bubonic plague among your friends and coworkers? Bad idea. Eat this, Amanda."

Amanda took the plate of noodles and dug in with a fork. Although she still had no appetite, she knew her body needed food to recover, and she hadn't had anything to eat since last night's chicken soup. "Thanks."

Mindy glanced at the blank TV screen in amazement.

"Do you mean to tell me you have a chance to catch up on all the soaps and you aren't even watching?"

"I'm sick, not on vacation," Amanda pointed out.

Mindy rushed to turn on the set and tune in her favorite. "Lord, will you look at him?" she asked, pointing to a shirtless hero soulfully telling a woman she was the only one for him.

"Don't listen to him," Amanda muttered. "As soon as you make one wrong move, he'll dump you."

"You *have* been watching this show!" Mindy accused.

Amanda shook her head glumly. "I was speaking from the perspective of real life," she said, chewing.

Mindy sighed. "I knew that rascal would be fooling around with Lorinda the minute Jennifer turned her back," she fretted, shaking her finger at the screen.

Amanda chuckled, even though she would have had to feel better just to die, and took another bite of the noodles Mindy had brought. "How do you know so much about the story line when you work every day?"

"I tape it," Mindy answered. Then, somewhat reluctantly, she snapped off the set and turned back to her mission of mercy. "Is there anything you want me to do at the office, Amanda? Or I could shop for you—"

Amanda interrupted with a shake of her head. "It's enough that you came over. That was really nice of you."

Mindy rose from the couch and put her hands on her slim hips. "I know. I'll make a bed for you on the couch so you can watch TV. Mom always did that for me when I was sick, and it never failed to cheer me up."

With that, Mindy disappeared into the bedroom, returning soon afterward with sheets, blankets and pillows. True to her word, she made a place for Amanda on the couch and all but tucked her in when she was settled with her magazines and the controls for the TV.

Before going back to work, she made Amanda a cup of hot tea, put the phone within reach and forced her to take more aspirin.

When Mindy was gone, Amanda got up to lock the door behind her, then padded back to the bed. She was comfortably settled when the telephone rang. A queer feeling quivered in the pit of her stomach as she remembered seeing Jordan in the restaurant the day before, felt again the electricity that passed between them when their eyes met. "Hello?" she said hopefully.

"Hello, Amanda."

The voice didn't belong to Jordan, but to Mrs. Prestwood. Amanda could pick up the keys to her house at the real estate office whenever she was ready.

Amanda promised to be there within the week, and asked Mrs. Prestwood to have telephone service hooked up at the house, along with electricity. Then she hung up and flipped slowly through the magazines, seeing none of the glossy photographs and enticing article titles. She was going to be living on the same island with Jordan, and that was all she could think about.

BY THE TIME Amanda recovered enough to return to work, half her notice was up and Mr. Mansfield had selected a replacement. Handing her her final paycheck, which was sizable because there was vacation pay added in, he wished her well. On her last day, he and Mindy and the others held a going away party for her in the hotel's elegant lounge, and Bob, Marion and Eunice attended, too.

That Friday evening, Amanda filled her car with boxes, one of which contained Gershwin, leaving the rest of her things behind for the movers to bring, and boarded the ferry for Vashon Island.

Since it was cold and dark in the bottom of the ship, she decided to venture upstairs to the snack bar for a cup of hot coffee. Just as she arrived, however, she spotted Jordan again. This time he was with his daughters, and the three of them were eating French fries while both girls talked at once.

Amanda's first instinct was to approach them and say hello, but in the end she lost her courage and slipped back out of the snack bar and down the stairs to her car. She sat hunched behind the wheel, waiting for the whistle announcing their arrival at Vashon Island to blast, and feeling miserable. What kind of life was she going to have in her new community if she had to worry about avoiding Jordan?

In those moments Amanda felt terribly alone, and the enormity of the things she'd done—giving up her job and apartment and borrowing such a staggering sum of money from her parents—oppressed her.

Finally the ferry came into port, and Amanda drove her car down the ramp, wondering if Jordan and the girls were in one of the cars ahead, or one behind. She didn't get a glimpse of them, which wasn't surprising, considering how dark it was.

When Amanda arrived at her new old house, the lights were on and Mrs. Prestwood was waiting in the kitchen to present the key, since Amanda had not had a chance to pick it up at the office. The old oil furnace was rumbling beneath the floor, filling the spacious rooms with warmth.

Amanda wandered through the rooms, sipping coffee from the percolator Betty Prestwood had thoughtfully loaned her and dreaming of the things she meant to do. There would be winter parties around the huge fireplace in the front parlor—she would serve mulled wine and spice cake with whipped cream. And in summer, guests could sleep on the screened sun porch if they wanted to, and be lulled into slumber by the quiet rhythm of the tide and the salty whisper of the breezes.

There were seven bedrooms upstairs, but only one bathroom. Amanda made a mental note to call in a plumbing contractor for estimates the next morning. She would have to add at least one more.

Amanda's private room, a small one off the kitchen, looked especially inviting after the long day she'd had. While Gershwin continued to explore the farthest reaches of his new home, she went out to the car to get the cot and sleeping bag she'd borrowed from her stepdad. After a bath upstairs, she crawled onto the cot with a book.

She hadn't read more than a page, when Gershwin suddenly landed in the middle of her stomach with a plop and meow.

Amanda let her book rest against her chin and stroked his silky fur. "Don't worry, Big Guy. We're both going to like it here." The instant the words were out of her mouth, though, she thought of the jolt that seeing Jordan and the girls had caused her, and her throat tightened painfully. "You'd think I'd be over him by now, wouldn't you?" she said when she could speak, her vision so blurred that there seemed to be two Gershwins lying on her stomach instead of one.

"Reoww," Gershwin agreed, before bending his head to lick one of his paws.

"Love is hell," Amanda went on with a sniffle. "Be glad you're neutered."

Gershwin made no comment on that, so Amanda dried her eyes and focused determinedly on her book again.

THE NEXT MORNING brought a storm in off Puget Sound. It slashed at the windows and howled around the corners of the house, and Gershwin kept himself within six inches of Amanda's feet. She left him only to carry in the boxes from the car and drive to the supermarket for food.

Since she'd prepared herself to encounter Jordan, Amanda was both relieved and disappointed when there was no sign of him. She filled her cart with groceries, taking care to buy a can of Gershwin's favorite food to make up for leaving him, and drove back over rain-slickened roads to the house.

The tempest raged all day, but Amanda was fascinated by it, rather than frightened. While Gershwin was sleeping off the feast Amanda had brought him, she put on her slicker and a pair of rubber boots she'd found in the basement and walked down to the beach.

Lightning cracked the sky like a mirror dropped on a hard floor, and the water lashed furiously at the rocky shoreline. Amanda stood with her hands in the pockets of her slicker, watching the spectacle in awe.

When she returned to the house half an hour later, her jeans were wet to her knees despite the rain garb she wore, and her hair was dripping. She felt strangely comforted, though, and when she saw Betty Prestwood's car splashing up the puddle-riddled driveway, she smiled and waved.

The two women dashed onto the enclosed porch together, laughing. Betty was only a few years older than Amanda, and they were getting to be good friends.

"There's an estate sale scheduled for today," Betty said breathlessly when they were in the kitchen and Amanda had handed her a cup of steaming coffee. "I thought you might like to go, since you need so much furniture. It's just on the other side of the island, and we could have lunch out."

Amanda was pleased that Betty had thought of her. Even though she had a surplus of funds, thanks to her own savings and the loan from Bob and Marion, it was going to cost a lot of money to get the bed and breakfast into operation. She needed to furnish the place attractively for a reasonable price. "Sounds great," Amanda said, ruefully comparing her soggy jeans and crumpled flannel shirt to Betty's stylish pink suit. "Just give me a few minutes, and I'll change."

Betty smiled. "Fine. Do you mind if I use the phone? I like to check in with the office periodically."

Amanda gestured toward the wall phone between the sink and stove. "Help yourself. And have some more coffee if you want it. I won't be long."

After finding a pair of black woolen slacks and a burgundy sweater, along with clean underthings and a towel and washcloth, Amanda dashed upstairs and took a quick, hot shower. When she was dressed, with her hair blow-dried and a light application of makeup highlighting her features, she hurried downstairs.

Betty was leaning against one of the kitchen counters, sipping coffee. "When are the movers coming?"

"Monday," Amanda answered, pulling on a pair of shoes that would probably be ruined the instant she wore them outside. "But even when all my stuff is here, the place is still going to echo like a cavern."

Betty laughed. "Maybe we can fix that this afternoon."

After saying goodbye to Gershwin, who still hadn't recovered from his stupor, Amanda pulled the ugly rubber boots she'd worn earlier on over her shoes, put on her slicker and followed Betty to her car.

Since the auction was scheduled for one o'clock, they had time for a leisurely lunch. Mercifully Betty suggested a small soup-and-sandwich place in town, rather than the roadside café Amanda knew Jordan frequented.

She ordered a turkey sandwich with bean sprouts, along with a bowl of minestrone, and ate with enthusiasm. She wasn't over Jordan, and she was still weak with lingering traces of the flu, but her appetite was back.

After lunch, she and Betty drove to a secluded house on the opposite side of the island, where folding chairs had been set up under huge pink-and-white striped canopies. Amanda's heart sank when she saw how many people had braved the nasty weather in search of a bargain, but Betty seemed to be taking a positive attitude, so she tried to follow suit.

The articles available for sale were scattered throughout the house—there were pianos and bedroom sets, tea services and bureaus, sets of china boasting imprints like Limoges and Haviland. Embroidered linens were offered, too, along with exquisite lace curtains and grandfather clocks, and wonderful old books that smelled of age and refinement.

Amanda's excitement built, and she crossed her fingers as she and Betty took their places in the horde of metal chairs.

A beautiful old sleigh bed with a matching bureau and armoire came up for sale first, and Amanda, thinking of her seven empty bedrooms, held up her bid card when the auctioneer asked for a modest amount to start the sale rolling.

A man in the back row bid against her, and it was nip and tuck, but Amanda finally won the skirmish with fairly minimal damage to her bank balance.

After that she bought linens, one of the grandfather clocks and a set of English bone china, while Betty purchased a full-length mirror in a cherrywood stand and an

old jewelry box. At the end of the sale, Amanda made arrangements for the auction company to deliver her pur-
chases, then wrote out a check.

It was midafternoon by then, and her soup and sandwich were beginning to wear off. Having lost sight of Betty
in the crowd, she bought a hot dog with mustard and rel-
ish and a diet cola, then sat quietly in one of the folding
chairs to eat.

She nearly choked when Jordan walked up, turned the
chair in front of hers around and straddled it, his arms
draped across the back. His expression was every bit as
remote as it had been the last time she'd seen him, and
Amanda prayed he couldn't hear her heart thudding against
her rib cage.

"What are you doing here?" he asked, his voice insinu-
ating that she was probably up to no good.

Amanda was instantly offended. She swallowed a chunk
of her hot dog in a painful lump and replied, "I thought
I'd try to steal some of the silverware, or maybe palm an
antique broach or two."

He grinned, though the expression didn't quite reach
his eyes. "You bought a bedroom set, a grandfather clock
and some dishes. Getting married, Ms. Scott, now that
Mrs. Brockman is out of the picture?"

It was all Amanda could do not to poke him in the eye
with the rest of her hot dog. Obviously he didn't know she'd
bought the Victorian house, and she wasn't about to tell
him. "It'll be a June wedding," she said evenly. "Would
you like to come?"

"I'm busy for the rest of the decade," Jordan answered
in a taut voice, his hazel eyes snapping as he rose from
the chair and put it back into line with the others. "See
you around."

As abruptly as that, he was gone, and Amanda was

left to sit there wondering why she'd let him walk away.
When Betty returned, bringing along two of her friends
to be introduced, Amanda was staring glumly at her un-
finished hot dog.

BECAUSE JESSIE AND Lisa were staying with Becky's parents
in Bellevue that weekend, Jordan was driving the Porsche.
He strode back to it, oblivious to the rain saturating his
hair and his shirt, and threw himself behind the wheel,
slamming the door behind him.

Damn it all to hell, if Amanda was going to go on as
if nothing had happened between them, couldn't she at
least stay on her own turf? It drove him crazy, catching
glimpses of her in restaurants, and in the midst of crowds
waiting to cross streets, and in the next aisle at bookstores.

After slamming his palms against the steering wheel
once, he turned the key in the ignition, and the powerful engine surged to life. The decision had been made by
the time the conglomeration of striped canopies had disappeared from the rearview mirror; he would go home,
change his clothes and spend the rest of the day in Seattle, working.

The plan seemed to be falling into place until an hour
later, when he was passing by that Victorian place Amanda
had liked so much. The lights were on, and there was a
familiar car parked in the driveway.

He met Betty Prestwood's pink Cadillac midway between the highway and the house. She smiled and waved,
and Jordan waved back distractedly, noticing for the first
time that the For Sale sign was gone from the yard.

He braked the car to a stop and sprinted through the
rain to the door, feeling a peculiar mixture of elation and
outrage as he hammered at it with one fist.

Chapter 11

꧁✦꧂

AMANDA HAD JUST CHANGED back into her jeans and a T-shirt when the thunderous knock sounded at the door. Expecting an enthusiastic salesperson, she was taken aback to find Jordan standing on her porch, dripping rainwater and indignation.

"Aren't you going to ask me in?" he demanded.

Amanda stepped back without a word, watching with round eyes as Jordan stomped into the warm kitchen, scowling at her.

"Well?" he prompted, putting his hands on his hips.

He seemed to have a particular scenario in mind, but Amanda couldn't think for the life of her what it would be.

She left him standing there while she went into her bathroom for a dry towel. Handing it to him upon her return, she asked, "Well, what?"

"What are you doing in this house? For that matter, what are you doing on this *island?*" He was drying his hair all the while he spoke, a grudging expression on his face.

Amanda hooked her thumbs in the waistband of her jeans and tilted her head to one side. "I own this house," she replied. "As for why I'm on the island, well—" she paused to shrug and spread her hands "—I guess I just didn't know I was supposed to get your approval before I stepped off the ferry."

Jordan flung the towel across the room, and it caught on the handle of the old-fashioned refrigerator. "Are you married to James?"

She went to the percolator and filled two cups with coffee, one for her and one for Jordan. "No," she answered, turning her head to look back at him over her shoulder. "I explained the situation to you. I was only trying to help James in my own misguided way. Where did you get the idea I meant to marry him?"

Jordan sighed and shoved his hand through damp, tangled hair. "Okay, so my imagination ran away with me. I tried to call you on Christmas Eve, and you weren't home. I had all these pictures in my mind of you lying on some secluded beach in Hawaii, helping James recuperate."

Although she was delighted, even jubilant, to know Jordan had tried to call her, she wasn't about to let on. She brought the coffee cup to him and held it out until he took it. "How would my lying on a secluded beach help James recuperate?"

"With you for a visual aid, a corpse would recuperate," he replied with a sheepish grin. His eyes remained serious. "I've missed you, Mandy."

She felt tears rising in her eyes and lowered her head while she struggled to hold them back. She didn't trust herself to speak.

Jordan took her coffee and set it, with his own, on the counter. "Don't you have any chairs in this place?"

Amanda made herself meet his eyes as she shook her head. "Not yet. The movers will be here on Monday."

He approached her, hooked his index fingers through the belt loops on her jeans and pulled her close. So close that every intimacy they'd ever shared came surging back to her memory at the contact, making her feel light-headed.

"I may have neglected to mention this before," he said in a voice like summer thunder rumbling far in the distance, "but I'm in love with you, and I have a feeling it's a lifetime thing."

Amanda linked her hands behind his neck, reveling in her closeness to Jordan and the priceless words he'd just said. "Actually, you did neglect to mention that, Mr. Richards."

He tasted her lips, sending a thrill careening through her system. "I apologize abjectly, even though you're guilty of the same oversight."

"Only too true," Amanda whispered, her mouth against his. "I love you, Jordan."

He ran his hands up and down her back, strong and sure and full of the power to set her senses aflame. He pressed his lips to her neck and answered with a teasing growl.

Amanda called upon all her self-control to lean back in his arms. "Jordan, we have things to talk about—things to work out. We can't just take up where we left off."

His fingers were hooked in her belt loops again. "I'll grant you that we have a lot to work through, and it's going to take some time. Why don't we go over to my place and talk?"

With considerable effort, Amanda willed her heart to slow down to a normal beat. She knew what was going to happen—it was inevitable—but she wanted to be sure they were on solid ground first. "We can talk here," she said, and she led him into the giant, empty parlor with its view of the sound. They sat together on a window seat with no cushion, their hands clasped. "I was wrong not to tell you I was seeing James again, Jordan, and I'm sorry."

He touched her lips with an index finger. Outside, beyond the rain-dappled glass, the storm raged on. "Looking back, I guess I wouldn't have been very receptive, anyway. I was feeling pretty possessive."

Amanda rested her head against his damp shoulder, unable to resist his warmth any longer, trembling as he traced a tingling pattern on her nape. "I thought I was going to die when I saw you at Ivar's with that corporation chick."

Jordan laughed and curved his fingers under her chin. "'Corporation chick'? That was Clarissa Robbins. She works in the legal department and is married to one of my best friends."

Amanda felt foolish, but she was also relieved, and she guessed that showed in her face, because Jordan was grinning at her. "You have your girls back," she said. "I saw you on the ferry last night."

Jordan nodded. "They didn't actually move in until a month ago. After all, they were used to living with Paul and Karen, so we just did weekends at first. And they're staying with Becky's parents until tomorrow night."

She tried to lower her head again, but Jordan wouldn't allow it.

"Think you could fall for a guy with two kids, Mandy?" he asked.

"I already have," she answered softly.

Jordan's mouth descended to hers, gentle at first, and then possessive and commanding. By the time he withdrew, Amanda was dazed.

"Show me the bridal suite," he said, rising to his feet and pulling Amanda after him.

She swallowed. "There's no bed in there, Jordan," she explained timidly.

"Where do you sleep?"

His voice was downright hypnotic. In fact, if he'd started undressing her right there in the middle of the parlor, she wouldn't have been able to raise an objection. "In a little room off the kitchen, but—"

"Show me," Jordan interrupted, and she led him back to where she slept.

"That'll never hold up," he said, eyeing the cot Amanda had spent the night on. With an inspired grin, he grabbed up the sleeping bag and pillow. "Now," he went on, grasping her hand again, "let's break in the bridal suite."

Amanda felt color rise in her cheeks, and she averted her eyes before leading the way around to the front of the house and up the stairs.

The best room faced the water and boasted its own fireplace, but it was unfurnished except for a large hooked rug centered in the middle of the floor.

Jordan spread the sleeping bag out on the rug and tossed the pillow carelessly on top of it, then stood watching Amanda with a mingling of humor and hunger in his eyes. "Come here, Mandy," he said with gentle authority.

She approached him shyly, because in some ways everything was new between them.

He slipped his hands beneath her T-shirt, resting them lightly on the sides of her waist; his hands were surprisingly warm.

"I love you, Amanda Scott," he told her firmly. "And in a month or a year or whenever you're ready, I'm going to make you my wife. Any objections?"

Amanda's lips were dry, and she wet them with her tongue. "None at all," she answered, and she drew in a sharp breath and closed her eyes as Jordan slid his hands up her sides to her breasts. With his thumbs he stroked her long-neglected nipples through the lacy fabric of her bra. When they stood erect, he pulled Amanda's T-shirt off over her head and tossed it aside.

"Let me look at you," he said, standing back a little.

Slowly, a little awkwardly, Amanda unhooked her bra and let it drop, revealing her full breasts. She let her hand fall back in ecstatic surrender as Jordan boldly closed his hands over her. When he bent his head and began to suckle at one pulsing nipple, she gave a little cry and entangled her hands in his hair.

He drew on both her breasts, one after the other, until she was half-delirious, and then he dropped to his knees on the sleeping bag and gently took Amanda's shoes from her feet. She started to sink down, needing union with him, but he grasped her hips and held her upright.

She bit down on her lower lip as she felt his finger beneath the waistband of her jeans. The snap gave way, and then the zipper, and then Amanda was bared to him, except for her panties and socks.

Her knees bent of their own accord, and her pelvis shifted forward as Jordan nipped at the hidden mound, all the time rolling one of her socks down. When her feet were bare, he pulled her panties down very slowly, and she kicked them aside impatiently, sure that Jordan would appease her now.

But he wasn't through tormenting her. He massaged the insides of her thighs, carefully avoiding the place that most needed his attention, and then lifted one of her knees and placed it over his shoulder.

Amanda was forced to link her hands behind his neck to keep from falling. "Oh," she whimpered as she realized what a vulnerable position she was in. "Jordan—"

He parted her with his fingers. "What?"

Her answer was cut off, and forced forever into the recesses of her mind when Jordan suddenly took her fully, greedily, into his mouth. She thrust her head back with the proud abandon of a tigress and gave a primitive groan that echoed in the empty room.

Jordan raised one hand to fondle her breast as he consumed her, and the two sensations combined to drive her to the very edge of sanity. She began to plead with him, and tug at the back of his shirt in a fruitless effort to strip him and feel his nakedness under her hands.

He lay back on the floor, bringing Amanda with him, and she rocked wildly in a shameless search for release while he moved his hands in gentle circles on her quivering belly. When he caught both her nipples between his fingers, Amanda's quest ended in a spectacular explosion that wrung a series of hoarse cries from her throat.

She sagged to the floor when it was over, only half-conscious, and Jordan arranged her on the sleeping bag before slowly removing his clothes. When he was naked, he tucked the pillow under her bottom and parted her knees, kneeling between them to tease her.

The back of one hand resting against her mouth, Amanda gave a soft moan. "Jordan—"

"Umm?" He gave her barely an inch of himself, but that was enough to arouse her all over again, to stir the fires he'd just banked. At the same time, he bent to sip at one of her nipples in a leisurely fashion.

Amanda groaned.

"What was that?" Jordan teased, barely pausing in his enjoyment of her breast.

"I want—oh, God, Jordan, please—I need you so much...."

He drew in a ragged breath, and she felt him tremble against the insides of her thighs as he gave her another inch.

She clutched at his arms, trying to pull him to her. "Jordan!" she wailed suddenly in utter desperation, and he gave her just a little more of himself.

Amanda couldn't wait any longer. She'd had release

once, it was true, but her every instinct drove her toward complete fulfillment. She needed Jordan's weight, his substance, his force, and she needed it immediately.

With a fierce cry, she thrust her hips upward, taking him all the way inside her, and at that point Jordan's awesome control snapped.

Amanda watched through a haze of passion as he surrendered. Bracing his hands on the rug and arching his back, he withdrew and lunged into her again in a long, violent stroke, leaving no doubt as to the extent of his claim on her.

Triumph came at the peak of a sweet frenzy that tore a rasping shout from Jordan's throat and set Amanda's spirit to spiraling within her. For a few dizzying moments she was sure it would escape and soar off into the cosmos, leaving her body behind forever. The feeling passed, like a fever, and when Jordan fell to her, she was there to receive him.

He kissed her bare shoulder between gasps for air, and finally whispered, "Don't mind me. I'll be fine in a year or two."

Amanda's breath had just returned, and she laughed, moving her hands over his back in a gesture meant both to soothe and to claim. But her eyes were solemn when Jordan lifted his head to study her face a few moments later.

"Do you think it will take a long time for us to get things ironed out, Jordan?"

He kissed her forehead. "Judging by what just happened here, I'd say no."

"Good," she answered.

He traced the outline of her mouth with the tip of one finger. "Will you give me a baby, Mandy?" he asked huskily.

Her heart warmed within her, and seemed to grow larger. "Probably sooner than you think," she replied.

Jordan chuckled and drew her close to him, and they lay together for a long time, recovering. Remembering. Finally, he bent to kiss her once more before rising from her to reach for his clothes. He gave her a long look as she sat up and wrapped her arms around her knees, then sighed. "We've got a lot of talking to do," he said. "Now that there's some chance of concentrating, let's go over to my place and get started."

Amanda nodded and grabbed her jeans and panties. Because her things were scattered all over the rug, she wasn't able to dress as fast as Jordan, and he was brazen enough to watch her put on every garment.

Fifteen minutes later they pulled into his garage. When a blaze was snapping in the living room fireplace, they sat side by side on the floor in front of it, cross-legged and sipping wine.

Amanda started the conversation with a blunt but necessary question. "Are you still in love with Becky?"

Jordan considered her words solemnly and for a long time. "Not in the way you mean," he finally said, his eyes caressing Amanda he watched her reactions. "But I'll always care about her. It's just that I feel a different kind of love for her now. Sort of mellow and quiet and nostalgic."

Amanda nodded, then let her head rest against his shoulder. "In a way, she lives on in Jessie and Lisa."

Jordan sighed, watching the fire. He told her about the accident then, about feeling Becky's arms tighten around his waist in fear just before impact, about the pain, about being in the hospital when her funeral was held. "I felt responsible for her death for a long time," he said, "but I finally realized I was just using that as an excuse to go on mourning forever. Deep down inside, I knew it was really an accident."

Amanda gave him a hug.

"Thanks, Mandy," he said hoarsely.

She sat up straight to look at him. "For what?"

"For coming along when you did, and for being who you are. Until I met you, I didn't think love was an option for me."

The rain began to slacken in its seemingly incessant chatter on the roof and against the windows, and Amanda thought she saw a hint of sunshine glimmering at the edge of a distant cloud. She linked her arm through Jordan's and laid her temple to his shoulder, content just to be close to him.

Jordan intertwined his fingers with Amanda's, and his grip was strong and tight. With his other hand he tapped his wineglass against hers. "Here's to taking chances," he said softly.

THE MOVERS ARRIVED on Monday, and so did the furniture Amanda had bought at the estate sale. She called in several plumbers for estimates on extra bathrooms, and that night she and Jordan and the girls sat around her kitchen table, eating chicken from a red-and-white striped bucket.

"I'm glad you didn't go to heaven," Jessie told Amanda, her dark eyes round and earnest.

"Me, too," Lisa put in, nibbling on a drumstick.

Amanda's gaze linked with Jordan's. "I could have sworn I visited there once," she said mysteriously.

Jordan gave her a look. "Dirty pool, lady," he accused.

"Uh-uh, Daddy," Jessie argued. "Amanda doesn't even *have* a pool."

"I stand corrected," Jordan told his daughter, but his eyes were on Amanda.

Tossing a denuded chicken bone onto her plate, Amanda stood up and bent to give greasy, top-of-the-head kisses to both Jessie and Lisa. "Thanks for being glad I'm around, gang," she told the girls in a conspiratorial whisper.

"You're welcome," Jessie replied.

Lisa was busy tilting the bucket to see if there was another drumstick inside.

Jordan watched Amanda with mischievous eyes as she dropped her plate into the trash and then leaned back against the sink with her arms folded.

"I suppose you people think I can't cook," she said.

No one offered a comment except for Gershwin, who came strolling into the kitchen with a cordial meow. The girls were delighted, and instantly abandoned what remained of their dinners to pet him.

When he realized he wasn't going to get any chicken, the cat wandered out of the room again. Jessie and Lisa were right behind him.

"Come here," Jordan said with just the hint of a grin.

"I've got no willpower at all where you're concerned," Amanda answered, allowing herself to be pulled onto his lap.

"Good. Will you marry me, Mandy?"

She tilted her head to one side. "Yes. But we agreed to wait, give things time—"

"We've had enough time. I love you, and that's never going to change."

Amanda kissed him. "If it's never going to change, then it won't matter if we wait."

He let his forehead fall against her breasts, pretending to be forlorn. "Do you know what it's going to do to me to go home tonight and leave you here?" he muttered.

She rested her chin on the top of his head. "You'll survive," she assured him. "I need a few months to get the business going, Jordan."

He sighed heavily. "Okay," he said with such a tone of martyrdom that Amanda laughed out loud.

Jordan repaid her by sliding a hand up under her shirt and cupping her breast.

Amanda squirmed and uttered a protest, but the steady strokes of his thumb across her nipple raised a fever in her. "We'll just have to be—flexible," she acquiesced with a sigh of supreme longing.

"We're not going to have much time alone together," Jordan warned, continuing his quiet campaign to drive her crazy. "Of course, if we were married, it would be perfectly natural for us to sleep together every night." He'd lifted one side of Amanda's bra so that her bare breast nestled in his hand.

"Jordan," Amanda whispered. "Stop it."

In the parlor, Amanda's television set came on, and the theme song of the girls' favorite sitcom filled the air. "A nuclear war wouldn't distract them from that show," Jordan said sleepily, lifting Amanda's T-shirt and closing his lips brazenly around her nipple.

She knew she should twist away, but the truth was, the most she could manage was to turn on Jordan's lap so that she could see the parlor doorway clearly. The position provided Jordan with better access to her breast, which he enjoyed without a hint of self-consciousness.

When he'd had enough, he righted her bra, pulled her shirt down and swatted her lightly on the bottom. "Well," he said with an exaggerated yawn, "it's a school night. I'd better take the girls home."

Amanda was indignant. "Jordan Richards, you deliberately got me worked up...."

He grinned and lifted her off his lap. "Yep," he confessed, rising from his chair and wandering idly in the direction of the parlor.

Flushed, Amanda flounced back and forth between the table and the trash can, disposing of the remains of dinner. After that, she wiped the table off in furious motions, and when she carried the dishcloth back to the sink, she realized Jordan was watching her with a twinkle in his eyes.

"In three days we could have a license," he said.

In the parlor, Jessie and Lisa laughed at some event in their favorite program, and the sound lifted Amanda's heart. The children would always be Becky and Jordan's, but she loved them already, and she wanted to be a part of their lives almost as much as she wanted to be a part of their father's.

She walked slowly over to the man she loved and put her arms around his waist. "Okay, Jordan, you win. I want to be with you and the kids too much to wait any longer. But you'll have to be patient with me, because getting a new business off the ground takes a lot of time and energy."

His eyes danced with delight as he lifted one hand for a solemn oath. "I'll be patient if you will," he said.

Amanda bit down on her lower lip, worried. "I don't want to fail at this, Jordan."

He kissed her forehead. "We'll have to work at marriage, Mandy—just like everybody else does. But it'll last, I promise you."

"How can you be so sure?" she asked, watching his face for some sign of reservation or caution.

She saw only confidence and love. "The odds are in our favor," he answered, "and I'm taking the rest on faith."

It was September, and the maples and elms scattered between the evergreens across the road were turning to bright gold. They matched the lumbering yellow school bus that ground to a halt beside the sign that read Amanda's Place.

The bus door opened and Jessie bounded down the steps and leaped to the ground, then turned to catch hold of Lisa's hand and patiently help her down.

Amanda smiled and placed one hand on her distended stomach, watching as her stepdaughters raced toward the house, their school papers fluttering in the autumn breeze.

"I made a house!" Lisa shouted, breathless with excitement as she raced ahead of her sister to meet Amanda on the step.

Amanda bent to properly examine the drawing Lisa had done in the afternoon kindergarten session. A crude square with windows represented the house, and there were four stick figures in front. "Here's me," Lisa said with a sniffle, pointing a pudgy little finger at the smallest form in the picture, "and here's Jessie and Daddy and you. I didn't draw the baby 'cause I don't know what he looks like."

Amanda kissed the child soundly on the forehead. "That's such a good picture that I'm going to put it up in the shop so everybody who comes in can admire it."

Lisa beamed at the prospect, sniffled again and toddled past Amanda and into the warm kitchen.

"How about you?" she asked Jessie, who had waited patiently on the bottom step for her turn. "Did you draw a picture, too?"

"I'm too big for that," Jessie said importantly. "I wrote the whole alphabet."

Putting an arm on the little girl's back, Amanda gently steered her into the kitchen. "Let's see," she said.

Jessie proudly extended the paper. "I already know enough to be in second grade," she said.

Amanda assessed the neatly printed letters marching

smartly across Jessie's paper. "This is certainly one of the nicest papers I've ever seen," she said.

Jessie eyed her shrewdly. "Good enough to be in the shop like Lisa's picture?"

"Absolutely," Amanda replied. To prove her assertion, she strode through the big dining room, now completely furnished, and the large parlor, where Lisa was plunking on the piano, into the shop. Several of her quilts were displayed there, along with the work of many local craftspeople.

Her live-in manager, Millie Delano, was behind the cash register. It had been a slow day, but there were guests scheduled for the weekend, and the quilts and other items had sold extremely well over the summer. Amanda was making a go of her bed and breakfast, although it would be a long time before she got rich.

She held up both Lisa's picture and Jessie's printing for Millie's inspection. The pleasant middle-aged woman smiled broadly as Amanda made places for the papers on the bulletin board behind the counter and pinned them into place.

Jessie, who sometimes worried that her fondness for Amanda made her disloyal to her mother, beamed with pride.

The girls were settled in the kitchen, drinking milk and eating bananas, when Jordan arrived from the city. "Is my family ready to go home?" he asked, poking his head around the door.

Jessie and Lisa, who were always delighted to see him, whether he'd been away five minutes, five hours or five days, flung themselves at him with shrieks of welcome. Amanda, her hands resting on her protruding stomach, stood back, watching. Her eyes brimmed with tears as she thought how lucky she was to have the three of them filling her life with love and confusion and laughter.

After gently freeing himself from his daughters, Jordan walked over to Amanda and laid his hands on either side of her face. With his thumbs he brushed away her tears. "Hi, pregnant lady," he said. A quiet pride made Amanda's heart swell.

"Hi," she replied with a soft smile.

He gave her a leisurely kiss, then steered her toward the door. Her coat was hanging on a wooden peg nearby, and he helped her into it before handing Jessie and Lisa their jackets.

Amanda was struck again by the depth of her love for him when, in his tailored suit, he dropped to one knee to help Lisa with a jammed zipper. She couldn't have asked for a better father for her child than Jordan Richards.

When the hectic family project of preparing dinner was behind them, and Lisa and Jessie had had their baths, their stories and their good-night kisses, Jordan led Amanda into the living room. They sat on the sofa in front of a snapping fire, with their heads touching.

Jordan brought his hand to rest on Amanda's stomach, and when the baby kicked, his eyes were as bright as the flames on the hearth. Amanda couldn't help smiling.

He smoothed back a lock of her hair. "Tired?" he asked.

"Yes." Amanda sighed. "How about you?"

"Beat," Jordan replied. "Personally, I don't see that we have any choice but to go straight to bed."

Amanda laughed and thrust herself off the couch. "Last one there is a rotten egg!" she cried, waddling toward the stairs.

* * * * *

BESTSELLING AUTHOR COLLECTION

CLASSIC ROMANCES IN COLLECTIBLE VOLUMES

New York Times Bestselling Author

LINDA LAEL MILLER

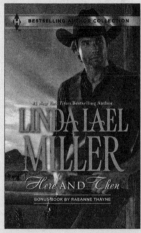

Rue Claridge never dreamed she'd find herself more than
one hundred years in the past…and in jail courtesy of
Marshal Farley Haynes. Fascinated by the rugged marshal, Rue
dreams of a lifetime with him in her modern world—but would he
choose her over everything he's ever known?

HERE AND THEN

Available November 13 wherever books are sold!

**Plus, enjoy the bonus story *Dalton's Undoing*
by *USA TODAY* bestselling author RaeAnne Thayne,
included in this 2-in-1 volume!**

www.Harlequin.com

NYTLLM1212

REQUEST YOUR
FREE BOOKS!

2 FREE NOVELS
FROM THE ROMANCE COLLECTION
PLUS 2 FREE GIFTS!

YES! Please send me 2 FREE novels from the Romance Collection and my 2 FREE gifts (gifts are worth about $10). After receiving them, if I don't wish to receive any more books, I can return the shipping statement marked "cancel." If I don't cancel, I will receive 4 brand-new novels every month and be billed just $5.99 per book in the U.S. or $6.49 per book in Canada. That's a saving of at least 25% off the cover price. It's quite a bargain! Shipping and handling is just 50¢ per book in the U.S. and 75¢ per book in Canada.* I understand that accepting the 2 free books and gifts places me under no obligation to buy anything. I can always return a shipment and cancel at any time. Even if I never buy another book, the two free books and gifts are mine to keep forever.

194/394 MDN FELQ

Name _____ (PLEASE PRINT) _____

Address _____ Apt. # _____

City _____ State/Prov. _____ Zip/Postal Code _____

Signature (if under 18, a parent or guardian must sign)

Mail to the **Reader Service**:
IN U.S.A.: P.O. Box 1867, Buffalo, NY 14240-1867
IN CANADA: P.O. Box 609, Fort Erie, Ontario L2A 5X3

Not valid for current subscribers to the Romance Collection
or the Romance/Suspense Collection.

**Want to try two free books from another line?
Call 1-800-873-8635 or visit www.ReaderService.com.**

* Terms and prices subject to change without notice. Prices do not include applicable taxes. Sales tax applicable in N.Y. Canadian residents will be charged applicable taxes. Offer not valid in Quebec. This offer is limited to one order per household. All orders subject to credit approval. Credit or debit balances in a customer's account(s) may be offset by any other outstanding balance owed by or to the customer. Please allow 4 to 6 weeks for delivery. Offer available while quantities last.

Your Privacy—The Reader Service is committed to protecting your privacy. Our Privacy Policy is available online at www.ReaderService.com or upon request from the Reader Service.

We make a portion of our mailing list available to reputable third parties that offer products we believe may interest you. If you prefer that we not exchange your name with third parties, or if you wish to clarify or modify your communication preferences, please visit us at www.ReaderService.com/consumerchoice or write to us at Reader Service Preference Service, P.O. Box 9062, Buffalo, NY 14269. Include your complete name and address.

New York Times bestselling author

SUSAN MALLERY

brings you a heartwarming tale for the holidays!

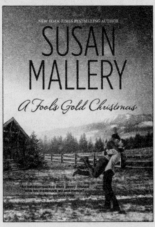

The unrelenting cheer in Fool's Gold, California, is bringing out the humbug in dancer Evie Stryker. She learned early on that Christmas miracles don't happen, at least not for her. Even when she's recruited to stage Fool's Gold's winter festival, she refuses to buy into the holiday hype.

Jaded lawyer Dante Jefferson is getting used to the backwater town he now reluctantly calls home, but the pounding of dancers' feet above his office is more than he can handle. However, when he confronts their gorgeous teacher, he's unprepared for the attraction that sears him down to the soul....

A Fool's Gold Christmas

Available in hardcover everywhere books are sold!

LINDA·LAEL MILLER

77661	BIG SKY MOUNTAIN	__	$7.99 U.S.	__	$9.99 CAN.
77681	McKETTRICK'S HEART	__	$7.99 U.S.	__	$9.99 CAN.
77677	McKETTRICK'S PRIDE	__	$7.99 U.S.	__	$9.99 CAN.
77643	BIG SKY COUNTRY	__	$7.99 U.S.	__	$9.99 CAN.
77642	McKETTRICK'S LUCK	__	$7.99 U.S.	__	$9.99 CAN.
77623	THE McKETTRICK LEGEND	__	$7.99 U.S.	__	$9.99 CAN.
77606	HOLIDAY IN STONE CREEK	__	$7.99 U.S.	__	$9.99 CAN.
77600	THE CREED LEGACY	__	$7.99 U.S.	__	$9.99 CAN.
77580	CREED'S HONOR	__	$7.99 U.S.	__	$9.99 CAN.
77561	MONTANA CREEDS: LOGAN	__	$7.99 U.S.	__	$9.99 CAN.
77555	A CREED IN STONE CREEK	__	$7.99 U.S.	__	$9.99 CAN.
77502	THE CHRISTMAS BRIDES	__	$7.99 U.S.	__	$9.99 CAN.
77492	McKETTRICK'S CHOICE	__	$7.99 U.S.	__	$9.99 CAN.
77446	McKETTRICKS OF TEXAS: AUSTIN	__	$7.99 U.S.	__	$9.99 CAN.
77441	McKETTRICKS OF TEXAS: GARRETT	__	$7.99 U.S.	__	$9.99 CAN.
77436	McKETTRICKS OF TEXAS: TATE	__	$7.99 U.S.	__	$9.99 CAN.
77388	THE BRIDEGROOM	__	$7.99 U.S.	__	$8.99 CAN.
77364	MONTANA CREEDS: TYLER	__	$7.99 U.S.	__	$7.99 CAN.
77358	MONTANA CREEDS: DYLAN	__	$7.99 U.S.	__	$7.99 CAN.
77330	THE RUSTLER	__	$7.99 U.S.	__	$7.99 CAN.
77296	A WANTED MAN	__	$7.99 U.S.	__	$7.99 CAN.
77200	DEADLY GAMBLE	__	$7.99 U.S.	__	$9.50 CAN.
77198	THE MAN FROM STONE CREEK	__	$7.99 U.S.	__	$9.50 CAN.

(limited quantities available)

TOTAL AMOUNT	$ _____
POSTAGE & HANDLING	$ _____
($1.00 FOR 1 BOOK, 50¢ for each additional)	
APPLICABLE TAXES*	$ _____
TOTAL PAYABLE	$ _____

(check or money order—please do not send cash)

To order, complete this form and send it, along with a check or money order for the total above, payable to Harlequin HQN, to: **In the U.S.:** 3010 Walden Avenue, P.O. Box 9077, Buffalo, NY 14269-9077; **In Canada:** P.O. Box 636, Fort Erie, Ontario, L2A 5X3.

Name: _____

Address: _____ City: _____

State/Prov.: _____ Zip/Postal Code: _____

Account Number (if applicable): _____

075 CSAS

*New York residents remit applicable sales taxes.
*Canadian residents remit applicable GST and provincial taxes.

H HARLEQUIN® HQN™

™ www.Harlequin.com

PHLLM1112BL